LIFE AND DEATH: NEW RULES

She screamed again. Billy plunged into the darkness. She was cowering in the corner, where the steel mesh met the stone. She was tall and flashy, clearly a hooker. He could hear her quietly sobbing as he veered toward her, could see the luxuriant blondness of her hair.

As the words "Are you okay?" began to slide from his lips, she moved her hands away from her face and he could see that she wasn't a woman at all, she was a clever reproduction, a pretty boy in drag, grinning wickedly at him, no tears whatsoever on that lovely phony face . . .

. . . and there was a noise behind him, and Billy turned just in time to see the other man hiss "*You're dead,*" thrusting forward with his hand.

The knife became a blur of motion. He felt the center of his breastbone shatter, felt the cold steel sliding inward. The world went luminous red.

And Billy Rowe went berserk.

He screamed, reaching out with both hands to grab his murderer by the collar. He beat the man's head against the wall, over and over, until the body slumped gracelessly to his feet.

Billy grabbed the hilt of the knife with both hands, tugged, felt the hooked end catch and the saw edge rasp, gritted his teeth against the horror and yanked. The knife came out.

There was no blood.

There was no pain.

There was no wound.

"Brash, bold and bloody, *The Cleanup* is a razor-sharp joyride into the dark alleys of Manhattan . . . and the darker sidestreets of the soul."

—Douglas E. Winter,
author of *Faces of Fear*

Bantam books by John Skipp and Craig Spector:

THE LIGHT AT THE END
THE CLEANUP

THE
CLEANUP

John Skipp and
Craig Spector

BANTAM BOOKS
TORONTO • NEW YORK • LONDON • SYDNEY • AUCKLAND

THE CLEANUP

A Bantam Book / March 1987

ISBN 0-553-26056-1

Published simultaneously in the United States and Canada

Bantam Books are published by Bantam Books, Inc. Its trade-
mark, consisting of the words "Bantam Books" and the por-
trayal of a rooster, is Registered in U.S. Patent and Trademark
Office and in other countries. Marca Registrada. Bantam
Books, Inc., 666 Fifth Avenue, New York, New York 10103.

PRINTED IN THE UNITED STATES OF AMERICA

KR   0 9 8 7 6 5 4 3 2 1

To Melanie Rose,
who waited for just the right moment
to arrive

ACKNOWLEDGEMENTS

The authors would like to thank an awful lot of people. So they will.

Tied for first place are: Lou Aronica, Amy Stout, and all the wonderful people in the Bantam organization; Adele Leone, Richard Monaco, and Richard McEnroe of the Adele Leone Agency; and the respective long-suffering mates of the authors, Marianne Walter and Lori Houck. Without any of the above, said authors might well be down on the Bowery somewhere, straining Sterno through a sock.

We'd also like, with a minimum of redundance, to thank: Kathy, Matt, Annie, Eva, Greg, our families, Alan, Sandy, Sean, Phil, Bay Ridge Typing & Copy, and all the other folks we mentioned last time. Special mention must be made of Jules, Judy, Jennifer, Johnny, Jan, Jimmy, Jane, Larry, Alfred, Claudia, Sherri, Niambi, Brian, Dave, the inimitable Robear, and all of the other good friends who make the Chelsea Commons the best neighborhood bar in the world.

No proper accrediting of this novel's source material would be complete without mentioning Andrea Dworkin, Bernard Goetz, Bob Guccionne, the Midtown Rapist, and all of the other exciting people who make this world such a fascinating and fun-filled place.

Finally, the authors would like to thank Merciful Providence for keeping them from killing themselves or each other in the extremely difficult year and a half that it took to write this sonofabitch.

THE
CLEANUP

PART ONE

NO BOTTOM

"Well, some folks get bent
In strange ways.
Like some folks seem meant
To feel the pain.
The sorrow gets sent
Down on their heads.
The sadness, it twists them.
They're never the same. . . ."

Billy Rowe
Twisted Toward Life

ONE

ON STANTON STREET

He was drawing a white chalk line around her body.

The cop started with her left foot, broadly tracing something that looked more like Frankenstein's workboots than the tiny, slightly decadent black heels that she wore. He outlined the curve of one delicate, fishnetted calf, stopping at the point where the right leg crossed over at the knee, then swept back down the right shin to describe another blocky piece of footwear.

There were nine other cops down on Stanton Street; their cars had cordoned off the area, slammed into park at jagged angles and left there, red lights arhythmically strobing. An ambulance had also arrived; a pair of paramedics leaned casually against the back, smoking cigarettes and tapping their feet.

Two cops were still digging around on the north side of the street, flashlights slicing into the darkness of the construction site. The rest were busy holding back the slowly-expanding crowd: tenants, almost exclusively, from the tenements that lined the south side. The low-budget hookers and johns had cut out at the sound of the sirens, leaving only a handful of Bowery bums to round out the inevitable vulture contingent.

The guy with the chalk had gone all the way up the back of her right leg. The line curved, almost lovingly, around the tight black slit skirt that adorned her outthrust

3

buttocks, then moved slowly along the perimeters of her zebra-striped blouse, her gracefully-arched back.

He had to stop at the pool of blood.

The kid's name was Billy Rowe, and he'd been staring out the window ever since they arrived. Shock. Understandable. He was their star witness, and what he had witnessed was nasty.

But Detective Frank Rizzo had spent the better part of the last ten minutes staring at the back of Billy's head. Which was terrific, if you liked shoulder-length scraggles of filthy blond hair. Rizzo did not. In fact, Rizzo disliked almost everything about Billy Rowe: his voice, his face, his scrawny frame, his shithole apartment, his idiot dog.

The only thing he liked was Billy Rowe's memory. It was fantastic. It was also the kid's most important characteristic, in terms of the investigation. It made everything else worth putting up with.

If not tolerable. Which it wasn't.

"Mr. Rowe," he said wearily, still addressing the kid's skull from the rear. "Just a few more questions, if you don't mind terribly."

"Just a minute," Billy said. He was lighting another cigarette off the butt of the last. It was the third in an unbroken chain of smoke that Billy'd dispensed in their short time together. He also had a quart of Bud that had been full when they met. It was almost empty now.

"Hey, no problem. We've got all night. Maybe I should just curl up in front of the TV or something." Rizzo pulled a cigarette of his own from his breast pocket, brought it to his lips, continued to speak. "Think you might be in the mood in a half hour or so?"

"You know somethin'?" Billy droned. He had a high-pitched voice, but it was dragging along its lowest register. "My roommate's an amateur comedian, too. You oughtta meet him. I'm sure that you'd get along famously."

"Frank. Leave him alone for a minute, okay?" This from Dennis the Menace, Rizzo's faithful protégé. Dennis Hamilton, of course, was playing with the dog. Dennis Hamilton was a perennial kid. Rizzo cast a sour glance at his junior partner, whose dark features were locked in a Stevie

Wonder grin as he tousled the ridiculous mutt's facial fur with vigor.

Hamilton had the uncanny knack of finding bright lights in the most repulsive circumstances. It was a wonderful quality. It pissed Rizzo off.

"Okay," the senior detective muttered. He took a deep drag and sighed out smoke, then cast his gaze around the charming decor of Billy Rowe's apartment.

It was disgusting. With the possible exception of *pigsty,* no word could peg it better. If you took a picture of it and enclosed the caption, "What's Not Wrong With This Room?", the answer would have to be, "Damned if *I* know!"

For starters, there was the laundry. It hadn't been done in at least two months. Every stinking bit of it was scattered across the floor, rumpled and sweaty and fetid as hell. It was joined, at his feet, by a sprawling jumble of miscellaneous junk: roughly a hundred albums and record jackets, disengaged from each other; a half-ton of comic books, paperbacks, and magazines; a *full* ton of notebooks and loose sheets of paper, all bearing the same neat cursive prose. Billy's handwriting, no doubt. God only knew what he was writing.

And then there were the empties.

It was something that Rizzo'd seen a lot of, since the Bottle Law. But this had to take the proverbial cake. There were hundreds of them, all over the room. Most of them were dusty. Most of them were growing slime.

There were some dog-eared posters on the walls. The only one he recognized was from Pink Floyd's *The Wall*, a movie he'd never had any desire to see. The rest of them were for groups he'd never heard of or political rallies for causes he'd never supported. Three Mile Island came up a lot. From the quality of the posters, Rizzo guessed that they were local, rather than national, affairs.

No wonder they never won, he mused. *Defeated on the home front. Overwhelmed by their own dirty laundry.* He grinned, thinking back on the ragtag legions that had over-run the '60's: glassy-eyed and scraggly-haired Utopians who spelled Hope with a capital D. They'd struck him as ridiculous then; and some things never change.

Nobody'd ever had to pick up after Rizzo, or admonish

him about cleanliness and godliness. God was a joke, but cleanliness was simply part and parcel of Taking Care Of Business. The maintenance of a good fighting machine. It was like exercise, a steady job, or changing the oil in your goddam car. Take care of business, or they mop the floor with you.

He looked at Billy Rowe again: a little '60's throwback, if ever there was one. Billy stood at five feet seven in his pulverized Adidas. His long, spindly hair trickled down from his head like thin strands of moist whole-wheat spaghetti. His beard was a thicket of stout, multicolored hairs; one of them, gray as an old man's coat, dangled crookedly from the right side of his chin.

He looked old: much older than his twenty-seven years. There were lines on his face that had no right to be there. It was obvious to Rizzo that the kid was drinking himself to death. He wondered if Billy had figured that out.

Rizzo wondered about a lot of things.

But he lost very little sleep over any of them.

The cop had opted to go around the pool of blood, resuming just below her elbow. She'd fallen with her arm tucked under her, as if she'd tried to catch herself and didn't quite have the strength.

Billy squeezed his eyes shut, rocked back sickly on his heels. Another sneak attack of vertigo. He heard the faceless drone of voices from below, mingling with the incessant scrape of chalk on asphalt, tracing its way along her sleeveless bicep, cutting inward at the shoulder to the crook of the neck . . .

(*cutting inward*)

His eyes snapped open. The room listed thirty degrees.

(*at the shoulder*)

It took a moment to pull himself back together. He drained the rest of his beer, trying to quiet the violent thrumming of his nerves. It didn't work. He doubted that anything would.

On the street, the chalk made a rounded and featureless sweep past the dead girl's profile. That was the worst part. Her mouth and one visible eye were still open. She looked like she'd just seen something terribly sad.

Billy found himself wondering, briefly, if any part of her could see the hand that held the chalk that cut in now under her chin, then swept out along her outstretched left arm and arced around the slender, curled, and lifeless fingers at its tip.

And if so, he hoped that it couldn't see him.

Bubba was great. That was Hamilton's opinion. Anyone who owned a dog that cool couldn't be all bad. Score one point for Billy.

Bubba was one of those undifferentiated mutts that seemed to have taken the most lovable characteristics of every breed in his genealogy. He was a gangly short-hair with a long pointy snoot and the kind of body that looked like it was made out of rubber. Bubba was a wiggler and a squiggler, foot-long tail continuously thrashing to left and right, wide-ass grin accommodating a constant panting and wheezing of joy at each stroke that he got. He was a people-lover, an attention-lover. He was also skinny as hell, but that just made him all the squirmier.

"Oh, you're a good fella, aren'tcha? Oh, yeah, you're a good boy." Skritch. Skritch. Hamilton listened to himself for a moment. *Why do dogs always reduce me to babbling?*, he wondered. It was a mystery of life. Why fight it? Skritcha skritcha. "Oh, yeah, you're a good—"

Bubba lunged forward suddenly and started lapping at Hamilton's cheek. He was a sloppy kisser, with lots of tongue. Hamilton grimaced and twisted his face away, laughing.

His eyes settled on Rizzo. Rizzo wasn't laughing. Rizzo was glaring at him, as usual. The man looked like Harry Dean Stanton: same haggard face, same mussy black hair, same rumpled demeanor and deadpan delivery. He was a persnickety old pain in the ass; he was also an excellent partner and a closet good guy, which he took great pains to conceal.

Bubba was wriggling and craning his neck to get at Hamilton's cheek. Rizzo let out a disgusted snort and flicked his ashes on a wadded-up T-shirt. Billy continued to stare out the window.

Poor guy, Hamilton thought. The disgust factor not-

withstanding, there were a lot of things about Billy that he
liked. He'd known people like that in college—intensely
creative, intensely sloppy—and seen a million of 'em while
working Homicide.

Billy was sharp, that much was for sure. His taste in
music said it all, so far as Hamilton was concerned:
progressive rock, progressive jazz, progressive funk and
traditional music from all over the world. From the Bothy
Band of Ireland to the Drummers of Burundi, with Mozart
and Zappa in between, and a healthy serving of Beatles and
Springsteens at the core. The only real difference between
their record collections was that Hamilton tended to keep
his in their covers and on the shelf.

And if Billy was really surviving as a musician, he was
probably pretty good. Just another guy with a talent and a
dream, banging his head against the walls of New York City.

Looks like the walls are winning, Hamilton mused,
staring out past their witness.

And into the flashing red October night.

The chalk line was complete. It made her look much
larger than she actually was. The paramedics wheeled over
a stretcher and a body bag, preparing to pack her up. They
flipped her over first.

And Billy turned away abruptly.

"Oh, Jesus," he moaned, features knotting in revulsion. He wasn't prepared for the actual wounds, staring up
at him in the hard light of the streetlamp. The maniac had
opened up her belly and poked holes in her chest; wet
things were threatening to tumble through the gashes. His
eyes squeezed shut, trying to drive out the vision . . .

. . . *and then the image coalesced for him with soul-
numbing clarity. It was a* face, *carved into her torso with
jagged-edged artistry. The twin puncture wounds above
her breasts were like eyes; the crooked gash across her belly
was a monstrous jack o' lantern smile, wide and brimming
over with—*

"No," he gagged, falling backward a step. Bile seeped
in through the walls at the back of his throat.

"You okay?" The black detective, his voice accompanied by the sound of movement and shifting debris. Billy turned to see that the guy was moving toward him, Bubba at his heels.

The vertigo, receding like a vanquished wave. "I . . . I just felt kinda sick for a second. It's okay." The bile lingered, made his voice thick and husky. He took a stab at clearing it, then continued to croak, "I just got a good look at the wounds, that's all."

Hamilton wrinkled his face. "Then don't look. You've seen enough."

"No, you don't understand," Billy said, looking into the cop's eyes. "I *want* to see it. I want to burn it into my memory banks. I want to carry those pictures with me for as long as I live. You understand?"

"Yeah." Hamilton met his stare. "I think I do."

Billy managed a half-hearted smile. Bubba ka-thumped through the rubble and jumped up to him, front paws resting on his chest, tail wagging ferociously. "Down, Bubba. C'mon," he murmured, then turned his gaze back to the street.

They were just loading the girl into the back of the ambulance. The crowd was beginning to disperse: the thrill was gone, and the rain was coming. In minutes, Stanton Street would be right back where it was, with no lingering traces of the tragedy to remind him, except . . .

Except . . .

The white chalk line, bright against the dark pavement: an empty thought balloon that he proceeded to fill with memory. . . .

The pictures were as vivid as a dream in progress. He could see all of Stanton Street spreading out before him: the blond black hooker in the purple hot pants, leaning against the Chrystie Street lamppost, adjusting her stockings; the head bobbing in the '67 Rambler at the curb; Fred Flintstone, one of the Bowery Boys, passed out on the sidewalk by the Ray Bari's Pizza Supplies parking lot; traffic whizzing by on the Bowery.

The darkness surrounding the construction site.

He was absently doodling with the strings of his guitar when she rounded the corner of Chrystie and started down

Stanton Street. He'd been doing it for roughly an hour and a half. It was not inspired, but it took his mind off his problems. Or tried to, anyway.

Fact was, his problems were the only things he could think about. They were various and sundry. They loomed behind his eyes.

The party, just for starters. There'd been five phone messages in the last two hours, reprimanding him for his absence. Three for Larry. One from Lisa. One from Mona herself.

It was important to Mona that he show up at the party. It was important to Mona that he show up looking decent. This party was one of the most important events in Mona de Vanguardia's life. She wanted to share it with him. She was his lover.

On the verge of what looked like success.

But he was out on the fire escape, doodling with his guitar, letting his answering machine do his dirty work for him. He was serenading the rats and roaches and bums and hookers and johns.

Until the girl rounded the corner and started toward him.

As soon as she hit the pool of streetlight, Billy recognized her. She was the ticket-taker at the 8th Street Playhouse, where he frequently took in his midnight movies. She had translated New Wave in epic fashion: the spiky hair and garish color/patterns made her genuinely hot, as opposed to the ugly pieces of modern art that many of her contemporaries had become. He'd joked with her, successfully, on many an occasion. She was a complete and utter sweetheart, from her sense of humor to her smile to her visual extravagance of beauty.

Billy remembered his heart's beating faster. He remembered the dull throb of his genitals, summoned by the thought of her. He remembered the subtle shifting of gears, the music from his fingers growing solid and strong as an audience worth impressing drew near.

She was weaving, just a little. Billy suspected that she was drunk. It was either that or 'ludes or smack, but he could always hope for the best. The blond black hooker stared after her, with what Billy deduced to be vague *contempt. The bobbing in the car continued, unabated. Fred Flintstone slept on.*

Billy was really jamming when she stepped into the circle of light directly beneath him. She paused there, smiling and staring at him. She was clearly impressed. She was clearly on drugs. She was clearly as lovely as he'd ever seen her.

He thought about asking her up. Of course. The nature of fantasy: imagine the best, imagine the worst. He thought about slipping inside her while she moaned and stroked his back. He thought about Mona, and the warm insides that he knew so well. He thought about Mona, at the party, pissed off. He thought about the fact that she would not be apt to walk in on them.

The girl was still down there, in the streetlight, smiling.

When the maniac came out of the shadows behind her.

Billy had perhaps a second of reaction time. He blew it. Not his fault. There was no jangling of the intuitive alarm, no screeching of violins. The rush from the darkness took less than three seconds. By then, it was too late.

The maniac was no taller than the girl . . . or Billy, for that matter. It wore an unseasonable gray trench coat and a battered gray fedora that perfectly shielded its face from Billy's view. It catapulted out of the shadows like a boulder besieging a castle, knocking her forward three feet when it slammed into her back. Its left arm slipped around her throat, effectively throttling any scream that she might have cared to make. Its right arm—gloved, like the other—held a short, distinctly pointed blade that glistened in the overhead light.

Billy watched her smile contort, become a soundless oval from which her tongue protruded. He watched the hand with the knife come down, then up, with a whickering sound too loud to be real and a spray of red too bright to be anything but. The blade had punched in just above her left breast; her body bent backwards at the waist, pelvis jutting outward as if in abandon.

Then the blade pulled away and came down again. Over her right breast, this time. More blood. A slightly more vigorous jerking.

Billy remembered screaming.

The third thrust of the knife plowed into her belly and lingered there, slicing painfully across the upper ridge of her pelvic bone. The gloved hand executed a ninety-degree turn there, wrenched sharply to the right. When the blade came away, there was something dangling from it, wedged at some minutely thin point between the grooves of the serrated edge. Then the knife, and its pitiful trailer of flesh, descended again.

While Billy continued to scream. He had leapt to his feet without even knowing it, standing half-bent over the metal banister. The guitar clanged and jangled at his feet, unheard and entirely unimportant.

And the knife came up. And the knife came down. And the body sagged, as the knife came up, and the maniac dragged her slowly back into the shadows. Her body, already essentially dead, flailed out in a last-minute race toward salvation. She broke free of its grasp, pitched forward with a shambling step. The knife slashed down again, catching her on the shoulder, digging deep and sliding away again. She stumbled forward, threw her right arm out in front of her, and fell. The maniac swayed behind her.

Billy screamed again. This time, the maniac heard him. It looked up, and the face beneath the fedora's brim looked startled and almost embarrassed. Billy couldn't see the eyes, but he distinctly picked up the trembling of the fat lower lip, the crooked and brittle-looking teeth in the wide-open mouth, the aspirin-sized dimple in the pudgy chin, the puny growth of the beard.

Then the maniac bolted, racing off toward Chrystie Street, the knife falling out of its hand and pinging against the pavement. The black blonde had already disappeared. There was a two-headed flurry of commotion in the Rambler's backseat; then it, too, dropped out of sight.

Voices began to shout from other windows, but Billy couldn't tell what they were saying. He was too busy screaming himself.

The word he was screaming was "Nooo. . . ."

The girl remained where she had fallen . . . as she would remain until the chalk line was complete, some *twenty minutes later. The girl was dead. And Billy had watched it all happen.*

Without lifting a finger to stop it.

The phone rang. It snapped Billy back to the present like the pay end of a whip. He turned to see that everyone in the room was watching him: Hamilton, Rizzo, Bubba. A trickle of sweat burned its way into his right eye socket. He rubbed at it, quietly cursing.

The phone rang again. "You gonna get that?" Rizzo inquired.

Billy shook his head. "That's what the machine's for."

Rizzo shrugged, looking at Hamilton. The phone rang again. Hamilton shot Rizzo a placating glance and was just about to say something when Billy and Larry's message kicked in at full volume.

There were two bars of electric guitar and hand-clap intro; then the voices came in, to the tune of "Rock 'n' Roll Is Here To Stay":

"Don't care what the neighbors say.
Roth and Rowe are here to stay.
We can't make it to the phone.
Leave your message at the tone.
BEEEEEEEEEEEEEEEEEEEEEEEEEEEEEEEEP"

Hamilton got a laugh out of it. Rizzo made a face. Billy and Bubba had heard it a million times, so they were unimpressed.

Evidently, so was the voice on the other end.

"I wish I could believe," it began, "that this means you're on your way over." A woman's voice, low and a bit on the frosty-cold side. "Actually, I'm glad that I *can't* believe it, because I'd only be fooling myself. It makes me wonder if I might not be fooling myself about a lot of things, Billy. Do you know what I mean?"

A soft click, amplified by the machine. A pair of horrendously loud beeps. And then silence.

Politely echoed by everyone in the room.

Except Rizzo, who grinned crookedly and said, "President of your fan club?"

"Man, I'm not in a very good mood," Billy snapped. "If you don't have any goddam heart, you could at least keep your fucking mouth shut." Then he turned to Hamilton and added, "Do you really have any more questions, or is he just here to tease the animals?"

"Just one thing," Rizzo said. The smartass was gone from his voice. It looked like the words had stung. "You say that you were out there for an hour and a half."

"Yes."

"And you didn't see the killer walk down the street at any time."

"That's right."

"Or sneak in through the construction site."

"If he did, I didn't see him. Right."

"So there's a chance that he was down there the whole time, just watching you, right?"

Billy nodded, said nothing.

"Who knows, maybe he liked your music." Rizzo gave an *anything-is-possible* shrug. "But one thing's for sure. He knew you were there, but he went ahead and killed her anyway. That's kinda strange, don't you think?"

Billy just stared at him. The air began to crackle.

"I guess he didn't see you as much of a threat."

Hamilton let out an incredulous hiss. Billy felt something threaten to snap behind his mind. He glanced at Bubba, who was watching him strangely. Rizzo started to talk again.

"But he might change his mind. And if he does, he knows where to find you. I'd think about that, if I were you. I'd watch my ass."

"What's that supposed to mean?" Billy's voice was clipped and even. The fury and terror were warring for control; he was struggling against them both.

"It means be careful," Hamilton cut in, hands raised in truce. "The way you describe him, the guy sounds like a psycho. We don't know what he's gonna do. So we'd advise you to lay low for a couple of days. Try not to be caught alone at night. Look over your shoulder a lot. Stuff like that." The black detective smiled a little. Billy didn't join him.

"And what are *you* guys gonna be doing?" A challenge.

"We can't offer you twenty-four-hour protection . . ."

"For that, you need a Speed Stick," Rizzo tossed in dryly.

". . . but we will have the neighborhood under surveillance, and we will have our phone lines open to you. If anything happens, you give us a ring, and we'll have men here in minutes." Hamilton's expression indicated that he meant it.

"Okay." Billy couldn't smile—he didn't have one in him—but he softened a little and nodded. "Okay. Is there anything else?"

"Yeah," Rizzo said, one hand motioning toward the floor. "Who does your interior decorating?"

"Why are you such a bastard?" Hamilton wanted to know. They were walking down the steps now, leaving Billy and his rubble for the hubbub on the street.

"There's something about wading through ten tons of shit," Rizzo said. "It makes me irritable."

"I think it's your arthritis. Have you been taking your downs lately?"

"Don't start in, Junior. I'll feed you to the press."

"Oh, Christ," Hamilton sighed. They'd be down there by now. Lots of flashing bulbs and rolling tape, microphones thrust in faces. "Okay. I'll be good. I promise."

"Always a fucking carnival when someone dies," Rizzo muttered, seemingly to himself. Then he turned to his partner and said, "And if we're lucky, no other lowlife assholes will murder each other tonight."

Hamilton bit back a response. He didn't like the way it was phrased, but he appreciated the sentiment.

It was something to hope for, anyway.

TWO

THE PARTY

Mona was pissed, but it wasn't insurmountable. Even if her darling sweetheart never showed up—*especially* so, the way she was feeling—there were a thousand kinds of fun to be had tonight.

Griffin Records was throwing the party at a posh new sushi place on Avenue A, right on the fringe of the danger zone in the Lower East Side. They had spared no expenses: open bar, open banquet. The only thing that was closed was the door.

But that hadn't stopped nearly nine hundred people from packing their way inside. The place was pandemonious. She couldn't believe some of the people who were there: Chaka Khan, Billy Crystal, Tom Petty, Billy Idol, Tim Matheson, Kelly Nichols . . . the list went on and on. Even Andy Warhol had stopped in for a couple of minutes, gauntly appraising the crowd.

The rest of the people were record execs, band members, other musicians, roadies and techies, members of the press, friends of the above, and numerous gorgeous women who were imported for the occasion.

And then there were the dancers. Of whom she was the star.

Mona de Vanguardia moved away from the pay phones and slipped gracefully into the crowd. Her profile had never been higher—all four videos from David Hart and the Brakes were playing tonight—and she caused a significant turning of heads as she slid toward the bar.

Which should not have surprised her, though it never really ceased to.

Dave was the star tonight, no question about it. But

she ran a close second for airtime on the videos. After *Something For Nothing*, the Powers That Were had decided to create a visual mythology around her. She was the woman that Dave always sang to. She was the woman who haunted his dreams.

It made for a uniquely powerful set of promo tapes from the band's first album, also called *Something For Nothing*. It also made for the biggest break in her long, occasionally sordid career.

Mona was twenty-seven years old. She stood at almost five feet five and weighed 113 pounds. She was a dancer by training and inclination, though she'd adopted acting and singing as potentially lucrative sidelines. It was starting to pay off. She was a truly remarkable dancer, and she could get away with the others.

But the thing that really sold her was her beauty. She'd finally had to reconcile herself with it, silly as it was. No matter how well she did anything else, they'd still be looking at her tits. So she'd adopted that as a sideline, too, and it had drawn top drawer.

Mona caught a glimpse of herself in the nonstop mirror that lined the walls. Places like this always had lots of mirrors. People were constantly checking themselves out. She joined them for a moment, appraising the wildly-teased black hair, the big brown eyes, the china-doll features. She'd worn a slinky black evening gown that made her Hispanically-dark complexion stand out. She liked her makeup, and was pleased that it was holding up.

It'll pass, she concluded, flashing a smile at herself. Christopher Guest caught it in the mirror and reflected it back at her. It *was* Christopher Guest! Her heart went giddy.

Then a hand squeezed down softly on her shoulder from behind. She looked up into the sharp gray eyes, the thin and classically-sculpted features of her roommate. "Any luck?" Lisa asked, and Mona turned to face her.

"Nope. Just the stupid machine. I swear to God, sometimes I'd like to pulverize that thing."

Lisa Traynor's beauty wasn't quite as exotic as Mona's— it wasn't her living, so she worked at it less—but she still had the capacity to effortlessly stun. Tonight, she'd gone to uncustomary lengths: letting down her Rapunzelesque expanses of wavy wheat-blond hair, consenting to provocative makeup, dressing to kill. She was similar to Mona in size and shape; but there was a chiseled intensity to her features, more forbidding than alluring.

That is, until she smiled, and the room lit up.

She was smiling now, soft and sympathetic. The hand on Mona's shoulder lingered. "Maybe you should just let it go," she said.

"Maybe I should just let *him* go," Mona countered, but she stared at the floor as she did it. Lisa's bullshit detector was excellent, and Mona didn't want to watch the little lights go off behind that penetrating stare.

"He's really depressed, Mona."

"So what else is new?" Mona sneered as she said it, feeling the anger boil back up within her. "He's been really depressed for the last six months."

"And you're tired of it."

"You're goddam right I am!" She caught herself yelling, pulled her volume back down. There were too many important people here, watching her. It would not do to lose one's cool. "I mean, I've been watching him sink so long now that I wonder if he's ever gonna come back up. And every time something good happens to *me*, it just knocks him farther down into the dirt. It's like he can't handle the idea that his girlfriend is doing better than he is."

"You know better than that." Lisa's hand dropped from her shoulder. "If we were talking about any other guy, I'd probably say yes. But Billy's not like that, and you know it. He's proud of you."

"Yeah. Obviously." Mona rolled her eyes and made an unpleasant face. "That's why he's here, leading my cheering section."

"Do I need to spell it out for you?" Lisa said, a bit on the disgusted side herself. "Okay. I will. Billy's not here because he's ashamed of himself. He knows how good he is, and it drives him crazy that he never got a deal. Dave intimidates him, without even trying. And Dave has the hots for you, which scares Billy even more. His self-esteem is running on *fumes* right now—"

"Well, great. That's just what I need." She could feel her cheeks burning, and that pissed her off even more. "I mean, this is my big moment in the spotlight! I worked like *hell* to get here! I'm supposed to be having the time of my life! But, no. Instead, I get guilt-tripped by you and my boyfriend, the self-made loser who's too goddam stubborn to make the concessions that would make him a star!"

Lisa looked weary. Her voice was soft, barely audible over the party's din. "Go have a great time, Mona—"

"No, no, no!" Mona was rolling now. "Not when poor Billy needs consoling! How can I have a good time when I know that my loved one is suffering so? My own victories *pale* in comparison to my dearest's terrible endless fucking anguish!"

"Laying it on a bit thick, aren't we?" Lisa's smile, in this case, was infuriating.

"*I just want him to be there for me.*" Her voice was deadly and level and low, and it sliced like a hot knife through butter. "I don't think it's fair that he should ruin this for me. If he can't put down his problems long enough to congratulate me on my successes, then piss on him. I don't need this shit. I'm tired of it."

Lisa shrugged and tightly smiled, conceding. It wasn't a victory. Mona could practically see the words *I can't talk to you, you're being a vindictive and irrational bitch, I leave you to your raving* etched across her roommate's face.

But it was the sympathy commingled with the resignation that made Mona ultimately turn away. Her own anger shamed her, and that was the last thing in the world she wanted to deal with right now. She was in her ostensible glory. She was surrounded by people who had done more than dream: they had *accomplished.*

And they were ready to welcome her into their fold.

If she would but dispose of her dead weight.

Dead weight like Billy Rowe.

"God, I need a drink," she informed the room at large. There were three active bars, strategically spaced throughout the place. She moved toward the nearest one, just to the right of the circle of people where she'd last seen Dave. At the center, of course.

Where he belongs, she told herself, fiercely grinning. *Because he earned it*.

Unlike certain other people I know.

On the inner periphery of that same circular crowd, Larry Roth was hanging out. Like Mona, he was digging on the wealth of celebrity that was wandering through. Cyndi Lauper and Jamie Lee Curtis were an underhanded stone's throw away, but the one he really wanted to rap with was Buck Henry. One comedian to another. Just for a minute. That wasn't too much to ask for, was it?"

Larry was a tall, fairly ridiculous-looking man. He bore a resemblance to his namesake from the fabled Three Stooges: same frizzy hair and shiny bald patch, same hook in the ol' proboscis. He'd done a fair amount of stand-up comedy in the last two years, but he'd yet to land a feature film or a half-hour in *Catch A Rising Star*. Sometimes he despaired. Tonight was no exception. He felt hopelessly outclassed by almost everyone he met.

But Dave Hart didn't do that to him, which was simultaneously nice and disheartening. He wanted to believe it was because Dave was just another asshole who'd stumbled on the right buttons and given them a push.

But it wasn't true, and Larry knew it. Dave Hart was hitting the big time because Dave Hart had the goods. The Brakes were hot, but it was Dave's material and Dave's presence that made it happen. And beyond that, Dave Hart seemed spectacularly unimpressed by his own sudden notoriety. He seemed warm and genuine, not at all the snooty holier-than-thou rock star that Larry'd expected. If you overlooked the expensive clothes and the continual cocaine-sniffle, Dave could have passed for any other extraordinarily handsome guy on the street.

Cyndi and Jamie disappeared behind a pair of rotund audio technicians. Buck Henry was still there, but he was talking to a beautiful woman named Veronica Vera. He was daunted by Buck's notoriety and Veronica's flagrant expanses of flesh. Maybe he could meet someone who knew someone and get introduced or something.

Or maybe I'm just whistling through my pale white cheeks, he told himself, turning his attention to the star's endless answering of questions.

"Yeah, well, we're lined up to tour with Huey Lewis and The News, starting in about three weeks. The record's out. The first video's out. It looks like we're made in the shade for awhile. But I still can't really believe it."

Believe it, shmucko, Larry silently appended. *You've got it by the balls.* He disliked the underpinning of jealousy that he heard in his own mind's voice, but he couldn't do anything about it. It was like trying to deny the existence of his prominent schnozzola.

He could understand why Billy hadn't shown up. It was spineless and stupid, and it was guaranteed to blow Billy's romance right out of the water, but he could understand it. Dave had taken all the steps that Billy had refused to—looking sharp, playing love songs that were three and a half minutes long, assimilating the sound and technology of the last five years—and made it pay off. Dave was playing Madison Square Garden, and Billy was playing Washington Square Park. Dave was holding down a $1,500-a-month loft on the Upper West Side, with money left over for coke; Billy was three months behind on his half of their miserable Bowery hole-in-the-wall, with barely enough money to keep him alcoholed and nicotined into submission.

Larry watched Dave work his crowd. It was something to see. Those big green eyes, that easy smile, the blond half-ton of cascading curls that framed his tanned and lupine features. Dave reminded Larry of the young Robert Plant: painfully handsome, brimming over with confidence and enthusiasm that was sublimely self-conscious. The women in the crowd had a tendency to squiggle when Dave looked at them. It made Larry sick; but again, he could understand it.

"We stepped in at number seven," Dave was saying, "with a bullet." Larry was half-inclined to fire one at his confidence-brimming head. "If we don't hit number one next week, our manager says that he'll eat his condominiums. Or his condoms. I forget." The crowd gave him a laugh.

I'll trade you, Larry thought. *You make bad jokes, I'll sell out coliseums. What do you say? I'm ready for anything.*

He had no idea how entirely wrong he was.

THREE

"ON YOUR OWN"

Outside, it was beginning to rain: big fat drops, the size of marbles. His guitar was still out on the fire escape, thumping and twanging as the water came down. But Billy couldn't quite bring himself to touch it.

Not yet.

It was an Ovation acoustic six-string with a pickup and a molded plastic back. Its sunburst finish had been mottled forever by a spilled beer at a keg party back in 1977. It had been up waterfalls and huddled around campfires at thirty-two degrees. If it couldn't handle a little rain, then fuck it.

But that wasn't all.

The big thing was that he blamed his guitar. For his lateness to the party. For the death of the girl. For the twelve years that he'd squandered on his fruitless quest for fame.

Billy Rowe sat on the edge of the bed. Another cigarette fumed between his fingers. Another quart of Bud hung snugly between his knees. He had watched the last of the cops depart, red lights trundling off to brighten other windows in the City of Boundless Opportunity. He'd watched the static darkness descend, once again.

Like the rain, which was coming more violently now. Like the violence, which was starting to reign.

"Oh, you're so clever," Billy said to himself. "You're so clever that it makes me want to ralph."

In truth, all the queasiness had pretty much vanished;

what remained was a lowly perception of self. Detective Rizzo, that bastard, had gotten through to him

(*i guess he didn't see you as much of a threat*)

in ways that ticked him off but were very hard to argue with. Especially when it came to

(*president of your fan club?*)

Mona, who would probably chew his head off if he showed up in this state. No questions asked: just an audible tearing of canines on flesh. She wouldn't wait to hear about the murder. She wouldn't wait to try and understand what he'd been through. She'd just take one look at him and then go out of her mind.

Which is exactly what I need, he thought, *to make the moment complete.*

Something large and fat thudded against the low E string of his guitar, sending a low thrumming into his ears. He set down the quart and stood up quickly. No vertigo. Nice. He moved toward the window that led to the fire escape.

Pools had formed over the front of the body; tributaries trickled down the neck. He guessed that maybe a quarter-inch of water had gathered inside. That was not good. The guitar was his only source of income; it was also his old and dependable friend, the vehicle of his self-expression.

Sudden shock—the realization that things could actually get worse—galvanized him into action. He grabbed the Ovation by its dripping neck, tipped it over, and started thumping on its back like a man burping a baby. He shook and tilted it, draining out every drop he could, then dragged it inside and looked for a towel.

There was one right next to his feet, of course. There were dozens of everything scattered across the floor of his room. *Need some filthy underwear?*, he asked himself rhetorically. *You got it! How 'bout a complete set of vintage Hendrix albums, all out of their covers? No problem!*

He stooped to grab the towel. Evidently, it had dried of old age. He made his way back to the bed with it and got to work.

Rizzo's contempt had proven contagious. Billy found

that he could barely stand to wear his own skin, much less sit in his goddam room. It *was* depressing; especially when one considered what it said about his present state of repair.

You're losing it, man, he told himself. *You're watching your life cave in all around you, and you're not doing anything to stop it. What you ought to do is grab a shower, toss on your cleanest clothes, and get the hell over to the party before you lose your girlfriend forever . . .*

Bubba barked.

"WAH!" Billy yelped, jumping a half-foot into the air. He came down staring in his stupid dog's direction. Bubba barked again, and then started to growl. At the bathtub. "What's the matter?" Billy asked.

And then the shower came on.

Bubba jumped back, yapping. Billy almost echoed the gesture. The shower came on at full blast, roaring into the old porcelain tub and splashing all over the floor. Thick plumes of steam began to rise from it. The water was hot.

But nobody had touched the shower faucets. Bubba was the only one close, and he was easily a yard away.

"Jesus," Billy droned, setting the guitar down on the bed and slowly rising. The steam was getting thick now; the water continued to thunder down. "This is weird," he muttered, nervously approaching. He grabbed the quart of beer off the floor, thinking vaguely about using it as a weapon.

The tub, like the only sink, was located in one corner of the kitchen, in classic tenement style. Bubba had backed across the room and was whimpering at the foot of the stove. He and Billy exchanged a nervous, searching look. There were no answers in it.

Billy stared, through the steam, into the bottom of the tub.

The rat was roughly the size of his foot, excluding the length of the tail. It was belly-up, legs twitching feebly, while the scalding water pummeled it from above. Its black-brown hair was slicked down, back-fur plastered to the white porcelain. Its mouth was open, the lower jaw jittering.

Except that it wasn't a rat . . .

"Omigod," Billy muttered, staggering backward, eyes wide. The terror was back; and with it, a kidney-punch of nausea. He tried to pull his thoughts together, but his mind refused to focus. Nothing felt real. Nothing made sense. When he closed his eyes, the darkness cartwheeled.

"No," he hissed, catching himself in mid-stumble. His eyes shot open and saw that he was falling, the sharp upper rim of the bathtub racing toward his face. He threw his hands up before him. The quart went flying. It shattered in the bathtub just as he caught himself at the rim, sending sploshes of beer and shards of glass up to spatter his face and hands.

You almost fainted, his mind informed him. There was a stinging pain in his right cheek, just below the eye; another on the back of his left hand. He swiped at them absently with the palm of his right, then fell back on his knees to the floor.

The rat was dead. A quick glance to his right confirmed it. The exploding quart hadn't fazed it a bit; it just lay there, jerking to the shower's choreography.

Except that it wasn't a rat . . .

The white-heat steamclouds were blistering, blinding. Hot water and sweat formed sparkling beads on his clothing, flesh, and hair. He leaned forward tentatively, waving his right hand in front of his face, trying to get a clearer view of the thing . . .

. . . and it was staring back up at him with eyes flat-black and lifeless, yellow dagger teeth grinning out from the pink cleft palate. Nothing about the angle or shape of the head was right: the ears, too long and pointed; the snout, too blunt and wide, with monstrous flaring nostrils. It looked like a wingless mutant fruitbat, the more he stared at it. Even its stiffening limbs were too long, and strangely jointed . . .

"Noooo," he droned, inching away from the horror, barely able to hear his own voice over the roar of the shower and the low thrum of terror in his mind. He could feel the madness, the nightmare delirium, sliding back into his brain like a dagger.

And the madness terrified him.

He couldn't bear it.

Not again.

"This isn't happening," he told himself. "I'm gonna turn off the water, and nothing will be there. . . ."

In his bedroom, something heavy fell over and shattered.

He heard chitenous, scuttling sounds.

"JESUS CHRIST!" Billy yelled, leaping to his feet. He was suddenly very much aware of the floor: the shadowed corners, the hiding places. He backed into the middle of the kitchen, heart thudding painfully in his chest. Behind him, Bubba was starting to yowl. Billy felt like joining in.

There was something in the room with them.

"Oh, shit." He could feel his balls constricting, feel the cold sweat prickling at his armpits and eyes. He backed up another step and then froze abruptly, while a full-blown poltergeist scenario played out inside his mind: the door slipping out of his grasp and slamming shut, then locking itself; cockroach-laden dishes rising up from the sink, winging themselves into the walls like kamikaze fighter planes; dirty clothes and record albums, circling in the air like a spiraling dolphin dance . . .

. . . *and things, scuttling quickly across the floor, closing in on his ankles with jagged teeth and glittering eyes* . . .

He was afraid to move, but staying was out of the question. Behind and to his left, Larry's room was entirely dark. *They could be coming in through the bathroom window,* he realized, sneaking a peek through the blackened doorway.

Nothing.

This isn't happening, he tried to tell himself. *This is crazy—*

Then the bolt lock on the front door unlatched.

And the door creaked slowly open.

Bubba wasted no time. He let out a squeal and raced through the opening, disappearing out into the hall. Billy watched, as the door swung wide, and the knob began to turn by itself. *Chika-chika.*

"Okay," he hissed. "Okay." His hands came up,

apologetic. He tried to watch his room, the shower, and Larry's room at the same time while he backed quickly toward the door. He knocked into Bubba's leash with his heel, picked it up automatically.

Whatever it was, it was already inside.

The door was for him.

He used it.

FOUR

THE PARTY, REVISITED

Mona sidled up to the bar and ordered a Tangueray and tonic. It arrived, vanished, and went back for a refill in the space of thirty seconds. The bartender had the good sense not to raise an eyebrow. She thanked him with a healthy tip and wandered back into the crowd.

She couldn't get Billy out of her head; that was the hell of it. Now that she was giving serious thought to dumping him, the memories were piling up like sandbags in a bunker's doorway. No amount of assault from the outside could get through.

It was just her, and her gin, and her mind's home movies.

Nearly fourteen months of them . . .

They met at a cast party for a low-budget splatter movie called *Sorority Slaughterhouse*. Mona had played the bitchy temptress who stole the show by getting a pitchfork through the face. Billy was a guest of the makeup artist, who'd done the life cast of Mona's face and been raving about her ever since.

As is often the case at New York parties of the talented unknown, the name of the game was Show 'n' Tell. Artists, actors, and models had their portfolios ready. Writers had

their manuscripts. And musicians had their demo tapes, if
not their actual instruments. The obligatory jam sessions,
solo performances, and sing-alongs went down, for what
seemed very much like forever.

Mona, of course, had a weakness for rock 'n' rollers.
Her last four boyfriends could have constituted a band, in
fact: bass, guitar, sax, and drums respectively. She knew
with painful intimacy what to expect from a relationship
with one; she'd seen more infidelity, slovenliness, drug
abuse, and fiscal irresponsiblity than she'd ever dared
dream possible.

But they were her obsession, and they were certainly
never boring. So whenever her heart got the urge to pull an
arrow from its quiver, it always aimed at a crazed musician.

She was surprised, but not displeased, to find that
Billy had entered her sites.

On the plus side, there was the little matter of his
talent. He was, far and away, the best performer in the
room. His repertoire of Beatles tunes, his catchy originals,
the soulful way his voice and guitar made even the worst of
his companions sound good: all of it weighed pleasantly
upon her heart, like the press of a lover's breast against her
own. And so far as she could tell, beneath the scraggly
clothes and hair, he was a rather attractive man.

Which brought her to the minus side: his absolute lack
of visual style. It was painful to watch such a gifted man so
oblivious to Manhattan's most sacred imperative. The other
musicians, however bereft, had at least the good sense to
sub image for imagination; Billy Rowe, on the other hand,
looked like he'd just finished sloppin' the hogs.

Mona hesitated, heartstring taut and arrow aimed. *Do
I really want to do this?*, she asked herself.

Then his tape came on, filling the air with his music.

Drowning out the audible twang of desire in flight.

The songs on his demo tape were multifaceted gems,
complex and beautiful. There were flaws: shitty drum
sound, spotty mix, eccentric arrangements, and occasional
overplaying. They were not perfect gems. But there was
spirit in the music. And talent. And vision.

Even Lisa, who basically viewed men as cock-mon-
gering subhumans, was obviously blown away by him. She

had him in a corner, and they were laughing their heads off about something; for a moment, Mona was concerned that her roommate was about to take a rare trip into heterosexuality. But no; when she walked over, the first thing Lisa said was, "Seduce this man. he'd be fun to have around. . . ."

Thanks a lot, Lees, Mona silently mused, pulling back to the very different party being held in the present. A middle-aged record exec winked at her; she returned a thin and empty smile, then stared down at her shoes.

There was no getting around the melancholy that the memories dredged up. They made her remember why she'd fallen for him in the first place; and why, despite all the many excellent arguments against it, she was in love with him still . . .

The music, he explained, was the demo tape from his rock opera, *The Real War.* It was, as he described it, his "dinosaur": a two-hour-long epic, three years in the making, that had proven utterly unmarketable. It was obvious to Mona that he was slightly embarrassed—evidently, he'd been told more than once that breaking into the music biz with rock opera was like attempting micro-surgery with a jackhammer—but there was also a surprisingly fierce pride in what he'd done that showed through.

Which led to a discussion of his reasons for writing *The Real War,* and the hard core of battle-scarred idealism that lay beneath Billy Rowe's every move and gesture.

"The real war," he explained, "is the battle against the madness within ourselves." He went on to describe the plot of his opera, which involved a conspiracy of enlightened men and women who, having conquered their own personal demons, were now determined to raise the global consciousness and prevent its Armageddon/annihilation.

Mona repressed her urge to scoff. Rock operas, changing the world: it all reeked of a '60's simpletonicity that she'd found little place for in her day-to-day life. But there was something contagious about his conviction: a simple faith in the ultimate goodness of his fellow human beings, and in the goodness of God, that touched a place inside her where the longing to believe was still very much alive.

Six years in New York had done a number on Mona's compassion. She'd stepped over too many urinating bums, fended off too many talent scouts who wore what brains they had in their scrotums, seen too much of the tough ol' world in action to maintain a bleeding heart. Most of the people she met had adopted a sort of cynical chic: coolness was the ability to laugh and shop while the rest of the world screamed and bled to death. If the Bomb comes down, make sure you're stoned enough to see the trails. When the going gets tough, drop a hit of Ecstasy and toddle off to Club Med for the weekend.

Billy Rowe was refreshing. Cop-show words like *honor* and *courage* slid off of his tongue with effortless panache and unquestioning power. He gave the impression that he was willing to die for what he believed in, and what he believed in was love.

They left the party together at one o'clock. By three, at her apartment, the beast with two backs was grinding its way into Heaven. The two hours between had been spent in the sweetest, slowest, most luxuriant, and excruciating foreplay either one had ever known: necks and nipples, tongues and toes, lips and fingers both north and south, all mounting together in an orgy of giving—both torrid and astoundingly tender.

He was *there* for her; that was the astonishing thing. Her life had been full of sexual athletes, most of whom would never make junior varsity: ball hogs, glory hounds, ignoring the cries of their teammates as they moved in for the score.

Now, for the first time, the words *making love* had finally lived up to their meaning.

Sleep came, finally, with the rising of the sun through her bedroom window. They did not dream; all their fantasies had been fulfilled. They remembered only that they were warm and happy and spent.

Together.

Where they seemed destined to remain . . .

"Dammit." The word hissed out of her, mournful and bitter. A tear had weaseled its way out of her left eye and

trundled down her cheek. More were poised and waiting. Her makeup was about to die.

Mona hurried to the ladies room, praying to God that none of the photographers caught her on the way. The glass of gin and tonic sloshed in her hand, a few drops spilling over, drunken analogue to her tears. If anybody noticed, they kept it to themselves.

The damage to her makeup was minimal. The three minutes she spent repairing it also went toward restoring her composure. Deep breathing helped. So did the drink. So did the moderate rekindling of her anger.

So what happened to that much-vaunted idealism, Mr. Rowe? Rhetorical question, phrased for herself alone. *What happened to the little Rainbow Warrior? You were the kid who got sent to the office every day: not for smoking or cutting class, but for standing up to the bullies in your peer group and the administration. You were the kid who quit school, got your diploma off a match pack, and sent copies to every teacher that ever jerked you around, with a note that read WHO NEEDS YOU? You were the young man who fought the nukes and the chemical dumps, threw benefit concerts, caused trouble for the Powers That Be in any little way you could.*

What happened to the Caped Crusader? The Ralph Nader of rock 'n' roll? She smiled unpleasantly into the mirror, imagining him there. *Well, let me tell you. He gave up. He crawled home with his stupid rock opera between his legs, took his phone off the hook, and opened the first of fifty thousand beers. He gave up, and he hasn't been heard from since. All we ever see anymore is his empty shell. I feel like the star of I Married a Zombie from Outer Space, and I hate it.*

So good-bye, Billy Rowe. I hope you get your shit back together someday. Send a postcard if you do; I won't be around to see it in person.

"There," she said out loud, squaring off with her reflection. "Now if I can only whip up the guts to say that in real life."

It wouldn't happen tonight. That much was virtually certain. Superman would be curled up inside a bottle somewhere, assuaging himself, making up excuses for his spectacular vanishing balls. Tonight, it was best to get him out of her system as quickly as possible.

And she knew just the man to do it.

Out of the bathroom, back into the crowd. Moving back toward the semicircle that was, yes, still very much in existence. The last of her drink was a vague buffer against the clank of dwindling ice cubes. She stopped for a refill, letting the gin perform a similar buffering against her conscience.

Then onward, again, toward the center of the gathering.

Toward Dave Hart, who stopped in mid-sentence and turned to beam at her. There were less than five seconds between the moment he viewed her and the moment of impact. It gave him just enough time to pucker his lips.

Of course, he had no idea that she was about to slide her tongue between them.

Mona kissed him with deliberate and thoroughgoing abandon. It took a couple of beats for him to believe what was happening, but he recouped admirably. She could almost hear the fireworks going off inside his mind.

What she *could* hear came to her in SenSurround: delighted laughter and applause, the steady *sniksniksnik* of auto-winders having a field day. The photographers and gossip-mongers had their scoop now. Everybody was happy. And she was just drunk and wickedly-pissed enough to join in their enjoyment.

Until the shouting erupted from the doorway.

"GET YOUR HANDS OFF ME, GODDAM IT! I'VE *GOT* A FUCKING INVITATION!" The voice sliced through the applause, the noise of the party, the kiss, with chain-saw subtlety. Mona pulled away from Dave abruptly, staring wide-eyed in the direction of the mounting conflict. She couldn't see over the heads of the crowd.

She didn't need to.

She knew who it was.

"Oh, God," she whispered. A block of ice appeared in the pit of her stomach; she felt suddenly dizzy and ill. The voice howled something else. It was drowned in the waves of excited babble.

"What *is* this shit?" Dave wanted to know. He'd

automatically wrapped a protective arm around her shoulders.

"I dunno," one of the nearby photographers said. "Some drunk. Looks like they're tossing him out . . ."

"Hold me," Mona whimpered. She could feel the blood draining out of her face, and her knees were going weak. Dave looked down, and his own eyes widened in shock and concern.

"Jesus! Mona, are you alright?"

"I'm . . ." *Am I going to faint? I don't know, I don't know, this isn't right, it isn't fair.* "I'm . . ." she tried again.

"Oh, baby," he muttered tenderly, holding her tight and moving her slowly toward the back of the sushi bar. "C'mon. We're gonna get you a seat. You're gonna be okay. Let's go."

She let him lead her, dimly aware that the commotion had died down, hearing wisps and snatches of laughing voices, descriptions of the ratty-looking nutcase, how his ass had hit the pavement, how he'd staggered away with his mangy mutt still tied up outside. . . .

Then she was crying, the sound mercifully drowning out all but Dave's sweet voice: a soothing flood of nonsense in her ears.

FIVE

PRAYER

Walking, walking, pulverized Adidas dragging his dead weight on their backs. Gray, rain-slick streets, drifting aimlessly past him like ocean fog. A half-moon, glaring baleful in the starless night sky, cold as the eye of a snake.

Billy Rowe, staring at the world through red and streaming eyes, a Vaseline-covered lens of pain that blurred

and distorted his vision. Billy Rowe, a brown-bagged q̄u̅
of Budweiser swinging back and forth between his h̄, ̄ ̄
his side, putting him in tune with the constant spinning,
spinning of the earth.

Billy Rowe, wandering alone through the last hour of
the darkest night he'd ever known.

While the freak parade marched by.

*On Seventh Street, between Second and Third Avenues, a drunken old sailor muscled his way toward Hell
and the East River. Massive arms on a spindly body, salt-and-pepper crewcut standing bristle-stiff atop his leathery
head, he swaggered and staggered blindly into the blackness while his lips muttered curses from his own private
lexicon of hate. His mind was gone, and his body was
dying, but his anger was a voodoo curse that propelled
him, horribly, forward.*

*At Astor Place, where the last street peddlers were still
hawking their clothes and records and junk for a spoonful
of oblivion, the rotting flower child was dancing. She could
have been forty, she could have been sixty: there was no
way of knowing. She probably didn't know herself. Her
eyes were as vacant as the parking lot to her left—too many
hits of acid, too many broken dreams—but she swayed like
an angel and she smiled like a saint while her little-girl
voice went* la la la la *to a fractured fairytale tune only she
could hear. There were flowers in her matted hair. The
petals were brown, and were sticking together.*

*Just off the corner of Bleecker and Broadway, a young-old man in piss-stained pants was dragging himself along a
cold brick wall. Blood flowed, copious, from a wound at his
scalpline. Apparently, somebody'd taken a bottle to him;
the cut was a jagged, semi-circular smile. He left behind a
trail of bloodstains that Billy followed for three blocks
before it veered off toward Houston Street and the
coldwater harbor below.*

There were more. There were more. Billy couldn't
stop to count the private Hells that were passing him by.
He was too immersed in his own. A gallon and a half of beer
swished and swilled through his innards, filling him with
acid bile. The world was spinning, and the cold sweat of
vertigo ran sickly down his flesh.

In his mind, it was worse: a gibbering collage of

haunting words and hideous pictures that ran together like lava and sputtering stone. When he closed his eyes, the images burned themselves into his retinas, draping ghostlike transparencies over his open-eyed sight.

And the voices refused to leave him alone.

(hit the road, twit, this is a private affair)

Billy was on the corner of Bleecker and Thompson, moving deep into the heart of Greenwich Village. Tourists and trendies, punks and preppies, bums and bohemians flooded the streets. He couldn't bring himself to look them in the eyes. He was afraid of what they might see.

(guess he didn't see you as much of a threat)

"Oh, yes," he laughed painfully. "I'm a scary guy, alrightee." He rocked back on his heels, drawing a speculative glance from the Oriental couple beside him at the curb. His eyes snapped shut . . .

. . . *and his rain-spattered guitar was rolling over on its side, sloshing a slow-motion river of blood down onto a video monitor that erupted in smoke and whistling sparks, and on the screen was Mona's face, screaming as the black static enveloped her* . . .

. . . and the light changed, and he opened his eyes as they started to shoulder past him. He went with the flow, let it buffet him forward, suffering the eyes that kept turning and

(are you alright?)

checking him out. At the opposite curb, Billy paused for a moment, one hand snaking out to a No Parking sign for balance. Bleecker Street did a lopsided carousel spin

(i said move it, asshole!)

and he felt his center of gravity lurch horribly to the side as he slammed into a pretty young woman with spiky wristbands and dayglo hair, who . . .

. . . *smiled at him sweetly, her hands clutching a five-foot length of small intestine that lolled like a tongue from the great smiling gash across her abdomen, and the woman was Mona, it was Lisa, it was the dead girl framed in the white chalk line, it was every beautiful woman he had ever known, and she* . . .

. . . called him an asshole and shoved him away. "I'm sorry," he muttered, stumbling west on Bleecker, the world

(dying i'm dying i'm)

spinning faster and faster, the bile in his stomach sloshing in sickening counter-motion. He felt the quart slip from his fingers, saw it bounce off the pavement and roll into the gutter behind a black Trans Am and . . .

. . . the squat form scurried deeper into the shadows beneath the car, its long naked tail whickering worm-like behind it as . . .

. . . Billy felt the first gag-reflex rock him from within. He stumbled over to a stoop, narrowly avoiding the seven-foot drop down the stairwell beside it, and . . .

. . . there were two more in the stairwell, scampering back into the dimness of the alleyway with their impossibly long front legs . . .

. . . and he sat down with a thud, eyes focusing and unfocusing in time with the hideous rolling motion in his gut. He turned and saw the lights from Café Figaro on the corner. They seemed to beckon him as he . . .

. . . turned and watched them stop, inches from the all-consuming blackness at the end of the alley, stop and turn to face him, rearing up on misshapen haunches, chittering at him . . .

. . . calling him by name . . .

. . . and Billy jumped up, lurching forward as the spinning world turned his legs to rubber and his bowels to jelly. He grabbed a parking meter for support, mind reeling like a baby on a raft in a whirlpool while his voice droned on and on, saying, "This isn't happening, this isn't happening . . ."

Every light on the street had a radiant aura; beams of brilliance speared his eyes. He gagged again, mouth filling with hot saliva. He spat it out, furious and terrified, fighting desperately to control the mutiny within.

Café Figaro loomed before him, with its promise of cappuccino and a comfortable chair, safety and sanity; at the very least, a dignified place in which to throw up. It was the best option he had.

He took it.

Something cleared in Billy's head when he opened the door. Every sweat gland in his body seemed to let go at once, soaking his clothes while they purged him of his madness. The voices in his head gave way to the din of the crowd, the gentle flute and Spanish guitar in the corner. The dim light of the room seemed to emanate from the smoky air it graced, a soft and omnipresent neon glow.

He took a couple of unsteady steps inward, one hand feeling along the wrought-iron railing that extended in from the door. The hostess, a tawny woman with an English accent and a WE ARE THE WORLD T-shirt met him at the end of the railing, appraising him carefully before leading him to a seat. Billy nodded and looked away; her guts weren't hanging out, but she wasn't smiling, either. And as he followed her past the hodgepodge of antique tables and throngs of Villagers, up the tiny flight of steps to the back of the café, it was clear that he still wasn't looking too good. Maybe worse.

Good idea, he thought. *Set me next to the men's room, just in case.* It pissed him off, but he couldn't argue with the logic.

"This all right?" she said. It wasn't really a question. The tiny marble two-person table was wedged into a cul-de-sac of booths at the very back of the room. He noted that she had specifically offered him the seat that faced the wall. *The better to hide you in, my dear,* he thought. It suited him just fine. He squeezed in, jostling the excruciatingly-hip couple behind him in the process, and began to casually peruse the wallpaper. It was a montage of French newspapers, thrown up and shellacked in a higgledy-piggledy fashion. Billy didn't speak French, was vaguely suspicious of people who did.

The hostess departed, pausing to toss an admonitory glance to the waitress. It was all lost on Billy. He stared at the empty chair in front of him, and the depression came flooding back. The voices were gone, and that was terrific; he could close his eyes without a nightmare vision looming, and that was even better. But the empty chair was, in a way, much worse. It was real. He couldn't blink it away.

The room began to spin, just a little. The word *no* hissed through the clenched fist that he pressed to his lips. He hated himself for getting so wasted, for being so weak, for standing by helplessly while people either conquered or fell all around him.

And the blackness welled up like Texas oil.

And his hands came up to cup his face in an attitude of prayer.

"Oh, God," he whispered. "Oh, God. Oh, God. Please help me. I can't take it anymore. I'm dying, the world is dying, and nothing that I've done has made a fucking bit of difference."

Tears rolled down his fingers and settled in his palms.

"I've tried, and I've tried, and I love you so much, and I always believed that you were guiding me toward my highest possible self. But then I look at the mess that I've made of my life, and I think *dear God, this can't be right*.

"It can't be. It can't."

Billy let out a deep rasping sob, followed by a flurry of clipped and shallow breaths. Tears spilled over his wrists and traced veinwork down his arms.

"That's why I'm begging you: Lord, God, Creator of the Universe, whatever you want to be called. I've lost control of my life. I don't like what I'm doing . . . I don't even *know* what I'm doing anymore. I only want to do the right thing." He searched himself as the words poured out, knowing that he'd spoken the truth.

"But I can't do it alone, I can't stand to be alone anymore. If you're there . . . if you're listening . . . please help me. I'm lost, and I need you to guide me back. I give myself up to you. I'm yours."

He listened to his words, and was immersed in the power, the *abandonment*, of the moment. It was surrender to a higher order, to something greater than the flesh and its demands.

Total surrender to the Infinite.

To the source of all light.

And darkness.

"I'm yours," he whispered, and the moment was more than enough. The room was still spinning, but that had become a joyous thing. He felt light and transcendent, a spirit cut loose from the mooring of self. *I'm having a flashback!*, yelled a voice in his mind. He dismissed it. This was heavier than acid. This was heavier than anything.

"I'm yours," he repeated with total conviction, not expecting an answer.

Not expecting a voice to say, "Billy, you wouldn't believe how long I've waited to hear those words."

SIX

CHRISTOPHER

The angel was beautiful, and more than beautiful; the word became ridiculous in context. All attempts at description became ridiculous. The angel was more than words could describe.

It was light given form. It was form in perfect proportion. It was kind of hard to tell, though, because the light was so intense: a gold so brilliant and unearthly to behold that Billy's saliva dried up in mid-swallow. Yet he stared at it—he couldn't *help* but stare at it—deeply enough to pick out the rainbow undercurrents playing across its core.

Its distinctly human core.

The angel's voice was sweeter than the New York Philharmonic's strings, more resonant than its brass and reeds together. It exuded a warmth that got under Billy's skin and went straight for the heart.

The angel was completely outside Billy's frame of reference.

And was sitting directly across from him nonetheless.

"Wuh," Billy said. It was really just the sound of his jaw flopping open.

"I beg your pardon?" the angel's voice chimed.

"Uh, buh," Billy clarified. He couldn't move. He couldn't speak. He could only stare through basketball eyes, mouth agape and senselessly flapping.

The angel's laugh could turn coal into honey. It pealed for a moment like ethereal bells. Then the voice said, "I'm sorry. I'm blowing you away," and . . .

. . . a man was sitting across from him at the table. He was unusually handsome—his hair baby-blond and rippling over his collar, his eyes icy-blue and sharp as diamonds, his tanned features bold and impeccably cut— but aside from the faint golden glow he emitted, he could have been passed off as mere flesh and blood. If flesh could be so lucky.

"Is that better?" the angel asked. His voice was music and exceedingly pleasant, but gave every indication of being merely mortal.

Billy nodded mutely.

"Then snap out of it, ace! I need to talk with you some." The angel winked conspiratorially and leaned back in his chair. For the first time, Billy noticed the dapperness of his dress: a loose but immaculately tailored suit of the finest linen Billy had ever seen. It almost hurt to look at it, made him feel as though he'd been dipped in slime.

Billy was still staring when the waitress arrived at last. "Can I get you something?" she asked.

Billy snapped to. "Umm . . . I'd like a cappuccino." He looked at the angel. "How 'bout you?"

The angel smiled, hefting a brandy snifter filled with liquid gold as galleano. The waitress gave Billy a look remarkably like the hostess's before turning away. Billy stared after her, uncomprehending.

"Uh . . . listen, Billy," the angel began. "Do you have any idea what's happening here?"

Billy slowly shook his head.

"Would you like to maybe hazard a guess?"

Billy shook his head again.

"Aw, c'mon," the angel *kvetched.* "I bet you ten to one that you'll nail it in six tries or less. Like stealing candy from a baby, kid. You can't go wrong."

Billy started to laugh. He couldn't help it.

"Be a sport," the angel persisted.

"I don't wanna," Billy wheedled, and they both laughed. "Nope, nope, nope . . . I don't wanna, because this is scaring the shit out of me. I've finally lost my mind, right? And none of this is really happening."

The angel stared at him thoughtfully for a moment. "That your first guess?" he finally asked.

Billy nodded.

The angel shrugged. "You got five more to go."

"Then I guess I'd . . . have to guess the same thing over again."

"Well, that's very thoughtful of you. Throw the rest of 'em away, and I can walk home a weiner." The angel rolled his eyes in a *why me?* gesture to the heavens, paused to light a cigarette. "Okay, you *are* crazy, but that isn't the correct answer. You got four more to go. You can do it, big fella!"

The angel drew deeply on his cigarette, blowing plumes of indescribably sweet smoke from his nostrils. Billy watched the smoke waft out, hanging luminously apart from the collective haze. The waitress returned with the cappuccino, and Billy noticed that the smoke seemed to *cling* to her somehow, leaving little tendrils trailing behind her like sargasso. She served him at arm's length. *Cooties,* he thought.

Billy mumbled his thanks as she fled. It was lost in the general din. He scanned the customer-laden tables that surrounded him. They seemed real enough. He looked down at his cappuccino: hot milk and serious coffee, whipped cream and a tubular cinnamon stick. It seemed real enough. He took a tentative sip; it was hot enough to burn his tongue.

But it didn't.

"Okay," he said at last. "I'll grant that I'm really talking to you. So I'll have to conclude that you're some wiseass who wandered over to my table and started playing with my brain."

"You mean like Hypno the Magnificent? 'Alla-kazam! You are a duck?'" The angel was clearly amused.

"Well, how the hell would *I* know?" Billy was getting upset. "Maybe you wandered by, saw the weird dude in the corner, and decided to have a spot of fun." He sat back in his seat and picked up the cup. It was still hot. He blew on it delicately. "Maybe I was just hallucinating the whole thing."

"That's a pretty half-assed theory, bub, and you know it."

"It's the only rational explanation I can think of."

"The rational mind is a backseat driver. You know that too."

"Yeah, well, maybe you just caught me on a bad day."
He lifted the cup to his lips.

"So let me ask you this," the angel persisted, smiling.
"Did you hallucinate the rats?"

Billy emptied half the cup right into his lap.

"WAH!" he screamed, flying backwards in his chair.
He slammed into the guy behind him, who slopped
mochaccino all over the tablecloth and into his girlfriend's
purse. They also screamed. Between the three of them, it
was loud enough to turn every head in the room.

"Such grace," the angel muttered. "Such economy of
motion."

Both the waitress and the hostess were on their way
over now, along with a busboy and a rather large dude in
kitchen whites. Billy was trying to apologize to the couple
behind him. It wasn't going over. He was launching into his
third round of, "Omigod, I'm so sorry—" when the hostess
cut in.

"What seems to be the trouble?" she demanded.

"I accidentally knocked into this gentleman and spilled
his drink," Billy said. "I'm sorry."

"He's a goddam loonie-tune!" yelled the man of the lost
mochaccino. "He's been sitting there talking to himself
since he got here!"

"Is that a fact?" inquired the hostess.

"Well, I, uh . . ." Billy glanced sharply over at his
companion. The angel had been whistling nonchalantly
throughout, but Billy had come to the sudden realization
that nobody else could hear it. "I know that this is gonna
sound a little weird, but . . ."

The kitchen help was fidgeting in his skivvies. He
looked like the kind of guy who liked to hit people. "You
want I should throw him out?" he probed delicately.

". . . see, I'm an actor, and I'm rehearsing this part
about a guy who hears voices. Plus, I got a little bit
plastered tonight . . ."

"You don't look drunk to me!" hollered Mr. Mochaccino. "You just look like an asshole!"

". . . and I sorta got carried away," Billy finished, but
the man's words bit into him. He didn't *feel* drunk any
more. The room wasn't spinning. His speech wasn't even

the tiniest bit slurred. "I'm sorry," he repeated, and the implications punched in further: he hadn't felt drunk since the whole weird conversation began.

"Buy them drinks," the angel suggested.

"Look," Billy said. "let me pay for that last drink and buy you each a new one, okay? I mean, that's the least I can do." He smiled apologetically.

All eyes went from Billy to his long-suffering victims, who looked at each other for a long dull moment before grudgingly shrugging and nodding their heads. The thug from the kitchen looked vaguely disappointed; everybody else was simply relieved.

The waitress moved to the casualty table for a new round of orders. The rest of them wandered away. Billy lit a cigarette, hoping the motion looked savvy and cool, then turned hesitantly back to the angel.

"Don't talk anymore," the angel said. "Seriously. Just keep all of your reactions in check. This is something that you're gonna have to get used to, so you might as well start now. Okay?"

Billy nodded.

"Don't even do that," the angel insisted. "Close your eyes, if that helps. Pretend that you're thinking. You do it all the time." He grinned. Billy turned away and took a drag, blowing it up at the ceiling.

"Great. Hold that pose. Now I'm just going to talk, and you're just going to listen. You'll have a lot of questions, but you'll just have to save 'em for later. I'm going to tell you some things that you'll need some time to think about before you can even get the questions right. So save it. 'Til the next time, you're all ears and no mouth. I mean it."

Pause. Billy blew a perfect smoke ring. The angel smiled.

"Terrific," said the angel. "Now listen up.

"My name is Christopher. You don't know me, but I know you very well. Now, sometimes you believe this, and sometimes you don't, but the fact of the matter is that you're a very special dude. And I do mean *very* special. In the scheme of things here on this ol' planet Earth, the extent of your potential purely boggles the mind." The angel leaned forward. "I should know. I've been assigned to you since the day that you zygoted into being."

Billy giggled, still staring at the ceiling. The couple behind him turned warily.

"I swear to God, Billy. You cut that out, or we'll both be riding in the rubber rodeo at Bellevue." Billy stopped, stifling another one, and turned to face the table. "Very good. May I continue? Don't answer that. Listen.

"What we're talking here is self-actualization. You have spent your whole life developing your personal power and a system of values to govern it with. The music, the movements, the schools, the jobs, the relationships, the tragedies, the drugs"—the angel waved his hands—"all of them were geared toward sculpting you into the man you were meant to be."

He paused. Billy was staring very hard at the table.

"There is, in fact, a man who you were meant to be. A particular man, with a particular job to do. A mission, as it were: the purpose for which you were born.

"You know that. You've *always* known that.

"And the time has come, Billy. To fulfill that purpose.

"To come of age."

Billy's eyes were closed, and he was shaking. The cigarette sat unattended between his fingers, half an inch of ash at its tip. Christopher gently removed it and snubbed it in the ashtray. Billy's lips tightened into the thin line between a grimace and a smile.

"When you surrendered to the Creator," the angel continued, "you opened yourself to the power of the universe. I know that sounds like cosmic crapola, but it happens to be the truth. You just brought me actively into your life; and in so doing, tripped open all your hidden doorways of potential.

"What you're going to find," the angel continued, "is this: as of this moment, you can do anything. And nothing can stop you. *Nothing.*"

A solitary tear tracked down Billy's right cheek. The nails of his left hand dug into his palm.

"God's truth," the angel said.

Billy's eyes were still closed, and he had trouble unclenching his teeth. "This is bullshit," he said very quietly, to himself. "This is a psychotic episode."

"Sorry."

"A wish-fulfillment fantasy."

"Your destiny."

"Bullshit."

"No. *Truth.*"

Billy felt the couple behind him turn again, and disregarded it. If he was really this crazy, their opinions no longer mattered. "*Listen,*" he hissed, his eyes snapping open.

And staring at an empty chair.

Billy's breath sucked in sharply. He half-stood before he remembered himself, cast his gaze wildly around the room. The guy behind him muttered something, and Billy shot him a withering glance before sitting back down in acute disorientation.

"Hey, asshole!" his favorite fellow customer growled. "You gonna—"

"Did I knock something over?" Billy asked. His voice sounded like a steel cable snapping. He whirled to face them. They visibly flinched. He could feel the terror pouring off of them. "Am I disturbing you? You want crazy, I'll show you crazy. I'll eat your goddam brains if you don't back off. Right now. Like *that.*"

Billy snapped his fingers. The man's features went blank. He found himself staring deeply into the man's eyes, heard his own voice speaking softly over the hum in his ears.

"We're fine now," he heard his voice saying. "I'll be leaving in a minute. Relax. Enjoy."

The man nodded stupidly, then turned back to his girlfriend, who looked like she'd just swallowed a ball-peen hammer. Billy nodded at her politely, then returned his gaze to the empty chair.

And the items in the center of the table.

There were two sheets of heavy-bond notebook paper stacked neatly before him, elegantly lettered in a luminous gold script. On top of them was a crisp twenty-dollar bill that had never seen the inside of a pocket.

He took them, very slowly, in his hands.

The twenty-dollar bill was newly dated. Everything was right, from Jackson's wicked pompadour to the tiniest curlicue. He laid it back down on the table gently, and began to read the note.

Dear hotshot,

Might be a good idea to bid adieu, at this point, before the giggle buggy gets here. Until we meet again there are just a few more things that I wanted to say.

The door has been opened, as it were, and there's no going back. Your life will never be the same. I can't answer all your questions now because you're not ready yet and you wouldn't believe me anyway. But trust me. I'm here to guide you. Always have been. Always will be. *You are never alone.*

As for your mission:

It's very simple. You have the gift. Learn to use it. Use it wisely. You have the power to clean up your life, clean up the streets, clean up the whole damned planet if you play your cards right.

Billy flipped to the next page. His heart was pounding.

Like I said: you can do anything, and nothing can stop you. That's the straight poop. *No limits.* No limits at all. You've been charged with an enormous power, and an enormous responsibility. You have been chosen because you are capable of using it wisely. And you will.

But the proof is in the pudding, my friend, and I suggest that you taste it promptly. There are no more excuses, no more reasons for waiting. Just the work to be done.

Just the work to be done.

Ball's in your court, ace. Take care, and be aware. I'll be keeping in touch.

Christopher

And that was the end of the note.

Billy stared at the pages for a long elastic moment,

then folded them neatly and stuck them in his back pocket. He picked up the twenty, held it parallel with the tabletop. It didn't even flop.

Great, he thought, laying the bill back down on the table. *That should take care of it.* Then he rose, feeling not the slightest bit dizzy, and walked out of Café Figaro.

That was when he remembered Bubba.

"Omigod." He pictured his poor squirmy sidekick, abandoned in front of the fucking hotsy-totsy too-good-for-Billy Rowe sushi bar on Avenue A. If some junkie hadn't gotten to him yet, Bubba was probably being served up as beef teriyaki for the gods of rock 'n' roll by now.

The image flooded him with panic. "You PUTZ!" he screamed at himself, clutching his hair by the handful. "Oh, Bubba. Oh, man. I can't believe I *did* that to you! I wish you were here—"

Behind him, someone barked.

It had begun.

PART TWO

BECOMING THE MAN

"Some folks is broke,
An' some folks is rich.
Some sit an' joke,
An' some sit an' bitch.
Some say they know,
An' some only wish. . . ."

Billy Rowe
Twisted Toward Life

SEVEN

RAT DREAMS

When Billy and Bubba got home, the rat-thing in the bathtub was gone. The broken quart was still there, of course—nightmares don't clean up after other people's messes—but the shower was off, and the monster was gone.

If it was ever actually here at all, Billy added, but he was too tired and bewildered to argue with himself. Too much had happened, too much of which made no sense at all. He would sort it out in the morning. If ever.

Bubba, for his part, did an exhaustive snoofling check of the premises. They got the waggle-tailed seal of approval: *no monsters here.* Billy peeled off his clothes, tossed them to the floor, and crawled into bed. Bubba joined him, cuddling close.

But even now, with the lights off and the sheet pulled up, Billy's mind mulled over the question: *Why me?*

And even now, as sleep began to seep in through his pores, his life was unfolding before him like a yawning cathedral that, in dreaming, he would wander.

From room to room to room . . .

Milwaukee, Wisconsin. 1960. Three months shy of three years old. In the pinstripes of light permitted by the venetian blinds, Billy could make out the details of the room: the light blue walls, the cheerful pictures, the bars

51

*and brightly-colored plastic playthings defining the para-
meters of his crib.*

He didn't know the meaning of the word fever. The
concept of one-hundred-and-eight degrees meant nothing
to him. And death was not in his vocabulary.

Nonetheless, the first two were part of him now, and
the third was not far away. In the hour since the family'd
left him to his nap, seven extra degrees of heat had welled
up from within, drenching his Pj's in sweat, making a fuzzy
muddle of his perception. He was too wasted to do anything
but whimper: a tiny sound, louder from outside than in.

Until the monsters started pouring down the walls.

Billy's little eyes widened in terror, and his already-
short breath hitched in his mucusoid chest. The monsters
were aware of it: gleefully so. They chittered and stared at
him as they descended from the ceiling, misshapen mouths
grinning and baring their teeth.

There were thousands of them. They enveloped the
walls in a semi-transparent, hallucinogenic swarm, poured
off onto the floor and began to race toward him: eyes
blacker than the darkness of the room, legs pounding in
soundless stampede-formation.

Nobody needed to tell him that the rat-things were
evil: no fairy tales, no Bible, no cartoon. Every speck of his
being burned and gleamed with the ancestral memory.

When the first of the horrors reached his crib, Billy let
out the first real scream of his life.

Then came the thundering of footsteps, the roar of
frightened voices. Light flooded in through the suddenly-
opened door. Mommy was there, and Daddy. They were
shouting to each other as they raced across the sea of
monsters. Billy could see them dimly through the bars and
the creatures that clung to them. He held out his arms, still
screaming.

Daddy's hand lay flat against his forehead, jerked
away. Daddy yelled something, yelled something else.
Mommy ran from the room. The rat-things yammered and
spat, tongues flicking . . .

. . . and then Billy was flying, Daddy's arms wrapped
tightly around him, the two of them moving out through the
doorway and into the hall. More thunder was booming

*from the water-room. It echoed madly in his head as they
rocketed toward it . . .*

*. . . and still the rats flowed down the walls in
torrents, shrieking their rage, piling up to Daddy's knees.
Daddy ignored them, plowed through them, fingers busily
unfastening the pressure cooker that Billy's pajamas had
become . . .*

*. . . and then the thunder was all, the ricochet/roar
of the bathtub's filling, the godlike booming of his parents'
voices as the last of his clothes were torn from his body and
he was plunged into the icy, fever-shattering water.*

*One of the monsters jumped in after him. He
screamed . . .*

. . . and it screamed . . .

"No, no, no," Billy's subconscious droned, aloud, as his
sleeping body thrashed in the sheets.

And the dream propelled him forward. . . .

*Buenos Aires, Argentina. 1966. Nine years old. Dad's
State Department had taken them across the equator,
through two years in a different land.*

A different world.

*The sky was the color of the Argentine flag: bright
blue, clear white clouds throughout. The last of the kids
were just making it down to the field. Three separate soccer
games were organizing themselves, Americans and Anglo-
Argentines of all grade levels mixing and matching. There
were kids hanging out on the bleachers. There were kids
chasing each other around. The half-hour recess was just
beginning.*

*Surrounding the field was a thirty-foot-high wire-mesh
fence, with another foot of curled barbed wire anointing
the top like a crown of thorns. Beyond it was a thirty-foot
drop, ending in a ravine that climbed eight feet back up
and resolved in a long straight line of abandoned railroad
tracks. Beyond that, on a ten-foot shoulder of dirt and
gravel, stood the hovels: eight of them, squat and ram-
shackle, constructed with mud and random outcroppings of
cinder block or corrugated tin.*

The people in the shacks were Chilean immigrants.

They had come all the way around the tip of the continent, avoiding the Andes mountains—through Tierra del Fuego, Land of Fire, the closest continental point to Antarctica— and then back up the Argentine coast, to camp outside the American school overlooking the Rio de la Plata.

Billy was three feet away from the fence, manning the scaled-down soccer goalposts. There were twenty minutes left to play in, and the game had already begun. Though the action was nowhere near him, Billy was absorbed in the scurrying at the far end of the field, where it looked like Donald Foley was about to boot one in.

Then the first military police vehicle had rolled down the hill beside the school, stopping at the dead end at the foot of the playground.

Another followed.

And another.

And another.

His team began to scream, "GOL! GOLÁSO!"; but Billy had missed Don's triumphant scoring kick entirely. He was staring at the first armed military men, mustachioed and sharply creased, getting out of the sedans and paddy wagon and moving along the railroad tracks.

One of them lit a torch. Another brandished a Thompson submachine gun. Two dozen others quickly followed suit, one way or the other. Billy moved away from the goalposts, wrapping his thin fingers around the thin gray wire of the fence. A few other kids came to join him.

It was the shouting of the children that alerted the Chileans. They had all been inside. Now the first one came out, just in time to catch a boot in the face from one of the officers.

The first real scream of anguish and terror was what brought the rest of the thousand-odd kids running toward the fence. A woman, evidently the bride of Bootface, had shrieked as her husband fell. The air was soon full of screams.

Billy remembered digging his face into the wire, trying to get closer to the madness at hand. Each hovel had sent out an explorer by now. All of them were facing extradition at best, imprisonment at worst. Both options promised violence and terror, delivered them up front.

The woman and her three children were dragged from the nearest hovel. The first torch twirled in through their doorway. Three doors up, a bald man raced out with a butcher knife in hand. The first gunfire went off. The man caved in at the knees and buckled, screeching and spraying.

He hit the dirt, and the children of Lincoln American School began to lose their minds. A howling erupted, hundreds strong, that overwhelmed the screams and automatic-weapon fire from below. Teachers were pressed up against the fence as well, now; some of them were also screaming.

Three other huts went up. Billy found himself wondering how mud could burn like that.

Then he spotted the monsters, for the second time.

Behind the madness.

Behind the smoke.

In the fifty yards between the hovels and the bank of the river, where river rats the size of cocker spaniels were rumored to dwell, Billy saw them. They were not rats. They were not anything that had been born of earthen egg and sperm. Their front legs were too long. Their heads and bodies were all wrong.

Behind him, the first end-of-recess bell ignited into sound. It put a ripple into everything: the voyeurs, the victims, the cops, the creatures. It was Pavlovian in its impact, jerking everyone to attention for a moment of disorienting conditioned response.

One of the soldier-cops paused only a second, then brought his billy club down on the head of the man from the seventh doorway. There was a pulping-melon sound.

And then the bell went off again.

The teachers at the fence were sobering up, joined by reinforcements from the administrative office. The back line of students was being peeled away, pulled from the fence and led back to their classrooms. Recess, as such, was over for the day.

The monsters began to dance.

Billy watched it all.

From the eighth and final doorway, a handsome Chilean in his mid-to-late twenties emerged with an Argen-

*tine flag in his hands. He waved it frantically, shouting over
and over,* "Yo soy patriota! Yo soy patriota!"

I am a patriot. *The words, like the horrors, twirled and
swirled through the air.* I am a patriot. *It seemed to amuse
the officer, who reached out and snatched the flag. He was
smiling as he kicked the Chilean, dropped the flag to the
dirt, ground it in with his heel, and then lit the last of the
hovels.*

*Ugly plumes of thick black smoke rose up toward the
heavens. An ugly smear of mud adorned the flag. Billy
couldn't get over how much they resembled each other.*

*The last of the illegal immigrants were being loaded
up. The last of the students were being dragged up the
steps. He couldn't get over the similarities there, either.*

*Dimly, through the smoke, he could still see the
monsters.*

*It took them five minutes to pry his fingers from the
fence.*

Tossing and turning, as the dream dragged him onward
and onward and down.

Thought his life.

And the first night.

Of the change . . .

EIGHT

THE TROUBLES

"Well, for starters," Larry said, "we're three months
behind on rent. Albert is threatening to throw us out,
which is nothing new, but he always means it. If we let it go
to four months, we're finished."

"I know," Billy said through a mouthful of foam.

"You know," Larry sneered. Billy went back to brushing his teeth. "Then you probably also know about the disconnect notice on the phone and the overdue electric bill. You may even have noticed that there's nothing in the house but beer."

"I thought you liked beer." *Shooka-shooka-shooka.*

"Oh, yeah, I love it. I want to eat, sleep, and fornicate it. Unfortunately, all I can do is drink it. And that's not even easy around here, because you usually get to it first."

Shooka-shooka-shooka. "This is all true, Larry. Keep going." *Shooka-shook.*

"Keep going!" Larry was working up his own lather now. His terry-cloth robe dangled halfway open; his hair was wild, and the eyes behind the glasses were slightly askew. "Well, then, how about the shit piled up in the sink? You're brushing your teeth on last week's dishes. You're up to your kneecaps in last year's garbage. You owe me two hundred dollars. You never have it, but you always have cigarettes, and you always have beer. You refuse to hold a steady job, because you're determined to make it as a musician; but you never bring home more than forty dollars a day, and you hardly ever make that, because you hardly ever stay out there more than a couple of hours.

"Meanwhile," he continued, "you ride on the dubious laurels of your fucking rock opera, which any industry person will tell you is a punch line in search of a joke that will make it funny.

"I've been watching you for almost seven years, man. I've been watching you make the grossest mistake a creative person can indulge in, year after year after year. You build the top of your goddam monument first, then try to fill in the rest of the thing before the apex crashes down on your pointy little head. Which it always does.

"And for an extra fringe benefit, you alienate all of the people who ever believed in you: Mona, Lisa, your family, me. You make us feel stupid for ever having believed it at all.

"Am I getting through to you, man? Do you hear what I'm saying?"

There followed a full fifteen seconds of silence.

"Huh?" Larry demanded.

Pause.

Shooka-shooka-shooka.

"*GOD DAMN IT!*" Larry bellowed. "*WHAT ARE YOU GOING TO DO?*"

Billy turned on the cold water and stuck his face under it, filling his mouth. Then he spit a couple of times, turned off the water, straightened, and turned.

"In case you hadn't noticed," he said, "that was a purely symbolic act."

"You brush your teeth of all responsibility." Larry laughed. "Clever."

"More like a cleansing," Billy said. His eyes were calm. His voice was steady. He was even smiling a little. "Rinse away the shit that clings to you, then start again clean."

"You might wanna try eating the shit instead."

"I swallowed a little."

"Whoa. Sorry I missed it."

"Listen. Larry." Billy was no longer smiling. "Cold water was part of the metaphor, too. To cool me off, lest I decide to kill you. Okay?"

"My heart! My heart!" Larry cried, staggering backward, clutching his breast. "The terror! It's too much!"

"Larry, I shut up and listened to you. Now you shut up and listen to me. *Everything you said was true*, alright? You've pointed out everywhere I'm fucking up, straight across the board. You're right. No argument whatsoever."

"No argument?" Larry was incredulous. Now he held his heart for a reason.

"Nope. I agree with everything you said."

"Why?" Larry asked, suddenly suspicious. "What's the matter with you?"

Billy smiled softly, a hint of hidden stress behind it.

"Come on," he said. "I'll show you."

Larry couldn't stop staring at the white chalk line. Billy knew how he felt. And then some.

The story of the murder had just been spun, in all of its intimate glory. It included his forcible eviction from Avenue A, which Larry had been somehow polite enough to keep from mentioning. It had *not* included Christopher or the rat-things, however; Billy hadn't quite reconciled himself to their reality yet.

Despite the fact that the note was still in his pocket.

Despite the fact that he knew it was true.

Billy had awakened this morning with the strangest feeling, so far from his customary state that he had to check and make sure that he was still himself. The feeling was one of *well-being*: his body rested, his mind acute, his spirit at unprecedented peace. He couldn't understand it, but he couldn't fight it, either—no more than he could wipe the blissed-out grin from his face.

And in the hour before Larry had awakened to assail him, something strong and clear had taken up residence inside him. It was the sense that his life was about to come together.

The sense of standing on destiny's edge, one step away from flight.

So when the ledger of sins had been read, Billy had been able to bite back his rage, throttle his defensiveness with an ease that was almost scary. Larry's amusing quip to the contrary, Billy *had* swallowed most of the shit. It was far from tantalizing, but it really hit the spot.

And the truth shall set them free, said a voice in his head.

Larry was speechless now, refreshingly enough. Billy took the opportunity to join him at the window, draping one arm around his shoulder, before speaking.

"Kinda gives one pause for thought, don't it?"

"I'd say." Larry's voice was barely there. He couldn't stop staring. Billy followed his gaze.

"I stared into the face of death last night, man. And it was a sobering sight. I feel"—hesitating—"like I've been knocked out of my body somehow. There's this incredible detachment. It's weird. It's nice. It's like there's this higher part of myself that experiences it all, but is somehow outside of it. Unaffected. Not jerked around, more specifically. You know what I—"

"You realize what this means, don't you?" Larry cut in.

"What?" Billy realized that Larry'd switched him off, somewhere along the way.

"It means we're gonna hafta be on the lookout for a

fucking maniac, man!" Larry said, his voice suddenly loud. He turned to Billy, eyes wide and distinctly frightened. "This is crazy! I mean—"

"I know."

"Do you really?" Larry turned, backed away, took Billy by the shoulders at arm's length. "I don't think so! God! *That guy knows where we live, Billy! He—*"

"I'm the one who saw it happen, remember? I think I know more about it than you do." His voice was low and deadly. His higher self was momentarily subsumed in a blood-red wave of anger. "Talking straight to me is one thing. Patronizing me is another. Just chill out and talk straight with me for a minute; we'll get this thing under control. Okay?"

"But—"

"*This is a life-or-death situation, yes.*" Billy's voice was cutting, intense. "I'm sorry that it's happening, but it wasn't my idea. Find another place to crash, if it makes you feel better. Wouldn't be a bad idea. If any nasty shit goes down, you won't want to be around for it."

"But *you do*, right?"

"I want to find him. Absolutely." Billy grinned, both enlightened and vengeful at once: the bottom line of balance. "But I have some other things that I need to do, too; and they pertain directly to the little speech you made a while ago. So listen.

"Here's my plan.

"I'm going out early every morning, and I'm not coming home until I've made at least a hundred bucks. Then I'm gonna clean the apartment until I nod out. Then I'm gonna wake up and do it again. By the end of the week, I'll have two months' rent and a spit-shined residence to pay on."

"Unless the maniac finds you." Larry's voice had lowered, but the terror was far from gone.

"In which case, I'll nail his ass."

"Of course."

"Just watch."

Their eyes were padlocked together for a long, unbending moment.

"Billy, you're nuts."

"That makes us even." Billy smiled. "And it makes me even with the whacked-out bastard who killed that girl . . . 'cept that I've got God and the NYPD on my side."

"They're just using you for *bait*, beanbrain! Can't you see that?"

"I'll tell you what *I* see, Larry. I see a week that will be completely thrown away if I run away and hide somewhere. Chances are good that the guy won't even come.

"And if he does . . . well, I've got it on good authority that nothing can stop me. So we'll see."

"You're fucking nuts," Larry maintained, but he had visibly lost the desire to debate it further. Which was fine with Billy.

"It's gonna be okay," he asserted.

"Honest to God, everything is going to be okay."

NINE

MONA AND LISA

When the phone rang, Mona was deep in the midst of a furious workout. Sweat flew from her forehead, arms, and back, spattering the hardwood floor and universal gym.

Lisa, meanwhile, was just lying on the sofa, skimming through Betty Friedan's *The Feminine Mystique* again. They were both clad only in T-shirts and panties; Lisa's shirt was purple, with tiny letters over her left breast reading NOSY LITTLE FUCKER, AREN'T YOU? Both the rotating fan and the old square baby-blue K mart special were going full-blast; humidity had crawled into the misery-zone, and 10 P.M. found the temperature lingering at an unseasonable eighty-two degrees.

The phone rang again. Lisa set the book down, a folded handbill for MRS. KAY: ASTROLOGY AND CARD READING, stuck in after page 312. It was the chapter called "The

Forfeited Self." The phone rang again, and she sat up, looking at Mona.

"Oh, Jesus," Mona sighed, tight-lipped with exertion and more. Her T-shirt was red, and said MY LAWYER CAN BEAT UP YOUR LAWYER. Her panties, like Lisa's, were black; but her legs were darker, and slightly less muscular.

"Whoever it is, I'll tell 'em you're in traction," Lisa said, getting up and moving through the living room. Mona nodded. The phone rang again.

Lisa walked through the doorless doorway, parted the delicate Indian-print drapes, and stepped into her bedroom. Beyond her, in the kitchen, the phone rang again. She stepped around the K mart fan and glanced quickly at her unmade bed, the blouse that Jody had left there. Flashes of last night's loving flickered, happy and excruciating, through her mind.

Jody worked for the video production company that taped Dave's videos. She had bright red hair and an incredible amount of freckles, spilling off of her face and down her neck and across the expanse of flesh revealed by her off-the-shoulder apparel. They'd kept glimpsing each other throughout the party, with increasingly-probing eyes and smiles. By one they'd struck up conversation together. By three they were in bed.

God, she was fantastic, Lisa silently enthused, moving into the kitchen. She caught the phone before the seventh ring.

"Mel's Lobster Emporium," she said.

"Hi, Mel," said the voice from the other end. "Can I speak with the lobster, please?"

"Billy!" Instantly, her conversation with Larry raced through her mind; the murder had been all over the news today, and it hadn't been easy to keep him off her mind. "How are ya? Are you okay?"

"Yeah, I'm fine. I made seventy bucks in the park today, playing. My head feels really clear, and my stools are firm." Pause. "How's Mona?"

"Never mind about her; I'm worried about you! Jesus, when I heard the news, I . . . it's just so horrible—"

"You talked to Larry?"

"Yeah . . ."

"Was he still scared half to death?"

"Aren't you?"

"Not really. Not for myself, anyway. I think I've seen the worst of it already."

"Knock on wood."

"The thing I'm *really* worried about is Mona. Does she still want to kill me?"

"Well, uh . . ." There were a couple of things that she couldn't tell him, and it didn't make her happy. She loved Billy, in her own way, as much as Mona did; the thought of keeping secrets from him sat in her stomach like a moldering thing. "She's very upset, to say the least. She's been loaded since nine last night."

"Did you tell her about . . . what happened to me?"

"Larry did. That was when she started hitting the tequila."

"Oh, great." Billy laughed ruefully.

"She doesn't know exactly *how* to feel," Lisa continued. "I'd advise you to have your shit together before you talk with her again. You are on very shaky ground."

"I understand what you're saying, but I'd kinda like to handle it differently. Think you could maybe get her on the horn?"

"I don't think that she wants to talk to you."

"Ask her."

"I don't think it's a good idea."

"Ask her anyway."

"What do you hope to accomplish?"

"I hope to get her so worked-up that she spills her guts completely. I hope to get her to scream her brains out. Maybe she'll be able to see more clearly once she gets it all out of her system."

"Thanks a lot, pal."

"Hey, I'm sorry. Put on some headphones or something. It'll all be over quickly."

"Yeah, but I'll be the one who has to console her when her eyeballs start leaking."

"You'll love it."

"That's true."

"You strumpet."

"Any chance to hold Mona is okay with me. Listen, let

me ask her." Pause. "Are you sure that you want to go through with this?"

"Absolutely."

"Okay. Hang on." She set the phone down on the counter, turned toward the living room, and paused for a moment. *This is going to be crazy*, she informed herself. *Hang on to your hat, toots. Here come de flood.*

She walked back through her bedroom. This time, her thoughts were only of Mona. She didn't know how much her roommate would reveal, but she was afraid on general principles. Mona and Billy had hit the bottom. If he succeeded only in blowing everything up forever, she would not have been surprised.

What will be, will be. That seemed probable enough. *If they break up, maybe she'll take up with Dave. Maybe I'll get her for a while.*

And if she stays with Billy, yahoo. When they're good, they're good. They could work it out. I'd like to see 'em try.

Lisa couldn't deny the little demon that yattered in her brain, drawing pictures of a naked Mona that gently undulated with her through the night. The image was completely irrespective of Billy; it also made her irrepressibly moist and warm.

Lisa parted the curtains and stepped into the living room. Mona was just sitting there, staring off into space. She looked gorgeous, but she did not look well inside.

"Your honey-buns would like to have speaks with you," Lisa said.

"Which one?" Mona managed a bitter smile, still staring off.

"The real one. The one who watches HBO here on a regular basis."

"What if I don't want to talk with him?"

"What the hell. Do it anyway."

"What makes you think," Mona said, staring straight into Lisa's eyes, "that he's my *real* honey-buns? Maybe I changed my mind."

Bullshit, Lisa thought, but she didn't say anything, opting to shrug instead.

Mona stared a moment longer, then got huffily up off

the universal and stomped over to the curtans, grabbing the tequila as she went.

"I'll talk to him," she said. "But I won't be held responsible for what I say." Then she disappeared, lovely ass and all, from view.

Lisa walked back over to the couch and resumed her horizontal sprawl. *The Feminine Mystique* was right where she'd left it, and she flipped back over to the place where she'd dropped it.

> The failure to realize the full possibilities of their existence has not been studied as a pathology in women. For it is considered normal feminine adjustment, in America and in most countries in the world. But one could apply to millions of women, adjusted to the housewife's role, the insights of neurologists and psychiatrists who have studied male patients with portions of their brains shot away and schizophrenics who have for other reasons forfeited their ability to relate to the real world. Such patients are seen now to have lost the unique mark of the human being: the capacity to transcend the present and to act in the light of the possible, the mysterious capacity to shape the future.

"*I'M SORRY, BILLY!*" came the scream from the kitchen. "*BUT I NEED A* MAN, *NOT A GODDAM CRIPPLE!*"

"Whoa," Lisa mumbled, letting the book slide shut.

"*CAN'T YOU JUST BE A MAN FOR ONCE? CAN'T YOU BE THERE FOR ME, FOR ONCE, WITHOUT COLLAPSING INTO A GODDAM HEAP?*"

I guess he's getting what he wanted, Lisa mused. *Poor guy.*

"I *HEARD* ABOUT WHAT HAPPENED!" Mona shrieked. "I'M *SORRY* ABOUT WHAT HAPPENED! BUT I CAN'T STOP THINKING THAT IF YOU'D JUST SHOWN UP AT THE GODDAM PARTY WHEN YOU WERE SUPPOSED TO, NONE OF THIS WOULD HAVE *HAPPENED!*"

Yeah, right, Lisa thought, almost angrily. *Like the girl would have lived if Billy hadn't been there to see it. Score one against Mona. That's stupid.*

Mona's next words were too quiet to hear. They stayed that way for a while. The fans droned on. Minutes passed.

And then the crying began.

It was a matter of moments before the curtain burst open and Mona came into the room, clutching her belly. Her face was full of pain. Lisa patted the space on the couch beside her and whispered the words, "Come here." Mona came. They held each other for a timeless stretch of time.

Mostly, Mona bawled her head off: a few words, denials, and curses punctuating each other, managed to cut their way through the sorrow. Throughout it all, Lisa kissed her hair, her forehead, her ears. The crying tapered down. The kissing continued. There was a long, moaning interlude.

"If you touch my tits," Mona whispered finally, "I'll break your hands."

"Wouldn't dream of it," Lisa murmured in response. "I just want to make you feel okay."

"I'll be okay in a couple of minutes. Honest to God, I will. As soon as I—shit . . ." A fresh tear started to roll.

"I love him, Lisa," she continued throatily. "I really, really love him. He's the greatest guy in the world. I just can't understand why he hates himself so much. And the murder . . . Jesus, I still can't believe that happened. . . ."

"I know." Lisa thought about the way Larry'd described it, complete with jack-o'-lantern torso. It wasn't hard to picture. She imagined being Billy, staring down. She imagined being the girl under the blade.

"But I just can't deal with it now," Mona continued. "I refuse to. Is that selfish?"

"I'd say."

"But don't you think that—" An agitated, mounting defense.

"Shhh. Shhh. I didn't say it wasn't understandable. So what are you going to do? Break up with him?"

Uncomfortable pause.

"I already did."

"Wow." *That* knocked the air out of Lisa for a second. "Really?" Mona nodded. "Are you going to stand by that, or are you doing it to scare him?"

"I don't know, I don't . . . I don't even wanna talk about it anymore. I don't wanna think about Billy, about Dave, about last night *period*.

"What I really want is some champagne."

They smiled at each other. "We have any left?"

"I brought a whole bottle back from Dave's. . . ." A tiny pang went off behind her eyes at the name. Then she brightened again. "So we've got plenty. You want some?"

"Only if we can come back in here and snuggle while we drink it." Lisa winked.

"And then, the oral sex."

"Don't tempt me, woman. I'll lubricate."

"I'll smear it all over my body," Mona purred lasciviously, but Lisa was sadly inclined to doubt it. All teasing aside, Mona always backed down in the end.

Well, almost always, Lisa amended, a smile flickering across her lips. There would always be that one night to look back on, no matter how fallow the future might be. She would not go to her grave without the experience of having made Mona groan and whinny and writhe. If that didn't get her into Heaven, nothing would.

Mona was staring at her, almost seeming to read her thoughts. She watched the *on* light click off behind Mona's eyes, and resigned herself to being a friend.

"Let's just get bombed and celebrate, okay?" she said, leading the way to the kitchen.

TEN

QUIZ

Billy stood very still in the center of the kitchen. The phone sat unheeded in his hand. He'd tried to call back, but Mona had taken the phone off the hook. Now a measured and mechanical voice droned endlessly through the tiny speaker: *if you'd like to make a call, please hang up and try again. If you need help, hang up and dial your operator.*

(DITDITDITDIT)

Billy stared at the receiver. The receiver stared back: a pair of huge black eyes that looked like they should have belonged to him. "Yes, operator," he said to no one in particular. "Get me the police. I'd like to report one extremely dead relationship . . . no, I'm not sure whether to call it murder or suicide. It hardly matters at this point, does it?"

(DITDITDITDIT)

"Yeah, well. I guess she got it out of her system, all right," he joked, quite distinctly to himself.

Nobody laughed. Billy hung up the phone. Not counting the cockroaches, Bubba was the only other one there: peacefully snoozing on the dirty laundry, blissfully unaware of the flailing his master'd just taken. Bubba grumbled and shifted fully onto his back: belly up, legs splayed, lost somewhere in Bubba-land. He covered his face with his front paws. Billy got a pang in his heart every time Bubba did that.

"Oh, Bubba," Billy murmured. "If you only knew . . ." A strange thought came to him. "Come to think of it, what *do* you know? Any idea what happened to you last night? Any idea what happened to *me?*"

Standing now in the brightly lit clutter of the kitchen, with nearly twenty-four hours between him and the events of the night before, it would be easy to dismiss it all as the product of an overworked and overactive imagination.

Except for the note in his pocket.

And except for the late, great Jennifer Mason, he reminded himself. The girl in the white chalk line and he had shared a post-mortem introduction, courtesy of every bodega and newsstand between Stanton Street and the park. Her picture . . . and the promise of more lurid details than he possibly cared to know . . . had assaulted him all afternoon. He'd finally broken down and grabbed the final edition of the *Post* during his last break.

There'd been four references to the "lone witness" in the text, none of them by name. Jennifer Mason, being dead and therefore defenseless, wasn't nearly so lucky in any respect. Her name, age, address, abbreviated history, and artistic aspirations (she'd been a painter) were all there in black and white.

Billy'd cried when he read it. Then he'd tossed the paper on his way back from the park.

But he'd kept the front page, *Wingo* ads and all.

Lest he forget.

Not that there's much chance of that, he mused. Nonetheless, he'd hung the front page up on his wall, right over his bed, where the cold sweat of memory would never be far away.

"Now all I need is a beer," he said, addressing a room that felt suddenly, claustrophobically small. A glance at his watch placed the time at 10:45. Just enough time to grab a six from Mateo's before they closed: a little fuel to ruminate over his possible futures with.

He headed for the door—quietly, so as not to disturb Bubba's beauty sleep—then moved out into the hallway and down the stairs.

Toward the night.

And the first of his tests.

The night was still hot, and unbelievably humid. He was dripping by the time he reached Mateo's bodega. So was the guy who was about to drop the iron gate. There was a bit of a hassle, but Billy managed to load up with his beer of choice before trundling out the door.

Elizabeth Street yawned before him, quiet but for the distant hum of traffic on Houston and Bowery. Billy liked this particular stretch, with its stolid working-class air: one block from the Bowery and its unending stream of sodden debris, perhaps a year away from the relentless SoHo gentrification that would ultimately displace them all.

"And good riddance to us," he said, sucking down a third of the bottle in his hand. It came out sounding far more bitter than he actually felt. He felt *good*, considering all the very good reasons against it.

Score one for Billy Rowe.

Billy finished the first bottle just as he hit Houston. The street throbbed with a constant flow of crosstown Saturday-night traffic. To his left lay Broadway and the Scrub-A-Dub Car Wash, still churnin' 'em out at 11:15. To his right was the Bowery.

And the bums.

They were out in full force tonight. Each one had a filthy rag in one hand and a can of windex in the other: weaving systematically between every car at the intersection, cheerfully smearing around the dirt on the windshields of their hapless, captive clientele. Seven days a week, twenty-four hours a day, three hundred and sixty-five days a year they were there: lining the corners, huddled around trash-barrel bonfires in winter, tucked in the shade of construction scaffolding during the dog days of summer, sharing bottles of Thunderbird and Olde English 800 as they laughed and chewed over the news and views of the permanently-excluded.

He was halfway across Houston when he heard the first scream.

"Oh, shit," he muttered, pausing on the median strip. The memory of the last scream he'd heard was still a flopping live wire in his head, spitting blue-white sparks of deadly intensity. Jennie Mason was still there, too: just barely alive enough to finish dying.

He would not let it happen again.

Billy ran across the rest of Houston Street, neatly skirting the traffic that roared toward him. A second scream pealed out, halfway to Bleecker on Elizabeth Street. He zeroed in on it, pushing forward . . .

. . . hoping that he wasn't too late . . .

They could have been a family, but it was difficult to tell. There was a man. There was a woman. There was a snotty-faced toddler in a beat-up stroller. There was a slate-gray Torino with a vinyl top that had been peeled like a deer in season: left front tire adorning the sidewalk, passenger door awkwardly dangling open. Arizona plates, but a New York City complexion. It would probably never see Arizona again.

The woman and child were wailing in unison; the man bellowed in counterpoint. He was tossing things from the backseat to the sidewalk as he roared: baby toys, a big box of Pampers, a battered vinyl suitcase bound shut in twine. Billy couldn't tell what the guy was saying, exactly, but it really didn't matter; his posture and pitch said it all.

The man was tall and lanky, with long greasy hair and a mean weasel-face that looked like it had been hit with a shovel. His blue-collar clothes were grime-encrusted, as if he'd just put in some time at a garage. The woman was a fading punkette: if before she was buxom—*zaftig*, even— now she was simply fat. Fat legs in leather pants stretched to the seams, fat arms poking out of a torn sweatshirt.

Fat face, swelling slightly in the two places where he'd struck her, large quantities of mascara tracking down her pudgy cheeks like cracks in old plaster.

The baby was a scaled-down model of her mother. Only the bruises were the same size; they took up a larger portion of the baby's face, were darker against the bright red infant skin. She howled like a banshee, kicking her stumpy legs. The man took a menacing step toward the stroller, glaring and raising the flat of his hand.

"*No, Rubin!*" the mother shrieked, leaping forward. Her loving man cracked her across the lips, hard enough to draw blood. It mingled with the spittle flecking from her lips as she staggered backward, squealing . . .

. . . *and Billy was close now, very close, a spark going off and igniting within him, a crackling surge of*

*Power unleased to make the air around him shudder and
seethe* . . .

. . . as Rubin stooped and scooped a battered Cabbage Patch doll from the sidewalk. He leaned over the
stroller, leering wickedly into the baby's face.

"Baby not happy?" he growled. "Baby want to *play?*"

The baby bawled. Rubin ground the doll into her face.
The mother howled and lunged at him again. Rubin
backhanded her, turned back to the stroller.

"Baby want to *play?*"

"Rubin want to *die?*"

Rubin whirled just as Billy straight-armed him in the
chest, staggering him back toward the car. Then Billy set
down his bag of beer and faced him, hands on hips.

"Who are *you?*" Rubin demanded. His red and black
piggy-eyes were rolling in their sockets. He was plowed in
the nastiest way; from the looks of it, it was nothing new.

"I'm Daredevil," Billy said. "The Man Without Fear.
Who are you?"

"GET OUTTA HERE, CREEP!" Rubin yowled, stepping forward.

"Nice name!" Billy enthused. "So appropriate, too."
He stepped forward as well. "How do you spell
that . . . ?"

Rubin swung. His right fist connected with Billy's
palm: the solid thwacking sound of one angry man's gesture.
Billy's fingers wrapped around the clenched fist's knobby
knuckles.

And started to squeeze.

"Drop the dollie," he said, eyes boring into Rubin's. It
was a lot like the night before, with Mr. Mochaccino:
Rubin's eyes were blank, and his own voice sounded
distant. Static licked the air.

"Drop the dollie," he repeated, squeezing harder.
There was the sound of small bones snapping. Rubin's eyes
bugged, and his jaw flew open wide.

The dollie dropped.

The punkette screamed.

Then something huge and sluggish plowed into Billie
from behind, knocking him forward. He let go of Rubin's
fist. Rubin screeched and dropped to his knees. Billy

kicked the box of jumbo Pampers and tripped over Rubin simultaneously. The box exploded, disposable diapers hurtling through the air. Rubin keeled over, still screaming and clutching his hand. Billy struggled to retain his balance. Flabby fists pounded into his back.

"Wait a minute!" he yelled. "What—"

"WHUDDAYA *DO* TO HIM!" the woman screamed. The words were nearly comprehensible. Billy spun around to face her, and she slugged him in the jaw: not hard enough to hurt, but the gesture itself was stunning. His hands came up by themselves. She punched him in the forearm.

"Hey!" he yelled. She came at him, fists flailing. "Cut it out!" She hit him again, and he pushed her back. She hit what was left of the box of Pampers, and went over with a squawk and a thud beside her two-fisted paramour.

Billy just stood there while Rubin and the punkette whooped in two-part harmony. He didn't know what to do. It had happened so fast.

But Rubin's hand was broken. That much was clear. It was swelling up like a purple balloon, and the fingers refused to unclench.

I did that, Billy's mind informed him. He staggered back, and the six-pack clinked against his heel. *I can't believe that I just did that. . . .*

Billy turned to grab the beer and met a pair of wide moon eyes. They pinned him for a moment, silencing his mind, forcing him to share in their open awe.

The baby was no longer crying. She was just *staring* at him, as if trying to determine what manner of life form he was. For the first time, Billy realized that the Power was for real: that he really was no longer an ordinary man.

"Omigod," he whispered . . .

. . . and then he was running, the shrieking meltdown of the happy nuclear family behind him receding as he ran and ran, toward Houston Street, away from what he'd done . . .

"Nice job, Crusher," the angel said, just as Billy rounded the corner. Billy screeched, nearly dropped his bag, and skidded to a halt. Christopher nodded, courtly.

"Oh, no!" Billy yelled.

"Oh, yes," the angel insisted.

A chain-link fence surrounded the lot on the corner of Houston and Elizabeth. Billy sagged against it, letting it support his weight. His legs didn't feel up to it at the moment. He blinked his eyes, hoping that Christopher would be gone when they reopened. No such luck.

"What do you want from me, anyway?" he groaned.

"Just a brief chat. About where you're heading."

"I'm heading *home*, man. That's the long and the short of it."

"In more ways than you know, my friend. But we still need to talk. Come on."

Wearily, Billy pulled himself away from the fence, and the two of them started walking toward the Bowery.

"You wanted to talk," Billy said, fishing a beer from the bag and twisting its head off. "So talk."

"Okay," the angel agreed. "Let's start with your little Killer Kowalski routine—"

"I didn't know what else to do! I mean, I didn't even know what I was doing!"

"I know. But now that you've got some idea of how strong you actually are, you're gonna want to put a bit more forethought in before you act. Not that I don't approve of how you handled Rowdy Rubin. *Au contraire!*"

"Jesus Christ, Christopher!" Billy shouted. The angel flinched. "I broke his goddam hand!"

"Be tough for him to beat up on the wife and kid for a while, though, won't it?"

"Well, uh . . ." Billy was forced to grin, despite himself. "I guess that's true."

"You know it is, Binky! And what's more, you could have killed him, which would have been really extreme. Or you could have hurt the woman when she attacked you. But you didn't.

"No, the only objection I've got to what you did is that you *ran* when it was over. You couldn't face what you'd done. And that's probably the most dangerous active flaw in your character."

"What do you mean?"

Christopher sighed. "You're a *runner*, Billy. You're a

great guy—otherwise, you wouldn't be in this mess—but you're a runner through and through. You run from your weaknesses, and then use your strengths to convince yourself that you're not really running. But you are. And that shit has got to stop.

"You're responsible for your actions, and the consequences of those actions. Example: you stepped in to prevent the abuse of a woman and child. In the course of it, you hurt somebody who deserved to be hurt. Oh, woe is me!" The angel wrung his hands extravagantly.

Billy suppressed a wave of rage. Truth was truth, but he wasn't in the mood to be mocked. "Whatever happened to good old non-violence?"

"Perfectly viable option. A lot tougher than the old eye-for-an-eye, that's for sure; if you plan to adopt it, you're going to have to work on that temper of yours. If that's the row you want to hoe, more power to you.

"Just remember that Jesus didn't go into palpitations when he tossed the moneylenders out of the temple. And nobody pissed nor moaned in Heaven when David greased Goliath's skids. I'm not ruling out compassion—without it, you're lost—but you can't fight the Good Fight without honesty and courage.

"So your running days are over. They've got to be. Do I make myself clear?"

"Yeah," Billy said. He felt properly humbled. "It's just easier said than done, that's all."

"What isn't?"

They had reached the corner of Bowery and Houston. The bums were everywhere. Billy knew that they couldn't see Christopher, but that was strangely okay: this was the one social circle in which talking to oneself wasn't only okay, but a primary qualification for membership.

The thought, as soon as it struck, dipped him headfirst into melancholy. He was painfully aware of how close he'd come to joining their shambling ranks: homeless, drunk, defeated. Contempt for their weakness, compassion for their lot: the two forces waged war within him. It was a conflict that he normally reserved for himself, and the realization of it flooded him again with that marvelous sense of detachment.

There but for the grace of God, he mused. *There but for the grace of—*

"You're thinking," Christopher interrupted. "That's good. Now let's see how well you think on your feet."

Billy looked up. One of the Bowery Boys was shuffling toward him. It was the infamous Fred Flintstone, in fact: those burly, slope-browed features were unmistakable. One grubby, broken-nailed paw was already outstretched. The whining entreaty was coming right up.

Billy didn't want to hear it. He didn't want to deal with it at all. Giving change to these guys was like a vote of affirmation: *Yeah, it's good that you gave up on life, here's your next bottle, try not to piss it all into your pants when you're done, okay?* He didn't want anything to do with it; avoidance had become his way of coping.

But Christopher's eyes were upon him, and Christopher's eyes missed nothing. Billy stopped in his tracks

(*your running days are over*)

and faced the bum, whose rheumy-red eyes said

(*there but for the grace of*)

nothing.

"Hey, buddy," Fred Flintstone began. "You gotta help me out."

Billy just looked at him.

The Power began to prickle at the air around him.

"C'mon, pallie," the bum persisted. "I need a bottle in the wors' way."

"I'm not your pallie," Billie said, the Power alive and warm within him. "But I know exactly what you need."

Terror flicked briefly in the derelict's eyes. His outstretched hand made a last-ditch attempt at retraction. Too late.

"And here it comes now," Billy said, taking hold of the hand with his own.

Healing Fred Flintstone took less than fifteen seconds. It was amazing to see how quickly and easily organs mended themselves when the Power was brought into play. Psychic pain was trickier; the only thing Billy had to fight it with was love. But he placed a warm fireball of light and hope at the core of the derelict's being, and hoped that that would be enough.

At the fifteenth second Billy looked up from his work. Christopher was smiling. Billy smiled back. The angel winked and vanished, leaving Billy to the burned-out husk that rose now, Lazaruslike, toward the land of the living.

Then Billy stood, still consumed by the Power of Light.

Yes, he said. I think it's time to go home.

It was easy, in that moment, to believe that the worst was over.

ELEVEN

RICKIE AND REX

"Say *cheese,* baby."

A muffled sob. A flash of blinding light, followed by the *whirrr* of tiny gears, pushing the little paper-and-chemical package through the slot. A keepsake.

Rickie sat back, admiring his handiwork. She was a great-lookin' chick, no two ways about it. Even in the dark, after they'd beat her face around a little, she still looked hot. He and Rex would be gone before the bruises really started to turn color; and besides, they had the pictures from when they'd fresh snagged her. Nice face.

Her body was fantastic, too. Nice tone. Real clean. Big firm titties with tiny nipples. A tight little twat with an authentic blond bush. It was everything they could ask for in a woman, really. They were happy as pigs in shit.

This had to be their lucky night.

"Baby, you gonna love this," Rex was saying. He was glad that Rickie always finished fast, tonight more than usual. He couldn't wait to put his pork into this one. "I guarantee, you ain't never had anything like it," he added, and began to unbuckle his pants.

It was the moment of truth, and he always looked forward to it. She'd pretty much stopped struggling since the last time he hit her—she was positively *tame* through Rickie's three-minute, four-inch performance—but that was entirely different. They *always* came alive again when he showed them what he had. It was, like, a unanimous thing.

Rex wasn't so hot to look at. Everything about him was big and ungainly: his twice-broken nose, his ears, his jaw. Slouching, he crested at an even six feet, and he weighed in at 235. His black, curly hair was unkempt and greasy. The rest of him tended to follow suit.

But he had a porn-star pecker, and that was a fact: eleven inches long, wide as the fat end of a pool cue. He was proud of the response it got: taut bursts of woman-breath, widening eyes.

He wished that her eyes weren't already swelling shut.

He remembered that they were fantastic.

Meanwhile, Rickie had dropped the camera—an SX-70 Sonar, real good for close-ups—and had picked up his knife. He was holding it to her throat, like he always did. Too hard. His pants were back around his waist, but he hadn't gotten around to hookin' 'em back up yet. He knew that he was just the warm-up act, and that the star was really antsy tonight. *If it wasn't for Rex*, he knew, *I'd never get any pussy at all.* It was something to keep in mind, no matter how much he hated it.

Rickie was scrawny and ratlike, almost completely the opposite of Rex: 108 pounds on a five-foot-seven frame, all coiled muscle and skinny bones. He had the same greasy curls and coloring, but that was where the resemblance ended. He was a whittled-down version, in every sense of the word . . . right down to his half-sized dick.

When Rex's pants hit the floor, and the girl began to moan, Rickie put a tiny little slice in her throat.

"If you make a sound, I'll kill you, bitch," he said. "If you try to get away, I'll kill you. You just lay there and *take it*, you hear me?" He was hissing now, every consonant sharp and deadly. "You just lay there and *take* it."

"Ain't a woman in the world can be quiet when *I'm* inside her, ace," Rex boasted. He knelt between her legs, hocked a large wad of spit into his hand, and lubed her up a little. "You know that by now."

Rickie knew. He tightened his grip on her hair when she squirmed, but he kept his mouth shut. He knew that Rex liked it when they made a lot of noise.

He also knew that *he'd* never get them to make that much noise.

Not unless he hurt them.

Very badly.

God, I hate you, Rickie thought. It applied to Rex, and to himself most of all, but it was intended for the woman and all of her kind. He hated the fact that he'd never made one cum, didn't even know how. He hated the fact that they only came to him when they wanted his money. He hated their beauty, their taste and their smell.

He hated the fact that they made him want them so badly.

Rex, on the other hand, didn't hate them at all. He loved them the way that he loved a good steak or a hot Trans Am. Rickie had heard Rex's motto a million times, forever linking the three in his mind:

Cars are for stealin', women are for fuckin', and steaks are for sizzlin' on the grill.

What could be simpler than that?

It was hotter than hell in the storage cellar, and it stunk like death and moldy cheese. That didn't seem to bother Rex. He leaned over the gorgeous blonde, slid his hands under her ass, and lifted her pelvis half a foot into the air. "You gonna love it, babe," he reiterated, and then painfully slipped her his first three inches.

She sucked her breath in sharply, whining, and started to cry.

Rickie put another tiny slice in her throat.

And then he did it again.

And then he did it again.

TWELVE

GUITAR DREAMS

In the dream . . .

His life's long corridor, stretching out again before him. Door after door after door, lining the walls to either side, inviting him to review the second-by-second-by-seconds of his life on Earth in segments designed with coherence in mind.

In the bed . . .

Billy Rowe, deeply asleep, motionless and silent but for the gentle susurration of his breath. Bubba, at the foot of the bed, deeply engrossed in dreams of his own. The sheets, wrestled aside by the heat and the unconscious vigor that the dreaming inspired.

In the room . . .

A solitary shape, floating just above the clutter.

Taking notes.

Buenos Aires, Argentina. 1967. On the occasion of his tenth birthday, Mom and Dad had stopped by the La Lucila music store and picked up a little something special. Already, his love of rock 'n' roll was firmly entrenched: Don Foley's older brother had clinched it by sending musical Care packages from the San Franciscan Summer of Love. Billy and Don were the only pre-teeners in the country who knew all the words to "Alice's Restaurant," could quote chapter and verse on the early Grateful Dead.

But Billy's favorite, far and away, was Jimi Hendrix. So he very nearly soiled his jeans when the wrapping paper unraveled to reveal his little something special. It was a sunburst Fender Stratocaster copy—the very one he'd ogled every day on his way home from school.

It was just like Jimi's.

And it was his!

So when the rest of the presents had been dispensed with, some 120 grueling seconds later, Billy hustled up the spiral staircase to his sister Becky's room, where the stereo was kept. A straight gray guitar cord had also been provided. He plugged into the jack, turned on the stereo amp, and laid his fingers on the strings for the very first time.

The guitar was wired for 220 volts. The amp was wired for 110. Even with the squat gray transformer between the amp and the wall, the guitar and the amp were not adjusted to each other.

When Billy touched the strings, every hair on his body stood on end. Painful electricity burned through his central nervous system, leaving no nerve ending untouched. He tried to let go of the strings. He couldn't. He was fused to the instrument.

And it was going to kill him.

His whole body was twitching when Becky finally raced over to the wall socket and unplugged the amp. The voltage had not been enough to kill him, but it had scrambled his own internal electronics to the point that he went in something like synesthesia: tasting colors, smelling sounds, his senses running together in nightmare psyche-delicide.

The family expected Billy's guitar-playing career to end right there.

They were wrong.

It was the night of guitar dreams, electric and wild: a lifetime measured in half-steps and whole tones, progressions both major and minor. In his dream, he raced down the years of practice and performance without end at the speed of an Eddie Van Halen solo. There were so many parties, so many jams, so many nights alone in the throes of rapturous composition. It was impossible to stop and relive them all.

It was enough just to taste the feeling.

And the feeling was freedom, the feeling was flight, the world a constantly-shifting wall of sound that he was

free to soar over on wings of song. To *be* the melody: that
was the thing. To rewrite yourself as the spirit moved you.
Improvising. Transmogrifying. Plastic. Explosive. A butterfly razorblade hootenanny howl of every passion and
emotion in the human repertoire.

A moment raced toward him. A moment to remember.
In the cathedral of his life, it was a sacred event. He paused
before it, entered it.

Remembered . . .

*Harrisburg, Pennsylvania. 1980. Twenty-three years
old. A dark, cloud-smothered sky cast its pallor on the
thousands who had gathered here today. But it could do
nothing to dampen their spirits.*

*It was March 28: the first-year anniversary of the
accident at Three Mile Island. In response, a number of
local anti-nuclearites had formed the March 28th Coalition. It was sponsoring the festival of music and messages,
the expression of solidarity, the media event. People had
come from as far as Alaska to inform Met Ed and the GPU
that their asses were in the populist sling.*

*A number of Big Names had cruised in for the
performance: Pete Seeger, Dick Gregory, Linda Ronstadt,
Stephen Stills.*

*But for these five minutes, on the early cusp of noon,
the stage belonged to Billy Rowe.*

*The name of the song was "We Are Going To Win." It was
an anthem for the '80's, and without a doubt the most
optimistic song he'd ever written. It had been written on
New Year's Day, to usher in a decade that he hoped would
make the '60's look like a pre-game warmup for evolution-
ary change.*

*The crowd was almost enough to make him believe it.
They were more than warm, more than enthusiastic.
Ninety-nine percent of them had never heard the song
before, but eighty-five percent of them were singing along
at the chorus. He had toyed with the idea of bringing along
a backup singer, but it was obvious now that he'd made the
right decision. He had all the beautiful voices he needed.*

*What drove him to doubt was the Coalition itself: the
most dogmatic, petty batch of neo-leftist glory-hogs he'd*

ever chanced to meet. Coming together with them had been his first real experience with the calcified dregs of The Movement, per se. For all their much-vaunted love of The People, they were as closed-in and cliquish as the fucking Masonic Order; and when it came to imagination, he'd seen more of it in the ads that read: DRAW BLINKY, MAKE BIG$$$!!!

Billy didn't much care for the March 28th Coalition. They didn't much care for him, either.

But there was a cause, which transcended the egos of Coalition and Billy alike. There was the crowd, which had traveled from far and wide to express its collective outrage and love of the Earth.

And there was the music, which in many ways was the heaviest thing of all.

The music, at that moment, was absolute magic. He had the crowd under his spell, but it wasn't quite that simple. The music had him by the balls, as well: his voice and his fingers were slaves to the song. It forced him through an extra singalong chorus that the crowd received with almost sexual ardor.

And that, of course, was when Max strode out onto the stage.

Max Fogel was the Grand Potentate of the Coalition. He was also the MC of its dog-and-pony show. He had a Karl Marx beard and a Karl Marx receding hairline to cover a brain that had stopped growing at roughly the same time that Karl Marx died. Billy often thought that Max would only achieve true happiness if someone slipped an R strategically into his name.

Billy stood at center stage, with a microphone aimed at his Ovation and another one at his face. He was concluding the brief instrumental interlude that led to the song's finale. Max came up to within six inches of the vocal mike and said, in a voice that carried through the speakers, "Your time is up."

For a very long moment, time seemed to stand absolutely still.

And the air around the stage began to crackle.

Billy looked out into the sea of faces; and for the first time, he realized how completely they were hanging on his every move. He looked at Max, saw how easily he could slice the man into fatty strips of bacon. There was an

*incredible sense of power in the moment: the sense that the
outcome of the entire event was squarely in his hands, as
surely as the guitar that he continued to play.*

I could devastate you, *Billy thought, staring Max
straight in the eye.* Right now. *Right in front of these
people.* Using nothing but your own swinish absence of
tact. You'd be too embarrassed to show your face in front of
these people again. It would be easy. It would be fun.

*But then he looked back at the crowd; and beyond, at
the cooling towers, barely visible through the haze hanging
over the Susquehanna River. That was the issue. That was
why they were gathered together: not to brand Max as a
walking turd, not to point out the hypocrises of the
Movement, but to inspire hope and feeling of community
among these people, so that there might someday be an end
to all the terracidal madness, nuclear and otherwise.*

And in that moment, Billy made his decision.

"Kids," he said, booming into the microphone. "I've
just been informed that my time is up. There's just about a
minute left in this song. I could stop right now, but I just
want to ask you: would you like to hear the end of it?"

"YEAH!!!" *came the thunderous response.*

"All right!" *Billy yelled. The crowd cheered. Max
glared. Billy blew him a kiss. He didn't give a fuck whether
Max was satisfied or not. The People had spoken, and it was
to them that Billy spoke as he sang the last lines of the song:*

> "Don't give up!
> We need you!
> Don't give up!
> We need you!"

Everybody but Max sang along.

So much for solidarity.

*They gave Billy a standing ovation when he left the
stage, but he could barely hear it. He was immersed in the
Power.*

And the knowledge that he had not abused it.

Faintly, very faintly, above the bedroom floor and the
dream-crowd's roar, a pair of invisible hands were also
applauding.

THIRTEEN

THE CLEANUP (PART 1)

Billy awoke to the sound of scuffling paper in the darkness of his room. He was up and on his feet in a flash, the cobwebs of dreamland trailing behind him. His hand shot out for the bedside lamp. There was fear in his belly and fire in his eyes as he stared at the sound and flicked on the light.

Bubba lolled his tongue stupidly, grinning, from the corner.

"Oh, Jesus," Billy muttered, letting out his own private grin of relief. *In a minute, my heart will stop thudding,* he assured himself. *God, I thought it was one of those things. . . .*

The dream resurged: the flood of memories. For a moment, he was back on the stage, reliving the fine high rush of triumph . . .

. . . and then he was back in his room, surveying the ruin, looking at the way his life had not so much stacked up as fallen all over the place . . .

. . . and then he was staring at the digital clock. It read 2:35. He felt wide awake. There were several hours of darkness left before the rest of the world awoke.

You can do anything, said a voice in his head. *Clean up your life, clean up the streets, clean up the whole goddam planet if you play your cards right.*

Suddenly, a number of things became remarkably clear.

In particular, where to begin.

(2:50)

There were 187 empty bottles in his room. He counted them as he lined them up in front of the bathtub. At an estimated six-pack a day, that took him back to nearly five weeks' worth. Most of them his. It had been that long since he and Larry had given the place a cursory cleaning.

The kitchen floor was covered, but his room looked almost naked. It was amazing how much space they took up. *If Larry wakes up and sees this, he'll go kablooee*, Billy cautioned himself, then stopped.

Because Larry's door was open, and the patented Larry Roth "Snore From Hell" was nowhere in evidence. When in full foghorning bloom, you'd hear irate neighbors pounding on walls, doors, floors, and ceilings. It never woke up Larry. He made more noise than a twenty-car pileup.

The prognosis was simple: no snoree, no Larry. The Smiley-Face Slasher had frightened him off. *Probably off boffing that receptionist*, Billy mused, grinning. *Nice piece of leverage, Lar'. Play on the ol' motherly instinct.*

In a way, it was too bad. Larry's snore alone would probably be enough to scare the killer off, if he ever dragged his ass around again. *Which I doubt he will*, he added.

But I wish he would.

Billy opened a Rolling Rock (188, he noted absently) and sat down on the rim of the bathtub. He turned on the hot water and stuck his hand under the faucet until his skin turned red and the steam began to billow.

It doesn't hurt. He was amazed by how calmly he was taking it. *I've never touched anything this hot for more than a second. I can feel it, but it doesn't hurt.* He took a long swig of beer with his other hand, lips grinning around the mouth of the bottle. *Look, Ma! No hands!*

Then he steadily, painstakingly washed out all 188 bottles, one by one. Many of them were simple rinse jobs, but quite a few boasted some startling and tenacious lower-life forms that clung to the bottom like barnacles. A few pieces of green stuff that looked like rotting bacon. A few flat black hash browns. And lots of flat little turquoise dots, like the ones you'd find on an old English muffin.

If I find something that looks like scrambled eggs, I'm in trouble, he mused, a little queasy. *I'll have to do a picture, call it "Breakfast On Slimeworld." It'll make me an artist of international stature.*

No such luck. Down the drain went his moldering fortune, in wave after colorful wave. He settled for the $9.40, his reward for cashing the empties in. They filled two Hefty bags. It took fifteen minutes.

(3:10)

Four more Hefty bags were filling up on the floor beside him: two for laundry, two for garbage. The laundry was winning, but not by much. It had been ages since Billy'd seen the floor. It looked nice, if somewhat dirty.

Between the pockets and the floor, he came up with forty dollars. A lot of other missing things turned up as well. He deferred them to the next step, whipping through the task with cool efficiency.

It took another bag to hold the clothes. He put them on the bag, then lugged the garbage into the kitchen. When he came back into the bedroom, it looked almost palatial. Another fifteen minutes had gone by.

(3:25)

He thought about everything else that remained to be done, from tidying and alphabetizing his records and tapes to the dishes to the laundryomat to getting all of his papers in order. Etcetera. Etcetera.

(3:26)

He said, "Fuck it," and wished that all of it were already done.

It worked.

(3:30)

He began to recover from the shock.

"Jesus Christ." They were the first words to make it out of his throat. In less time than it would have taken to blink an eye—and far too fast for his eyes to have seen it— the place was clean. *Completely* clean. Even the cockroaches, living or dead, were gone.

The dishes were washed and dried and in their places. The stove—a nightmare, by anybody's standards—was immaculate for the first time since its arrival on Stanton

Street. The floors were mopped and waxed and shiny. The
garbage bags were gone entirely.

All the laundry bags were gone, as well: the clothes
clean and pressed and put away. Nine dollars and forty
cents were neatly stacked on the floorspace where the
returnables had been. All his records and tapes and papers
were filed: in alphabetical order, of course.

Samantha Stevens, you got nothin' on me, he mused,
beginning to giggle, visions of a twitchy-nosed Elizabeth
Montgomery dancing in his head. It was too weird. He
spun around and around in the center of his room, laughter
mounting into hysteria, simultaneously boggling at and
accepting how easily all physical law had been superseded.
The old Firesign Theatre line came back to him: *everything
you know is wrong.* In the context of the moment, truer
words had never been spoken.

Then he glanced at his desk, and the hilarity stopped.
The twirling stopped.

His heart nearly stopped.

There was a neat stack of papers on his desk. He knew
what it was, even before he got close enough to read the
first page. "I gave you away, three years ago," he muttered,
barely able to whip up the wind. The pages didn't react,
one way or the other. They just stayed where they were.

On the desk.

Before him.

There was a tattered leather chair in front of the desk.
Billy eased himself into it. He was shaking. He couldn't
help it. He was frightened. He couldn't help that, either.
The light in the room was beginning to shimmy, and he felt
himself slipping back . . .

. . . *to that summer in '77, just before the nervous
breakdown, on his friend Jeffrey's porch, on acid, while the
jam session blasted inside and the world blasted out all
around him and the only thing he could do was pour out his
soul onto page after page after page* . . .

It was the poem. The I'm-ready-to-die poem. The
dear-God-please-explain-what's-going-on-because-I-can't-
stand-to-live-anymore poem that he'd written on the eve of
the madness that had nearly destroyed him. In its own
strange way, it was the last time he'd prayed . . .

. . . before the night in Café Figaro.

When Christopher had come.

"You were looking for clues?" Billy asked himself rhetorically. His voice was high and quavering.

He started to read.

God is a fool
Of the worst sort
Twisted labyrinth maker
Weaver of the fabric
In which we are
So hopelessly entangled
I think
"God, can't we stop dancing
Even for a second?
Whirling like fools for
Your clownish entertainment?"
But no
We are of the fabric
We have no choice
So we dance
Fools all
Propelled by God/Great Bozo's
Heaving breath . . .

"You realize, of course," Christopher said from behind him, "that them's *fightin'* words."

"WAH!" Billy yelled, jumping a foot out of his chair.

"The place is lookin' good. You might wanna take up housekeeping as a second career."

"Don't sneak *up* on me like that!" Billy took a couple of deep breaths to steady himself. "Man, don't they believe in knocking where you come from?"

"No doors, no windows. You get out of the knack of needing privacy. If you know God's always watching, what's the sense in pretending you're ever alone?"

"Christopher, you bring me solace when skies are gray. I always hoped that angels were just like you."

The angel smiled. "Think you might wanna be one when you grow up?"

"Nice job, if you can get it."

"You're executive material, kid. Take it from me."

"Yeah, well, great. So what do you want from me, anyway? To what do I owe the ex-treme pleasure?"

"You found the poem."

Pause. From Billy, a nervous swallow.

"You put it there, didn't you?"

"Who, *me*?" The angel feigned alarum.

"It's important, isn't it?"

"You tell me."

Christopher just stood there with a cunning little smirk. The more Billy stared at it, the more inscrutable it became.

"Yeah, okay," Billy sighed. "It's important. You bastard."

"So keep reading. Don't mind me. I'm just gonna doodle in my notebook for a while."

"You do that," Billy growled, lighting a cigarette with jittering fingers. The ashtray, for once, was empty and visible. It reminded him, again, of just how absolutely everything had changed.

Then he turned back to the poem, all seventeen handwritten pages of it, and allowed it to pull him back.

Into the madness.

(3:55)

Why? That was the question at the bottom of those seventeen screaming pages: a big fat pain-wracked metaphysical *why*. It read like a poem, but in fact it was a hysterical letter to God the Father, asking: why is the sky blue, Daddy? Why do people have to die? Why do I have to eat my vegetables? Why? *Why?* WHY?

No other question can make you crazy quite so thoroughly, quite so easily. It made short work of the twenty-year-old Billy Rowe. He'd been completely unable to accept the answer, the only real answer there was.

Now, nearly eight years later, a whole new batch of *why* questions had arrived: Why do men go around murdering women? Why am I being tailed by angels and demons? Why is any of this happening at all?

Billy could accept the answer now.

Because. He whispered the word in his mind. *Because that's just the way it is.*

And it was such a relief to acknowledge it, to embrace the penultimate truth of it. *Because that's just the way it is*. So simple that it sounded like it said exactly nothing, when it was actually saying everything that needed to be said.

"So I have the Power," he said out loud. "And my time has come."

"That's correct," Christopher chirped from behind him. "You still had a couple of guesses left from the other night, you know. So . . . you win!"

Billy laughed. He'd almost forgotten that Christopher was hanging out. "So what's the Grand Prize?" he inquired, tidying the stack of paper on his desk.

"My never-ending respect."

"Oh, terrific!" Billy sneered, beginning to turn. "Couldn't afford a lifetime supply of Snickers bars, I gath—"

He stopped.

The room was empty.

". . . er," Billy concluded, blinking. Then he noticed the notebook, suspended roughly three feet above the floor. A silver pen was moving across one open page. It seemed to be doing it all by itself.

"Cut that out!" Billy yelled.

"Oh! Sorry." Christopher reappeared, the notebook and pen in his hands. "Just trying to be inconspicuous."

"Well, don't. Things are weird enough as it is." The cigarette he'd lit had smoldered to death in the ashtray. Billy lit another. "So, now what?"

"I'm not the one to ask, big fella. Ask yourself. Are you done for the night?"

"Not exactly, no. What, did you plan to hang around and watch?"

"You got a problem with that?"

"Matter o' fact, I do," Billy said. Christopher looked wounded. "Aw, Snookums. Don't get me wrong. You're delightful company. It's just that there's stuff I have to work out by myself."

"Absolutely true." Christopher pocketed his writing utensils and stood. "You're starting to relax now, aren't you?"

Billy grinned sheepishly. "Yeah. I am."

"You'll be fine. Just get yourself on center and in focus. You're off to a terrific start."

"Thank you."

"My pleasure. So I'll see ya later, huh?"

"You bet. Take care—uh, wait!"

"What?"

"I . . . I gotta ask you something." Billy could feel himself hunching into an I-know-this-is-stupid posture, couldn't help himself.

"Shoot."

"Is God male, female, both, or neither?"

"Yes."

Billy laughed. "That's what I thought. Thanks!"

"No problem." Christopher grinned, saluted. "Later!"

" 'Bye!"

It was just like saying good-bye to any other friend, except that this one didn't have to use the stairs. Christopher vanished without so much as a *poof!*, heading off toward God knows where.

Wonder if I could do that?, Billy mused. He thought about materializing in Mona's bed, on top of her. Would she ever be surprised. The thought was so appealing that he almost considered giving it a try.

Then a picture formed in his mind's eye; and in it, Mona was not alone when he popped into the room . . .

"Shit." Dave's face sucked all the joy out of the fantasy. The happy phone call from earlier danced back into his brain with golf shoes. He grimaced against the vision, the sounds, the sensations. It didn't stop them from coming, but it gave him something to do.

She dumped you, man, said a voice in his head. It sounded petty. He listened to it anyway. It was loud. *You're inconveniencing her, and she loves you so much that she's left you to go crazy on your own. Lotta fucking compassion. Great girl. You bet.*

A slightly less bitter voice spoke up. *That's ridiculous,* it said. *If she didn't love me, she wouldn't have put up with my decay for so long. She just can't believe that she's having to deal with this at the most happening time of her life.*

If you weren't such a shmuck, said an old, tired voice, *you'd get yourself a total overhaul. Look at you! Look at your—*

Billy smiled. The click from inner to outer was loud and clear.

"You're old tapes," he informed his conscious mind. "You're talking like nothing has changed. You're telling me the room's a mess when I cleaned it up an hour ago. CATCH UP!"

His thoughts, stunned and chagrined, were still for a moment.

When the picture of Mona came back, he was in it, and Dave was gone.

And when he opened his eyes, Billy saw himself reflected in the windowpane: Grampa Moses, with the 50,000-year-old beard. It occurred to him, for what seemed like the first time, that he hadn't really seen his face since 1974, and that most of the people he was close to now had never even seen it at all.

"Mona," he said, very softly, to himself. "I'm gonna get you back, baby. If it's a new man you need, I will become that man. For you."

The next phase was clear.

And the cleanup was only beginning.

FOURTEEN

LOVE AND WAR

They had just finished hearing about how girls just want to have fun when Mona started hooting from the living room. Paula glanced up from her storyboards with customary contempt. Lisa smiled, recognizing the reason for the hooting at once.

"Come on," she said to Paula, who sat beside her on the bed. "I want you to see this."

Paula Levin reluctantly rose from the mattress. She looked like she'd been carved out of cinder blocks by a pissed-off Nazi neorealist: chunky figure, ashen complexion. Her broadest smile was a tiny curl at one end of two profoundly-tightened lips. She was not smiling now.

The two of them moved into the living room, where Mona sat cross-legged in the middle of the floor. MTV was firing through Manhattan Cable and into the Sylvania, which then pumped it into the room. Dave Hart and the Brakes were providing the sound.

And Mona was dancing across the screen.

"That's you," Paula said. Mona nodded, grinning, eyes glued to the tube. On the screen, her long black hair had been teased into an ebony stormcloud that whooshed and billowed around her face. Her metallic-blue eyelids were flown at half-mast, partially veiling the dark eyes that fired hunger at the camera lens. She wore a black satin gown that clung desperately to her curves, yet flew liquidly up her thighs at the coaxing of a hand.

Lisa, as always, gaped while she watched Mona dance. There was something so exquisitely sensual about it, a fairy-tale perfection that the eye could scarcely believe. In motion, Mona was magic, and Lisa was constantly under her spell.

Paula, on the other hand, was less than enchanted. She was virtually glowering now. It was almost enough to wipe the smile from Lisa's face. But not quite.

Mona disappeared from the screen, and Dave replaced her. Lisa had to admit that he looked gorgeous, too, in a rock star kind of way. The band was behind him, and he copped an *el serioso* stance as he began to sing:

"Given all the time you'd need,
  Could you offer more than you'd receive?"

Cut to a living room scene, where a grittier Dave sat on a threadbare couch with a blonde who was cute, but rather plain by comparison to Mona. The blue light of a TV screen flickered on their faces as, off-screen, Dave's singing voice continued:

"Given all that you'd require,
  Could you find that object of desire?"

And Mona was there, on the TV within the TV, provocatively bopping to the sound. The camera focused on her wickedly-smiling lips, her moist tongue's seductive flicking.

Paula grunted and stomped her foot. It was not meant to be in time with the music.

"What?" Lisa said, glancing sharply over at Paula, who was puffing herself up like the Goodyear Blimp of wrath.

"This is repulsive," Paula asserted, then turned somewhat contemptuously toward Mona and said, "How does it feel to be an 'object of desire'?"

"Slightly better than being the object of contempt," Mona countered. She was smiling.

"You don't think the men who produced this video hold you in contempt?"

"No. I think they respect me enough to employ me . . ."

"As a slut."

". . . as an actress who's portraying an object of desire," Mona threw back steamily. "And I think you've got a wise fucking mouth."

Lisa winced. This had turned ugly with remarkable speed. She tried to think of some way to get Paula out of there, but it was too late. The battle was engaged. Her attention retreated to MTV, where Dave was singing:

"You want something for nothing
With nothing that's taken away."

On the screen Dave was kneeling in front of his TV in a gesture of supplication. The blonde came into the picture with a fresh beer for him. He kissed her perfunctorily, took the beer, and continued to stare at the tube.

"Do you have any idea what this song is about?" Mona was saying. She was mad, but she was also enjoying herself. Lisa tried to wipe the smile off her face and failed. The encounter was fascinating. She watched.

"Of course!" Paula began.

"I doubt it," Mona cut in. She took a deep breath and continued. "It's about this guy who's got a perfectly wonderful girlfriend, but . . ."

"He treats her like chattel—"

". . . he's got fantasies about the perfect woman who will be forever young and forever beautiful, and who will fuck his brains out day and night."

"And you're her!" Paula crowed triumphantly. "You're the woman who will put herself out there and feed their twisted fantasies!"

"I assume you don't have fantasies."

"They don't involve the subjugation of women."

"No, they involve the subjugation of men. I guess that's a whole lot better."

"Men are pigs. And when you play into their hands like that, you become the swill on which they feed. You degrade all women with your behavior."

"And you," Mona said, "are a belligerent cunt. That's a more positive role model, I assume."

For a long crackling second, it looked like Mona was going to get hit. The thought made Lisa very nervous. Mona was tough and agile and strong, but she depended on her looks for her livelihood. A black eye would not do.

The doorbell rang. "I'll get it," Lisa said, grateful for the interruption. *Don't kill each other while I'm gone*, she was tempted to say, but the words wouldn't come. She blasted toward the door, thinking about the nature of the conflict, wondering who she disagreed with more.

Bottom line: she didn't like men much more than Paula did. She'd learned a healthy distrust for most of them as early as junior high, when the hooting and the hitting-on grew in tandem with her breasts. And then, years later, the rape had confirmed it. Men *were* pigs, by and large: even the best of them would toss you down and prong you, given half a chance. They automatically assumed superiority, the right of possession. They didn't seem to understand that women were people, too.

But what Paula didn't understand was that Mona wasn't doing it for the men. She was doing it for herself. She was using what she had to make her way in the world. Despite a billion ugly experiences of her own, Mona was still turned on by men; and she wasn't above sleeping with them if she thought it might get her where she wanted to go. She used them as much as they used her. It was parity. And if she could handle it, more power to her.

Because Mona was as much of a feminist as anyone. She believed in equal opportunity and equal pay. She believed that women should be allowed to develop into full human beings, not squeezed into an empty-headed and exclusively nurturing role. She held those truths to be self-evident, and took them in the same stride that she took her beauty. The only time they came up was when confronted by a power-tripping Neanderthal male, at which point she fought as hard as Paula or anybody.

So, yeah, Paula was a bit of a jerk sometimes (but only on days that ended with the letter Y). On the other hand, she was a film director of unquestionable power and daring. *Between Our Thighs* was a blistering attack on male supremacy, and had probably caused more screaming matches than any other film in the history of feminist cinema. Lisa was honored to be editing the next Paula Levin film. It was worth the occasional grating unpleasantness.

So long as they don't kill each other, she silently concluded. Then the doorbell rang again, and she pushed the buzzer that unlocked the downstairs doors. She held it, the nasal *BRAZZZZZZ* droning in her ears, until the inner door closed and the footsteps started up the stairs. Then she let go of the buzzer, opened the apartment door, and looked to see who was coming.

The guy was short and thin, with a Mick Jagger haircut and the kind of multilayered, vaguely *Road Warrior*esque clothing that had become all the rage. There was something vaguely familiar about his handsome, clean-cut face, but she couldn't put her finger on it.

"Hello?" she said, skrinching up her own face scrutinously.

Then he smiled, and the shock of recognition hit with such sudden, swift intensity that she staggered for a moment, breathless. A huge smile of her own bloomed over her face, and she started to call his name.

"Shhhhh," he hissed, bringing one finger to his lips and winking.

* * *

The video was almost over, but it didn't really matter anymore. She'd seen it before, and she'd see it again, whereas a good fight with Paula Levin didn't happen every day.

"See, that's just the point," she was saying. "I'm not against pornography. I don't think the evidence backs you up. I mean, rape was going on in the days of Attila the Hun! You think that the hordes were all sitting around reading *Hustler* magazine? Come on!"

Paula sneered. "That's such an infantile argument. Pornography doesn't make men vile. Men are already vile. Pornography just encourages them, and gives them the means to control and dehumanize women."

"It dehumanizes men, too! Can't you see that? Christ, you talk as if men were completely happy with the way things are, when most of 'em are actually pretty miserable—at least as miserable as the women they're supposed to be oppressing."

"And here's living proof!" called a male voice from Lisa's bedroom. *Oh, Jesus. Billy,* Mona thought, all the wind going out of her sails. She felt suddenly queasy, and her eyes were riveted on the curtain as she waited for the moment of truth.

But the guy who came into the room wasn't Billy. He was the same size and shape, but his hair was stylish and his face was clean-shaven and his clothes weren't filthy or ragged or—

"Omigod." All one word, barely audible above the music. "Omigod." She just stared. She couldn't stop.

Billy did a little wiggling sashay, threw up his hands, and froze. "TA-DAH!!!" he announced, beaming obscenely.

"Mona, I've got someone I'd like you to meet," Lisa said, coming up beside Billy. She was smiling, too. It was threatening to be contagious.

Fortunately, Paula was not. It was nice to have a sobering influence in the room. For one brief flickering moment, Mona almost liked Paula. Then it went away, and she returned her gaze to Billy.

"Wuh," she said. It was the only thing she could think of.

"A new primitive form of greeting," Billy muttered to Lisa, who nodded sagely.

"Wuh . . . what *happened?*" Mona elaborated.

"I mugged a student at the Fashion Institute and stole his clothes."

"And his hair," Lisa added.

"Yeah, it's terrible. There's this naked, hairless kid lying unconscious in the stairwell—"

"That's not funny," Paula interjected.

"Oh, yes it is," Billy begged to differ. "You should see him."

"Billy!" Mona was exasperated now. The shock was mellowing into a more rational utter confusion. "I don't understand. I—" She gave up, stood there shaking her head with a pained and pleading expression.

"Well, to tell you the truth, ma'am," he drawled, "I heard you might be auditioning for a new boyfriend, and I wanted to try out for the part." He gave her a frank, disarming grin, and shrugged. "That's basically it."

"He slipped me a ten-spot," Lisa said, addressing Paula, "in hope that we could go work at the Commons for a while."

"Ve vant to be alone," Billy purred. Then he cast a questioning glance at Mona and squeaked the word, "Okay?"

Mona didn't know what to do. The weird thing was, there was no anger in her. It had all taken a nap or something, gone off for a week at Club Med. The only things left were awe and a giddy exitement.

Billy looked *great*: that was the marvelous, terrifying thing. It was hard to believe that it was actually him. He looked easily ten years younger, and he was absolutely radiant with confidence.

There was no way she could say no to him, although she couldn't say yes either. She couldn't speak. Her head gave a little teensy nod, eyes baby-doll wide.

"Terrific," Billy said, then turned to face Paula. "And who are you?" he asked, extending his hand. "I don't believe we've met."

"Paula Levin," she said, taking his hand and squeezing it to the threshold of pain. Billy squeezed back with equal strength, grinning hugely.

"Oh, you're kidding!" he enthused. "I sat through *Between Our Thighs* twice! It was a fan-tastic movie!"

Paula looked skeptical. "Why are you saying this?" she finally asked.

"'Cause it's true! I really enjoyed the movie. I dragged as many male friends as I could to see it. You should have seen their faces. They were furious."

"And you?" Paula wanted to know. "Were you furious, too?"

"Absolutely. But I loved it. There's something about getting kicked in the nuts for an hour and a half—it really makes you think about where you stand."

"And how," Lisa contributed.

"But you didn't agree with it," Paula probed.

"I agree with a lot of it. A lot of it is over the edge, but that's okay. I'm a firm believer in overkill." Paula snorted. Billy continued. "It doesn't make for good philosophy, but it's great for entertainment."

"You ready to go?" Lisa asked Paula, who was starting to seethe.

"Where?"

"The Chelsea Commons. It's this great little bar on the corner. Good food and drink, terrific atmosphere, peaceful enough to work in." Lisa winked and gestured. "C'mon. You'll love it."

Paula turned—reluctantly, it seemed—and followed Lisa out of the room. Lisa waved 'bye. Paula didn't.

"Maybe we'll come down later and argue some more!" Billy called after them. Mona laughed despite herself. He turned to her and mimicked a Paula-glower. It looked like a shaved and none-too-bright gorilla.

"Now you stop that!" Mona cried. The laughter was painful. He couldn't resist one last slack-jawed grimace. "You're incorrigible," she added.

"Yep, that's me," he said.

The apartment door slammed shut. They heard footsteps descending the stairs. The laughter vanished in a puff of thin air. Mona was overwhelmingly aware of the fact that she was alone with Billy, something that she'd told herself would never happen again. But this—this was Billy and *not*-Billy. It was very hard to deal with. She was very much off-balance.

Billy sensed his advantage, and it almost annoyed her. The only thing was that he had *earned* his confidence; if she hadn't broken up with him, if things hadn't gotten so crazy already, her immediate and total reaction would have been one of pride and joy. It was the suddenness of it, the both terribly-bad and terribly-apt *timing* of it, that left her floundering in the violent sea of her own emotions.

"Can you talk with me now?" he asked her. The clown was gone. The man she loved was back.

For the first time in ages, she mused. *Goddam it.* "Okay. I'll give it a whirl."

"Thank you." He smiled, cautious now, and motioned to the floor beside her. "May I sit down?"

"Sure."

He sat. He did not touch her.

"Let me start," he said.

She nodded.

"I'm gonna try and make this quick, so we can go back and forth for a while. Damn, it's hard." He sighed and wiped a little genuine sweat from his forehead. Then he nailed her with his eyes.

"You see, it's like this. I was sinking. You were watching me sink. You tried to help. You couldn't. You were rising while I was sinking, and we couldn't reach each other's hands."

Tears were starting to form in Mona's eyes. She wished them away. It didn't work. She turned, for a moment, to look at the TV. *Something For Nothing* was just about to end. She was dancing away from Dave and going out the door as the little letters flashed that said: *Dave Hart and the Brakes, "Something For Nothing," SOMETHING FOR NOTHING, Griffin Records.* The moment was so poignant, so absurdly appropriate, that she let the tears stream down her face without lifting a finger to stop them.

"Oh, baby," Billy said. He reached out to wipe the wet trails from her cheeks. She flinched for a second, but didn't stop him. His fingers came up wet. He brought them to his lips and licked them clean.

"Turn the TV off," Mona sighed.

"Good idea." Billy reached over with his newly clean fingers and twiddled the knob. The screen went blank. Silence draped itself over the room like a cool satin sheet.

"The man you loved wasn't sinking," he said. "The man you loved had his shit together. He wasn't a star, but he wasn't a failure. He still had his pride. He was striving for something . . ."

"The man I loved was you," she gasped. The tears were really pouring now. It wasn't so bad. It was a pain she could appreciate.

"Yeah, well, I'm back," he said. "And I'm not going down for the count again. I swear to God, Mona."

"I love it when you say my name."

"Mona . . . Mona." He smiled. She smiled. He took her hair in his hands. It felt incredible. He massaged the sides of her head. She almost died.

"Billy Rowe," she said.

"I want to be your man. I want to be *a* man. I'll do anything in the fucking world to keep you. Do you believe me?"

"I want to."

"That's good enough for me."

He was starting to cry now, too. She leaned forward suddenly and licked the tears from his face. He licked her back. The conversation ceased.

The floor was uncarpeted. For now, it didn't matter. There was no way on Earth that Mona would break the action for any reason. They settled back down into a prone position, he slightly on top. They kissed, almost frantically.

Billy pulled away for a second and then started again, gently this time. There was the wonderful experience of time standing absolutely still. His hands were on her face. Her hands were on his back. Slowly, she brought one of her hands around and dragged it lightly down his chest, his belly, to the final resting place at his crotch.

It was hard as a hammer and soft as satin. She gloried in its touch, burrowing under his waistband. He groaned into her mouth and brought his own hands down to lightly trace the roundness of her breasts, her nipples. They got hard and soft as well. He put them softly through their paces.

It was very important to get out of their clothes. The best thing about clothes was dispensing with them. She went for his belt first, unbuckling it with blind grace. He brought his hands down to her waistband and eased it toward her ankles. She lifted her hips in clear cooperation, waited for her jogging pants to disassociate with her completely. Then she deftly unsnapped and unzipped him, began to echo the gesture. When she got to his knees, he kicked his boots off, and the rest of the process went entirely unimpeded.

Next came the shirts. No problem at all. Neither Mona nor Billy were wearing a bra, which speeded things up considerably. Both of them were beginning to sweat. Neither of them minded. It gave them some juice to work with.

Billy's lips worked their way from her lips to her chin, her chin to her throat, her throat to her shoulder to her armpit to her nipple on the left-hand side. She let out little *oooing* sounds. They intensified as he moved to the right side of her bosom.

And then down.

And down.

And down.

There was a brief stretch, between the time when his lips reached her hot and nether to the point of first coming, where the bad times flickered across the private screening room of her mind. It was like reading road signs at ninety miles per hour. They didn't mean anything. They had nothing to do with the fact that he was driving her crazy with his fingers and lips and tongue, that her highly-trained body was helpless now to do anything but shudder and grind, that all of reality was funneling down to fingers and tongue and fingers and tongue and the warm wet beast of sweet thunder and fire that was being lured now, lured up from the depths within her, climbing up to meet and mate with his tongue, flood his mouth with cries of liquid ecstasy . . .

. . . and then she was coming, and the bad times were gone, the bad times had never existed, nothing existed outside the orgasmic reality of her flesh and his sweetly relentless technique that plied and probed and stroked every last gleeful secret of desire from her lips . . .

. . . and then the riding was ending, the long graceful

segue back to earth and the hardwood floor, the muscles uncoiling, the tension hissing silently out of her like steam from a safety valve. Mona found that she'd recovered the power of speech, did not choose to exercise it yet. Billy was still easing her down, and she felt like she had time.

All the time in the world.

Then he stopped, looked up, and grinned at her across the solid plateau of her belly, meeting her gaze between the twin peaks of her breasts. "Mmmm," he said.

"You, my dear, give the best head in the universe."

"Look who's talking."

"Do I have to prove it?"

"I dare ya. I *double*-dare ya!"

"Just let me catch my breath. . . ."

"Hey, don't worry. I'll catch it for ya." He crawled up over her and sealed her with a kiss. She could taste herself. The beast within her reawakened, crying Billy's name.

"Oh, baby," she said, drawing her lips away softly. "I don't know how I could ever have let you go."

"You had a little help."

"Yeah, but—"

"Forget it. It's over." He kissed her once, quickly, then pulled back, smiling. "I believe we have a serious competition going on."

"Oh, yeah." She slid out from under him and rolled him onto his back. "We're going into the top of the first inning in today's double-header," she droned in her best Joe Garagiola voice. He started to laugh, and that was when she got her lips around him.

"Oh!" he gasped. She could feel him tensing. "You're not doing anything to strengthen your case, you realize."

But Mona opted to continue speaking in tongues. It was the best, the most beautiful way of telling him how much she loved him, how happy she was that he was back, how proud of his return from the land of the lost.

And for a brief, puzzling second, she could have sworn that she heard his voice, inside her mind, whisper *Mona, I love you, too*.

FIFTEEN

PLAYING TO WIN

Five forty-five on an overcast Tuesday afternoon, and Billy was smiling. It had been a good day, in every respect. His cash intake had been phenomenal. He was slated for another late-night rendezvous with Mona. His playing had opened in top form and gone straight uphill from there. The response of the crowds had followed suit.

But the bottom line on his smile was *control*, pure and simple. *For once*, he mused, *I feel like I've really got a handle on this. For once . . .*

It had started around five-thirty this morning, just as the first faint tendrils of dawn were inching themselves across the sky. Billy had left Mona's, and their torrid reconciliation, with the promise of later and greater ground to be covered tonight. The walk down from Chelsea had been inspiring rather than tiring; something about the flavor of Manhattan at dawn filled him with a sense of imminent purpose. He felt like he'd gotten the drop on the town.

He'd hit Stanton Street, taken Bubba for a walk, and grabbed his gear. Then he'd hopped a cab down to South Ferry, grabbed a large coffee and an egg on a roll, and grabbed a prime spot on the Staten Island ferryboat of his choice for the rush-hour shift.

It was a great way to start the day: a solid three hours of cruising back and forth in the harbor, playing and singing to boatload after boatload of captive listeners. It was also a very lucrative route, and it had been a long time since Billy'd gotten up the gumption to drag-ass out of bed and do it.

But today was different.

Everything was different.

After rush hour, six round trips, and $47.50 later, he had ambled up to Liberty Plaza and scored a choice spot catercorner to the jutting twin shadows of the World Trade Center. By eleven-thirty he was happily serenading the endless streaming hordes of the financial district as they fled their cloistered air-conditioned cubicles for a half hour of lunchtime release. Billy competed for sonic primacy with a half-dozen other acts: jazz trios, hip white funksters, comedians, and magic shows.

But there had been no competition. Not really. Billy played and sang like an angel, garnering the lion's share of the crowds.

And the money.

By two o'clock, Billy had it in the bag. He broke as the last of the lunch crowd trickled by, pausing to accept compliments and cash from a bevy of receptionists. "We're twenty minutes late, our boss is gonna kill us, and it's *all your fault!*" one particularly well-rounded redhead informed him. He resisted the urge to take phone numbers first and ask questions later.

Three o'clock had found him back on Stanton Street. A couple of slices from Original Ray's pizza, a leisurely shower, a change of clothes, and a half hour of play with his fur-covered buddy had left him just enough time to hit Washington Square Park for the fun-filled evening set.

As he set up, he couldn't stop thinking about how beautifully the circuit worked. It was a good routine, the struggling artist's equivalent of a regular job. He'd first envisioned it last summer with Junior, the black sax-playing friend of his. Junior had readily agreed that it was a great idea.

Today was the first time that he'd actually pulled it off.

And, God, does it ever feel good, he thought. *It feels so good to be in control of the situation. Man, if I keep this up, I'll be able to pay off Albert and score some new goods for my act.*

Like the man says: I can do anything.

He set up on the eastern perimeter of the basin that was the hub of the park, his amp surreptitiously camouflaged by his jacket in response to a recent edict regarding noise pollution. The law was rather selectively enforced, according to the officer's convenience: one never knew when terror might strike. His effects were on the pavement before him; a battered "silver bullet" microphone balanced precariously on a wobbly stand before him. It wasn't much, but it was all he had left after the crippling rip-off last year.

Not to worry, he reminded himself. *Better things are a-comin' soon.*

Still, a parade of expensive pro-audio gear danced through his mind as he began his first set: a carefully-selected amalgam of Beatles, Jackson Browne, and Steely Dan guaranteed to generate maximum crowd consciousness. He felt good tonight. He'd play anything.

Hell, he said to himself. *I'd even play* "Stairway To Heaven."

The music swelled. A crowd started to form.

And Billy smiled.

By seven-fifteen Billy was in a state of complete and utter awe. He'd expected the crowd. He'd expected the enthusiasm, and the high that came from riding the fixed point of a group awareness. After everything else, he'd even expected the money that came piling into his guitar case, mesmerizing Bubba with the clinking and jingling of coin on coin on bill on coin.

He had not expected the kid.

And the kid was fucking *hot*.

Uninvited accompaniment was a fact of life for a street player. There was always someone who would inevitably come up and want to join in. Sometimes they brought an instrument. Sometimes they just wanted to sing along. Trouble was, most of them had the musical finesse of a tractor-trailer full of pigs, locking up at eighty miles per hour; and they invariably hung around until the end of the set, scaring off the audience and suggesting that you oughtta form a team. Sometimes you felt lucky if *all* they wanted was half of the money.

So when the kid wandered up, a battered flute in his hand, Billy simultaneously winced and thanked God that it wasn't something louder. If worse came to worst, he could always turn up and drive the intruder away by outblasting him.

But the kid was HOT. He couldn't be more than fifteen, and he looked like an outtake from *Menudo*, but he followed every nuance and subtle shade of color that Billy threw out. He laid back when Billy sang and screamed through the breaks; he followed chord changes without even having to look. He just hunkered down over that tarnished tube of silver and blew like Ian Anderson from Jethro Tull, rocking back and forth in boneless tandem with Billy's driving steel pulse.

After a while, Billy stopped playing songs. He just *played*: sliding from key to key, mood to mood, with no warning and no clear idea himself of what the next direction would be. It was musical barnstorming, and it was pure magic. The kid followed him every step of the way.

The crowd loved it.

Billy stepped away from the microphone and let the kid take the helm. The music soared. The crowd swelled. They were completely surrounded by now, nestled inside one of the little niches formed by the abutments, with people before, behind, above and below them. All rapt. All ears. The basin of the park was turning into a benign maelstrom of swaying flesh.

Then Billy looked up, hands on automatic, and saw a park ranger whizzing toward them on a modified golf cart. He got a sudden flash of good ol' Max Fogel, stomping out of the wings at the TMI event; and it occurred to him that, once again, he was presiding over something bigger than all of them. There was energy here, in amazing proportion; and if it ended badly, things could turn very, very ugly.

The kid turned to him, dark eyes large and rueful. He kept playing, but the words "Oh, shit" came clearly through the flute. Billy laughed, still playing as well, and mouthed the words *I'll take care of it*.

He knew what he had to do.

The ranger was babbling into his walkie-talkie at the edge of the crowd. They could see a police cruiser pull off Fifth Avenue and ominously onto the path, on an intercept course.

The crowd swayed. The ranger pushed his way into its periphery, sending little waves of nastiness rippling in his wake. Billy felt the crescendo building, building. He dug into the guitar with a flurry of furious handwork, strumming up and up the neck while the kid blew wild, arcing trills around the changes, growing in intensity by fractions of a second . . .

. . . and at precisely the right moment, with only a cursory nod of confirmation, ended *ensemble*: Billy letting ring a cascade of delicate harmonics; the kid, a breathy trill.

Sealed with a kiss.

The crowd went apeshit.

It sounded like Madison Square Garden. The applause was deafening. People started milling around, tossing money and shaking hands and patting backs and saying *you guys are great, how long have you been together, why haven't you played here before, my god, that was incredible* . . .

. . . and then the ranger was there, puffing himself up authoritatively, getting ready to deliver his ultimaxim. Billy stared into his eyes and *pushed*, just a little.

The ranger's eyes went blank.

You put up one hell of a fight, there, officer, Billy thought, stifling the urge to giggle. Then he sent a little message to the ranger's brain, and listened to the playback from the ranger's lips.

"Excuse me," the ranger said. "I just wanted to tell you that you guys are really great."

"Well, *thank* you," Billy gushed. The kid was stunned. Most of the crowd reacted the same.

"No problem," the ranger continued, still blank-eyed. "You can jam all night, as far as I'm concerned. You're great."

The cop cruiser, seeing everything under control, went on its merry way.

"Thanks again," Billy said, letting go of the control. The ranger looked ill for a moment, then grinned weakly and staggered back to his golf cart.

"What happened?" the kid wondered out loud. Billy turned, saw the glaze in those dark eyes, and understood for the first time since the jam began.

I made it happen. Not a matter of pride. Just a matter of fact. *That kid never played so well in his whole goddam life. I made it happen!*

But that wasn't all. The kid's eyes were glazed, oh yes; but they hadn't been Vacu-formed like the ranger's. There was new light behind them, bright with quantum realization. He may never have played that well before, but he would again. That much was radiantly clear.

"Oh, nothing," Billy replied, winking and jerking his thumb in the ranger's direction. "That was just one of our biggest fans."

The kid nodded like a man getting street directions in a foreign language: too embarrassed to admit that he didn't understand.

He'll have to live with that, Billy mused. *And I wish him all the best*.

They're great, she told herself.

Christine Brackett stood watching the two musicians as they milled about in the aftermath of whatever had just transpired. *Whatever* it was, she knew, it was significant. It had been a long time since she'd seen or heard anyone on the streets who was worth following up on; *ages* more since she'd been to Washington Square Park. It was such a burn-out haven: a mecca for those determined to live in the barefooted past.

Or those who came of age too late, she thought. It was difficult to avoid noticing that a lot of the hippies and free spirits lounging on the grass and smoking it couldn't have been much past Captain Kangaroo when The Movement was in full bloom.

Still, she made it a point to cruise through from time to time. You never knew what might pop up. *And it's good to see where you've been*, she added. *It helps you see where you're going.* . . .

Christine was going to hit the nearest pay phone in about ten minutes and inform Roger that today was his lucky day. Roger was her boss, her lover-of-sorts, and the major rock around her neck in the business.

And Roger was in trouble. Good ol' boy-wonder-can-do-no-wrong Roger Ferris was in deep, deep trouble. Roger did first-string A&R for Polynote Records, and his last three surefire big-time discoveries had burned a trail straight to the bottom of the cut-out bins in record time (but not before sucking thousands of Polynote dollars right up their collective noses). The Powers That Be were not currently pleased with ol' Rog; rumor had it that his ass was literally on the firing line.

All of which suited Christine just fine, except . . .

Except that Roger was her boss.

Except that Roger was her lover. Of sorts.

And except, most of all, that Roger could be and usually *was* a relentless, petulant son of a bitch; and if he went, he just might try to take anyone within reach along for the ride.

Her, first and foremost.

So Christine Brackett, a sleek and intelligent woman of thirty-four, flipped back her shimmering and tastefully-streaked blond hair, clipped a five-dollar bill to her business card, and approached the two musicians with the silly-looking dog tied to the guitar case. Smiled her best winning smile. And prepared herself to plant some hooks in their unsuspecting psyches with a grade-A *schmooz*.

With the right producer, and a solid backup band, they might just be the next wave in a turbulent business. They might just save Roger's quivering butt. And hers, in the bargain.

Besides: if anyone deserved to be heard, they did. They were *great*.

SIXTEEN

BEDROOM-EYE VIEW

Beep-beep.

Mona's clock dutifully announced the time. 2 A.M.

Beep-beep.

Duty done, it resumed its measured tracking of microseconds, face aglow as it stared up at the ceiling fan from its place on the nightstand in the darkness of her room. Nobody paid it the slightest bit of attention. It ignored them right back.

In the bed, time was standing still.

Billy was on his back, holding on for dear life to the headboard rails of her big brass bed. His eyes slid shut, but he could still see with excruciating clarity: willow-arms wrapped around her head's black mane, small breasts tight against her sleek and straining body as she rose and fell, rose and fell, Rotoscoped in Technicolor across the insides of his eyelids. She set the pace, controlling both horizontal and vertical; the best he could do was aid and abet as she thrust him deep into rubyfruit Heaven, again and again and again. The air was alive with animal ecstasy, funky sound, and scent colliding. He white-knuckled the rails, hooting and grinding and fighting like hell to forestall the inevitable uncoiling in his balls, the lunatic game-show host in his brain that said *ladies and gentlemen, it's that time again!*

And they shuddered, in unison, as the moment was upon them; and the onslaught of orgasm sealed itself in one long soul kiss. Their bodies stuck together, slick with sweat and sweet tongue-nectar. Their breath hitched, joyous and ragged. Muscular tremors echoed through them like gunshots through Carlsbad Caverns.

"I got . . . a question," Mona barely managed.

Billy smiled. "I think I . . . know what it is." Still gasping as well.

"How come we're so goddam good together, no matter what else is going on? Can you figure it out?"

"Nope. But I'm not about to complain."

Mona nodded, then slowly pulled out from around him. "Oh," they agreed in unison. She flopped over on her back beside him and stared up at the ceiling fan, whistling mutely overhead. The soft breeze was cool on their naked bodies. The temporary silence was golden and sweet.

"Earth to Billy," she called out softly, at last. They rolled onto their sides and faced each other, fingers reaching out gently to stroke each other's flesh.

"I don't want to stop touching you," he said.

"So who's stopping you?"

"I don't never ever ever want to stop."

"That might become awkward when I'm dancing."

"How about if we trade skin grafts?"

"Oh, God." She sighed and rolled away for a second. "You know, loving you is not the easiest thing I've ever done."

"No pain, no gain."

"No *brain*," she said, pointing at his skull. He made a Mongoloid face. She rolled her eyes and looked away; when she turned back to him, her mock exasperation had been replaced by honest concern.

"You're afraid of something, aren't you?" he asked her quietly. She took a moment before nodding. "You wanna tell me about it?"

"I don't know. Let me think for a minute."

"Come on. Confession is good for the soul."

"So is silent meditation."

"So's an electric carving knife. Out of the three, I'll take confession any day."

"Okay, okay." She turned away sharply. "You wanna know what I'm afraid of?"

"That was the general idea."

"I'm afraid of what's going to happen to us. I really am. It just seems like everything else about our lives is drifting apart . . . like love is just about the only thing we really have in common. And I don't know if it's enough, all by itself, to keep us together."

Billy let out an enormous sigh. She turned to look at him, but now *he* was turned away, eyes glued to the whirling blades of the fan.

"I'm just trying to be realistic," she continued. "This is a major turning point in my life . . ."

"And mine."

". . . and I don't really know what the future has in store," she continued, as if he hadn't interrupted. "Dave's talking about taking me on the road, you know. What happens if I'm gone for four, five months? Are you supposed to just sit around and wait for me?"

"As if I wouldn't do that anyway."

"But why should you have to?"

"Because the woman I love has something important to do, and I've got plenty of my own stuff to do, and why the hell *shouldn't* I wait for you? Jesus! It's not like I've got something better to do!"

"Don't get upset."

"Who's goddam fucking upset?" he asked. Then he laughed. She didn't join him. It wasn't all that funny. "No, listen, baby," he continued. "I don't know how much loving me restricts you. That's not what it's meant for. All I can rightly claim on you is first dibs; and even then, only for as long as you're into it. If you meet someone along the way, just make sure you don't tell me who or where they are, because I'll have to kill them."

"You're so understanding."

"Gentle too." Pause. "Is that all?"

"I don't know. I . . ."

"Is it Dave?"

"Well . . ." Long pause. "There is that little matter, yes."

"He's got the major hots for you."

"That's true."

"And vice versa?"

"Ummm . . ." The words *a little* appeared in her mind. She found them tacky, and refused to say them. It didn't make them go away.

"I heard that," he said, grinning ruefully.

"Heard what?"

"'A little.'"

"*What?*" For a second cold terror stole through her. Then she figured that her face must have betrayed her. "So you're a mind reader now, huh?" she said, struggling to sound nonchalant.

"I have many powers, my dear, of which you are scarcely aware."

"Like the power of presumption."

"For example." He gave her an intimate, conspiratorial wink.

"And what if I were to tell you that I don't want Dave . . . that I don't want anyone but you?"

"I'd be thrilled, of course." He smiled. "But I wouldn't stake my life on it lasting forever. Like you said: we don't know what tomorrow may bring. And I've got a long way to go before I'm bankable enough to pull an equal load with you."

"So?"

"So Dave *is*."

"Again"—a bit heatedly—"so?"

"So I'm not any more of a chump than you are. If love were enough, we'd be married by now. It's got to be backed up by action, both for each other and for ourselves.

"I'm not even remotely successful right now. You are. Dave most certainly is. If you've gotta talk realistic, then you've gotta cop to the fact that Dave can take care of you much better than I can. He can *help* more than I can. He's got something in the neighborhood of 87,000 clear advantages over me."

"But he doesn't love me like you do."

"How *does* he love you?"

"I'm not sure you could call what he feels for me love at all. He *says* he loves me. . . ."

"But he says that to all the girls?"

"Just about." She laughed. "Not really. Mostly he charms them into bed, gives them autographed records, and waves bye-bye. Or at least that's what I hear."

"But he's more serious with you—"

"You know something?" she cut in abruptly. "You sound like you're trying to sell me on him. And I'm not so sure that I like it."

"I'm just trying to be realistic." He had the good sense not to mimic her voice. "And I want you to know something."

"What?"

"I want you." His eyes came around to bore into hers now. "I want you forever. Till the day I die." She tried to look away. He wouldn't let her. His hands held her face in position. "And I am going to do everything within my power to both earn and keep you. But I will not be held responsible for dragging you down."

"Okay."

"If you go with the rock star, I'll understand."

"Okay."

"I'll kill myself, but I'll understand."

"I'll kill *you*!" she exclaimed, grabbing his throat with both hands. He rolled onto his back and let his tongue loll out limply. She giggled and squeezed. He gurgled and flailed. She threw herself on top of him and kissed his lips into silence.

"Be a rock star," she whispered when their mouths disengaged. "You have what it takes. I believe in you. Whatsername from Polynote believes in you. Everyone who really knows you believes in you . . ."

"So what else do I need?"

"Round Four," she whispered slyly.

"Oh, God," he groaned, face contorted in mock-horror. His limp penis shuddered in agreement. "It'll never play the violin again!"

"Don't be so sure," she replied, taking him in hand. She made two expert motions, and Billy made sounds that he didn't even know were in him. Paganini arose, for the fifth time tonight; in the interest of fair play, Billy dipped a pair of rigid fingers inside her.

"Never stop," she moaned. Her face glowed, in profile, beside him.

"Never ever," he agreed.

Then they came together, once again.

In earnest.

As if for the last time.

SEVENTEEN

CHRISTINE

Six hours and as many Old Peculiers later, Christine had a fairly good idea of how to package things. Her earlier attempts to locate ineffable Roger Ferris had come to naught, and she was damned if she was going to leave this message on his machine.

So she opted to forge ahead on her own, brainstorming a packaging-and-marketing strategy that would singe his short hairs. By two-fifteen she had a solid preliminary concept.

She also had one Old Peculier too many.

It wasn't that she was drunk; it was just that the smoke and clamor of the pub was exceeding its normal bounds. Which were considerable. Her eyes were red, her concentration was flagging, and the preponderance of yuppies and junior-yups was making her queasy. When the door swung open and another half-dozen piled in, she decided to take her leave.

The floor tilted a little more than she'd expected. She lurched a teeny bit, narrowly avoiding the waitress's fully laden tray, veering into a trio of undergrads instead. All of them took a moment to glare at her. "Life's a bitch," she informed them solemnly. "And then you die." They blanched visibly.

No big deal. The world went on. The waitress was long gone, and the undergrads grabbed her vacated table. Maybe she was drunk, after all. *No*, she thought. It was just that the place was so ungodly crowded, the tables packed together like dead lemmings at the bottom of a cliff.

The clientele of the Peculier pub was alarmingly young and painfully normal. Preppies, rapt in their collegiate cocoons, plus a spattering of their fully metamorphosed elders in primo yuppie form. No matter how she approached it, it was hard to take. She'd grown up in an age when the young people at least made a *pretense* of caring more for principle than capital; naive and bubble-headed though it was, they'd been light-years ahead of anything these droids had to offer.

Christine was thirty-four: she'd reached the flower of her youth in the psychedelic defiance of the '60's. She'd been to Woodstock. She'd roamed the Village, bare-footed and blasted on purple microdot and the metaphysical message of love, burning into her nervous system like a neon tattoo. She'd fallen deeply for the music, which seemed to offer so much: a sense of purpose, a sense of unity.

A sense of hope.

It had taken another decade for her to put the pieces together. But she had straightened up, working her way into the business, accepting and adapting to the changes in taste and the times that were an inevitable part of forward motion. She'd been too young for the last one. She was determined to be ready for the next, which she felt was imminent. And she'd worked toward that readiness with a willful tenacity that would've terrified half the people in this room.

Six more clean-cut college proto-droids reeled in through the doorway as she reached it. She slid out past them and into the night.

It was 2:25 in the morning.

The Greenwich Village nightlife was tapering off. Scattered pockets of pedestrians and scanty traffic passed her on her way down Waverly, heading for the cozy little Jane Street brownstone she called home. Her long blond hair shimmered in the passing streetlight; next to the illuminated headlights and neon logos for Miller and Stroh's, it was the brightest thing there.

As she made her way toward Jane Street and Ninth Avenue, she thought about Roger and the crazy sex-and-drugs-and rock 'n' roll business in which she had become embroiled. The rock 'n' roll was a consummate blast: it was great to be so close to the heart of the big-name acts, even from the tangential perspective of administrative assistant. Just being that close was more than a rush, she felt; it was an implicit facet of her unfolding destiny.

And the drugs weren't really a problem; not for her, at any rate. She'd gone through all that years before. She had about as much desire to do coke as she had to flush gold bullion down the toilet. And as for the psychedelics, well . . .

What did Alan Watts say?, she thought. "Once you've gotten the message, hang up the phone." Drugs were no big deal.

But the *sex*—

Something scuttled in front of her. She gasped as a rat the size of a football scrambled out of the gutter to her left and across the street. It wobbled into the shadow of an illegally-parked truck and was gone.

"Speaking of Roger . . ." she muttered, and giggled in spite of herself. After all, she was letting him get away with being such a scumbag. She was partly to blame. But only a little.

"It's necessary," she told herself. She treated Roger's twisted needs with the same acceptance that a Grailer would grant a swamp that lay in the path of the Quest: an unpleasant, and unavoidable, leg of the journey. And never mind the stink.

Which was why she'd let Roger fuck her into promotionability. Which was why she'd put up with the ropes and the rubber and the hideous lingerie and the insipid misogynistic fantasies.

Which was also why she was a little afraid of backing away from him now, even though he was beginning to disgust her beyond the pale. She was too damned close. Too close to moving into a position of clout. Too close to her destiny. *It is not,* she reasoned, *the worst concession I've had to make since Utopia showed me the two-by-fours propping up its false front.*

On the other hand, she added, *maybe it is.*

Because Roger Ferris was a scumbag, and no shimmering vision of her glorious future could mince her around that fact. He was smooth and funny and really sharp (so long as you ignored the subtext); he was handsome and charismatic (so long as you stuck to the surface); he was good at his job, and he knew how to treat people (so long as you weren't his subordinate). And *forget* about bed.

Past the first thirty seconds, it was hard to like Roger. All you could do was acknowledge him as an integral part of the landscape. He was there, immutable, and you would either have to go through him or somehow get around him if you wanted to get anywhere at all.

She'd found a way through him. It had worked, but it wasn't pretty.

She wondered if she would ever feel entirely clean again.

Christine Brackett turned briskly onto Greenwich Street and the last leg of her journey. She felt, deep in her heart, a small shred of the Light: a speck of innocence kept clean and glowing as a halidom to her youth and a portend of her destiny. She was a good bit less than thrilled with the world in which she lived, and the Light that shimmered at the core of her being had been growing slowly dimmer for a long long time.

But she didn't want to die.

So when the sudden rush of motion came out of the tiny construction site, behind and to her left, her spirit flared up like a Roman candle. She started to spin, body tensing in accordance with adrenaline and the will to survive. Her eyes, as always, focused on her assailant with psychotropic clarity—

The gloved hand clamped down on her throat, squeezing off her air supply, holding her painfully in place. There was a striking and total gestalt flash of the face: sunken eyes hiding under the shadow of the hat's brim; piggy nose, puffy lips, and fat jowls; an Italian grandmother's growth of beard, wispy and thin, with a dimple the size of a pencil-tip eraser at the chin.

Christine Brackett tried to scream, but no sound would come. The killer had seen to that. Her body refused to move, though her mind and her spirit screamed for her to *run!*

But it was too late for that.

The blade whirled. It put a blackhead-sized dimple in her flesh, sliced through it, forging the way for the widening and serrated edge that sawed a great puckering groove through her left lung and lodged within her exploding heart before the pain had a chance to register in her brain.

And that was only the beginning of the end.

EIGHTEEN

THE CITY OF HOPES AND DREAMS

Billy awoke, from a dreamless sleep, to the lilting strains of the garbage trucks on Tenth Avenue. The leap from sleep to wakefulness was clean and instantaneous. No fog. No fatigue. Not a thought in his head.

Mona's clock, still bright-faced on the nightstand, pegged the time at 4:35.

The garbagemen were as loud as the trucks. They didn't give a shit. They had, Billy realized, one of the most hideous, thankless jobs in all of Manhattan, keeping eight million people from being buried under their own excremental excess.

On an ordinary night, Billy might have been pissed. But this was no ordinary night. All of his senses were crystal-clear. Every creak of the truck's grinding jaws, gnawing rot. Ever flapping-jawed joke or complaint from the men. Every garbage-can bang or Hefty-bag fling. The idiosyncrasies of the engines. The rumble of rubber on damp concrete.

Most of all he was aware of Mona: the heat and scent and sight of her, beside him in the bed. There was something so impossibly perfect about it, so unspeakably beautiful, that his rational mind was uncustomarily pleased to be silent while his senses drank her in.

I love you, he thought to her, smiling. His right arm was around her curved shoulders, holding her close. The light through the window was sufficient to reveal every curve of her body through the covering of the sheets. Her face, in sleeping, was tension-free: soft, oblivious, too gorgeous for words. *This is almost too good,* he told himself, tasting her on his tongue.

But I gotta get up, another voice, also his own, informed him. *No way I'm gonna get back to sleep. I'm wide awake.*

Quietly, carefully, he pulled his right arm out from under her, eased himself away. She let out a short, sweet mewling sound, curled herself around a pillow, and was still again. It was clear there would be no waking her; not even the fifty-megaton rumbling of the trucks was enough.

It took a minute to assemble all his clothing off the floor: it had been rather literally thrown off, in all directions. The whole ordeal of dressing silently in the dark was slightly arduous.

Cleaning up my room was easier, he mused. It prompted a laugh that was hard to swallow. The thought *wish I were already dressed* flashed across his mind.

And, of course, it worked.

And then he went *naw,* and silently undressed, and then put his clothes back on again by hand. It was too easy.

Billy took one last adoring look at Mona, then snuck out through the door. Grabbed his jacket off the living room couch. Tiptoed through Lisa's room, thinking *God, this must be beautiful-woman Heaven* as he peeked at her sleeping form.

In the kitchen, he paused to write a note.

And then escaped.

Things were quiet in the city of hopes and dreams as he meandered down Tenth, toward the meat-packing district. There, he knew, the bloody-bibbed blue-collar men were already at it, pre-packaging corpses for the daily feast. A cabbie cruised by, eyeing him speculatively; Billy shook his head, and the cab went by.

Walking was the shit.

Walking.

And thinking.

He couldn't help wondering why the cabbie had come to New York City. Was he an artist? A writer? A fashion designer? A would-be reigning prince of the commodities exchange, where the howlers on the floor fed on a steady diet of Maalox and cocaine?

New York was a pilgrim's city. It was Jerusalem. It was Mecca. It was the East Coast's question to the West Coast's answering Hollywood, the dreaded bugaboo and sacred icon of worshipers from all over the world.

There were people who had been born here, most assuredly: part and parcel of the fabric, no more nor less apt to make or break. There were people who grew up squarely in the thrall of the dream. But most had come from Saigon or Puerto Rico, London or Marrakesh, Eugene or Tucson or good old York, Pa., dipping more and more multitudinous influence into the constantly-melting pot.

The pilgrims had come, one and all, with a hope. And a dream.

And I, he noted, *am no exception*. He knew why he'd walked into the Belly of the Beast: for the money and fame and impact that his music might bring. Just like Mona, with her dancing. Just like Larry, with his jokes. Just like Lisa, with her film work.

Just like everybody else.

But now it's different. It was an Irish coffee kind of thought, sobriety and delirium working at crossed purposes in the same steaming cup. *I can do anything*, he added.

But what am I going to do?

Billy cut east on the winding ribbon of West Fourth Street, taking the well-traveled path toward home. There were gay men, staggering and swaggering away from Westworld and the rest of the Crisco-and-handcuff emporiums. There were punked-out preppies in trashy threads, loudly enjoying the night. There were trashed-out derelicts in rising numbers as he made his way east, having forsaken their dreams in favor of liquid oblivion. There were handfuls of the upwardly mobile, taking their own sedated risks.

An invisible line called Broadway separated the west side from the east. He crossed over it at Bleecker and made his way into the home of the Bowery Boys. They were still out there with their rags and bitches, an endless scuttling at the bottom of the barrel.

Wish I could help you all, he mused. *Wish I had just a minute to spend with each of you*.

But I don't. There aren't that many minutes left in my life.

There are too many of you.
Too many broken dreams.

A quick scan of the populace showed no trace of Fred Flintstone. He took it as a good sign. Maybe ol' Fred was getting his act together. Billy wanted to believe it.

"God bless you, man, wherever you are," he prayed out loud, and then crossed the Bowery at Houston Street. The boys tried to hit him up for change. There were too many of them. He just smiled and kept going, across Houston and down to the corner of Stanton Street.

A strange little pang went off as he rounded the corner. It took him a moment to place.

Then his mind raced back over the four short days since everything changed, focused back on the event that had triggered it all.

The construction site.

The murder.

The girl.

"Jesus," Billy whispered. "Four days." So much had gone down in so short a time. It was more than vaguely incomprehensible.

But the thought of Jennifer Mason had all but vanished from his mind, and that was not a nice realization. It seemed more than callous. It seemed obscene. What, for all his miraculous Power, had he done to avenge her death? Had the killer been found? Had Billy lifted even a finger to try?

Not exactly.

It hurt. He walked slowly, now, along the construction side of Stanton, dredging up the memories, running them over and over.

Pausing at the spot where the killer had hidden. Peering deeply into the shadows, as if to sniff out any lingering trace.

And then turning to stare at the faded chalk line, barely visible now, yet strangely more enduring than the blood . . .

. . . and then he was back on the fire escape again. The flashing steel, the puckering wounds. He could see the sputtering smiley-face take shape, see the absolute intention behind it.

He could see the lower half of the killer's face, a bristly-jowled half-moon of rotting teeth and dimpled chin. He could see the vague alarm in the flopping-open jaw, almost feel the caught-with-the-pants-down humiliation.

And the madness, churning wormlike, within . . .

Then he was back on the sidewalk: his memory refreshed, his spirit sickened. He looked up at the fire escape, trying to imagine the maniac's perspective

(*guess he didn't see you as much of a threat*)

as he stood down there in the shadows, waiting for his moment to arrive. . . .

Then he glanced down the block, in the direction of Chrystie Street.

The blond black hooker was there.

There was a long, crackling moment of contemplation. She hadn't noticed him. She was just leaning against the lamppost, as always, long sleek legs exposed up to her micro-mini-skirted ass. It wouldn't be hard to approach her; getting information, on the other hand, might turn out to be a bitch.

Unless . . .

"We'll find out," he muttered cheerfully. Then he turned and meandered on down to the corner.

The hooker's brown eyes impassively tracked his movement toward her. It occurred to him that she'd never seen the new Billy Rowe before. He was hitting her from out of the blue, and that made things all the better.

"Hey," she mumbled as he approached. Not a whole lot of enthusiasm. "You wanna date?"

Billy smiled. "Yep," he said.

Her big eyes widened, then narrowed abruptly. As a low-budget Tina Turner clone, she wasn't bad at all. The lips and the legs were exactly right. The cheekbones came close. The wardrobe and hair did what they could.

The biggest difference between them, outside of their incomes, could be seen most clearly through the eyes. They were big, and they were beautiful.

But they were absolutely empty.

"Blow job cost you fifteen," she said. "You wanna fuck, it cost you twenty-five. Anything extra, the cost goes up. Okay?" He nodded. She shrugged. "Let's go."

She turned toward the row of parked cars at the curb. There was a calculated swivel to her hips, not entirely unattractive.

The hooker stopped, of course, in front of the '67 Rambler that had not budged since the head-bobbing night of the murder, nor for many moons before. A nervous shudder rippled through him at the thought of getting in. It was a combination hotel room and petri dish on wheels.

"You mean the jiffy john," he said, half-smiling. If she got the joke, she didn't let on. Maybe it just wasn't funny to her. She opened the door to the backseat. He took a deep breath and entered. She slid in after him. The door banged shut behind.

Billy was overwhelmed by the smell. It was obvious that the Rambler's windows hadn't been opened in quite a while. The stench of funk and dead emotion was stale and acrid as a freshly disinterred grave. It was not even remotely sexy. He tried to ignore it. He couldn't.

"So whadda you want?" It wasn't a question. It was far too weary for that.

Billy thought about it for a moment. He watched her, as he thought. She had no love for what she was doing, and she had no love for him. Head or tail: flip a coin for the ten-dollar difference. That was all the difference it made to her.

He imagined lying on top of her, his pants to his knees, his hands wrist-deep in the rancid upholstery. He imagined slipping it to her, and that was where his imagination ended. It was too weird. It was too much. It was like trying to imagine what it would be like to drink from a gutter, dig a sandwich out of a garbage can and eat it.

For a moment, he had thought about getting behind her experience, going into her mind, reigniting her soul. That moment had passed.

He didn't want to know what it was like to be her. He just wanted out of the car.

"I wanna . . . talk to you for a minute," he said. His throat felt thick, and his voice was crusty as the Rambler's interior.

"Aw, shit." The hooker didn't even look surprised. She turned around and reached for the handle on the door, writing him off.

"No, wait." His hand went to the wad of bills in his pocket. He flashed it at her. "It won't take long, and I'll make it worth your while."

"Yeah. I bet." She let out a sneer that had nothing on Tina Turner.

"Five minutes, ten dollars. You don't even have to do anything. Just answer a couple questions. Piece of cake. Okay?" He peeled ten ones off the top of the deck, held them out to her. "Okay?"

She took the money, stuck it in her purse, and waited.

"Okay," he said, nodding. "This is about the night of the murder."

It was not what she expected. Her flickering eyes betrayed her. "What about it?" she asked.

"I saw it happen. So did you. I just want to know if you saw anything that I missed."

"I didn't see shit." Her face was made of stone. "And I don't talk to cops."

"I'm not a—"

Without warning, she turned and reached for the handle again. His reaction was automatic and impossibly fast. Her wrist was in his hand before either of them knew it happened. She spun on him, furious.

And then her eyes went even blanker than they already were.

"Think hard," he said, no longer asking. "You'd been out on the street for hours that night, and somebody else was in the car. Did you see the guy who killed that girl . . . I mean, did you see when he got here?"

She shook her head weakly. There was sweat on her brow.

"Have you seen him around here before?"

"Noooo." Barely a whisper. The sweat on her brow was cold. He was sure that she was sure she was going to die.

"I'm not going to kill you," he assured her, smiling. "I just want to find the killer. You understand me? That's all I want."

A shudder ran through her body. A little bit of the tension went with it, on out.

A couple of things became clear to Billy. The first of them was that this entire encounter had been absolutely useless: blow ten dollars, scare a hooker half to death, and come out of it even dumber than before. Not what you'd call a successful endeavor.

Which left him here, in the Communicable Diseasemobile, with a terrified woman and a possible piece of unfinished business.

I've already got her under control, he thought. *I might as well make it count for something.*

He looked at her. Fear and the Power had stripped away her tough veneer. What remained was one desperately unhappy human being, with a job that made the Tenth Avenue garbagemen's life-styles seem princely by comparison. The compassion he'd been unable to find before came to him now.

Like the warmth, flowering out of his hand and into her soul.

"What's your name?" he asked.

"Roxie."

"Roxie, you've got to get out of this line of work."

"I can't." She choked, and her eyes began to moisten. Without her defenses, her emotions were raw and open as a plateful of sushi.

"You can do anything," he insisted, squeezing harder on her wrist. "I know this for a fact."

"I *can't!*" she repeated, the tears starting to flow. He could feel her inner walls collapsing, taste the anguish like blood on his tongue. She slumped toward him, and he took her in his arms, letting her cry it all out on his shoulder.

And as he held her, he caught their joint reflection in the rearview mirror. And it was strange, it was strange, it took him back in his mind to all those sweaty-palmed teenage drive-in movie days, where the backseat was the arena for a different blend of lust and terror, a more innocent blend . . .

. . . and he wondered about this woman/child, collapsed in his embrace. Where she grew up. How her home life was. The nature of her adolescent storm. He wondered what had led her here, to the city of hopes and dreams, to leave her so hopeless and dreamless.

"Roxie," he murmured. Her sobbing had subsided to a

steady low level. "If you could do anything, what would you do?"

"I . . . I don' know." She sniffled as she spoke, and he could see that she was thinking.

"Any place you'd like to go. Anything you'd like to be."

She shook her head. "I don' know. I can't think. . . ."

"Well, you give it some time," he said, so soft. "And you think about it. If you need help, look for me, cause I'll be around.

"And I will help you. Honest to God, I will.

"See, I can do anything, too."

She looked up at him, then, as he leaned his face toward hers. Fear was her most basic and powerful reflex; it made her recoil slightly as he brushed his lips against her forehead, as if it were the kiss of death that she was expecting.

When, in fact, it was the kiss of life.

NINETEEN

A MOMENT'S PEACE

One hour later. The tears on his face had not yet dried; they had only changed in shape.

He was up in his apartment, savoring the roominess and cleanliness of it, loving the way the first rays of dawn crept slowly in through the windows. The long shadows held no terror for him, just a bittersweet medley of melancholy and joy, balancing each other and translating as inner peace.

The Real War, in its entirety, was playing on the stereo. Of all the three-hundred-plus songs he'd written over the years, the material from the rock opera was far and away his favorite. It was full of the fire and conviction that had pulled him out of the madness: crazy enough to believe in a better world, tough enough to show the hardships of ever attempting it.

And that was how he felt this morning: crazy, tough, and optimistic. He was also a bit overwhelmed by the magnitude of his task, no matter how he sliced it. Sure, he could touch the Fred Flintstones and Roxies, single out individuals from the millions of potential charity cases in New York City alone; sure, he could dissuade the cops from busting up his performances; sure, he could even break the bones of an occasional Rubin, if it came right down to it.

But what can I do on the large scale?, he wondered. *What can I do to affect more than a handful of people at a time?*

The obvious answer was pouring out of the speakers: his music. It had touched more people than his physical body ever would. It was his one true talent, transcending his ability to make friends or a mess or both.

But is it direct enough?, he asked himself. *Can a person really change the world with music? God, I wish I had the answer to that one. . . .*

As if in answer, Christopher appeared.

"Nice guitar," the angel said. "Who's playing it?"

"I thought you knowed all, and seed all," Billy answered dryly. He was pleased with himself for not having jumped. Yes, he really *was* adjusting.

"Yeah, but sometimes I forget. That you?" Billy nodded. "Man, I'd forgotten how good you were."

"Am."

"Is." They laughed. "Yeah, it's really too bad that you didn't keep after your music. It's great stuff. It would have lived forever."

"No signs up saying I can't still do it," Billy countered. A pang had gone off at the use of the past tense. "In case you hadn't noticed, I'm getting hot again."

"But you've got to admit that your material's a bit outdated."

"So I'll write new stuff! What's the big deal?" Billy noticed that his voice was rising in both volume and pitch.

"Hit a tender spot, did I? So solly, grasshopper." Christopher brought an apologetic hand to rest over his heart. Somehow, it just didn't look too sincere.

"What, are you trying to tell me that I shouldn't rock 'n' roll?" The volume and pitch were down, but the irritation still came through loud and clear.

"A Billy Rowe without rock 'n' roll is like a day without sunshine," the angel said, in perfect imitation of Anita Bryant. It was a new one on Billy. He laughed, despite his anger. "But let's just say that the music alone will not fulfill your mission."

"Okay," Billy said, momentarily cooled out. "But I've just been thinking about that, and—"

"I know. I read your mind."

"Oh, terrific." A desperate throwing-up of hands. "So why do I even bother talking to you?"

"It's good therapy for you."

"Oh, Christopher. You're so terribly kind." The anger was back, deepened by resentment. "How come I can't just read *your* mind, save us both some jawing power?"

"My mind doesn't work like yours. Sorry. It's just one of those limitations you'll have to learn to live with."

"Wait a minute." Mind clicking into overdrive. "I thought you said that I could do anything."

"Okay. Sorry again, this time more truly." The sincerity was evident on Christopher's face. "When I said that you can do anything, that was part absolute fact and part frame of reference. Compared to what you *thought* you could do, you're virtually unlimited. Compared to all there is to be done in the universe, well . . . you've got to work your way up to a lot of stuff. That's all."

"So I can't just instantly make everyone blond and tan?"

"Not right away, no."

"Damn." Smiling bemusedly. Letting it fade. "But seriously: If music isn't it, and I can't just *think* the world into a better place, then what can I actually do?"

"Like I said before, ace: one step at a time."

"Fuck that, Christopher! I wanna do something now!" He slammed his fist against the palm of his other hand, then clenched them together. "I need to know what I can do! I need a strategy!"

"So use your better judgment. Nobody said that you couldn't do *that*."

"Okay." Billy closed his eyes and rubbed his forehead for a moment. He thought about all the people he knew and never seemed to be able to help . . .

. . . *and then he thought of Jennifer Mason, the human monster on the street below, and his helplessness at saving either of them from the horror of their moments together* . . .

. . . and he said, "What about the killer? What if I find him? Do I wipe him out? Do I turn him over to the police? Do I perform an insta-healing on him so he never does it again?"

"Up to you."

"You're an enormous help."

"Sorry, Poopsie. I thought you knew. If you want somebody to tell you what to do, join the army. Get a respectable job. Last I heard, free will was what made the world go 'round."

". . . and 'round and 'round and 'round, without anybody knowing for sure that they're doing the right thing. So, great. I'll make something up. I'll trust my goddam intuition."

"Good idea."

And Billy got a good idea. It came in a massive intuitive flash, translated from thought to word to deed so quickly that he didn't even have time to consider it.

"Okay," he said. "I want everyone in New York City to know thirty seconds of peace—"

"*NOOOOO!*" Christopher screamed, but it was already too late. The Power welled up and out of Billy in a wave so far beyond anything he'd experienced that he felt like he was going over Niagara Falls in a barrel, whipped suddenly over the brink and sent madly dashing toward the thunderous rocks below . . .

. . . and then the pain hit, an unbelievable agony that shrieked through every nerve in his body and then focused on his chakras, the centers of energy that ran from his crotch to the center of his forehead. It was white-hot pain, blinding and intolerable, a thousand times worse than the cross-current zap from his Argentine guitar and no less reluctant to allow him reprieve . . .

. . . and then darkness, complete and blissfully oblivious.

While, in the city that surrounded him, his dream began to come true. . . .

Peace, draping like a heavenly veil over all of Manhattan, sucking the hate and the driving passion from over eight million people in the space of a second.

For more than eighty percent, it came to them in their dreams. Nightmare was vanquished. As was Freudian doubt and guilt. As was all of the irrelevant nattering that occupied so much unambitious dreamscape.

But for the waking, the shift was another thing entirely.

Cab drivers, perennial cranks at the wheel, went suddenly calm: no need to honk or scream obscenities. Their passengers, too, were suddenly stripped of their anger at straying spouses, troublesome partners, mutinous underlings, intimidating bosses, that asshole in the LeSabre that refused to go more than thirty mph. All-night deli waitresses found themselves without a complaint by or against them. Janitors found themselves at one with their brooms. The pimps and patrolmen of Times Square found themselves smiling at each other, for no other reason than that it felt good to do.

A professional hit man named Vic Scampetti watched his mark leave the Gramercy Park Hotel at the moment the peace settled into him. His Smith & Wesson Model 3000 shotgun was pumped up and ready. The gimp—an overextended dealer to the stars who'd stepped on a couple of the wrong toes—was in his sights . . .

. . . and then a ripple ran through the universe, muddying his vision, putting a pinprick of pain in the middle of his forehead. It was over in a second. What replaced it was an incredible sense of well-being. He looked at the twelve-gauge in his huge dark hands. He looked at the kid he was supposed to blow away. He looked at himself in the rearveiw mirror.

Then he set down the shotgun on the seat beside him.

It didn't seem right, all of a sudden. Killing just didn't seem like the right thing to do, that's all. He didn't agonize over it. He launched into no chorus of mea culpa, mea culpa. *He very simply decided that he would not off the kid. Dino would just have to understand.*

Vic started up the Eldorado and pulled slowly away from the curb. He felt better than he could remember feeling in all of his thirty-seven years. Ahead of him, the kid had crossed over to the north side of Gramercy Park, heading west in a loose, shuffling dance step. Vic grinned and turned right at the corner, pulled up alongside the kid, and leaned partway out the window. "How ya doin'?" he called out. The kid began to smile . . .

. . . and then the headache slammed into him with full crushing power, an avalanche of pain that turned his vision lava-red. His foot slammed reflexively down on the brakes, making the world lurch around him. Beside him, the kid had staggered back against the wrought-iron fence that surrounded the park, clutching his temples and whining. Vic was suddenly flooded with hate and an even more seering confusion, thinking *what the fuck am I doing, I'm s'posed to kill this guy, I must be goin' crazy* as he picked up the Smith & Wesson and braced it against his shoulder, aiming.

The kid saw what was coming. He started to scream. His open mouth made a perfect target. Vic aimed for the bull's-eye and squeezed off a shot. There was no need for a second. His tires squealed as he pulled away.

And pain settled over Manhattan like a Portuguese Man o' War.

The peace had lasted for thirty seconds, precisely.

The first thing Billy saw, when he awakened, was red. Then the details of his room began to swim into view, limp and rubbery. The headache was steady and torturous now, as he'd always imagined a migraine would be. He moaned, and the sound was like a needle in the brain.

Then Christopher was leaning over, with an expression that he'd never seen the angel wear before. Not the anger and concern, both represented in equal batches: it was the *fear* that was a stranger there. He had never seen Christopher afraid before.

"Don't talk," Christopher said. The words thudded

dully against Billy's eardrums. "You just lay there and go to sleep. You stupid little putz."

Billy tried to cast a questioning gaze. It hurt too much to move his face.

"Dammit, you've got to *listen* when I talk to you." The voice was soft and deadly, completely bereft of humor. "You could have fried yourself out just now. Did you know that? You could have just scrambled your brains for good. Then you'd be of no use to yourself, to me, or to anybody else. You got that?"

Billy thought about nodding, then raised his arm up weakly with an okie-doke sign.

"Good." Christopher smiled, but it didn't fool anyone. "Now get some sleep. You're gonna need a lot of it to get over this thing. But you'll be alright, okay? I promise you'll be alright."

It hurt too much to smile. When Billy tried, it turned into a grimace. The lights went out, and Christopher vanished. He was alone in the dark with his pain and an all-consuming, soul-numbing fatigue. He tried to think about what had happened. It didn't work. Sleep welled up like a great dark ocean and quietly washed him away.

In his dream, there were chittering things in the room that tittered and called him by name. . . .

TWENTY

SOCIAL CALLS

Tuesday morning. 8:45. Billy was sitting on the edge of his bed, massaging his temples, watching the sun attempt to claw its way through the sky's impenetrable layer of clouds. The sun was losing. Billy wasn't surprised.

He shifted his gaze to the wall, and the front-page shot of Jennifer Mason. It was an older picture, from her prepunked-out days. He could imagine the reporter at the door of the familial abode, saying *excuse me, ma'am, but do you have any pictures of your late daughter for the final press edition?*

Her hair was long, but her face was the same: a perfect-toothed smile, bright eyes beaming out from their impeccably madeup settings. Her face was warm and wonderful, even in grainy black and white. She looked great.

One hell of a lot better than she looks now, he thought, and then put a lid on it. There was no point in endless recriminations, inevitable though they were. They did no good; and besides, his head hurt too badly. He didn't need any more pain.

Still, he couldn't stop staring at her photograph.

As the air in the room began to tingle.

"It's not fair," he said, "that this should have happened. You were too young, too beautiful, too cool. It doesn't make sense. It isn't fair.

"I wish that we could have you back again . . ."

. . . and then she was there, less than a foot from where he sat, leaning over him and smiling, arms folded across her belly.

"Oh, you can have me back," she said, *stepping closer. "You can have anything you want. The question is . . ."*

She held out her arms to him, prepared to embrace him.

". . . how much of me do you want?"

As her belly opened up in a great wet smile, and her insides tumbled toward him . . .

. . . and then Billy awoke with a start, eyes snapping open like a vampire in a Hammer horror film. There was a scream on his lips that died in the transition; it fell back into his throat, became a painful lump that was hard to swallow around.

"Jesus," he croaked.

And then the downstairs buzzer rang.

Bubba awoke, from his place at the foot of the bed. He and Billy stared at each other in blank-eyed confusion. "Damned if I know," Billy said conversationally. His head clanged as he said it. The words *you could have fried yourself out just now* replayed in his mind, bringing the memory of the cause of his pain back with it.

The buzzer went off again. It felt like vigorously-applied steel wool on the inside of his skull. He dragged his gaze over to the clock on his desk. 8:45.

Then he looked up at the picture of Jennifer Mason. Wishing nothing whatsoever.

"Alright, already," Billy muttered as a last buzzing barrage assailed him. He struggled to his feet, teetered there a moment, then moved painfully to the window and peered down at his guests.

Detectives Hamilton and Rizzo stared unhappily back at him.

Let this be another bad dream, he thought, blinking a few times just in case. They didn't disappear.

His keys were in his pocket. He hadn't managed to undress before losing consciousness. He was not about to walk three flights of steps: down would be bad enough, but back up was inconceivable.

He was also not about to yell. So he fished out the keys, dangled them outside the window, pointed at them with his other hand, and then let them drop to the pavement below.

Thereby buying himself a minute of throbbing shut-eye before the interrogation began.

Eight-fifty found Larry Roth firmly planted behind his desk at the saintly offices of Front Line Media. He was fresh from the steaming shower and sheets of Brenda Porcaro's apartment, where eight weeks of seductive pre-production work had come to slam-bang fruition. Brenda was the receptionist for Front Line, and had clearly been hired on the basis of her scenic, rather than secretarial, attributes: the theory had been advanced, by none other than Larry himself, that she would fail the pencil test not because her breasts sagged, but because the pencil would be too damned happy to ever want to fall.

Larry smiled and leaned back in his chair, despite the monster headache that both he and Brenda had awakened with this morning. A large cup of light coffee, an egg on a roll, two extra-strength Tylenol, and a day's worth of flimflammery were laid out before him. He popped the painkillers and washed them down, thought once more and fondly of Brenda in motion, then steeled himself for the business to come.

First on the list was to read and answer the previous day's pressing mail: largely inquiries from the Better Business Bureau, the Postal Inspector, and the Attorney General's office. Front Line Media had a vast array of scams and swindles, all of which fell short of actual mail fraud. But not by much.

Today's allegations included several probes into the "Erotic Art and Literature Society," which bought up remaindered books of truly awful art (featuring naked women) for a dollar apiece and sold them through their bogus publication, *Better Lifestyles*, for only $14.95 (plus $3.00 shipping and handling).

There were a lot of pissed-off art enthusiasts out there wishing to confer with "Felix Cunningham," Larry's alias on this particular project. He was in charge of "Customer Relations," which essentially made him Front Line's first-string flak catcher and shit shoveler. He had an alias for every scam they pulled. It gave the illusion of a vast media empire, protected him from possible retaliation from dissatisfied customers, and helped him distance himself from the fact that he was instrumental in bilking thousands of people out of millions of dollars annually.

After all, he was a comedian, not a shyster. This was just something to keep him alive in the days between now and the Big Break. There were those who did not approve, Billy among them; but it cost him very little, in either sleep or self-esteem.

It's a living, he mused, then bit into his sandwich. Contemplating the vagaries of business ethics was difficult with the rich flavors of butter, salt, egg, roll, and Brenda Porcaro alive in his mouth. He plowed through the sandwich, and made sizable headway with the coffee before the first letter of rage made its way before his eyes.

And that, of course, was when the phone began to ring.

* * *

"C'mon. Answer the phone," Billy hissed. "Please . . ."

It was obvious to Dennis Hamilton that Billy was pretty fucking upset. For starters, they'd brought him some of the worst news he could possibly have heard. On top of that, his headache appeared to be monumentally worse than the ones the two detectives had been complaining about since roughly five-thirty this morning.

Crowning it all was the fact that Frank was being a king-size prick.

As if to illustrate this, Rizzo said, "I love an air-tight alibi."

Billy whirled, still holding the endlessly-ringing phone to his ear. His free hand jabbed an outstretched finger in Rizzo's direction. "You know what I like about you, man?" he snapped. "Nothing! Not a single goddam thing!"

"Watch it, kid." Rizzo was pretty close to the wire himself. "You're starting to annoy me."

"SO FUCKING WHAT!" The phone rang another time, senselessly, before Billy slammed it down. "You think you don't annoy me with your glib patronization? You think I want you in my face? Think again!"

Hamilton stood, getting ready to intervene. He'd been kneeling beside good ol' Bubba again, skritching away; but Bubba had tensed and recoiled at the roar of his master's voice, gone into fight position. If Bubba expected trouble, then Hamilton thought it wise to be ready as well.

"I mean," Billy continued, "why would I kill someone who wanted to give me a record contract? It doesn't make any sense! She's one of the *last* people I'd want to kill, if I wanted to kill anyone at all! Why would I do it? Huh?"

"You tell us," Rizzo said. His temper was on a tooth-skin tether.

"I *can't* tell you, because I didn't have anything to do with it!" Billy bellowed. Hamilton saw the next Rizzo retort coming from a mile away, saw that nothing more than spleen-venting was going to come from either side . . .

. . . and so he let himself drift back to the reason for their visit: the body they'd found in the Greenwich Street ditch, with that horrible fucking *face* carved across her.

But that wasn't the worst.

The worst was that she had been *chewed*: that she'd fallen or been thrown into the construction site culvert and lay there unnoticed for a good four hours, which was plenty of time to become part of the food chain. The rats must have found her fairly quickly, working on her arms and her legs and her face.

But not the torso. Oh, no. Not the goddam leering jack-o'-lantern grin, which was left clear as day to greet them this morning. The little bastards had gnawed her extremities to the bone in half a dozen places, but they'd left the psycho killer's carving intact, as if . . .

. . . as if they were framing it.

Dennis Hamilton shuddered involuntarily. His head throbbed in much the same way. He lit yet another cigarette, his fourteenth of the day, in a day just under nine hours old. Then he tuned back into the cheerful debate, still in progress.

"Listen, Rowe," Rizzo was saying. "I don't know what to think. All I know is that we're sitting on two bodies in the last four days, and that they've got only three things in common: they were all attractive young women, they all were carved up like Halloween pumpkins, and your name kept coming up. Now, don't you think that's a little strange?"

"Of course I do! What, do you think I'm crazy?"

"The thought had crossed my mind."

"Frank. Stop." Hamilton was massaging his own head now; Bubba was still on combat alert. "This isn't going anywhere."

"Why don't you make fun of my apartment?" Billy yelled. "It was good for a laugh last time! Why don't you kick my dog? *That* might be fun!"

"That's enough out of you, too, Mr. Rowe," Hamilton snapped. It didn't need to be loud to cut. "My head is killing me, and I don't think I can take any more of this. Okay?"

Billy and Rizzo both glared at him for a minute; then, seeming to realize they had something in common, they both turned away in embarrassed resentment. It gave Hamilton another minute of blissful silence in which to try and make his skull stop clanging.

"You're gonna have to come down to the station with us," Rizzo said at last.

"Why?" Billy wanted to know, but both of their volumes were down.

"We want to have a composite drawing done," Hamilton cut in, hoping to keep it that way, "of the killer's face."

"What I saw of it," Billy added.

"That's right. And we want to keep trying your girlfriend: not because we think you did it, but because it would be nice to establish positively that you didn't. You understand."

"I guess." Billy didn't look happy, but he did look resigned; and he was evidently burned out on the hollering, as well.

Hamilton tried to match the kid with the bristling bundle of loose nerve endings he and Rizzo had questioned on Friday. Not an easy task. It went beyond the shave and snappier dress, beyond the trendy hair. It went beyond the almost-frightening metamorphosis of his shithole apartment, which was now neat as a pin.

No, Dennis Hamilton thought. *It runs deeper than that. There's something new going on inside that boy. Something intense.*

Something scary . . .

Rizzo was aware of it, too. It was obvious that he didn't know what to do about this new Billy Rowe, and it was weirding him out. Big chunks of Rizzo's reasons for disliking Billy had been defused when they walked in the door; but the dislike had persisted—intensified, even—to the point where rational discussion was impossible. That was not Rizzolike. It did not bode well for the joy factor of the next several hours, much less the investigation as a whole.

"Let's go," Rizzo said, moving toward the door. Hamilton nodded, and Billy surprisingly did the same. Bubba took it as his cue to sashay toward the door, as well; Billy had to catch him, hold him close, and explain that their morning constitutional was being temporarily postponed.

Then out the door, down the stairs, into the street and the dark green late-model Plymouth parked illegally at the corner.

Just as Billy's phone began to ring.

* * *

"Damn," Dave muttered, retracting the antenna of his Extend-a-phone and setting the receiver back down in its cradle. The morning's gray pallor seeped in through the living room windows of his spacious West Seventy-Ninth Street abode. The sky looked a lot like the inside of his head felt: murky, gloomy, completely miserable. Not even the ficus trees, ferns, and other foliage—calculated to lend a sense of airiness and lightness—could put a dent in the ugliness.

Dave Hart sat squarely in the middle of his sprawling home studio, rubbing his forehead like a magic lamp. His three wishes were firmly in place.

I wish I didn't feel so bad. I wish I knew what the hell was going on here.

I wish Mona would answer the goddam phone.

None of them seemed on the brink of coming true. He kept rubbing anyway, just in case. All around him, the bright LED eyes of his machinery watched: four-track porta-studio, digital drum machine, all manner of computerized, synthesized ultra-high-tech audio gear. His eyes focused on the monitor: the waveform of his last keyboard program was displaying itself in endlessly replicating patterns.

Like my life, he mused. *Like my life.*

He'd been up since quarter of six, wrestling with this stupid headache and his feelings for the sultry Ms. de Vanguardia. It was coming together in song-form, with reasonable success: a cool chord progression, a decent skeletal rhythm section down on tape. And the words were coming with remarkable ease:

You got a skinny little man somewhere,
And he loves you a lot,
But he's not takin' care of ya.
It's been draggin' on too long.
You go to work, and he goes out to play.
Then he takes you to dinner, but
You wind up payin', honey.
Don't it strike you that it
Might be wrong?

* * *

Mona!
I fell in love when you
Came dancing across the screen.
Mona!
I could feel your body shakin'.
What does it mean?

Dave was also trying to forget the dream he'd had. He wasn't having very good luck with that. At all.

It was too fucking weird. He'd been up late: MTV had slated a special back-to-back screening of the Brakes' videos, and he'd had the band and some friends—*sans* Mona—over to celebrate. They'd partied heavily through the whole show and after; Dave had finally stumbled to bed around four. His consciousness sank like a stone, aided by the combination of high-grade Jamaican and a bottle of Moët champagne.

And the first tendrils of the dream had wrapped around his brain. . . .

At first it was good, so good: the world evaporating, shrinking away till there was nothing left but the two of them. No stardom. No fame. No interference. Just Dave, and Mona, and the taut, ceaseless friction of skin on skin.

And his music: the way it sounded in his soul, before the hit factory in his brain took hold and molded it into product. *It was timeless and eternal, flowing out of his fingers to caress her as mere flesh could not.*

She danced for him. For him alone. Dancing away, then toward him again, with that same I-want-you ferocity that she'd brought to his videos and his bed . . .

. . . and then they'd felt the eyes upon them.

Cold eyes. Cruel eyes. Watching them.

Hating them.

Dave ran to Mona, screaming through airless lungs across a vast black distance. She turned to him, arms outstretched . . .

. . . and in the second before their fingers clasped, his hands began to twist and gnarl. He recoiled, still screaming, watching in helpless horror as his fingers welded together, bubbling and steaming—

"No," Dave said, fighting off the memory. It was ridiculous that a dream should strike such terror in him. He looked at his hands. They were good as new. Better, actually: no new set of hands could possibly pull off the musical acrobatics that his ten highly-trained digits could perform automatically.

They looked so delicate, though; he had to admit it, holding them to the light from the lamp beside him, seeing the red beneath the webbed skin between. Ten little skin-and-bone twigs, suitable for snapping off and using as kindling—

"No. No. Cancel. Stop." He squeezed his eyelids shut, felt the dull thudding in his brain sharpen to crystal clarity. When he brought his hands up to clutch his skull, the fingers felt brittle, arthritic. "*NO, dammit!*" he yelled, holding his hands away from him suddenly, as if fending off the grip of a strangler.

There were a couple of bottles of Kirin beer in the fridge. Dave got one out and cracked it open with trembling, alien fingers. He downed half of it in one long pull, took a deep breath, and finished the rest. Then he repeated the process.

By the end of the second bottle, the dull thrumming in his head had returned, and his hands felt only marginally other-directed.

It was his third such bout, since he'd awakened.

Sedated again, Dave's thoughts flickered over more cheerful matters. A four-letter word imposed itself immediately, beginning with M and ending with O-N-A. There was a definite smile to be had from the thought.

Until he pursued it deeply enough. At which point he got depressed again.

Mona was back with her do-nothing boyfriend. He could feel it in his bones. At best, that meant a future of upset rehearsals and dampened celebrations, as she ministered to his perpetually floundering ego. At worst (and Dave grimaced at the thought), it meant watching her sink further and further into a destructive relationship that could jeopardize everything: her career, her happiness, her future.

If neither of those prospects thrilled him, the idea of sitting on his hands while Mona went down the dumper was even less appealing. He knew damned well that she'd used him on Friday to get back at Billy; but he also knew that he'd felt *something* pass between them, beyond mere bodily fluids. A spark. A little *ping!* at the bottom of his heart.

A chance: perhaps his last.

Because Dave Hart was wasted on one-night stands, endless parades of brainless chippies who couldn't see beyond the star to the man. The love in him ran deeper than that, and it had been far too long since that part of him had been addressed in anything but his tunes.

He wanted one woman, one woman alone, to give himself to completely.

And that woman, without a doubt, was Mona.

No problem, said a voice in his mind. *All you have to do is steal her from her poor long-suffering loverboy.* It placed a moral porcupine in his hands, prickling and squirming as he tried to hold on. Other voices, not his own, informed him that he was a heartless and mercenary scumbag.

"Fuck you all," he said. "If it's a choice between him and me, I choose me. Q.E.D."

And let us not forget, he added, *that even an "object of desire" can have an opinion of her own.*

He decided, once again, to find out what it was. Dave lit a smoke as he moved toward the phone, plucked the receiver from its cradle, and punched in Mona's number.

The phone rang once, twice.

Halfway through the third came the sound of the receiver on the other end, lifting.

"Hello?" he said, grinning. "Mona?"

"I'm so glad you called. I was just thinking about you."

"Yeah, I bet you were, asshole. I been thinking about you, too. Like, f'rinstance, how you and your buddy would look in a pair of body casts."

Larry frowned, his headache coming back. This was not going well at all. But then, his monthly conversations with Albert never did. As landlords went, Albert rated somewhere between Mickey Mouse and Mussolini. He was a squat, stinking dwarf of a man whose pleasant demeanor was matched only by his lustrous personal hygiene. It was

Larry's considered opinion that Albert's underwear was embroidered, not with the days of the week, but with the months of the year.

For the moment, Larry kept his opinions to himself. It was bad business to insult someone who you owed back rent to . . . especially when that someone had passkeys and a penchant for hired help.

Very nasty hired help.

Larry poured on the smooth, effluent FM-dj tones with which he customarily jerked off creditors from both the private and professional sectors. It was an act akin to pouring Dom Pérignon on a turd. "Albert," he crooned, "there's no need to get hysterical—"

"Historical?" Albert sputtered. "*I'll* give you historical, asshole! If you're not paid in full by Friday, you're HISTORY!"

"But—"

"No *buts*, Buttski! Where I come from, IOU and DOA spell the same fuckin' thing! You read me?"

Larry winced. Albert was being witty. It was always nauseating when Albert got witty. "Loud and clear," Larry murmured, swallowing down the first saline burst of bile.

Albert hung up then, abruptly. Larry gave thanks for God's small favors, briefly, before allowing himself the luxury of fury.

"Fucking idiot," Larry hissed into the dead receiver. Exactly who he was referring to was open to debate: Albert, for being one; Billy, for acting like one; his humble self, for allowing things to degenerate to this state.

Even Brenda, of the vast *poitrine*, for letting the schmuck get through in the first place. He had his finger on the page button, ready to feed her the full brunt of his executive rage.

Then his mind strayed to the previous night, and the image of twin flesh zeppelins effectively put the brakes on his anger. *Better to fuck her tonight*, he chuckled internally, *than to fuck with her now. Am I right?*

Absolutely.

He shifted internal gears, inclined himself toward more pressing matters.

Picked up the phone.

Got an outside line.
And dialed.

"First Choice Messenger Service. May I help you?"

It was always a riot to listen to Ralphie on the customer line. It was like watching a toad do a Sir Laurence Olivier imitation. "Caviar on a Cheez Doodle," Lisa muttered, repressing the urge to swear.

Ralphie glared, went on pretending. Lisa pulled her clipboard from the black canvas bag cinched around her shoulder. *Wishful thinking,* she told herself. *Coupled with the Boy Scout Motto.*

She did not like working for First Choice. It had landed on her by default. When Your Kind Of Messengers, Inc., had sold out to First Choice, part of the deal had been that all the hot-shit messengers went along for the ride. Most of the messengers were not so wealthy that they could afford a payless job-hunting interim. Lisa was among the majority.

And so she had found herself peddling madly through the streets of Manhattan at the behest of the sleaziest batch of motherfuckers ever to design their own business logo. Hoods, losers, popeyes, and hopheads surrounded her every time she came into the office. It made her ill. It made her furious.

It made her a little over two hundred a week.

Until Paula's money came through, that would have to do. Even afterwards, she'd have to bike for somebody: one did not get rich on two or three editing jobs a year. But there were four-score-and-seven-odd other messenger services in Manhattan, and any one of them had to be better than this.

"Here's one for you, babe," Ralphie croaked, hanging up the phone and turning to her. "Front Line Media, 1775 Broadway. Move yer pretty ass."

"As soon as you waddle on over here and give me the ticket, I will."

Ralphie smacked his lips, exposed his greenish choppers. "Why doncha come in here," he crooned, "an' *take* it."

"Messengers aren't allowed behind the counter," she answered frostily. "That's one of the many rules."

"In your case, I think we can—"

"No, I don't think so." Cutting him off. "Rules are rules. You should know. You've made so many of them."

It's hopeless, she mused. *Casting pearls before swine.* The proverbial swine were clearly in evidence, leering and snickering in their pen. Five guys, every one of them malignant and brainless. *Yeah, I wanna get caught in the back there with you, alrightee.*

But I wouldn't want to clean up what was left of you, when I got done.

"So are you going to give me the run or not?" she wearily inquired.

"She got a temper, don't she?" Ralphie said, elbowing the goon beside him. The pigpen erupted with *haw-haw-haws.* "Whatsamatter, baby, sisters not treatin' you right at night?"

"Okay," Lisa. The words *I don't have to put up with this shit* stayed right where they belonged: inside. It would only fuel their pinheaded fire. She turned to leave . . .

. . . and walked straight into the flower.

Lisa's heart skipped a beat: she flinched involuntarily. Things thrust into her face always freaked her out a little.

Then she smiled. It was okay.

It was her little friend.

"Ooooooo, Stanley!" Ralphie catcalled, leering at Lisa. "Looks like Stan the Man's got a serious jones for you, missy."

"Better watch out, Stanley! Her girlfriends might beat you up!" yelled another.

"Yeah, Stan," chimed in a third. "You wouldn't wanna get decked by a dyke!"

"You guys are incredibly fucking clever," she snapped, then turned back to the flower-bearing outcast before her.

Stanley Peckard was a strange blend of Peter Lorre and Wally Cox. There was the bug-eyed toadishness of the former, clothed in the anal-retentive chic of the latter. And like both of them, he was essentially brain-dead.

But he was a little sweetheart, and that was a fact. Beneath the natty little suit, with all its buttons buttoned . . . beneath the polka-dot bow tie and the graying, spit-combed hair . . . beneath the anachronistic simp/wimp exterior, there beat a heart as sweet as cotton candy.

And it was true that he had a terrible crush on her: every time she walked into the room, his eyes got shiny as marbles. It was usually only a matter of moments before he produced the day's present: a plastic toy, a whistle, or (as he'd done one day, when her Flair had gone dry during checkout) a felt-tip pen.

And today, it was a flower. *A hot flower*, she noted. He'd obviously nicked it from one of the well-tended beds that skirted the traffic islands of Park Avenue. There were dirt smudges on his knees. *Probably a major adventure for him*, she thought.

The flower was still in front of her face, quivering. She accepted the offering, taking it gently from his hand. "Thank you," she said. "You made my day."

Stanley beamed like a jack-o'-lantern, showing crooked, brittle teeth.

There was a thimble-sized dimple in the middle of his chin.

TWENTY-ONE

SHARP!

The day rolled on, another link in the endless chain clamped firmly around the neck of Stanley Peckard. He hustled back and forth at the beck and call of Ralphie, bow tie tight against his neck as he wore his Kinney loafers down to nubbins on the unforgiving cement. At least a dozen times in the course of that minimum-wage day, he wanted to cut loose and shove that tie right into his pocket where no one would see, unbutton his shirt and roll up his sleeves.

But he couldn't. He was working, and when you worked you had to look

(*sharp!*)

good, or you'd never get ahead. Mother had told him that, and he'd never forgotten. Not even after she died.

It was okay. He'd cut loose tonight. Tonight was gonna be somethin', alright. The very thought of it was what got him through the day. It made him happy.

Stanley hummed a little tune, one of his favorites. He must have heard it a million times, on the TV:

"Here's to good friends.
Tonight is kind-a spec-ial . . ."

By 5:05, he was all checked out and ready to roll. He stepped out onto Park Avenue and headed south, toward Thirteenth Street and home. He walked fast, sprightly, not taking time to enjoy the tall buildings, or the park with its funny squirrels who would come up and grab a nut right out of your hand if you let them.

By 5:25 he was home; a rundown six-story dump on Thirteenth, east of Avenue A. He hustled up the four flights of stairs as fast as his scrawny legs would carry him. The stairwell reeked of Clorox and Night Train-scented urine, but he refused to let it bother him.

Tonight was kinda special.

Stanley Peckard had a date.

By 5:45, he was back on the street. It wasn't time yet. Oh, no. But he had something he had to do, and he had to hurry.

By 5:55, he made it to the store, a sigh of relief melding with the ragged catch in his breath. It was very rude to show up for a date without a present, and this store was his favorite place to shop. They closed at six: he'd have to be quick. No time to browse amongst the aisles and aisles of bright, handy helpers and special surprises.

Luckily, he found just the thing: in the back, by the cash register. On a neat little counter with a magnetic strip, put there to keep everything neat. It was really special, had practically jumped up and shouted his name as he walked past.

He held it in his hand now: six inches long, with a real wooden handle. Stainless steel. Shiny.

And, in tiny, incised script, the name.

A classy name. For a classy date.
Master Carver.
She was going to love it.

There were demons in his head. It wasn't that hard to figure out. Sometimes he was barely aware of them; sometimes he was aware of nothing else. But he always knew, in what remained of his mind, that there were always demons dancing in what used to be his brain.

And they were always, always hungry.

He stepped out of E&H Hardware on Second Avenue, his present pressed tightly against his breast. There was a butcher shop on the corner, closed for the night. Rows upon rows of polished stainless steel hooks hung in the window, patiently awaiting the new day's wares. He looked at them like a child staring at a mantelful of Christmas stockings, and whispered something so quietly that only the demons could hear.

"Pieces of meat," he said.

Then he headed for home.

To wait for the night.

And his date.

On the screen . . .

They were dancing again. The boys and girls. Tight curves in tight, tight denim, grinding and churning. Ocean behind them. Sand at their feet. Pouting lips and primal teeth.

As always, he watched the girls. He could feel their pulse.

In the room . . .

A plush comfy chair with a skin of green vinyl, right in front of the flickering tube. A fist-sized hole in the bulky right arm, showing fluffs of white padding and deep gouges in the wood. A big-assed indentation where the seat had conformed to his sedentary weight.

To the left, a coffee table strewn with paper bags and white deli napkins, empty TV dinner trays that glistened blue in the phosphor-dot light. More of the same, scattered on the dull, stained carpeting around it. Beyond, against

the wall, a ratty Colonial-style sofa. A stinking, rumpled
trench coat and fedora, slung haphazardly across it.

On the wall, above the sofa . . .

A pair of grainy black-and-white photographs. Press
clippings, festooned with lurid, blaring headlines. All
suspended by fresh cellophane-tape tatters, asymetrically
applied.

They were his bestest girls. He had made them
famous.

He had made them smile.

At the door . . .

Demon light, blinking in through the keyhole. The
doorknob, twisting. With no earthly hand upon it.

They were calling him. Impatiently. Hungrily.

Calling.

He moved around the coffee table, past the chair,
toward the door. The knob stopped turning as his hand fell
upon it. But it was warm.

As warm as flesh.

On the screen . . .

The dancing stopped. The light flickered out.

In the room . . .

Little things were moving.

They brought him his hat and coat.

There were demons in his head, and they made him do
things. He wasn't sure whether he liked the things they
made him do or not, but that was entirely beside the point.
They took him to work, and they brought him home. They
made sure that his bills got paid on time. They kept him
quiet, and when he did speak they put words in his mouth
that kept people at a distance. They protected him from
anyone who strayed too close, who interfered with the
Plan.

They led him down the stairs and into the night. They
caught a cab for him at the corner of Fourteenth and
Avenue A. They took him sufficiently far afield, as they
always did for his dates.

And, as always, they made the driver forget his face.

* * *

The demon voice came unbidden.

Not a voice at all, really. More a certainty, that telltale prickle at the base of the skull, telling him that

(*this is the place*)

it wouldn't be long; any minute now. He fidgeted and cast about nervously, actually stepping off the sidewalk to cross the street, and

(*WRONG*)

the tickle was instantly a hot needle, poking bleeding holes in his brain. He wheeled around to face the mouth of the doorway beside him. The needle softened, became a tickle again, and he felt

(*much better*)

like he'd better get a move on. He didn't want to be late, be

(*a disappointment?*)

accused of standing her up. He'd never do that. He'd

(*done it before*)

find a place to hide and surprise her. Maybe she'd

(*like that*)

smile for him.

He picked his spot carefully: within easy reach, yet safely obscured in the blackened mouth of the doorway. He fished a grubby handkerchief from his pocket, mopped his brow daintily, and shoved it back in.

He thought about his date for a minute. He'd never seen her. He never did. At least not beforehand. That was one of the rules.

But he knew how to make them smile. You just had to look

(*SHARP!*)

good and you had to be

(*SHARP!*)

strong and you had to bring them

(*SHARP!*)

surprises. Then they'd smile for you.

They always did.

There was a song in his heart, as there often was. He began, very quietly, to sing along:

"You got the look
   I want to know bet-ter . . ."

Listening to the footsteps, clicking up the street.

"You got the look
   That's all to-ge-ther . . ."

He peeked out. Someone was coming. He wondered if
it was her, and
   (!!!!!!)
the cluster became a white-hot bolt of molten pain that
burned like a headful of boiling oil. He fell back against the
wall and clutched himself, trying trying trying not to cry
out.

The demons didn't like it when he cried out.

It spoiled the surprise.

He sank back into the shadows and waited for the
delicate footsteps to recede, to stop ripping meaty holes in
his brain. They did both, moving toward and past him, each
step gouging across, then receding into the empty expanse
of his head.

Finally, she was gone. The bolt was a tickle again.

And he was very very happy.

Because in the midst of the pain, They had shown him.

This was a first. Why They'd chosen to reveal her face
was a mystery that diminished in light of the fact that he'd
seen her: a flickering image as clear as the reflection off of
still, clean water . . .

. . . and she was sleek and slender, with lots of leg
and lots of darkdark hair. . . .

He could hardly wait.

She was going to be his *bestest* girl.

The music in his head was much louder now, a regular
Super Bowl of voices, jeering and cheering by the millions
and billions. Peeking out from the shadows, he could
almost see her coming, hear the clickclickclicking of her
heels.

Stanley Peckard was excited. She was
   (SHARP!)
practically smiling already.

TWENTY-TWO

THE WAR, IN EXTREME CLOSE-UP

Paula Levin's apartment was a hole in a wall on the corner of Sixteenth and Ninth, but she'd managed to stuff it quite admirably. Every inch of wall space not covered by bookshelves was smothered in photo murals of the most prurient sort imaginable: kiddie-porn, dogs and ponies, hog-tied women being raped by men in leather masks, and so on.

Lisa was stunned.

"Disgusting, isn't it?" Diane said. She was grinning.

"That's the whole point," Susan continued. "If we're going to fight them, we have to be able to face them unflinchingly."

"But—" Lisa began.

"No buts," Paula intoned, stepping out of the kitchen, a gallon of wine and four glasses in her hands. "It's a fact that you'll simply have to face."

Not necessarily, Lisa thought, but she kept it to herself. She was looking at a picture of a beautiful blond woman, blindfolded and in chains. The woman was giving Technicolor head to the barrel of a .357 Magnum.

It was an infuriating photograph, no doubt about it. Lisa had seethed while seeing such exploitative displays over the years. But something even weirder than that was going on here.

And it had to do with these women.

They'd gotten together this evening for a pre-production meeting for *Pieces of Meat*, the next Paula Levin film. As the script had not actually been written yet, this was a combination brainstorming session and process of unification. Paula had stressed the importance of "being of one mind" on this project; Lisa had seen the sense of that, been more than happy to oblige.

Now she wasn't so sure.

"Have a seat," Susan Silver said. She was Paula's producer and cowriter. They'd met less than five minutes ago, but already Lisa had the impression that talking to Susan was a lot like using a nail file on one's teeth. She was serious and shrill and utterly sexless, despite the fact that her features were not at all unattractive. The offer, potentially sisterly and caring, had the ring of a Nazi inquisitor.

"Just a minute," Lisa said. She had dragged her attention back to the wall-smothering murals. Two prepubescent girls were licking an ugly man's dick, right next to a triple-penetration shot of porn star Ginger Lynn. A full page of bondage titles like *Beat The Bitch* and *Cheerleader Gang Bang* were neatly centered within a potpourri of ads for sweaters and liquor and cars, all featuring large-breasted goddess/models.

Lisa could understand what was going on, could even appreciate the artistry behind it. The problem wasn't with the feminist transmogrification of the imagery at all. It was the notion of using the shit as wallpaper that disturbed Lisa. It was like a Jew, papering his room with outtakes from Auschwitz. There was something unhealthily obsessive about it.

"Try the wine," Diane said. "It helps. Believe me." She winked at Lisa as she spoke, playful and sly.

Diane was a complete mystery to Lisa. She was cute, she was funny, she was not dogmatic, and she was not involved in the film. She said that she was just in town for a few days, and wouldn't say why . . . the closest she would come was "to cause all kinds of trouble" . . . which did nothing to explain why she was hanging out with Paula and Susan. From the looks of it, they didn't even like each other all that much.

"Wine sounds good," Lisa said. "Don't mind if I do."

"Fine," Susan said. "Then perhaps we can get down to business." No expression whatsoever played across her face.

Paula, equally brick-faced, poured the wine.

"Alright," Diane said, pulling out a chair at the table for Lisa. She was a wild little pixie, and that was a fact: big gray eyes in her little round face, shaggy chestnut pageboy, and perpetual elfin grin. As she was the only friendly element in the room, Lisa couldn't help but respond.

"Thanks," Lisa said, smiling back. Diane winked. Lisa sat. Diane took the seat beside her, pushed it just close enough to be obvious.

"I propose a toast," Paula said, holding her glass aloft. The others echoed her gesture. "To the end of male supremacy, and male atrocity. By whatever means necessary. Once and for all."

Paula and Susan were two of a kind. They had the same cold, piercing eyes. And as they lifted their glasses, both of them silently stared at Lisa. Diane was staring, too, but she was beaming as she did it.

Lisa felt very much like a paramecium, under microscopic scrutiny. It was not a pleasant experience. It reminded her horribly of being alone with the guys in the dispatch office, outnumbered by aliens that she didn't even *want* to understand.

Do I want to do this film?, she asked herself. *Do I want to work with these people?*

Do I want, refining the question, *to hang around a little longer, and let the next half an hour decide?*

Lisa nodded, forced a smile, and raised her glass.

They clinked their glasses together. Diane drained her glass in one gulp. Paula and Susan merely sipped. Lisa felt compelled to fill the middle ground.

The glasses went down.

And Paula began the meeting.

"You all know," she commenced, "that *Pieces Of Meat* is concerned with the violation of women, and that we intend to go all-out in its description. Over a hundred recent case histories have been compiled by Susan and myself in the last six months: over a hundred instances of torture, rape, and murder, in New York City alone.

"The problem is this: we've had a hard time finding a story extraordinary enough to win us over. A hundred-odd corroborations are wonderful, of course; but the budget we require cannot be generated by that kind of patchwork product."

"We need *a* story," Susan added. "One story that will serve as an illuminating metaphor for all of the others."

"Something sensational," Lisa said, nodding. She felt she understood.

"NO!" Paula and Susan shouted simultaneously. They stared at each other, then, and Susan deferred. "Sensationalism is the male perspective. It's a usury mode, devoid of human feelings. *Poignancy* is what we're after, and they are two entirely different animals."

"Sorry," Lisa said. She would debate the truth of that later, in private.

"There have been a few cases that came terribly close," Susan said. "But there were always problems. Dead women, for example, are extremely hard to interview. And the people they were close to have shown an unfortunate reticence to talk about it."

"Which is why," Paula added, staring directly at Lisa, "we are looking for people within our personal circle of contacts. Someone whose people *will* be willing to talk." Pause. "Have you known anybody like that?"

"Not right offhand," Lisa countered. "I know people who have had bad experiences, but I'm afraid that they'd fall under the more mediocre, less poignant jurisdiction."

"And Linda Lovelace has already been done," Diane quipped, grinning.

Paula and Susan glared at her for a second. She shrugged and poured herself another glass of wine. Again, Lisa found herself wondering what these people were doing in the same room together.

But Diane's statement had triggered a thought in her mind.

"Why not use someone from the actual porn industry?" Lisa asked. "If you could find the star of *Beat The Bitch*, for example . . ."

"The women in pornography don't like to speak with us," Susan said, and the tiniest whisp of a smile played across her features. "They've been completely brainwashed by the men who enslave them. Many of them actually think that they're providing a valuable service."

"Just like your friend," Paula said, "the dancer."

Lisa fought down a surge of anger at the mention of Mona, instantly realized that that was what Paula's comment had intended to make her betray. For one extremely brief moment, she was tempted to shame by the weight of those eyes; then her own mind spoke up, and what it said was *who the hell do these people think they are?*

She glanced at Diane, and something came clear. *Diane handles those two just by being herself. She doesn't let them rattle her. She doesn't let them intimidate her. Why should I?*

"Yep," Lisa said, just a tad sardonic. "Just like poor old Mona."

Then she smiled and turned her gaze back to the walls. The blonde was still sucking on the gun barrel. Lisa wondered if the woman had been forced to take that picture; if she was one of the handful of beautiful women who actually *like* to suck on gun barrels; or, most likely of all, if she was just like everybody else, doing unsavory things because sometimes you need to if you want to stay alive.

Right now, Lisa was leaning toward that answer herself.

"May I have some more wine?" she said.

The next picture showed her screaming through a mouthful of blood and broken teeth, while a huge stud plowed into her from behind. There was no question as to the authenticity of the photograph.

The blood was real.

The stud was Rex.

And Rickie had taken the picture himself.

It was the brunette that they'd done the other night. She wasn't as sweet as Saturday's blonde, but then who the hell was? She'd been good enough to fuck. And she had a little screechy voice that made her a pleasure to hit and cut . . .

Rickie was getting quite a collection together: five bitches in the last two weeks, for a grand total of eighty-seven decent photos. Most of them occupied the back of his socks-and-underwear drawer, but the very best were enshrined in the plastic pockets of his wallet.

There was a time when he'd enjoyed looking at other people's mass-produced fictions: movies, videos, peep shows, magazines, live sex performances at Show World. But they had never been enough, not really; they had never really *involved* him, in the way that his adventures were involving him now.

"HEY, *PENDEJO!*" Rex yelled from the next room. "YOU GONNA JACK OFF TO DAT SHIT ALL NIGHT, OR ARE WE GONNA GO OUT AND *PARTY!*"

It wasn't a question. Rickie grinned and slid shut his drawer. The wallet was already in his pocket.

The camera was already around his neck.

And the night was just beginning.

TWENTY-THREE

THE CHOICE

The lighting was soft in the Chelsea Commons. Warm shadows filled the room, snug against the darkly-burnished woodwork and brick. A few of the regulars were lined up at the bar, laughing and drinking and giving each other the business. Very few of the tables were occupied at eleven on a Wednesday night.

Mona and Dave shared one of them.

"This is a nice place," Dave said. "It feels comfortable."

"It is comfortable. Lisa and I come down here all the time. It's great to have a neighborhood hangout, where the men don't hit on you and the bartender knows how you like your drinks."

"Hear, hear!" Dave trumpeted, holding up his glass: Dos Equis on ice, with a wedge of lime. Mona clinked her shot of tequila against it. "The waitress didn't even give me a funny look when I ordered."

"They usually do?"

"All the time. Somehow, I survive it." He shrugged, winked, and took a defiant swig of beer with ice and lime. "Anyone doesn't like it, they can complain to God. See how much good it does 'em."

Mona downed her shot, and they were silent for a moment. The comfort of the Commons notwithstanding, she was anything but relaxed. The tequila was for drowning all those little butterflies in her stomach. It was doing okay, but they weren't dead yet.

I want to have a good time, she told herself. *It's ridiculous to get this uptight. Dave's a good guy. I've been working with him, off and on, for months. We've had a great time. Why should this be any exception?*

Because he wants you. Another voice, inside her mind.

Yeah, but he's always wanted me.

Yeah, but now you've let him in once. That changes everything, and you know it.

But can't I just have a regular evening with him, like friends?

Surprise! Not for a long, long time. And what about Billy. . . ?

She shut herself up. Dave was looking at her curiously.

Am I that transparent?

Yes. Shut up.

"What's the matter?" Dave asked.

"It's nothing."

"Of course. And so is the Berlin Wall."

Mona sighed and said nothing. Dave sighed and reached across the table for her hand. She almost jerked away, then abandoned herself to his touch.

She missed the fact that he had almost jerked away, himself.

"You're worried," he said, "about what's happening between us."

"Yes."

"Howz come?" He grinned. "I thought we were pretty terrific. . . ."

The front door came open and banged shut in a second. Mona looked up, instinctively pulling free of Dave's hand. Four people that she didn't recognize walked in. When she looked back down, Dave's hand was lightly balled into a fist.

"Oh, Dave. I'm sorry." This time, she reached over to cup his fist in her hands. "It's just that . . . I just get nervous that—"

The door swung open.

And Billy walked in.

He saw them at once. There was no missing Mona's look of frozen horror. In the instant their eyes met, he could see what was going on, how she felt about it, and what his presence did to the dynamics of the evening.

It had not been a terrific day for Billy. After nearly five hours in the precinct house, he'd gone home and slept off the last of his headache. Not a note had been strummed nor sung; not a penny had been made.

And now he had walked into this.

Billy nodded slightly and gave Mona an I'll-be-over-in-a-minute gesture. Some of the people he'd met in his frequent pit stops to the Commons were hanging out. He went over to say howdy, grab a Rolling Rock, give Mona a sporting chance to pull herself together.

And swallow the bile, welling up in his throat at the thought of facing down Dave. Mona's companion hadn't seen him yet—had *never* seen the new, improved Billy Rowe—but the reverse was not true, and Billy was not cheered by what he felt to be coming.

Already he could feel the Power gathering force within him. It was like standing under high-voltage power lines: the same prickling static charge, making his short hairs stand on end. *Wonder what would happen if I put a lightbulb in my hand?* he mused, nearly laughing, and then the fear overwhelmed his sense of humor.

He was terrified of letting himself go, because he was pissed. There were thoughts in his head, violent and vengeful, that were just fine and dandy so long as they stayed there. Dave's face, exploding. Dave's cock, falling off. Dave's cock, slowly growing from the middle of his forehead while his rock-star hands turned into flippers—

NO!, his mind screamed, clamping down hard on the

pictures and the Power. He no longer had the luxury of innocent ugly thoughts; the leap to actuality was too easy, too impossibly spontaneous.

Calm down. Calm down. It was almost like a mantra. *Relax. Drink your beer. Drink your whole damn beer before you dare to go over and face them.*

Billy tipped his head back and poured the beer straight down his throat. He'd gotten reasonably good at it as a teenager, where one of the j.d. rites of passage was being able to shotgun a whole can of beer without gasping or choking or spraying all over the floor. Concentrating on his throat took his mind off of Dave. The bile washed down.

In a minute, he was ready.

"Wow," Dave said. He was absolutely stunned. "That's the same burn-out Billy I've been hearing so much about?"

"Uh-huh," Mona muttered, but her head was shaking. She had her eyes glued on Billy as he ordered another drink. There had been a long cold moment where she could almost *feel* the rage pouring off of him in jagged, cutting waves. It was over now—she'd most certainly imagined it—but the realization did nothing to alter the fact that she was suddenly, inexplicably afraid of him.

Don't come over here, she heard herself silently begging. *Please, Billy, don't make another scene.* It was inevitable—the wish was ridiculous—but she couldn't help wanting to write the script, make her boyfriend flash an understanding smile and then turn to walk out the door.

As it turned out, half of her wish came true; the smile that she'd hoped for, flashing toward her. The other half of the wish went diametrically in reverse.

As is often the case, with wishes.

"Oh, shit," she groaned as he started toward them.

"There goes the neighborhood," Dave contributed, shrugging.

"Dave. Please." She cast a panicky glance at him, then returned her gaze to Billy. "Be cool. Don't bait him. If a fight starts, I don't think I'll be able to handle it."

"Swear to God," he said, holding up both hands in solemn testimonial. All of his fingers were crossed. Mona didn't laugh. "No, really," he assured her.

And then Billy was standing at the head of the table, gazing at them both.

"Hiya," Billy said. His smile was strained, but nearly halfway genuine.

"Hi," Mona peeped, averting her eyes.

"How ya doin'?" Dave concluded, offering his hand. "You're Billy, am I right?"

Billy looked at it for a second before taking it and answering. "Yeah. And you're Dave." They shook.

"And, of course, we both know Mona," Dave said.

The handshake stopped.

The handgrip held.

The air itself began to hum.

For Mona, it was like being caught in the middle of an enormous static electrical charge: her hair felt like it stood out four feet from her head, rigid as porcupine quills; her skin seemed literally to crawl along her bones. The terror was back, much stronger than before. All she could do was stare at the two men before her: one gritting his teeth in a mask of fierce exertion, the other blank-eyed and twitching like a fish on a stick.

For Dave, it was as if throbbing white-hot tongs had been rammed into his brain, pincing and slashing the living gray matter into a pudding that slithered and screamed. The pain was nova. His nerve endings crisped down to blackening bacon. His flesh seemed to sizzle and steam. There was nothing but the agony, complete and killing. The rest of the world, up to and including the chair on which he writhed, had never existed at all.

And for Billy, it was a bucking bronco ride through the memory of Dave Hart, single-minded as a bullet through the brain. He didn't see the seconds leading back to what he sought; they were a blur and less, irrelevant as the scenery whipping past a blind man's window.

When the image came, he froze from within, the pain welling up to rival Dave's own. It was a XXX feature that rolled through the projector of Billy's mind in flames, showing all that there was to be shown and then melting into lava that wore sputtering canyons in his own brain,

*making his own nerves cinder as the scream tore its way
from his throat . . .*

The handgrip broke.

The bar went silent.

They stared at each other, alive and in pain; Mona and
Dave falling back in their seats, Billy weaving slightly on
his feet. The blood seemed to drain from all three of them
simultaneously, leaving a trio of wide-eyed boggling ghosts.

Then Dave cried out, "MY HANDS!" and fell forward
across the table. Mona let out a tiny scream and reached
forward, cradling the back of his head. Her eyes looked
crazy, and her face wrung itself into a mask that was
anything but beautiful.

Billy reeled back, hitting the empty table behind him.
Rubin and the punkette and their baby loomed up sickly
behind his eyes, a nightmare paraphraseology that made
just enough sense to wipe him out.

"WHAT DID YOU DO TO HIM?" Mona screamed,
making the moment complete. The spark that went off
when he locked eyes with her made his hair want to
spontaneously combust.

And his mind was a crazed mosaic of words, the web of
a spider on acid, spun misshapen from the fabric of life and
left to gibber at the backsides of his eardrums, saying,
*Omigod, I lost control, I didn't want to know what I just
learned, I didn't want to see her on top of him, smiling, I
didn't want to know what he felt for her at the moment that
he—*

"I didn't do it," he said, little more than a whisper. He
broke his gaze away from Mona's. Dave's hands were not
smoking. He was too freaked to be relieved by the absence
of horror. "I swear to God, I didn't," he reiterated, sliding
away from the table and backing toward the door.

Then he turned and ran, the distance closing quickly,
the gawking foursome by the door no more than an asterisk
for a footnote that would never be read as he blasted past
them, silent scream unheard, the door flying open and
ushering him into the night's black weighty mass. . . .

TWENTY-FOUR

THE HORRORS

The horrors all began promptly at 11:45, with a choreographer's sense of sweep and synchronous motion. Above, the sliver moon was one perfect curling claw; the chill wind was humid and thick as the air from a punctured lung. Emptiness seemed to crowd the streets, making them feel close and paranoiac even in the absence of other people.

It was a perfect night for the horrors. They had waited too long for just such a night.

But the waiting was over.

Their moment had come.

Mona waved good-bye to the back of Dave's head as the cab lumbered up Tenth Avenue. She still had no idea what had happened. She couldn't imagine being able to figure it out.

But Dave had been fish-white, going on green, when she'd led him out of the Commons. The headache that all of Manhattan had shared was back, a million times worse. He'd barely been able to walk, much less kiss her good night. And the conversation he'd intended to have was completely beyond him, until further notice.

What happened? her mind demanded to know, nerves still tingling from proximity to the Power. The pictures refused to go away, flashing before her with rapid shutter-speed, piling up like 8 by 10 glossies to crowd her skull. She kept seeing Dave: the emptiness of his eyes, the slackness of his flesh . . .

. . . *and she kept seeing Billy, his terrible intensity shifting suddenly into anguish. She kept seeing him scream,*

166

terror huge in his eyes, hand yanking away from Dave's as if it were burning . . .

. . . just as the crackling air subsided . . .

. . . and she kept seeing him, croaking denials, staggering backward like a drunk and then racing out of the room . . .

Mona lit her last cigarette with trembling fingers, crumpled the pack, tossed it into the can on the corner. *The deli closes in fifteen minutes,* she heard herself think. *You want more cigarettes. You're gonna need 'em. Let's go.*

She looked in through the window. Almost everyone in the bar was watching her closely. She could understand that. She'd be watching her, too. Embarrassment claimed a toehold on her psyche, quickly shaken loose by the sheer maddening strangeness.

Mona pointed at her cigarette and made an I'll-be-right-back gesture. Jules, behind the bar, mouthed the words *be careful.* The regulars at the bar nodded soberly in agreement. She nodded back, gave a feeble smile, and headed east on Twenty-fourth Street.

Almost every street in Manhattan is a valley, lined on either side by five- to one-hundred-story cliffs. West Twenty-fourth was no exception. To her right, London Terrace Apartments loomed up and up above her, thirty-some stories and an entire city block of it, comfortably redolent with old-style class. On her left was a straight line of well-kept brownstones, their fenced-in front yards steep with shadow.

It was a safe street, quiet and fairly well-to-do. Mona couldn't remember having been scared on it before. But the cold made every sensation clear, too clear, amplifying the click and scuffle of her footsteps. No traffic passed, either on foot or on wheels.

And the fear of Billy was still fresh in her mind. It didn't make sense, when she stopped to look at it—no *way* could Billy have caused what happened—but she couldn't shake the feeling that it had come from him somehow, that he was the terrible power's source.

"Oh, Billy What's wrong with you?" she heard herself whimper. But the still night smothered her words.

And Billy wasn't around to hear them.

* * *

Stanley Peckard stood in the sunken doorway, with the broken glass and plaster at his feet. He had a dazed look on his face, a raptuous idiot grin made all the more chilling by the cold glint of steel in his hand. He was listening to the click-clicking footsteps, approaching now, coming slowly into range.

It was her.

She was beautiful: her dark hair long and sumptuous, her brown eyes wide above china-doll cheekbones. Delicate nose. Pursed and lovely lips.

And those long, long legs.

Just as They had told him she would be.

The black leather clung tightly to the hilt of the Master Carver, ensheathed his sweaty hand. His brittle-toothed grin intensified as the girl came within five feet of him, four feet, three . . .

In the darkness behind him, the Little Ones began to sing. The girl didn't hear them.

The girls never did.

Billy was moving fast, as if his feet were trying to keep pace with his mind. No chance. Try as he might, he couldn't walk at the speed of thought.

And his thoughts were in overdrive, describing Grand Prix circles and loop-dee-loops around the racetrack of his mind. Fear and guilt were in the lead, dragging a mass of confusion behind them.

He was scared for Dave most directly: there had been a frozen moment in which he'd been certain that Dave was dying. He'd *felt* it: the Cuisinarted brain, the spot-welded fingers. It was with him still, like a ghostly image on an old black-and-white TV, overlapping the sense of his own legs pumping as he turned left on Fourteenth Street, right on Washington, down the cobblestoned center of the meat-packing district.

Then there was the little matter of his future with Mona. He didn't know what she'd felt, but he knew that she'd felt *something*. She'd made it pretty clear when she screamed.

WHAT DID YOU DO TO HIM? The voice was lunatic,

shriekish, clawing at his skull from within. It made his stomach squirm like a bubble of swamp gas bursting. He knew that he'd frightened her in a way she couldn't possibly explain. It didn't matter. It would still weigh against him. The vaguest fears are the hardest ones to fight.

Billy was surrounded by squat, enormous gray warehouses of death. The one on his left went anonymous, from where he stood. The one on his right was called Golden Packing. The air on Washington Street was no less ponderous than the air in the Twenty-fourth Street canyon, but it was already ripe with the smell of corpses.

Overhead, and to his right again, ran an upraised bridge of sorts: former railway, former roadway, he couldn't be sure. Green-leafed foliage reached over the top at various points. The stretch was clearly overgrown, long out of use. It met with an upper story of Golden Packing at one point, ended with a clearly more recent brick wall, resumed on the other side of the building. And so on and so on, off to the vanishing points both before and behind him.

There were a pair of pay phones down at the corner of Washington and Little West Twelfth Street, lit from within and caught in the circle of streetlight. Little West Twelfth Street had always cracked him up, made him wish he could take Elmer Fudd on a tour of it. *Widdow West Twewfth Stweet*, said a voice in his head, tempting him to laugh.

But his eyes were on the pay phones, for some reason that he couldn't get a handle on. He paused in the middle of the street, fumbling a cigarette from his pocket, staring at the phones. He got a Lark 100 in his mouth, dug for a match, couldn't find one.

He lit the cigarette with his mind.

It was so easy. It was *too* easy. It was starting to scare the shit out of him. He felt like a time bomb with no legible timing mechanism, an event just waiting to happen . . .

(*mona*)

He stopped: feet, heart, breath, completely. It was not his voice. It was not her voice. It was not even a human voice. But

(*the knife*)

it was real; and though he had no idea what was going on, he knew it was bad, and he found himself eyeing the pay phones and thinking *if I can catch her before she leaves, it'll be okay, it's got to be okay. I refuse to accept that I wouldn't be able to know in time . . .*

. . . and then he was running, the Power was mounting, the trippiness making the cobblestones seem to glow and his feet to glide smoothly above them, on air, the phone booths whitely luminous and floating closer, himself leaping up onto the curb and reaching for the first phone, grabbing the receiver, bringing it up to his ear . . .

. . . thinking *I'm gonna get you in time, baby. Nothing bad is going to happen to you.*

I promise.

Too late.

There was, of course, one building on the block that was neither a brownstone nor remotely well-to-do: 411 West Twenty-fourth. It was shorter than the others, at only two stories; it had a peeling face of painted-white wood, metal bars like saw-toothed waves over the feeble doors and broken windows, a long history of excretia from the neighborhood down-and-outers. One of them was slouching in front of its doorway now, taking a characteristic whiz. She watched him for a moment as she passed.

Noting, in the final second, that the padlock on the metal gate had been neatly snapped in two . . .

. . . and then the hand was around her throat, cutting off her air, making the scream that tried to wail out of her throttle and die on its way from her lungs . . .

. . . as the gate screeched open with a sound that the night absorbed, and she found herself sliding backward into a room full of fragmented glass and plaster . . .

. . . and the Master Carver came down, perfectly aimed, slicing six inches into the apex of her breast and then out again, sliding over through the steaming air to wetly pierce the other side in flawless, susurrating symmetry . . .

Billy heard the scream, and the phone slammed back down. His mind, his mind reeled, his mind went crazy as it tried to nail the source of the sound: it was right behind him, it was far away . . .

Then the scream came again, source unquestionable now. It was coming from the loading docks behind him, a sprawling expanse of asphalt draped in the shadow of the obsolescent bridgework above. The darkness of it was impenetrable. He peered into it: afraid to run in blindly, not knowing what else to do.

Something long and sleek and ratlike raced across the pavement, chittering.

"Oh, shit," Billy moaned, staring back at the comforting brightness of the phones for a second. *Call the cops*, he heard himself think. *Dial Emergency, 911* . . .

Then she screamed again, and he knew that the cops would never get there in time, *he* wouldn't get there in time if he didn't get off his fucking ass and GO . . .

. . . and then he was plunging into the darkness, the asphalt sloping downward beneath his feet like a slow descent into Hell. Dimly, his eyes began to pick out the details of the loading docks: the wall of black steel mesh to his right, light twinkling starlike through the million tiny holes; the rows of massive concrete pylons holding up the bridge; the piles of garbage and rubble against the walls and the pylons; the girl . . .

She was cowering in the corner, where the steel mesh met the stone. She was tall and flashy, clearly a hooker, long white legs under a short black shift, long slender hands clutched over her face. He could hear her quietly sobbing as he veered toward her, could see the luxuriant blondness of her hair. *She's alone*, his mind informed him, and he began to wonder why . . .

Then he was upon her; and as the words, "Are you okay?" began to slide from his lips, she moved her hands away from her face, and he could see that she wasn't a woman at all, she was a clever reproduction, a pretty boy in drag, grinning wickedly at him, no tears whatsoever on that lovely phony face . . .

. . . and there was a noise behind him, and Billy turned just in time to see the other man hiss, *"You're dead,"* thrusting forward with his hand.

One second, frozen in time. The knife, insanely clear in the darkness, seeming to hang in stasis even though he knew that it was moving toward him. Eight inches of flat black nonreflective steel, serrated along the top edge, hooking upward at the tip, with blood-gutters running down the sides.

Then time unfroze. The knife became a blur of motion, too fast to follow with his eyes. He felt the center of his breastbone shatter, felt the cold steel sliding inward, sawing back a second, punching through again. The world went a blinding, luminous red.

And Billy Rowe went berserk.

"NOOOO!" he screamed, reaching out with both hands to grab his murderer by the collar. *"NOOOOOO!!!"* he repeated, whipping the man around and smashing him into the black steel mesh with a resonant booming sound. The grip on the knife slipped away. The blade stayed where it was, wedged to the hilt in Billy's chest.

The killer's name was Bobby Ramos. He was twenty-four years old. This was the third time that he and his little playmate, Johnny, had set up and skewered some well-meaning chump. It was getting to be a habit. The first two guys had gone down without so much as a squawk, and he saw no reason why this one should be any exception.

He never got a chance to find out.

Because Billy Rowe screamed and grabbed Bobby Ramos by the ears, wedged his thumbs into the holes, and proceeded to beat the man's head in against the wall, still screaming, the first blow raising a faint fracture line across the back of the skull, making the stars dance in front of Ramos's eyes, the glazing eyes that stared into Billy's and saw *red* there, inhuman and glowing and mad . . .

. . . and then his head hit the wall again, putting the lights out forever, putting a seven-inch vertical crack in the bone, the black steel mesh denting inward and splotched with blood and meat and hair, but that wasn't enough, because Billy was dying and this fucker had killed him and control no longer mattered, control was a joke from the past, nothing mattered in the whole spinning universe of rubble and filth and screaming drag queens and screeching demons but the knife in his chest and the head in his hands and the fence that thrummed and bowed in now as Billy split the skull in half against it, staving in the back of the head, letting the pulped red brains seep out, mashed through the tiny holes in the fence, oozing sluggishly down the other side . . .

. . . and then there was nothing left to destroy, and the body slumped gracelessly to his feet, and Billy fell forward against the fence, fingers sliding in through the gore-smeared holes and hanging on, heart thundering in his chest like an elephant stampede. He had not been aware that he'd been screaming the whole time.

It took him almost a minute to stop.

Silence fell over the loading docks. If the queen was still there, she was no longer breathing. Billy took the time to get his own breathing under control. He was afraid to open his eyes. He was afraid that he wouldn't be able to.

Very slowly, he did it anyway.

The knife was still there, jutting from his chest like an extra tit. The body was there, too, brainless and stinking. He gagged and pulled his fingers from the fence, staggering south and closer to the street. The smell went with him, soaked into his hands and his clothing.

But there was no pain; and in that instant, Billy realized that he wasn't going to die, he was *never* going to die, Christopher had been telling the truth in saying that nothing could stop him.

He was never. Going. To die.

But I can kill, Billy thought as he dropped to his knees on the pavement. *I can kill*. Dry-heaving, bent double at the waist, clutching his belly. *I can kill*. Like a nobleman in the last throes of *seppuku*, with the knife still in his chest.

And that was when the monsters began to applaud.

Pitta-patta-pitta-patta. They were tiny-flippered sounds, pockmarking the bloated silence. *Pitta-patta-pitta-patta*. Perhaps fifteen pairs of paws in all, slapping together with evident glee.

And then, of course, there were the high-pitched chittering sounds.

Just as he'd remembered them.

All his life.

Billy opened his eyes, and they were there: easily fifteen of them, clustered in the darkest section of the lot. There was a wrought-iron stairway leading up to the abandoned bridge. The heaviest concentration of garbage and rubble was at its base. The monsters seemed to prefer it there, too.

Their shapes were vague; they blended in too well with the shadows. But he could see their eyes, and that was the most terrifying thing of all. Because they were the same flat and utterly-soulless black that he remembered them to be, but he was seeing them clearly in total darkness. As if they were *blacker* than black, blacker than any shade this world could produce.

Blacker than Hell.

And all of them were staring at him.

Billy scuttled backward on his knees, hit the wall. The cheering grew wilder, more enthusiastic. He didn't think he had any screams left, but one forced its way out with astonishing conviction. The screeching got wilder, seemed almost to mimic him.

"GET THE FUCK OUT OF HERE!" he roared.

"*HERE! HERE!*" a few of them called. The rest continued to titter or mock his scream.

"LEAVE ME ALONE!"

"*'LONE! 'LONE!*" yowled a single voice, more singular and chilling than the others. "*LEE ME 'LONE! LEE ME 'LONE!*" Gales of hysterical gremlin laughter ensued, punctuated by screams and sounds that Billy couldn't begin to understand.

A few of them began to move toward him, and that was when Billy remembered the knife. He grabbed the hilt with both hands, tugged, felt the hooked end catch and the saw edge rasp, gritted his teeth against the horror, and yanked. The knife came out, blade black and nonreflective as it was when it went in.

There was no blood.

There was no pain.

There was no wound.

One of the demons was up on its stubby hind legs, forelegs kicking like a palomino's, misshapen head thrown back in laughter. Billy let out a cry and hurled the knife, sent it whickering across the loading docks with incredible speed. The dark shape split in half and crumbled. A few of the others converged on it. They didn't look like they were trying to be helpful.

Then the feeding sounds began, and the madness became a bright gem in Billy's forehead that lit from within. He scrambled to his feet and ran, heading back toward a Little West Twelfth Street that would never amuse him again. The taunting voices of the horrors followed him for over a block, then receded. He ran the rest of the way with only his own voices to torment him.

At the corner of Eighth and Greenwich avenues, Billy came across his first living human being: an elderly matron with a pair of pitiful Pekinese. *"You can't see me,"* he hissed, and it was true, though the dogs continued to yap like crazy.

It remained true, through the rest of the miles and twenty minutes home.

They couldn't see him.

They couldn't see the blood.

TWENTY-FIVE

A NORMAL LIFE

The door was swinging open when Billy reached the top of the stairs. It was Christopher, radiant and dapper as always, framing the doorway in pale white light. There was compassion on his face and a quart of Bud in his hand. He held it out to Billy, a gesture of pacification, and said, "Here, muh man. Come on in. I'm so sorry—"

Billy's hand was a blur of arcing motion. It struck the quart and sent it exploding against the wall. The angel had no reaction time. Billy's hand whipped back up, striking Christopher across the face. Then Billy stepped up within an inch of him and hissed, *"Get out of my way, God damn you to Hell."*

Christopher's eyes went wide for a second, bearing anger and hurt and the tiniest flicker of fear. Then he blinked, and only a trace of melancholy remained to mar the calm. He didn't speak. He didn't budge.

"*Didn't you hear me?*" Billy went on, a little louder. "*I said to get out of my goddam way.*" His eyes were red and huge and crawling with pain, but they never left Christopher's for a second. The stairwell was rank with the stench of death, still caked over him; violence raged through his body in shuddering waves.

When the angel failed to respond, he swung again, this time with his fist. Christopher caught it with the flat of one hand and held it; not painfully, but very very securely.

"*FUCK YOU!*" Billy yelled, his last thread of control snapping. He struggled to free himself from the grip. He couldn't.

Throughout it all, their eyes were locked; and little by little, Billy felt the righteousness of his anger slip away. It didn't stop feeding the fury, but it whipped the carpet out from under it. He felt less centered and more insane, the longer he stared into that unwavering blue.

And then the tears started to roll, and he couldn't handle that, so he poured every last ounce of his strength into breaking away, and it worked, and he went stumbling past Christopher and into the kitchen, where he landed on his knees and proceeded to cry his head off.

A barking, bellowing roar erupted from the bedroom doorway. He looked up through streaming eyes to see Bubba, the dog's fur hackled on the rigid, quivering body. Bubba seemed to be looking right through him, not recognizing him at all. The yowling corkscrewed into his ears, stuck razors in his spine.

"*BUBBA, SHUT UP AND GO TO SLEEP!*" he screamed.

And Bubba fell over on his side with a mute, almost comical thud.

Just like that.

Billy stopped in mid-tearfall, staring. For a second, it looked like Bubba wasn't even breathing; he crawled closer, saw the gentle rise and fall of the breast, and relaxed slightly. *If Bubba died*, he thought, *that would be it. That would be absolutely all she wrote*. The thought raked screeching fingernails across the blackboard of his mind.

When he closed his eyes, there were pictures to augment the sound, pathologically vivid: skulls crumpling like beer cans, caving in like buildings in the throes of demolition. The full horror of what he had done came back, as it had a thousand times before in the hundreds of thousands of seconds since the slaughter out back of Golden Packing.

And the tears came back.

With a vengeance.

"He smelled you, but he couldn't see you," Christopher said from behind him. "That was a big part of it. Mostly, though, I think it was the blood. It was driving him crazy." Pause. "It's not doing wonders for me, either."

Billy pivoted on his knees, very slowly, to face Christopher. He was still crying, but a wide, incredulous skeleton grin slowly spread across his features. He held out his hands, as if in praise of Allah.

Twin bubbling fountains of blood erupted from the palms of his hands.

"So how do you think *I* feel?" Billy cried out, the blood rolling down his arms and splashing over onto the floor. "How do you think I fucking feel, huh? I've got chunks of that guy under my *fingernails*! I—" He broke down then, bringing his still-gushing hands to his face, completing his baptism in gore.

"As I recall," Christopher's voice intoned, "the man was trying to kill you. Technically, in ordinary mortal terms, you'd be deader than a doornail right now.

"Given the choice, I think most people would be glad that you walked away and he didn't. If you hadn't stopped him, he'd have just gone along his merry way, robbing and killing as much as he liked, until somebody *else* put a stop to him. Do you understand that?"

Billy understood perfectly. It didn't stop the blood from pouring, and it didn't stop the tears. The sobbing and stigmata went on and on. Like Christopher's voice. On and on . . .

"You want to know why the monsters were there, don't you? You want to know why they applauded. Well, let me tell you.

"They're waiting for you to go over the edge, Billy boy. Believe it. They're waiting for you to fuck up royally. Know why? Because you've got the Power now, and the Power can go either way. Much as the Light wants you, there are things out there in the Darkness that want you just as badly. And if you're not very careful, they'll get you.

"That's why you've got to get yourself under control."

Control, it occurred to Billy, was the one thing he didn't have. He didn't have a grip on the Power. He didn't have a handle on his life. He couldn't even take the reins on his own emotions. All three of them could go skittering out from under him at any moment, and all he could do was gawk at them like a starving cartoon character with a plateful of Mexican jumping beans.

"You've been out of control for a long time, Billy. You couldn't get your career off the ground, you couldn't maintain a relationship, you couldn't even clean up your room. The closest you've come to coming to grips was a couple of days ago, before you pulled that dumbass stunt with Peace on Earth, Good Will to Man. And you haven't made a smart move since."

Billy snuffled a little, calming slowly. The bloodfall mellowed down to a trickle, then stopped. He was listening to Christopher now, getting caught up in the sense of the words despite himself.

But the anger would not go away. Like the Power, it made a sizzling gumbo of the world: ingredients whipped together into a savory but undifferentiated stew. It tasted too good to let go of, and it satisfied a hunger that lay deeper than the pit of his stomach.

"I got a question," he heard himself saying, the voice sounding labored and pained.

"Go ahead."

"Are you trying to tell me"—and his voice hitched for a second—"that it's *good* that I killed that guy, only I sh-should have been tidier about it?"

Christopher was silent for a moment. Billy wiped the blood from his eyes and opened them. The angel was just looking at him. No expression. Just looking. Billy felt something tighten within himself.

Become solid.

And the sobbing stopped, sudden and irrevocable. He could feel the Power, the vibratronic tingle of it, wiping away all doubt and leaving clarity in its place. *You're on to something*, said a voice in his head, and he was inclined to believe it.

"No, really, Christopher," he said now, smiling. "I'd like an answer to that one. Was my mistake in killing the man who stabbed me, or in getting so out-of-control about it? I mean, is going around killing criminals what you really want me to be doing? Is that the name of the game?"

Christopher sighed. "We just want you to do what's right."

"And what's right?" Billy yelled. "Is that up to me, with my noted proclivity for having no handle whatsoever on how to do things right? I mean, why did you give me the Power in the first place if I'm such a goddam idiot? It doesn't make *sense*, Christopher! It's almost as if I were *designed* to fuck up, and you were sorta sent along just to depress me while I do it! You know? It's like somebody's playing a nasty practical joke on me; and if that's true, then I don't wanna hang around for the punchline. I'm sorry. This shit is for the birds."

"You can't be saying this." Christopher looked stern, more than a little upset.

"*Read my lips*," Billy said, and the malevolence of his smile was genuine now. "I don't want your goddam Power anymore. You can take it and shove it right up your righteous little ass. Next time you talk to God, you can shove it up His ass, too. I never joined Jews for Jesus, and I won't join Assassins for Jesus, either. I don't want it. You can have it. Just get it the hell away from me."

"It's not that easy." The angel was shaken. Billy was thrilled.

"What do you *mean*, it's not that easy? The Lord giveth, and the Lord taketh away: that's what I always heard. Well, *taketh it away*, my friend! And take your smiling self away with it! Go see the editors of *Soldier of Fortune* magazine! I'm sure they'd love the opportunity to clean up the streets for you!"

"I said it's not that easy, Billy, and I wasn't exactly kidding."

"How so?"

"Because the Power is *yours*. It has *always* been yours.

I didn't bring it to you; I came along to instruct you when you awakened the Power yourself, by calling for help. You might recall the desperate moment itself."

A bright bubble of shame burst in the neighborhood of Billy's heart, thinking back on the night where it all began. "But I didn't ask for this," he croaked. For a moment, he felt like the Hindenburg in the deflating moment before it exploded.

"Yeah, but you sure got it, didn't you? So maybe you ought to listen up for a moment."

"And maybe I won't." All the air wasn't out of Billy yet. "Maybe I'm tired of listening to you."

"Maybe you are, but that doesn't change the fact that there are still a couple of things you maybe oughtta hear."

"Like, for instance?"

"Like, for instance, that you can't go back. No matter how badly you may want to, and I don't even entirely believe *that*. The simple fact is that you have gone off like a lantern in the night. You have been seen. And they are not going to let you go. They will be watching you, just as I will be watching you. Forever."

"And who are they?"

"The demons." There was a chill in Christopher's voice that had no problem filling the room. "As I've said before, they want you. And if you don't get your head together fast, they will have you in every way that there is to be had. *Comprende?* They'll have a field day with you, with all the Power you have. It'll be the greatest thrill of their miserable lives."

"So what," and Billy was trembling as he said it, the faces of the rat-things phosphorescent in the dark grooves of his brain, "am I supposed to do?"

"You're not *supposed* to do *anything*, asshole! I thought I made that clear! This is *your* immortal soul we're talking about, and the choice is up to you. But I've got a couple of friendly advisements to offer.

"And the first one is to give up the dreams of the old Billy Rowe."

"WHAT?"

"Read my lips," Christopher said, mimicking Billy's voice. "If the old Billy Rowe didn't die in the moment he got the Power, he died in that loading dock off of Little West Twelfth Street. His illusions should have died with him. If you keep them alive, that is your own complete and absolute folly."

"What illusions? What are you talking about?"

"Well, for one thing, you might as well forget about leading anything like a normal life. There will be no house in the country. There will be no loving wife with 3.2 smiling children in the yard. And there will be no rock 'n' roll Heaven either. You might as well kiss it all good-bye, because it ain't gonna happen."

"SAYS WHO?" Billy shrieked.

"SAYS GOD!" Christopher shouted back, equally as loud. "You wanna argue? You go right ahead! Makes no difference to me! Frankly, I'm getting tired of stating the obvious to someone who doesn't even appreciate what he's got! I wish we *could've* given the Power to the editors of *Soldier of Fortune*, because at least they've got some fucking balls!"

"You want some fucking balls? Okay! Here they are!" The rage grafted neatly onto the fear, making a hybrid that was all too familiar. "If I'm stuck with the Power, I'm stuck with it. Fine. But I'll be God's pal forever if He could arrange to take your scum-sucking face out of my life from now on. Because I don't like you, Christopher. I don't like you at all. I don't like your fucking advice, and I don't like the cutesy-pie radiance of your awe-inspiring presence. If I'm supposed to choose what's right and what's wrong, then my first official choice is that I'd rather lick Satan's *balls* than look at you for another goddam second! Alright?"

Christopher stared at him, furious and unquestionably hurt.

"ALRIGHT?" Billy reiterated.

"Then you probably will," Christopher said quietly. "Lick Satan's balls, that is. Your choice. He'll be thrilled. I will not. So it goes."

"Just get out of here," Billy said. "Now."

The angel nodded once and then vanished. Billy watched him go. The room went silent, save for Bubba's quietly-rasping breath. Billy watched his best friend's unconscious expansion/contraction of lungs, with particular emphasis on the ribs that caged them.

How easily they could snap.

Christopher had said quite a number of things, all of them intended to strike the marrow. But the one that stuck with him most heartily said *you might as well forget about leading anything like a normal life*.

And that was, of course, when the phone began to ring.

PART THREE

THE CLEANUP

"Some folks make love.
Some folks make none.
Some folks too twisted
To love anyone."

Billy Rowe
Twisted Toward Life

TWENTY-SIX

THE MONSTER SEED

The young man's eyes were balls of red-stained glass, shiny and more than slightly mad. The tender flesh around them tended more toward maroon; he'd been rubbing them quite a bit, from the looks of it. Betty Ward was not surprised. She'd seen that look a million times.

There were twenty-three people in the Emergency waiting room of St. Vincent's tonight. Most of them were wearing variations on the theme. A lot of grief, a lot of pain, a lot of stone terror and stunned disbelief. If she read a dozen sordid romances a week for the rest of her life, Betty Ward would derive one-billionth of the high drama to be found in any given night behind the receptionist's desk.

There were so many ways to die. She'd never imagined it before. She'd never had any occasion to. Unless you were riding the actual line where life and death lay balanced, with a functional reason for being there, it was a morbid and ignoble preoccupation at best. Or so she had always felt.

But every night in Emergency featured a cavalcade of punctured lungs and ruptured spleens, common coronaries and switchblade tracheotomies. People got wiped out in their cars and in their beds, by strangers or loved ones, in nearly equal proportions. Scarcely an hour went by when somebody didn't die, somewhere in the neighborhood of St. Vincent's.

Which meant that the waiting room was always inhabited by at least a handful of anguished souls, either trying to be brave or giving up completely, thereby running the gamut of variations on the Look.

Which the young man before her embodied at this moment.

He had a few of the other common characteristics as well, particularly for the one-to-five A.M. stretch: unshaven, disheveled, a kind of I-am-not-awake-yet bewilderment about him. She was accustomed to untucked shirts, unzippered zippers, and wildly tousled hair; she was accustomed to stuttering, rapid eye movements, flickering expressions that were heartbreakingly unconscious.

But there was something slightly different about this young man: something that she found in one out of a thousand cases or less.

He scared her.

"I'm looking for Mona de Vanguardia," he said, voice stressed up into the higher registers. "I understand she's here."

"Let me look," Betty said, grateful for a chance to get away from those eyes, wondering what it was about him that made her heart beat harder than usual. It was rarely something that a finger could be put on; the human race had a hefty repertoire of subtle gestures that separated the men from the monsters, the boys from the beasts. She would have to watch him closely if she wanted to peg the telltale signs.

And she didn't want to watch him that closely. Not at all.

The name in question flickered past her vision as she scanned down the pages of her logbook. She went back up and locked in on it, at the same time remembering that somebody else had been in for Ms. de V.: a lovely, Verushka-like young lady with lots of running mascara. The patient had been moved to room 617 when a cursory examination diagnosed her as merely serious. When Verushka'd heard that, she'd left shortly thereafter.

Maybe that'll cheer him up, Betty thought, *and he'll go away, too*. Sometimes, even the scary ones reverted to human form when they heard some happy news. She whipped up her best professional smile before returning her gaze to his . . .

. . . and then she was caught in a rush of white light and weightlessness, of soft fingers probing a mind she could no longer place as resting somewhere above her shoulders . . .

. . . and she heard a soft voice say I'm not here, you haven't seen me . . .

. . . and then she was blinking, momentarily dizzy, at the twenty-two people in the Emergency waiting room. The dizziness passed.

She wondered what it was.

Room 617 had a drab brown door that was perhaps fifty yards from the nurse's station. Even invisible, he was a bit nervous about opening and closing the door. He did it anyway, with no noticeable ill effect.

Six-seventeen had four women in it, all separated by white rack-mounted partitions. A quick sensing through the air revealed that Mona was to his far right. He walked toward her, soundless and unseeable, rounding the partition and pausing for a moment of sudden, complete emotional slaughter.

Oh, Jesus, he silently moaned. *Oh, God, please give me strength . . .*

There were no tubes up her nose, thank God. No bleeping monitors of brain wave or pulse. She had an IV hooked up to her, but other than that, she could have been simply sleeping.

Except that the woman in the hospital bed looked nothing like Mona at all. The face was all wrong: nose flat and misshapen, lips distended and huge, the features puffed out and hideously discolored. She looked for all the world like a Mongoloid child.

I don't understand why they didn't just kill her! Lisa's voice screamed in his memory. *They came so goddam fucking close!*

The voice cut off. Silence flooded his ears, broken only by the quiet breaths of the four unconscious women. The dim streetlight through the blinds was the only illumination; thin strips of light sliced through the broad stripes of

shadow draped across her. Billy fought down the urge to
scream and cry and tear down the walls.

As he moved, very slowly, toward her.

And it was strange, because his own encounter with
blood and death had receded to a numb and muzzled
portion of his brain. Thinking about it was like remembering an old movie that he'd seen once, long ago. It was
shadow. It wasn't real. It held no pain for him whatsoever.

All his capacity for pain and been directed toward
Mona.

And that was the other thing: he no longer felt bad
about killing Bobby Ramos. His only regret was that he
hadn't done it to the miserable cocksuckers who'd done this
to her. Before it happened.

Before they were born.

Oh, baby, his mind whispered silently to her. *It's
gonna be okay. I'm gonna make it okay. I will heal you.*

And then, so help me God, I will make them pay.

Billy knelt beside her, letting the Power take over,
clearing his mind of everything but the task at hand.

His fingertips came to rest on her sweat-moistened
temples.

His consciousness merged with the nightmare in her
mind . . .

. . . *and she was falling backward, the massive hand
around her throat, cutting off all airborne dialogue between her lungs and her brain, heels dragging down the
three concrete steps and then into the gutted building. No
time to react. No chance to fight back. Just the inexorable
strength from behind, hauling her across the broken glass
and plasterboard that littered the filthy godforsaken
floor . . .*

. . . *and then there was a second of freedom, maybe
less, really no time at all before the second man was there,
driving one fist into her belly, knocking the wind out of her
as she fell back and he laughed and held something up in
front of her face . . .*

. . . *and he said* say CHEESE, *baby . . .*

. . . *and then the light went off, unspeakably bright,
lasting only for a second and then flooding the darkness*

with puke-green polka dots that danced and flickered across the first man's face as he spun her around, features indistinguishable, fist all too clear as it came up to her face and connected with her nose, the shattering of bone and cartilage deafening in her ears, the pain needle-bright and more blinding than the flashbar, the floor coming up to flatten and slice her before she even knew she had fallen . . .

. . . and she knew what they were going to do, could taste the red inevitablity of it even as her fingers wrapped around the jagged shard of glass and jabbed blindly at the first shadow to fall across her. No use. No go.

The feel of the huge hand, encircling her own and squeezing. The feel of the glass, sinking to the bone in her fingers and palm. The feel of her wrist, bending backward and snapping like a crisp, gigantic carrot, the sound of it flat and faraway . . .

. . . while Billy watched, gritted teeth grinding, body thrumming and taut as a knot in a high-voltage cable. It was hard to tell where his own anguish left off and Mona's began. He was seeing through her eyes, feeling through her nerves, experiencing through her heart and mind and soul. He *was* Mona, living the horror for the very first time while she dragged herself through it again.

There was a part of him, though, that remained himself throughout. It was a part of himself that he barely recognized; but, once inside, he felt very much at home there. Its gaze was cold as a serpent's eye, detached as the man behind the camera, intent as a predator sighting out its prey. An old Spanish saying ran over and over in an icicle-thin and deadly voice:

Revenge is a dish best served cold.

Like a mantra. Over and over.

Revenge.

As he watched.

Is a dish.

And he watched.

Best served cold.

As the horror went on and on . . .

* * *

The little one had a knife. He used it to slice her clothes off. Her eyes were rapidly swelling shut, so she couldn't really see it; but she could feel the cold blunt edge of it slide the length of her torso while the blade sawed a lightning-bolt fissure down the middle of her pullover dress. When he got to the leather belt, he hacked his way through it, driving the hilt repeatedly into her belly. She whoofed out air that felt like ground glass in her throat.

The big man was behind her, pinning her arms, grinding his huge erection against his zipper against the back of her head. He was the main reason why she didn't scream. He had informed her that, if she did, he would kill both her and whoever was stupid enough to try to help. She was inclined to believe him. He didn't sound like he was kidding.

But part of her, incredibly, was still being cagey. After the initial onslaught, time had slowed to a snail-like, Sam Peckinpaughian crawl. In that subjective universe, she had plenty of time to think. Maybe too much.

Maybe just enough.

I have fucked before, *she told herself*, to get what I wanted. And right now, what I want is to survive. *It wasn't enough to allow her to pretend that she loved it, but it was enough to make herself shut up while she retreated to a private place inside herself, where the fingers that roughly tore off her bikini panties and laid her bare couldn't really touch her at all.*

That was the rest of what kept her from screaming.

Her semiclosed eyes had adjusted to the darkness now, and the little green dots were gone. She could clearly see the little man as he rose above her and pulled down his pants. She could see his dark skin, his oily black hair, his thin mustache. She could see his eyes, also oily and black. She could see the dull gleam of his unbrushed teeth.

She could see his puny genitals, the cock standing up like a flesh-colored Magic Marker. The words you are fucking pathetic *slipped through her mind and out of her mouth, subjective time notwithstanding, before she could stop them . . .*

. . . and then he landed on her stomach with both naked knees, and time sped up again drastically. His fist

was a blur in the instant before it slipped beneath her vision and slammed into her teeth. She quite distinctly felt four from the top and two from the bottom shatter, felt the nerve endings scream in the moment before their deaths, felt the flood of blood and broken bone. She spat in something like a gag reflex, then swallowed involuntarily. Five teeth went out. One tooth went down. She had no idea which ones were which.

Then the fist came back and flattened into an out-stretched palm. He spat into it. She watched it come down as he slid his knees off of her. She felt it sluice against the lips of her vagina.

The tooth got lodged in her esophagus. She started to choke, helplessly, feeling its sharp edges tear into her muscle meat. The big man lifted her slightly, pounded a fist against her back. The tooth clawed its way back up her throat, flew out into the open air with an escort of blood and saliva that trickled down her chin and spackled her naked breasts.

And then he was inside her.

The little man with the little dick set the rhythm. She was barely even there. The part of her that had been pulled back by the pain detached again, retreating back to that private place where the fuckings-over could be measured reasonably, with that modicum of detachment that had enabled her to survive dance teachers and casting directors and potential investors and anyone else who . . .

. . . ever dragged her into an abandoned building and beat her and ripped her clothes off with a knife . . .

. . . and that was when the metaphor broke down, because there was no comparison, there was no way to justify this in terms of the other, there was no way to justify this at all. Hatred infused her, numbing and cold. And though her senses were addled, she forced herself to consciousness with all the ferocity of will at her disposal.

I can't stop you now, hissed a voice in her mind, as she pried her swollen eyes open to take in and memorize every detail of their faces. But I'll get you later. Oh, yes, I will. I'll have your balls on a steaming platter.

And in that private place, where no one could touch her, the visions of tactical fucks from the past were replaced by visions of vengeance . . .

* * *

. . . that Billy shared, unaware of the terrible tension in his own body, the mass of sweat and steel he had become. He had, in that moment, no thoughts or sensations but hers . . .

. . . and then Pencil Dick came, grunting and mewling, and Billy was amazed by how distinctly he could feel the jism squirting, a surprising amount of it, making the last several sputtering strokes slide less painfully in and out.

I know you now, Billy thought, staring up through Mona's eyes into that narrow, sweating face. *I know you by smell, motherfucker. Now all I need is your name . . .*

As if in answer, the big guy who held her pinned said, "Come on, Rickie Ricardo. It's time for Big Rex to babaloo . . ."

The little guy got off her, and the men began to trade places. The knife was back in the little guy's hand; he held it to her throat as he slid behind her, whispering, you love dat, baby, you love dat magic motion *while his partner said* she ain't seen nothin' till she seen Rex do his stuff, *and it came to her in an incredible sickly surge of madness that they were competing, she was the playing field for their little fucking contest, my-dick's-bigger-than-your-dick taken out of the locker room and into the streets. The anger boiled up again, outrage at the sheer mindless atrocity of it. She started to jerk forward, a roar in her throat . . .*

. . . and that was when Rickie Ricardo cut her for the first time, yanking her head back by the hair with one hand, letting the knife trace a thin shallow line of trickling red beneath her chin. He was better with the knife than he was with his cock. The cut was expert. The pain it brought, searing as it was, paled in comparison to the terror it produced. Everything changed when the knife cut her throat.

Everything.

They're going to kill me, *she realized.* I'm going to die. *The knowledge drove her back to her secret place, but it wasn't the same there anymore. The numbness had spread, it had taken over, even her thoughts stared out in frozen horror as Rex unhitched his belt and unzipped his jeans and yanked them to his knees.*

Omigod, *she whispered, and that was when Rickie cut her again. Then she started to cry, and he cut her again, saying* you make a sound and you're dead, you unnerstand me, bitch, one sound and you're dead . . .

NOOOOOO!!! Billy screamed inside his head, but it didn't do any good, it couldn't stop what had already happened, and so he screamed for no reason other than because he couldn't help it as Rex lowered that stinking bulk over her body and then rammed that monstrous stinking thing inside . . .

. . . and she almost screamed, and Rickie cut her again, and Billy could feel it, he could feel it all, the slivering pain from the cut-after-cut, the unspeakable rending agony of her vaginal walls, the complete and utter violation of it, the absolute assurance that it couldn't go on much longer, she couldn't take any more, it would kill her, please, soon . . .

. . . and it didn't stop, and it didn't stop, and there was a high moan writhing in her throat that the knife couldn't stop no matter how many times it sliced and sliced because something was building up inside of her now, a tidal wave of molten lava, a razor-toothed climax of anguish that had nothing to do with sex or joy but had everything to do with the end being near, the beautiful peaceful black dying end . . .

. . . and the pictures started flashing through her mind once again, but this time Billy saw *himself* in bed with her, *Dave* in bed with her, *Lisa* in bed with her, some guy he didn't even *know* in bed with her . . .

. . . and they were wonderful memories, but they didn't help at all, the reality of the moment poisoned them, made them ugly and pathetic and sad . . .

. . . as the thunder boiled up to its peak . . .

. . . and then she was fading, she was fading, her thoughts and her body and the world just going away, borne on wings of black black evernight . . .

* * *

. . . and Billy collapsed in a heap on the hospital floor, nerves aflame. He couldn't stop shaking. He could barely breathe. The pain in his nose and his mouth and his throat and his wrist and his back and his groin still throbbed at him like the phantom twinges of an amputated limb.

But in his mind, it was the worst, because the rage and the terror and the hatred and the pain and the helplessness-unto-death of it had engraved itself on his central nervous system with sulfuric acid, burning a little deeper with every passing second. There was no escaping the pictures, the heartless brutality, the utter devastation of it.

He had come as close to the female experience of rape as any man could ever dream of coming.

And it was still only the tiniest micro-scintilla of what Mona, and all of the millions before her, had come to know firsthand.

And he knew that he would never be the same.

Not ever. Not ever.

Again.

Oh, God, I'm sorry, he heard himself thinking. *Oh, baby, oh, Jesus, I'm so sorry I can't believe this I can't believe I let this happen to you . . .*

. . . while the cold part of his mind, the serpent-eye view from within, reminded him that *he* had not done it, any more than he had been the white man who drove the Indians down the Trail of Tears or wore the white hood while the nigger was a-danglin' from the tree . . .

. . . and as he lay there, with the hospital tile cold as a corpse's lips against his cheek, Billy began to feel the calm again. It was a terrible calm, like the eye of a hurricane; but his thoughts could assemble coherently within it, and that was all he needed or dared to expect.

In only a very few minutes, he was ready.

Clambering back up on his knees, though his nerves were still frying. Seeing, through eyes now well-adjusted to the gloom, the physical evidence of the nightmare.

Reaching, then, for her temples once more.

Sending, now, instead of receiving.

He could feel the Power move through him. Out of him. Into her.

And he began, without a sound, to speak.

Mona, his mind's voice said. He felt the ripple of her unconscious receptivity. *Mona, I love you*, he continued. *You are going to be okay. I swear it.*

He heard her sigh, from deep within. So far, so good. He let out a heavy sigh of his own before continuing.

I won't take away your memory of what happened. I'm not even sure that I could, but I'm not about to try. You will want to remember. You've gone through too much to forget.

His fingers, traveling down to the bridge of her broken nose.

But I will atone, as best I can, for this.

As the membrane and cartilage and nerves realigned themselves, burst capillaries sucking spilled blood back in and sealing themselves up seamlessly.

And this.

Fingers moving down to the mouth now: the swollen lips, the bloodied gums, the shattered bits of bone. Fingertips, tapping her own deep regenerative powers. Tapping them into overdrive.

As the swelling receded. And the torn gums re-knit. And the teeth grew, quite perfectly, back.

And this.

Tracing the knife wounds across her throat and shoulders and breasts.

The wounds, diminishing into puffy-red and temporary scar-tissue traceries.

And this.

Mending the broken wrist, the slit flesh of the hand.

And this.

Reaching down to lightly cup her battered vulva in his hand. Not daring to tiptoe inside. Sending wave upon wave of healing Power from without.

From within.

As the damage and pain receded from the savaged vaginal walls.

And finally this, he said, dragging his fingertips up the length of her body, dealing with the many glass and plasterboard lacerations before coming to rest once again at her temples.

I will avenge you, he said . . .

* * *

. . . and in the final moment before the connection broke, from deep within her stunned sedation, she could feel the one micro-scintilla of male anguish that the connection made possible quite distinctly. She could feel the conviction behind his vow. She could feel the Power. It heartened and undermined her, all at once.

Alleviating certain terrors.

And magnifying others.

TWENTY-SEVEN

CONUNDRUM

"**J**esus fucking Christ Almighty," Dennis Hamilton muttered, sucking deep on a stale Winston and wishing, not for the first time in the last week, that he'd picked another line of work.

Her name was Marcy Keller, and up until roughly three hours ago, she'd been a real looker. That was all behind her now. As was everything else, save a trip to St. Vincent's in a zip-lock bag and whatever lay beyond the pale.

Dennis felt sick. To the stomach. To the core. *Fuck Rizzo and his sour little pep talks*, he thought. This was *not* getting any easier to handle, and exposure was *not* desensitizing him to the miserable mindless brutality. If anything, it was *heightening* it: following him home, ragging him, making him wish that he could find the little son of a bitch before anyone else did. He wanted to toss the little fuck right off the World Trade Towers, watch him splut against the cold hard pavement below.

All he got for the wanting was an excess of bile and a lot of lost sleep. Things were not looking up.

Dennis looked up. Two rival news crews were close to duking it out, jockeying for primacy and the most lurid angle to feed to the late-breaking reports. The media was turning this whole thing into a Christian-eating lion trip, digging into the pasts of the victims, drawing elaborate conclusions about the killer on the wispiest of theories, even battling over what to call him. The Smiley-Face Slasher. The Happy-Face Killer. The "Have a Nice Day" Assassin. Every pea-brained TV station and newspaper in town had their pet names, which they hoped the public would adopt as their own. The press conferences were circuses, with the blatant Battle of the Monikers practically superseding the quality of the information being gathered.

Not that there was much to gather, or much of any quality. It harkened back to Son of Sam, and Hamilton's rookie days at the periphery of the armada assembled on behalf of *that* particular psycho. Hundreds of men and millions of man-hours, just spinning their wheels until the guy screwed up.

And that, perversely enough, was their only thread of hope. This nut case, whatever else you might want to say about him, was certainly ambitious. Three girls in five days: not the work of a slouch. And if he kept it up at that pace, they were bound to get lucky soon.

But they, including Dennis, weren't feeling very lucky just now.

He looked over at the murder site. Rizzo was walking toward him. Marcy was tagged and bagged and ready to roll. The news crews were off and running, hot to be the first to feed her memory to the aforementioned lions.

"C'mon, Junior," Rizzo said, placing an uncharacteristically sympathetic hand on his shoulder. "We've done everything we can here."

"We didn't do shit," Hamilton countered.

Rizzo shrugged, conceding it. "But we still have to get back to the office."

Dennis Hamilton nodded sourly, tossed his butt, and followed his elder partner back to the car. The faces of the dead girls haunted him, tattooed in neon across his inner eyelids, pleading for justice every time he closed his eyes.

And he wished that it were not his responsibility.

And he wished that he could accomplish it.

And he wished that he could lay down the badge, the rules.

Just for a minute.
Or maybe forever.

Lisa stood at the sink, filling the teapot and letting the tears stream down her cheeks. She'd been home for over an hour, but sleep was out of the question. There'd be no sleeping tonight. There'd be nothing but tears and fears and pointless recriminations.

Coupled with one absolutely unshakable conclusion.

Never again, her mind whispered, the words like knives. *Mona, I would die before I let that happen to you again.*

She'd been down this road twice now, and that was two times too many. The first time was hers. Almost six years and three thousand miles of scar tissue stood between that night and this, but the rage and betrayal lay like a dead animal at the bottom of a well: just beneath the surface, poisoning her perceptions and lending the ring of truth to her basest fears. About men. About herself.

About life.

No great drama, she told herself. *Paula and Susan would pass on it in a second.* Nonetheless, it was her story, and she let her mind glide across its contours like a blind woman reading braille. Remembering . . .

Remembering . . .

She was a sophomore at Cal Tech, involved in a semester-long research film project with two fellow sophomore/cronies. *What were their names?* She snorted derisively, all the while going through the mindlessly soothing motions of making tea.

Roy. Gordy.

She'd never forget them. Ever. Their names poked her brain full of little bleeding holes in the wee hours of those nights that she fell prey to morbid introspection. Roy and Gordy. Her two fuzzy friends. They'd sweated and slaved together for three months: a lot of late nights hunched over the moviolas in the labs, a lot of grace under pressure. A lot of late-night bitching and drinking sessions at Gordy's apartment, which was three blocks from campus and had a great stereo. A good place to decompress after an evening of editing film that delved into the breeding and feeding habits of great white sharks.

They grew close. She couldn't help it. Gordy was sweet, and oh so shy. And Roy . . .

Lisa shuddered.

The water boiled.

She always knew in her heart that it was Roy's idea. She couldn't prove it, of course—hell, she couldn't prove *anything*—but she knew.

It was another late night: they'd just finished the third reel, which scored a major point in proving the casaul relationship between aggressive behavior and the shark's propensity for sneak attacks. They were feeling really good, so they partied it up at Gordy's, doing endless Seven-and-Sevens with The Police blasting through the speakers. She remembered passing out on the couch, a full-tilt buzz on.

She woke up in Gordy's bed. Naked. With Gordy and Roy.

It was feeding-frenzy time.

With her as bait.

The memories flooded up and out of her psyche like a wave of projectile vomit. Gordy and Roy: drunk as lords, mean as snakes, hooting and grunting and trying to convince themselves that her struggles were for fun. Gordy and Roy, capitalizing on the moment of her maximum vulnerability to rut and suck and chew and thrust. Violating her body. Violating her trust. Making her hate something that shouldn't, *shouldn't* be hateful.

Making her hate them.

Eventually she passed out, a merciful black wave of alcohol-and-shock-induced overload. They continued onward for some unknown time longer, leaving her with only a scattered, lurid gestalt of the nightmare.

She still couldn't stand to have things thrust in her face.

And the next day, it was as if nothing had happened. *Nothing.* No apologies. No acknowledgments. Just business as usual.

She'd left before the week was out. And in no small sense she'd been running ever since. Away from that night. Away from herself. And toward . . .

Mona . . .

Lisa stifled a sob, back in her kitchen again. She could

feel the rage boiling up inside her, like the water whistling painfully through the teapot's tiny hole. She thought of Mona's beautiful face, swollen and broken and bruised. She thought of Mona's neck and breasts, limned in crisscrossing arcs of blood.

The cup in her hand bore a picture of Snoopy and the words THIS HAS BEEN A WONDERFUL DAY. Lisa let out a shriek that was barely human and winged the stupid motherfucker into the wall.

And as the cup shattered, so did her paralysis.

Slowly, Lisa turned and left the kitchen, unfastening her clothes as she went. She was down to T-shirt and panties when she reached the living room. The light bulb in the ceiling buzzed as she turned the dimmer down to candlelight level. It didn't faze her. Nothing could faze her now.

She hadn't known what to do about it, six years ago. She knew what to do about it now.

Lisa: in the dim light.

Lisa: eyes fixed on the middle distance, moving with fluid determination across the broad expanse of floor. Strike. Block. Position. Kick. Breath controlled, in perfect synch with the rhythm of the movement.

Lisa: lost in the movement, one with the movement, mistress of the movement. Punch. Roll. Position. Kick. Her body fluid and slick with sweat, illuminated only by the halogen streetlight outside the window and the faint glow from above. Performing *kata*, her formal warrior's rites, as prescribed by her *sensai*, her instructor.

Lisa: five-year brown-belt devotee of jujitsu, working through her fury by endless repetition of the ritual cycle, until her body thrummed like a tight steel wire.

An hour later, it still wasn't enough.

She ended the *kata*, bowing ceremoniously to the implied presence of her *sensai*: a handsome woman named Gloria who lived in Brooklyn. Her body felt charged, alive, in a state of balance.

But her soul still screamed for atonement.

She stared across the living room at the makeshift bookshelf affair, so common to the young and struggling. Six tiers of shelf, constructed wholly of unvarnished pine boards on cinder blocks. She crossed the room in four long strides and started pulling the books off, tossing them unceremoniously to the sofa. Humor, history, art, and politics all fell in a jumbled heap.

The complete works of Andrea Dworkin, Susan Brownmiller, and a host of other militant feminist ideologians fell in with scarcely a second glance. Lisa had no need, right now, for their tireless screeds on the nature of the condition. Lisa knew the nature of the condition. She had lived it.

Right now, she needed to do something about it.

When she had emptied and dismantled the case, she set about the rearrangement. Four of the blocks, stacked two on two, with a meter of space between them. One board, laid lengthwise across.

Perfect.

She stood before the display, staring at it fixedly as she centered her weight.

Paused.

And with a short, clipped *keai!*

(*never again!*)

she broke the board cleanly in half, using the heel of her right hand.

Without stopping, she moved the blocks closer and laid the halved board back down. Again, the *keai!*

(*never again!*)

and a swift downward thrust of the elbow. The board fell in quarters.

Her heartbeat was up. Wordlessly she set up two of the blocks, and placed the four quarters in a neat stack atop them.

She'd never done four boards before, particularly not such short ones. Didn't matter. She cleared her mind, took a short cleansing breath, and *KEAI!*

Eight pieces of wood clattered to the floor.

Lisa rose slowly, measuredly, like a diver in a decompression tank.

And then she did it again.

And then she did it again.

TWENTY-EIGHT

BROTHERS AND SISTERS

At 11:05 the following morning Mona de Vanguardia was released from St. Vincent's with no complications whatsoever. The chart at the foot of her bed gave her a clean bill of health. The pharmaceutical department gave her a healthy batch of downs. There was no charge for her overnight stay. The doctors and nurses and orderlies and security guards all waved and smiled and said good-bye.

Billy took care of everything.

Bubba was waiting at the curb when they came through the revolving doors. He went into an animated cha-cha-cha when he saw them, without any help from Billy. Mona very nearly smiled.

They caught a cab on Seventh. Ordinarily, Bubba would have been a problem, but Billy took care of it. The cabbie didn't mind a bit.

All the way home, Mona was stiff and silent and distant. Billy had reached for her at one point, as she stumbled on her way out of the hospital elevator. The scream in her eyes had made it quite clear: she did not want to be touched.

"Okay," Billy had said. It was the only word exchanged between them.

It was the only moment in which their eyes had truly met.

Okay, he repeated silently, watching the gray scenery whip past below the same sky-smothering layer of clouds. He didn't know how much she remembered of his visit last night, how much of a shadow lay between the point where she'd blacked out, broken, and the point where she'd awakened in a considerable state of repair. He could not—

would not—apply the touch that would enable him to know.

Any more than he would ply her with words.

Any more than he would erase the memories altogether.

This one is yours, he continued, addressing her in imaginary, internal conversation. *This is the fight that only you can win. I have spared your body disfigurement and months of painful healing. To spare you any more would be to spare you the chance to grow.*

And you would never forgive me for sparing you that.

There is integrity in facing the pain. There is integrity in facing the horror. Everything that my life has taught me has been confirmed in the last few days.

I will not rob you of your integrity.

No matter how much it hurts you.

No matter how much it hurts me.

The rear window on the right-hand side was open just enough for Bubba to poke his snoot through the crack. Billy held him close, basking in the animal warmth, the simple purity of living and loving that was Bubba's natural state of being.

Billy needed that warmth, now more than ever.

As their journey drew to a close.

Dave Hart had been ringing the outside doorbell for nearly two minutes when the cab pulled up at the curb beside him. He had a lingering dull ache in his skull, a staggering amount of dread in his heart, and a huge bouquet of flowers in his alien-feeling right hand.

When Bubba jumped out of the backseat, he thought *what a funny-looking dog.*

When Billy followed, he thought *omigod,* and the flowers nearly dropped to the pavement.

When Mona emerged behind them, he clung to the flowers with all his might, and the dread became a living thing that crawled inside his chest.

"*Mona,*" he whispered, taking two steps toward them. For all the power of his singing voice, that was all the wind that he could whip up.

"Dave," Billy said, engaging the eye contact that Mona would not. "Be cool, okay?"

The first thing Dave felt was a tingling in his hands, hot and balming as Ben-Gay lotion. The second thing he felt was a burst of instinctive terror as the dog came loping toward him.

Then a bright light went off inside his head; and when consciousness returned a split second later, the fear was gone.

Which was good, because that was when Bubba jumped up, forepaws bracing against Dave's chest, checking him out with canine exuberance. Dave laughed, automatically stroking the blunt head with one hand, holding the flowers away with the second.

Mona wordlessly moved past him, to the door. Her keys were already in her hand. Billy walked just behind her, pacing her, gauging her steps for any sign of weakness or loss of balance.

None came, and the door swung open. Billy made a *c'mon, you guys* motion that was, from Dave's perspective, surprisingly warm.

The four of them went up.

"I can't believe you people," Lisa was saying as she moved like a dervish from the sink to the stove. "And I think that you should leave before she gets here. Okay?"

"Not okay," Paula said. Susan was right beside her. "I don't think that you've given us a chance."

"I haven't given you a chance!" Lisa yelled, a rat-a-tat of humorless laughter on its heels. She whirled and aimed a finger at Paula's head. "I gave you the chance to be a decent human being when I called and told you that I wouldn't be able to make our meeting this evening. Twenty minutes later the whole gang is here, trying to hustle me into letting you talk to her!"

"We don't 'hustle,'" Susan informed her coldly. "That's a male sup—"

"BULLSHIT!" Lisa erupted, slamming her fist against the stove. Susan's wire-rimmed glasses seemed to fog, just a little. "You've got it all figured out, don't you? Anything that sounds bad is male supremist dogma; then you go ahead and do the same thing, only you use a more flattering set of catchphrases. What *do* you call what you're doing here? 'Enlightened self-interest'?"

"You're letting your personal feelings get in the way," Paula said, low and measured. "This is a *war* we're fighting here—"

"I've got news for you, sister," Lisa cut in. "When you lose your compassion, you've already lost the war."

The sound of ascending footsteps was audible from the stairwell. All eyes shifted to the doorway. Lisa hissed through her teeth; it was too late to boot them before Mona's arrival.

"If anybody says one single word to her," she said, "I will break their fucking necks."

The sentiment had a second to soak in before the door swung open . . .

. . . and then Bubba was through the door and madly cruising. He *loved* it here at Mona and Lisa's. He loved the smell: the air alive with perfume and incense and musky-sweet girl sweat. Bubba always reverted back to puppy-hood when he came over to visit.

Right now, that entailed doing multiple laps around the kitchen table. Lisa was there, bubbling over with sudden happy noise. He did another turn and then jumped up at her, burying his nose between her breasts as she skritched behind his ears.

But there were other people here—new people, strangers—so he jumped back down and took another wild spin, then zeroed in on the big chunky one. She was in heat, just now. Bubba always loved it when that happened.

Without a moment's hesitation, he drove his nose into her crotch, while he humped against her left knee with gay abandon.

"GET OFF OF ME!" Paula screamed, pushing at the dog with both hands. It fell back, looking startled and stupid. "GET BACK, I SAY!" she continued, bringing her right foot back to deliver a kick.

"Bubba, no." A calm male voice, from the doorway, softly authoritative. The dog backed away, and the man walked into the room. It was the one who had sat through *Between Our Thighs* twice, the dancer's boyfriend/audi-tionee. He didn't look nearly as slick as he had the last time they'd met.

But he looked easily twice as intense.

And he didn't look happy to see her. At all.

Paula took a glance over at Lisa, whose eyes had widened to nearly the size of Susan B. Anthony dollars. The editor was staring out into the doorway, with a very strange mixture of shock and joy on her face. Paula spent a moment trying to understand why.

And then Mona came through the door.

She was not on a stretcher. She wasn't even on crutches. There were no visible bandages swathing her at all. She wasn't even missing any teeth.

"Mona," Lisa said.

But Mona didn't acknowledge her roommate. She didn't acknowledge any of them. She moved straight ahead, with measured steps, toward the door to Lisa's bedroom and beyond. It was clear to Paula that the woman was definitely in pain; Lisa's ludicrous threat notwithstanding, this was obviously neither the time nor place to talk to Mona about anything.

Tomorrow would be better.

And the day after that.

And every day, from then on.

Until she got what she wanted.

Even barring the regrettable absence of a broken nose, Mona was perfect.

Past the first choked utterance, Lisa found herself completely unable to speak. She had to steady herself against the stove as Mona disappeared from the kitchen and the door slid shut behind.

It's impossible. They were the only words that could form inside her mind. She was terrified, she was overjoyed, she was stunned to the marrow of her bones. She felt like a set of china that had just had the tablecloth ripped magically out from under it without shattering.

But I saw her. The new thought crept in, with a power and a set of images all its own. She could distinctly see the shattered teeth, the misshapen knob of purple flesh and cartilage between the eyes and mouth, the terrible abundance of dried and still-flowing blood, as the paramedics had borne her best friend's wreckage from the ruin of 411 West Twenty-fourth Street.

She turned to Billy, who was still standing just to the left of the doorway, and was amazed to see Dave standing there, still clutching the floral bouquet. The sight of Billy and Dave together was only slightly less strange than the sight of the reconstituted Mona. It did nothing for her attempts to hinge herself firmly back in reality.

She wondered briefly if this weren't all an extremely perverse dream.

"No," Billy said, as if in answer. "Not a dream."

"But I—" she began.

"It looked worse last night than it wound up being," he cut in. "That's all."

"*But I—*" she tried again, a bit more frenzied.

"Not now," Billy insisted, a chilly trace of smile on his lips. "We've got company. And I guess I'd like to know a little bit about that." He turned a cold gaze toward Paula and Susan. "You here to offer your condolences, or what?"

Lisa turned toward the women, who showed no reaction whatsoever to what he'd thrown. *Masters of the unified front*, she noted. *They wouldn't give him the fucking time of day.*

The man who brought the victimized woman home is the enemy, simply because he's a man.

How many layers of bullshit are there between the truth and me, anyway?

Dave had been feeling very much like an outsider throughout it all. That internalized status sense had not changed a whit. But he felt himself being sucked, more and more, into the drama as it unfolded before him.

The women were, doubtless, the feminists that Lisa was affiliated with. They were Movement people, all the way: no-nonsense clothes, no-nonsense hair, no nonsensical makeup whatsoever. They were determined, intelligent, and brittle as day-old bread. All of that was obvious at a glance.

The big surprise was Billy: more succinctly, how much he was finding himself impressed by the guy. This was the loser that Mona had so often described; this was the man whose handshake had precipitated the most profound and hallucinogenic headache of his life. This was the guy who he had been totally prepared to steal Mona away from, if only for her own good.

That opinion was rapidly, if not happily, changing.

Because Billy was dealing with the situation in ways that Dave doubted very seriously he'd be able to match. When he'd first heard about the rape, it was overload-time: too much weirdness, too much panic. Dragging himself downtown, to her apartment, had been—*to thine own self be true*—one of the most difficult experiences of his life. Short of thrusting his flowers forth, he'd had no idea as to what he would do.

But Billy was on top of it, and that was impressive. And Billy had not been a prick about his presence, which was more impressive still. Billy seemed to have all of the ramifications of the nightmare under control.

Down to the feminists, whose presence seemed entirely suspect, to say the least.

Which was the most impressive thing of all.

"C'mon," Billy was insisting. "From you, silence is bullshit. You're more straightforward than that. Talk to me."

"You couldn't possibly understand," Susan said.

"The impossible is my frame of reference," Billy said. "Why don't you try me."

It wasn't a question. As intensely as the two women were staring him down, Billy was matching them, and more. Dave felt his respect start to border on camaraderie; and he found his composure inching steadily back.

"I know," he said. "You're selling Girl Scout cookies, door to door."

Billy let out a hoot of laughter. Lisa groaned, then shot him a look that said *please, don't start.* The other two women flared up like safety matches off a barnyard door.

"And what are *you* here for?" Paula threw back, pointing at the flowers. "Sloppy seconds?"

Dave broke out in a spontaneous, furious sweat. "I'm here because I love her!" he blurted. Billy's eyebrows raised, and the word *oops* flickered across Dave's mind; but it was too late to worry about, and it was the truth.

"Whereas you two," Billy said, "look like a pair of

Army recruiters. And if that's true, then I just gotta say that you've got the worst sense of timing I've ever seen."

"Tacky," Dave agreed. He and Billy exchanged rueful grins.

"That's enough," Lisa said, striding into the middle of the room. "I think you should all leave now."

"But—" Susan began.

"I don't care to discuss it, Susan." Her voice was as steady and cutting as the flame from an acetylene torch. "I don't care to discuss it with anyone, okay? This isn't a political debate. This isn't the fucking *Don Rickles Show*. The last thing Mona needs right now is to listen to the four of you take potshots at each other. In case you've forgotten, there's a wounded human being in the next room.

"And Mona comes *first*." She was addressing the women now, Dave could see. It was his guess that Billy had been right about the Army recruiters. "That's the bottom line: Mona comes first. Understood?"

Everybody nodded, though some seemed more apologetic than others. Dave, for his part, felt properly chagrined. He'd come here full of anxiety and concern, only to wind up teasing the dykes. It was stupid. It made him feel petty and small.

"Just one thing," Billy said. "I want Bubba to stay here with you." Lisa looked at him, expressionless. "You can't be here all the time, and he's a good watchdog. He can take care of her, and keep her company. I think she'd like it."

"Okay." Lisa nodded. There was a shadow of a smile on her troubled face. "And we'll talk later, alright?"

"Absolutely."

"And would you give her these," Dave said, indicating the flowers, "for me?"

"Sure." Lisa's smile was nearly halfway to normal as she took the bouquet. "I'm sure she'll like them, too."

"We ready to go?" Billy said.

"Ready when you are."

"Okay. Let's go."

Dave had never actually let the door slip shut behind him. He turned, and Billy followed. The words *and you girls might want to leave her some pamphlets* crossed his mind, and quite wisely decided to stay there.

When the door closed behind them, he wiped the lingering sweat from his forehead and said, "Jesus, that was intense."

Billy nodded solid agreement. "I don't know about you, but I could use a beer."

Dave smiled. "We talking Chelsea Commons?"

"Sounds good to me."

They started down the stairs, together. Dave boggled at the pleasant strangeness of it. There was something absurdly appropriate about having a drink with Billy now: a truce, rendered under the shadow of atrocity.

"Billy," he said, pausing midway down and turning to fix the other man with a penetrating stare. "Is she going to be okay?"

"Yeah," Billy said, smiling melancholy confidence. "I think she's gonna be fine. It's just gonna take a while."

"You're taking care of her." Not a question: an assessment.

"Yes."

"You've probably gathered"—and Dave was stunned by the ease with which the words came out—"that I'm a little bit crazy about her, myself."

"That's okay." Billy put his hand on Dave's shoulder and gently squeezed. "There's no such thing as too much love in the world."

"You're a good guy."

"So are you, man."

"Will you marry me?"

Billy stared, dumbstruck, then laughed. "Good to meet you, Dave. At last."

"Alright!" Dave enthused, offering his hand automatically. Billy took and shook it. "Now let's go get blasted, whaddaya say?"

"Alright!" Billy echoed.

It didn't occur to Dave until much later that his hands, for the first time in days, felt like his own again.

TWENTY-NINE

WAR ROOM

Billy! read the big angry letters of the note. ALBERT CALLED ME AT THE OFFICE TODAY. HE SAID THINGS THAT WERE NOT NICE. HE THREATENED ME WITH BODILY HARM IF THE FULL $1000 ISN'T IN HIS HANDS BY SIX TOMORROW EVENING.

I WILL JUST BARELY HAVE MY PART OF THE MONEY TOGETHER. I CANNOT AND WILL NOT BAIL YOU OUT. AND IF YOU DON'T HAVE THE REQUISITE CASH TOGETHER, I WILL RIP YOUR FUCKING EYES OUT WITH MY TEETH.

The note was signed, LOVE, LARRY, and it was hanging squarely in the middle of Billy's bedroom door, where he couldn't possibly miss it when he came home.

P.S., it concluded, THE APARTMENT LOOKS GREAT, I'M AMAZED TO SAY. LET'S SEE IF WE CAN KEEP IT.

Billy gave Larry a full sixty seconds of serious thought. Larry came up wanting. Billy was not surprised. Threats from *anybody* rang kind of hollow these days, and Larry was certainly no exception.

Let he who is without sin . . . the Good Lord's voice began. Again, Larry was a joke in the scheme of things. Diverting flak from the Better Business Bureau was not Billy's idea of the cleanliness next to Godliness.

It was copping a slimeball excuse for not doing what is right.

And that shit couldn't be tolerated.

Anymore.

But there were more immediately important things to dwell on, Billy knew. The covering of debts, for one thing.

Even if the debt was owed to Albert, who hadn't given a righteous shit about anyone but himself since his six-year-old self had discovered the joys of pulling wings off flies.

You did not renege. You did not go back on your word. It was an imperative as basic as breathing.

If you don't have a code . . . he thought, and the thought drove him back to where he'd been before the note had so pleasantly jarred his consciousness. Yes, money was important. Yes, living up to your obligations was important. And that was the bitch.

He had to figure out what his obligations really were.

Billy tore the note off the door, folded it twice, and stuffed it into his pocket. Then he walked into his room and shut the door behind him.

The weighing of his priorities.

And the straightening thereof.

Was about to begin.

There was only one chunk of wall space in the room that was suitable for hanging things on. It was his poster wall, occupying the space between his desk and the doorway. Relics from his past festooned it like barnacles on a long-since-sunken ship.

It was time for them to go. He told them so as he took them down. The March 28th Coalition poster was the first to come down, rippling in terror and the Stanton Street breeze as he laid it gently on the floor.

Then came his old band posters. There was a terrible appropriateness to their fall. *And there will be no rock 'n' roll Heaven, either,* Christopher had said. Christopher could eat a dozen elephant turds, so far as Billy was concerned; but there was still a disconcerting rightness to what he'd said, in light of Billy's successes to date.

All none of them, he heard himself thinking. *All none of them worth mentioning.*

It was a bleak thought, but it passed with relative ease. All but one of the wall's posters were draped across the floor, editing each other by overlap. The only one left was for Pink Floyd's *The Wall*: the screaming face it depicted looked very much like the agony submerged so deep within him.

Mona's rape.

The three dead women.

His own murder.

And the man he'd murdered himself.

What remained on the wall, once *The Wall* came down, were the press clippings for Jennifer Mason, Christine Brackett, and Marcy Keller. The last one was of particular morbid interest to him, just now.

Marcy Keller had looked almost exactly like Mona.

And there was a warning there. Oh, yes, there was. He could almost hear the nasal screeching of the demons, saying *we let your girl off easy this time. She only got raped and beaten and slashed within an inch of her life.*

But she could be dead, and then what would you do? Think about it, holy man.

Think about it.

He was thinking about it, alright. He didn't know what to *do* about it, exactly, but the thought was definitely there. How could he protect her, short of being with her constantly? How could he do that and still pay the rent, much less accomplish anything else?

"That's easy," he muttered to the walls. "I can't." It was not a happy admission. It left him with only one course of action.

As if I ever had any choice.

Billy rolled the posters up into one fat tube, slipped a rubber band around the whole of it, and slid it under his bed. There was a pile of file cards next to his right knee, several cardboard-mounted packs of thumbtacks just beyond them, a black Flair in his pocket. He had everything he needed for a low-tech simulation of *Dr. Strangelove's* legendary war room.

And it was war that he was contemplating.

Most definitely.

War.

The pen came out. Uncapped. Held ready. He took the stack of file cards and set them on his knee. He wrote *SMILEY-FACE SLASHER* on one, set it down on the floor. He wrote *RICKIE AND REX* on another, set it down beside the first. Stared at the two, in juxtaposition, for a moment. Thought about them for quite a bit. And then started to write again.

SHORT TERM, he wrote in huge letters that encompassed the next card. He set it down above the other two, centered. *LONG TERM*, he wrote on another, setting it well àpart from the others.

Good, he thought. *This is where we get a handle on what's happening. This is where we assume some real control.*

Another category occurred to him: *IN GENERAL*. He wrote it on two cards, set one down beneath both the long- and short-term categories. Then he did the same with two cards that read *IN SPECIFIC*. *SMILEY-FACE-SLASHER* and *RICKIE AND REX* went under the short-term/specific column. What followed came easily. He was on a roll.

RAPE, *MURDER*, and *THEFT*, each with their own cards, went under short-term/in general. *WAR, STARVATION*, and *POLITICAL IMPRISONMENT* went under long-term/in general. Nothing under long-term/specific as yet. There would be, he felt quite sure. Given time.

How? was the next question that occurred to him, dragging its friends, the five *W's*, behind it: Who, What, Where, When, and the ever-popular Why. It occurred to him that everything on his lists was kind of grim. Not good. *I will not go over the edge on this.*

He took a breather, moving into the kitchen for a sixteen-ounce Bud which he carried back into his room. He noticed that there were two empty quarts and six empty cans lying around, along with one complete dirty wardrobe and a spare dirty T-shirt to boot. The beginnings of decay. *I'll have to take care of that*, he told himself, and then returned to the matter at hand.

Good thoughts. Positive visions. He oriented himself toward them. *LOVE*, he wrote, then copied it three more times and put it under every heading. *MONA*, he wrote once, then hesitated for nearly a minute and wrote again, placing it under both specific columns. Then *MUSIC* went down twice, posited as a general thing.

He ran into an impasse.

Why are there so damn few specifics?, he angrily demanded of himself. The first word was the best one, and he pursued it down several other avenues. Aimlessly.

But something was starting to coalesce now in the back of his head. A worldview. Something to hang his strategy on. He smiled, his creative juices churning. Another beckoned.

What are you going to do?, he asked himself, staring at the growing tree of logic before him. He focused on the short-term/specific pile, and the impasse came back. He didn't know how to find them. He didn't even know who they were. He had faces—*half* a face, in the case of the slasher—but there were an awful lot of faces in New York City.

And plenty of places to put them in.

Out of frustration he turned to the short-term/general column. *RAPE. MURDER. THEFT.* They were easier. Oh, God, so much easier. *What* was taken care of. *Why* was entirely self-evident. *Who* presented him with an empty thought balloon, a chalk line waiting to be made flesh. *When* was something that dangled, savory, at the tip of his tongue.

He turned his attention to *where.*

That was interesting. He smiled as he speculated. His own neighborhood was ripe, and that was a fact; but in the scheme of things, nobody gave a good goddam about what happened to assholes in the Lower East Side. Same went for Harlem. He could probably kick some shit in the neighborhood of Little West Twelfth Street; but Bobby Ramos and his sweetheart notwithstanding, he had no particular vendetta against homosexuals. And there were worse places in the city, without a doubt. More poignant places, with regard to where he aimed.

Parks. The word resonated in all the right ways. *Where do the scumbags hang out at night?*, he asked himself, and the answer squatted firmly in his hand. *The parks: Washington Square, Madison Square, Union Square, Bryant—*

And the answer came to him, and it was so obvious that he had to choke back the laughter. Visions of Charles Bronson danced sugarplum-like before his eyes.

Yes, he thought, draining his beer and setting it down on the floor, like all the ones before it. *Yes,* he reiterated, clapping his hands with glee.

Yes, he concluded, grabbing his jacket against the cool October night, and into the first phase of the plan.

THIRTY

A STROLL THROUGH CENTRAL PARK

Billy dallied for a moment at the northernmost tip of Grand Army Plaza, just looking. There was the Pulitzer Fountain and the Plaza Hotel, 9 West Fifty-seventh and 767 Fifth, the heart of high-rising pulse-of-the-nation Manhattan spread out before him. There was power here, immense and ever churning, beautiful and terrible and deep as any ocean.

Even now, with the ten o'clock moon above, when most of the action had been taken indoors or to another part of town, the southeast corner of Central Park was a vital and vibrant artery in the life of the city and the world. He could feel the force that moved mountains and nations. Pushing. Pushing.

When he'd first moved to New York, all those many years ago, he'd tasted that hot coppery charge in the air and fallen in love. *Here, I can do anything,* he'd told himself with absolute conviction.

And now, at last, it was true.

"Look out, baby, cuz here I come," he informed the towering skyline. He felt like David, on a battlefield crawling with blank-faced Goliaths. He was not afraid. He was amped to the gills.

He was ready.

Billy quickly looked both ways, checking for cops or oncoming motorists, then crossed over to the first pedestrian path and headed in toward the zoo. There was a fresh quart of Bud in his hand; he took a swig off it as soon as the Central Park darkness enveloped him.

Scarcely ten yards down the path he noticed a jumble of jagged white outlines painted across the pavement. For a moment he was startled, then the *Village Voice* article came back to him. Some artist, making a statement about nuclear war and Ground Zero, had taken upon himself the task of painting crude figures of humans and other animals—a dog, and something that was either a cat, a squirrel, or a very large rat. One crude figure reached out for another. Just like Michelangelo.

Billy snorted and shook his head. High art tended to do that to him. And though he grew faint at the very thought of hurting the artist's feelings, he doubted that these little slapdash outlines had put an end to nuclear war. They didn't even make him *think* about nuclear war.

They made him think about Jennifer Mason, and the considerably more gifted cop who'd drawn the white chalk line around her body. He drank to their memory and then pushed on.

Moving deeper into the darkness.

Kennan Wyeth was tall and thin, with a healthy head of dusty-blond hair, a wicked tan, and a faceful of deep, gritty lines that time and trouble had bequeathed him. He hated to shave. His beard grew in darker, but never seemed to get past the bristle stage. He thought it made him look like Don Johnson. He was wrong.

Tonight, Kennan sported a black leather jacket, black Motorhead T-shirt, black peg-leg jeans and ankle-high engineer boots with lots of little silver chains. He also wore an eight-inch blade in his back pocket. It kept him warm when the world turned cold.

The world had turned absolutely frigid, just lately, for poor old Kennan Wyeth. Try as he might, she refused to put out for him. Lord knows that he *tried* to hold a steady job: the bitch just wouldn't cough up anything that would hold his interest. He was a restless soul, with big dreams, none of which involved shit jobs or going to school.

Kennan Wyeth was thirty-four years old. Most of the last sixteen had been spent playing Ping-Pong with Riker's Island. He agreed with the social workers who blamed society, even though they were a bunch of drippy rats' assholes that he hated almost more than the judges, cops, lawyers, screws, and pederasts they tried to save him from. Society was to blame for his seven counts of narcotics possession, three counts of assault with a deadly weapon, five counts of resisting arrest, and one count of second-degree murder. It was a liberating insight.

So when Kennan spotted the dicklick lounging on the wall of the Gapstow Bridge, he had no moral quarrel with himself. Society was to blame for what was about to happen.

With any luck, society would never even find out.

The pond was still close enough to Fifty-ninth Street to catch the light from the city. The surface of the water twinkled like a million rippling knives. Tall, lush trees surrounded the inner rim of the park, and he walked in their long shadows, several hundred yards in. He moved quietly through the grass, and he wasn't easy to see. He was banking on that.

The Gapstow Bridge was at the north end of the pond. It was just a little pedestrian affair: solid stone, roughly twenty yards across. The walls were four feet high at the ends, higher in the middle. The lounger was toward the end, where the mouth of the bridge came up in a kind of monumentlike thing. The lounger had his back against it, feet stretched out in front of him on the wall, just smoking his cigarette and drinking his beer and staring a hole in his shoes, from the looks of it.

His back was to Kennan, who came within fifteen yards before he hit the pedestrian path. The sneaking up part was done.

"Hey," Kennan said, boot heels clopping as he sauntered over to the kid. He had a thin, adenoidal voice, heavily steeped in Brooklynese. His lips sneered when he spoke. He thought it made him look like Jimmy Dean. Wrong again.

The kid didn't respond. He just kept smoking and drinking and staring straight ahead. Kennan didn't like that.

"Hey, kid," he repeated, within five feet now. "You got a hearin' problem or sumpin'? I'm *talkin'* to ya!"

No response. Kennan was definitely unhappy now. He

noticed that the kid also had a leather jacket and needed to shave. He didn't let those similarities blossom into feelings of brotherly love.

The switchblade in his pocket felt very warm indeed.

He was now within a foot of the kid, practically right in his face, and there was still no response. The asshole didn't even look up. Kennan felt a wave of something unsettling rush through him, bit back on it hard. He'd seen harder cases before. They all bled when you stuck them.

"Listen, prick!" he yelled, unable to get the slight quaver out of his high-pitched voice. "You betta *listen* when I talk ta ya!"

Then the kid went to take another swig, and that was all she wrote. Kennan let out a snarl and swung, a back-handed slap that sent the quart spinning off to shatter on the rocks some thirty feet below. *That* got a rise out of the little shit; he let out a snarl of his own and whipped his face around.

But by then, Kennan had the knife out, its keen point hovering an inch from the kid's nose. "Ya money, asswipe. Let's have it," he said . . .

. . . and then the kid had a hold on his knife hand at the wrist, so fast that Kennan didn't even see the blur. He gasped, tried to draw back, couldn't. There was no give in that grip.

The kid's other hand was coming around now, open palm aiming straight at the outstretched blade. Kennan's eyes bugged out. *This ain't happenin'*, he heard himself thinking. It sounded stupid, even to himself.

The blade punched in through the palm and came out the other side like a blood-smothered jack-in-the-box. The kid didn't even flinch. He pushed even harder, hand sliding down the cold steel, closing in on the hilt.

Kennan began to burble something that even *he* didn't understand. His bladder let loose in a prickly warm flood, adhering his jeans to his legs. He watched the impaled hand slide the final inch, felt it close around his own. The grip was no less solid for having had its muscles slit. He felt his knucklebones strain against his skin.

But the kid's face was the worst. There was no pain in it, and no mercy. It was the face of a judge, or a demon, or both. When it smiled, Kennan's size 39-D prison-issue asshole began to flutter like a headless chicken.

"No," the kid said. "You got that backwards, man. You're supposed to give all of *your* money to *me*."

It took a minute for Kennan to divine the perfect sense of that. Then he galvanized into action, left hand swooping down to his right pants pocket, head bobbing like a doggie dashboard ornament. He fished out a crumpled wad of bills—fifty, sixty dollars' worth that he'd only just scored this evening—and handed them over. The hand holding his wrist disengaged to accept the money. The hand with the knife through it stayed right where it was. So did Kennan.

"Terrific," the kid said. "What's your name?"

"K-K-Kennan." Face slick with sweat and tears and snot and drool. "K-K-Kennan W-Wyeth."

The kid smiled again, pocketing the money. "Well, it's been a pleasure doing business with you, K-K-Kennan. Have a nice day . . ."

. . . and suddenly he was flying, the kid flipping him up and flinging him like a beanbag over the side of the bridge, in rapid headlong pursuit of the late quart of beer. He felt his hand lose its grip on the handle of the knife, felt the iron grip let go of him at the same time, felt the wind whistling around his ears. The streetlight, fainter beyond the bridge, still glistened softly on the water that he raced toward like Superman. *I'm gonna land there*, he heard himself thinking. *I'm gonna miss the rocks. I'm gonna be okay* . . .

Wrong again.

". . . an' dat was when I hadta cut loose from the bitch," Dewayne Peterson complained. It was nothing new. Either was the story, which—barring constant revision and twisting of facts—Richie Grover had suffered through thirty times in the two weeks since Dewayne's wife split with the children.

Richie rolled his eyes and sucked on the joint. It was low-grade Colombian, the same shit he dealt. But it gave a righteous buzz if you smoked enough, and he had. Coupled with the Thunderbird, it melted down his inhibitions and made him feel like the stinking High Lord of the Universe.

"Dewayne," he croaked, still holding in the hit, "you so full o' shit dat it hurt."

"Suck mah big black dick," Dewayne retorted cleverly, reaching for the joint.

"Suck it yo'self, you so Goddam big." But the joint changed hands, and silence resumed.

The park was quiet at night. Peaceful. All the street noise was far away. Sitting down by the lake, with the cool grass beneath them, it was almost possible to forget how fucked up your life was.

Richie looked at Dewayne, and Dewayne looked back. They'd been hanging out together since they were old enough to pronounce *mo'fo'*, grown up on the same block of East 108 Street, gotten into much of the same kinds of trouble. Sometimes they got on each other's nerves like crazy, but they had enough in common to keep them together.

Both of them were black, broke, and twenty-three in America. Both of them were high school dropouts. Both were minimum-wage messengers who still lived at home; even Dewayne, with one child and another on the way, was still stuck at Momma's indefinitely. They had mutual tastes in drugs and music. They also shared a profound hatred of the white-dominated world.

So when they saw the beautiful white chick walking across the Bow Bridge, less than a hundred yards away, an identical idea pinged in both of their heads. It was too cool to be true, and both of them knew it.

When Dewayne's mouth opened to let out a coyote howl, Richie slapped an urgent finger to his lips and shook his head *no-no*.

She was coming straight toward them.

All they had to do was wait.

She was tall and blond and unspeakably well-proportioned. Her tits were as big as they could get without turning sloppy. Her hips were profound, in the best sense of the word. The jogging suit she wore had money written all over it, and it clung to her body like a sausage skin. Her flesh was white as cream. Her hair hung to her ass.

"What da fuck she doing here?" Dewayne whispered.

"I don' know. Shut up." Richie's answering hiss was

popsicle cold. She was stepping off the bridge. She could have been stepping off the cover of *Vogue*. It would have made just as much sense. As if sense mattered.

If there was one way to get back at the white man, raping his women was it. It gave him the coldest, boldest satisfaction available. Richie couldn't stop smiling, anticipating his dive into that sweet white meat. It made him hard. It made him wiggly.

Dewayne snubbed out the joint on the bottom of his shoe. Uncharacteristically good thinking. The less they did to tip her off, the better. She was walking down the pedestrian path that led within five yards of where they crouched. With any luck, she wouldn't see them until they were already up her ass.

Then she turned, following the path that led deep into the Ramble. Dewayne let out a muffled curse that Richie nearly echoed.

Until he thought about the choice she'd made.

Alright, he silently cheered. *Alright.*

Because the Ramble was the deepest, darkest place in the park: a real live maze of twisty pedestrian paths, leading to the heart of the mystery that was Central Park at night. The trees grew thickest there; the shadows fell most heavily. You couldn't even see the buildings.

In was the most private place in the park. And the scariest, for the cops and everyone else.

At night.

"C'mon, man," Richie hissed, dragging himself to his feet. Dewayne grinned, catching the drift. She had disappeared up the path, was inextricably in the Ramble now. They stole after her in a sublimely cautious half jog, were swallowed by the darkness themselves.

The path curled and ascended. They followed it up. Even so, it took a minute before they spotted her again. Dewayne smacked Richie lightly on the arm, flashed him a glance that consigned stealth to blackest Hell. Richie nodded, grinning fiercely.

They took off, full-speed.

The woman froze, half-turned toward them. Richie couldn't read the expression on her face, but he guessed it wasn't mild amusement. Then she started to run, those long legs pumping. The chase had officially begun.

"Damn!" Richie hissed after only a second. She was *fast*. They'd gained a couple of yards on her with the element of surprise; she'd won it back at once. Dewayne surged forward, keeping pace with her, but Richie felt himself falling back slightly, cursing. The whole damn trail was uphill, for one thing; for another, he'd been drinking and smoking too much for a long time. It all came together to wreak havoc on his stamina.

The woman reached a fork in the path and veered toward the left. Dewayne tore after her. Richie let out a tight-lipped grimace that was meant to be a smile. The fork to the right was a slightly shorter route to the selfsame place. If he pushed, he might even be able to beat them there.

And what a wonderful spot it was.

Richie veered to the right, pushing, pushing, the path listing south and then veering rather sharply to the left. Not twenty yards ahead the land began to level off. Already, he could see the roof of the altar on which they would sacrifice the woman's right to choose.

It was a pagodalike shelter, one of fifteen summerhouses built throughout the park in the 1860's. It was an octagonal structure, open at either end, with a solid and ornate roof and floor. The support beams were not squared-off slabs of featureless timber, but unhusked and knotty tree trunks whose branches reached up to merge with the ceiling. There were no walls, but six of the eight sides were lined with benches and handrails.

The whole thing came off looking primitive but complex, organic yet meticulously sculpted. It was as if the thing had grown, full-blown, from a mutant seed. It was 125 years old, and had held up nicely. It didn't look a day older than the dawn of Time.

The path was plateauing under Richie's feet when the woman popped out of the darkness to his left. Dewayne was maybe five steps behind her. There was no doubt that everyone was feeling the uphill sprint, but she had tired more quickly than her pursuer. It was a matter of seconds before Dewayne had her nailed.

Richie was bummed. He had been hoping for more than sloppy seconds, but it didn't look like it would work out that way. It was like playing Capture the Flag. There was no question that Dewayne was gonna have first dibs.

She was six feet into the summerhouse when Dewayne pounced onto her back. Her knees buckled under his weight, and she collapsed to the floor. She didn't scream. Even through his disappointment and exertion, Richie found that somewhat strange.

He entered the structure just as his friend flipped the woman over and used his knees to force her legs apart. She struggled like crazy, but it didn't do any good. Richie came to a halt beside them, staring down at her savagely snarling face.

Something wasn't right there. She seemed almost to be smiling. He knelt to get a closer look, and dread exploded in his chest like a fragmentation mine.

Because she was smiling, oh yes, and the smile was literally growing across her face, bones creaking as her jaws elongated and her long sharp teeth jutted outward. Her eyes were slit-irised balls of luminous gold; they fired out beams of light that bored straight into Dewayne's, making them glow as well . . .

Richie was no stranger to the sleazoid movie theatres on Forty-second Street. Next to kung fu fantasies and jack-off spectaculars, horror movies were his favorite things to watch. Staring at the creature transforming before him now, he couldn't help thinking about the vampire chick in *Fright Night*, the transformation scenes in *The Howling* and *An American Werewolf in London*. He'd never been seduced enough to believe what he was seeing.

He believed it now.

Dewayne's mouth flopped open, but no scream was forthcoming. The only sound was something like a leaky radiator. His body had gone rigid. It started to jerk and twitch and shudder. The tight curls of his hair seemed to tighten and writhe like tiny, black snakes.

Then jagged lines of searing brilliance began to etch themselves across his forehead, blood rolling from the trenches of flesh they cut, blazing from within. Richie fell back, screaming, but he couldn't drag his gaze away from the horror.

A word was forming, letter by letter, as if branded onto

Dewayne's face. One word, in large block letters of hellish fluorescence.

RAPIST.

Dewayne jerked to his feet suddenly, though Richie knew for a fact that his friend was dead. Invisible fingers seemed to yank the corpse's belt open, yank down the zipper, drag the pants down to the knees. Something wet splutted down with them; in death, a final load had dropped. The body just stood there while the creature climbed out from under it, then toppled face first to the ground and lay still.

The monster smiled at Richie.

Richie screamed and began to run.

Out of the shelter, the altar on which his friend had been sacrificed instead. Down the path, away from the way he'd come, away from the nightmare behind him. The path itself, zigging and zagging in a subtle downward motion. The creature, loping after him on all fours like a hound of Hell.

A pond opened up before him. The water looked black and fetid. Richie stumbled and fell straight into it, and struck his head on a rock less than three feet under. The universe went dull and indifferent for a moment; just long enough for him to realize that he was swallowing water. Then he pulled himself together, and his head broke the surface just in time to see the monster hit the surface of the pond.

There was the *ka-boom*ing of a cannonball off a high dive, the requisite pillar of gushing spray. Richie whirled and screeched and ran in hideous slow motion, hands frantically dog-paddling before him. Underwater, no one can see you piss your pants. It was the only reassurance he had.

He was less than a foot from the other side when the hand closed around his ankle.

His throat sucked in for the power to scream, and got a quart of black water instead. It jetted up his nostrils as well, gagging him, flooding the inches around him with hundreds of anguished bubbles. He waited for his life to flash before his eyes, but there was nothing but darkness, nothing but darkness and the solid weight of the monster that held him now, grabbed him by the forearms and dragged him to the surface.

The monster was a man.

Richie sputtered and coughed and drooled, eyes bulging.

The monster was a man: no longer a woman, no longer the thing that had slaughtered Dewayne. The monster was a man with pale white skin and light brown hair and piercing eyes. It smiled at him as it reached for his throat and pinned the back of his head to the shore, leaning close.

"*Now you know what it's like,*" the monster said. "*Fun, huh? Did you ever think about what it was like to be on the receiving end of a fucker like you?*"

Richie shook his head crazily back and forth, not in answer to the question.

"*Well, now you know. Or maybe you don't.*" The man/ monster probed its gaze into his own for a moment. Richie remembered what that gaze had done to his partner in crime, slammed his eyelids shut abruptly. The voice continued, its source mercifully invisible.

"*No, I don't think that you've quite grasped it yet.*" The voice was smooth, ebullient, remorseless. "*You need something more explicit. More dramatic, shall we say.*

"*No problem.*"

Richie felt himself begin to change.

It started with the burning of his skin. That would have been bad enough. The burning of his skin was like a trillion tattoo needles at once. Then he felt and heard his own bones stretching: spine, hips, limbs, skull. There were no words for the pain he felt. There were no rational sounds in his head at all.

And all the while, the Power thrummed through him like a turbine's roar. It numbed and disassociated him from the paling of his flesh, the jutting of his breasts, the widening of his hips and the recession of his genitals into the newly formed wet slit across his groin. He couldn't feel his hair grow blond, flow down past his shoulders. He most certainly couldn't feel the change in his apparel.

Until the thrumming stopped.

And the voice said, "*Look.*"

And he found himself staring at the reflection in the water.

At the man who looked almost indescribably happy. At the woman, whose goggly eyes stared blankly back up at him.

At the woman who he and Dewayne had assaulted.

At the woman who he had become.

"In a way, you're getting off easy," the man/monster said. *"If you make it home, you can have a wonderful time with yourself.*

"If you make it home," it repeated. And winked.

Richie Grover staggered backward, hit the edge of the pond, and clambered up onto the shore like a crab. By increments he realized the nature of his fate. He saw his brand-new firm white tits, shimmering in their expensive jogging togs. He sensed the immensity of Central Park, sprawling all around him like a great dark jungle full of wild and horny beasts. He envisioned his appearance at the door of his parents' apartment, the *what-the-fuck* expression on the face of whoever opened the door.

"You'd better run," the man/monster advised him, *"before you start looking good to me."*

Then Richie ran, trim and hairless feminine legs propelling him forward. He heard Billy's laughter and his own heart pounding, alive in his ears like tribal drums.

As he ran deeper into a park that had never seemed so black and merciless.

As he ran deeper into a darkness that had no end.

THIRTY-ONE

THE WOMAN'S VERSION

By one o'clock, Billy had seven hundred dollars in his pocket and thirteen bloodred notches on his soul. Larry was deep into the now-ritual breaching of Brenda Porcaro. Albert was placing a call to some business associates, with regard to a pair of wayward tenants. Stan "the Man" Peckard was placing himself squarely in the front-row balcony seats of the Variety Photoplays, just in time for the thrilling climax of *Objects of Desire* ("PLUNGES THE FINAL INCHES INTO *TOTAL* SENSUALITY!!!"). Dennis Hamilton was sitting alone in a stylish Upper West Side bar, struggling with his gut feelings about one William Rowe. Dave Hart was sitting alone in his stylish Upper West Side apartment, struggling with a song of unrequited love.

And Mona was alone, in a drugged and battered dreamworld.

Where the nightmare never ended.

But only changed in shape.

Lisa sat curled on the sofa, polishing off her tenth greyhound of the day and wishing she still smoked. Enough vodka and grapefruit juice for one more drink remained; any minute now, she would stagger into the kitchen and polish it off.

She had been drinking slowly and steadily since noon, pacing herself so that she never got too drunk or too sober. The result was a steadily thrumming buzz that stripped away her inhibitions but left her coordination largely intact.

She'd spent three hours, all told, playing with good ol' Bubba. She'd spent another four hours just holding him while she cried her silly head off. Reading was out of the question; five bites of a cheese-and-sprout sandwich were all that she'd managed to put down. There were always more bookshelves, but she was afraid of waking Mona.

That left her with the TV set, which had been running on low volume throughout the day, where she could occasionally lose herself for up to five minutes at a time.

It left her with way too much time to think.

The news came on, a low simmer of global atrocity that Lisa tuned out with ease. She shifted her attention to the piles of books surrounding the sofa, the dismantled shelves, the imperfections in the white ceiling. There were a number of tiny hairs on her fingers that demanded careful scrutiny . . .

. . . *And there was Mona, playing across the private*

screening room of her mind: a thousand luminous freeze-frames that alternately assuaged and assailed her sight. Dancing, provocative as Original Sin, in the Dave Hart video. Crying, as she announced her breakup with Billy. Moaning buckets, as she was fingered to orgasm. Grinning fiercely, as she spoke her piece to Paula on the subject of the male-female dynamic.

Unconscious, with her face battered out of all recognition.

Walking expressionless through the kitchen, with the outer damage miraculously gone . . .

"Shit," Lisa hissed. Her mind's spinning wheels had dug a psychic Grand Canyon of futility over the last thirteen hours. How could she answer an insoluble question? How could she explain the inexplicable?

"That's easy," she murmured. "I can't." It was the most unsatisfactory explanation imaginable, but she was stuck with it. The only one who could answer her questions had been asleep for thirteen hours, and she was not about to interrupt that healing slumber. She would rather go crazy first.

Which was convenient, since that's exactly what she was doing.

There was a last cool swallow at the bottom of her glass. She brought the cold glass lip to her own, tilted it back.

And Mona's face appeared on the TV screen.

Lisa choked. Most of the greyhound made it back into the glass; a few sweet sticky drops spritzed onto her hand, her knees, the floor. She let out a series of pain-wracking coughs that doubled her over, then shot to her feet too quickly. Gravity and vertigo conspired to knock her back on her ass.

She fought them down, staggering on unsteady legs toward the tube. The anchorwoman's face had replaced Mona's; it wasn't nearly as nice, but it filled her with an equal measure of dread. *Don't let me have missed it*, she prayed to God and Channel 4 as she crashed to her knees before the set and flipped up the volume.

". . . was the third victim of the Smiley-Face Slasher," the newswoman said. "It followed by one day the killing of Christine Brackett, a thirty-four-year-old employee of Polynote Records . . ."

"Shit," Lisa hissed again, her fingers moving back to the volume.

Then a trio of black-and-white photos were montaged across the screen, and Lisa stayed her hand. They were pictures of the three dead women; and the one on the far right was Mona.

But not Mona.

"Whoa." It was the only thing she could think of to say. The resemblance was absolutely uncanny. Even with the volume up, she couldn't hear the woman's voice over the sudden manic prattle of her own internal ones.

She was comparing the time of Mona's assault with the time of Marcy Keller's death. She was comparing the death of Marcy Keller to the death of Jennifer Mason. She was comparing the man who had witnessed Jennifer Mason's death with the man who had brought Mona home today. They were like three different colors of thread in an elaborate embroidery, interweaving and overlapping and coalescing into a pattern far grander than the sum of its parts.

A composite drawing.

Of Billy's face.

"It doesn't make sense," she informed herself, while the woman informed her subliminally of the Slasher Task Force now being assembled, citywide. "Not really. I mean, what could . . . could Billy have to do with it? It—"

A terrible moaning sound erupted from behind her. She whirled, sloshing the last recycled slug of greyhound across the floor. It didn't matter.

The sound came again.

It was coming from Mona's room.

In the dream, she was surrounded by fire. Rats with gargoyle faces were skittering and screeching across the walls and floor and ceiling, their mottled fur ablaze. Something huge and terrible stood just beyond them, in the center of the flames. Staring at her.

Smiling.

And Billy was there, directly before her. He was

covered with blood. There was no way of knowing whether the blood was his own or somebody else's.

It's not so bad, he told her gently, his gore-smothered fingers reaching out for her throat.

And she screamed, left hand coming under-and-in to cup his forearm, right hand smacking down on the outside to lock the elbow . . .

Lisa's reaction was instinctive, requiring not a second of thought. She broke the hold and jumped back, in a fighting posture: body balanced, arms curled and ready, eyes burning holes in her assailant.

All in the thoughtless second.

Before Mona began to cry.

It took several seconds more for Lisa to ease herself back to the world of the wounded. Part of her mind was boggling at the fact that Mona had executed the arm-bar so well, from out of deepest slumber; part of her was fighting the adrenaline rush, the training she had so deeply ingrained.

I taught her that move, a voice in Lisa's head reminded her. *A second later and my arm would have been in pieces.* There was an element of pride in that; there was also an element of terror.

Mona was turned away from her, curled into herself like a babe in the womb, pillow muffling the violence of her cries. Lisa just watched, helplessly aware of just exactly how helpless she was.

"Mona," she said softly, tiptoeing to the edge of the bed. "Mona, baby, I'm sorry I scared you." She sat down gently on the mattress, her eyes never leaving Mona's arched and painfully-spasming back. "And I want—"

"*DON'T TOUCH ME!*" Mona shrieked suddenly. Her body writhed over to the far side of the bed, still facing away. Her sobs, unmuffled, were as loud as the scream.

Lisa was on her feet before she knew she had moved, backing away from the bed and into the doorway. "I . . . I'm sorry . . ." she managed to get out, her own tears returning to haunt her. "I'll be in the . . . the other room if you need me. . . ."

Then the power of speech was beyond her, too, and

she stumbled back into the living room. She landed on the sofa face first, using the cushions to muffle her own sobs while her thoughts spun relentlessly forward.

Don't touch me. Lisa knew those words quite well. Oh, yes. *Don't touch me.* That had been her message to the world for the twelve months following good ol' Roy and Gordy. There'd been a thousand miles of terror to crawl through before she could even submit to a woman's touch. And even then, the voice had still been braying in her head: *don't touch me, don't touch me, don't touch . . .*

The words ignited hatred in Lisa, hot and cold as an icicle impaling her heart. It was directed at the faceless men who'd done this to Mona. It was directed back across the years at Roy and Gordy, dispersed throughout the ages at every man who ever so much as contemplated rape.

And it was directed, with surprising strength, at Paula Levin.

Yeah, right, she hissed at an imaginary Paula, who her mind's eye had made even blockier and uglier than life. *Now's a good time to talk to her. Kick her while she's down. She might just snap; she's got enough rage and pain. Make a good little soldier out of her. Bend her to the cause. Never mind her heart.*

You ever been raped, Paula? She was aware that her mind was getting catty. *So fucking what? I doubt it. God only knows why feminism became the issue for you. Couldn't make the football team? Couldn't make the Joint Chiefs of Staff?*

She told herself to shut up; this was getting out of hand. But she couldn't shake the certainty that Paula was every bit as much of a user as the male supremists she rallied against, the sluts she labeled traitors.

And she wondered what kind of dirt Paula had, blanketed over by her self-righteous morality . . .

Diane Beekman's opinion of Paula Levin was a bit more dispassionate, and quite possibly a bit more accurate. Being ugly and obnoxious was no picnic, after all; intelligence only made it worse. Diane had a pretty good idea why Paula was the way she was.

Diane, on the other hand, knew all about being desired.

Daddy had desired her like crazy.

Right up until the end.

Diane was standing at the heart of Hell's Kitchen. Eighth Avenue and Forty-second Street formed an enormous concrete cross beside her, bustling with maggots both on foot and on wheels. Junkies and dealers and perverts, mostly male, surrounded her at the curb.

She hoped that they would follow her, one and all.

The light changed, and the little green WALK sign illuminated on the north side of Forty-second. Her pace was brisk, despite the cargo strapped to the inside of her coat. The garish lights of Show World were directly before her, attention-grabbing as the pink center of a *Hustler* centerfold. She moved toward it, grinning.

Waiting for the pink to turn red.

Show World was New York's foremost sleaze emporium, with four stories of jack-off entertainment for the lonely, loveless man-about-town. Floor number 4 featured live sex shows, mostly boring. Floor number 3 hosted an infinitude of booths where girls danced or talked dirty while pathetic men greased the weasel. Floor number 1 contained much of the same.

At this time of night, those three floors would be closed, and all the working girls would be gone. Which was perfect.

Floor number 2—the ground floor—was the one that she wanted.

She went in through the Forty-second Street entrance. The Show World Bookstore splayed itself out whorishly before her. There was sign at the door that boldly proclaimed UNACCOMPANIED FEMALES NOT ADMITTED. It failed to daunt her. She'd been in there twice before.

Enough to scope it out.

She had no problems with the man at the bookstore counter. With her heavy winter coat and boyish features and boyish haircut and jaunty Stetson, she could as easily pass for a pretty boy as a cute and adventurous girl. Either way, it didn't matter.

She walked through the store, letting her gaze dance along the wall to her left. Lots of videotapes and big glossy-covered magazines. Most of them featured big dicks in or on their way to one or more feminine orifices. She clocked them off in her mind as she moved: blowjob, blowjob, blowjob, straight fuck, blowjob, blowjob, anal, anal, blowjob, and an interesting triple penetration.

The effect was simultaneously titillating and droning. *One thing about porn*, she told herself merrily. *You can love it or hate it, but you can't help but react to it.* At the same time, the endless repetition of it was like a local anesthetic to the crotch.

The fantasyland inside one's mind is where the real action is.

In her own fantasyland, the sight of all those cocks in mouths triggered the inevitable memories of Daddy. How many hundreds of hundreds of times had he forced her to perform that act? There was no way of counting. They were like the rows and rows of magazine covers, blurring into each other like grains of salt in a shaker.

And, as always, she was biting it off: the hot blood in her mouth . . .

But no. The explosions were better. The explosions were more real. For every dream of biting one off, she had blown off a dozen more in real life.

And that was better. Yes.

Oh yes indeed.

The guy at the token booth that led to Show World proper was just a bit more of a problem. It wasn't her femininity; it was the fact that she'd brought in her own twelve-ounce can of Pepsi, sheathed in a brown paper bag. "You can't bring that in here, baby," he informed her. "You wanna Pepsi? Get it outta the machine."

"Just let me finish it, okay?" she said. "I'll get my next one from the machine. I'm gonna be here for a while." She looked him straight in the eye as she spoke, unwavering. His gaze didn't waver, either, and for a second she was scared. The can was critical to the plan.

"It won't kill you," she continued, smiling. "Who's gonna give a shit, right?" She gestured at the thirty-odd droneheads wandering from video booth to video booth. He followed her gaze, and nodded perfunctorily. The little green light of victory went off within her.

"Alright," he said, smiling back at last. He was a tall,

skinny black man with a purple turtleneck sweater and junkie eyes. His teeth, when he smiled, were enormous. "But it still cost you a dollar to get in."

She slapped down a five and said, "That's how many tokens I want. Like I said, I'm gonna be here awhile."

The token black's grin increased. "You like to watch, huh, baby?"

"I *love* to watch," she assured him.

"Okay," he said, laying the requisite tokens before her. "You need any help with that, you jus' let me know, okay?"

"I'll be thinking about you," she said, breathing the words and leaning close, "when I'm alone."

He laughed wickedly, appraising her. Not a bad laugh at all. "You *crazy*," he said.

"You don't know the half of it," she agreed, winking and scooping up the tokens.

Then she was beyond him, in the L-shaped corridor where the video booths reigned. They were the size of tiny linen closets: strictly one-man operations. A door. A seat. A blank video screen or two. And a series of token slots, allowing for two to four options.

As always, she couldn't believe how many ugly, lonely men were wandering the corridors around her. Even at this hour, there had to be thirty in all. It was, as always, pathetic. If she could have afforded to feel for them—if her capacity for sympathy hadn't died in the comfort of her own home, oh those many years before—her little heart would have bled by the bucketful.

As it is, she informed them silently, *I'll leave the bleeding to you.*

Then she turned her attention to finding the right booth for her own purposes.

There were so many. It was hard to choose. Since she wouldn't really be watching, anyway, some of the edge was off; on the other hand, there was so much that she'd never actually seen. The paucity of forbidden sights beguiled her. Should she go for the double bill of *Tina's Sudsy Blowhole* and *Teenage Enema Queen*, or opt for the more conventional interracial thrills of *Plantation Owner's Daughter* and *Black Magic, White Bitch*. Such a quandary. She could easily spend an hour agonizing over it.

But she had less than eight minutes left.

Diane finally settled on *Daddy's Little Girl* and *Family Fuckathon*; they were only too appropriate, and she'd never seen them before. She opened the door, confirmed that someone hadn't just left it open in the hope of finding a partner, then stepped in and shut the door behind her.

She liked the lock on the door. It was so convenient.

The first thing she did was slip $4.75 worth of tokens into Slot A and push the button (her last token was a souvenir). Then, in the clear light provided by *Daddy's Little Girl*, she opened her heavy coat and looked inside.

There were two more Pepsi cans inside, strapped carefully to the neighborhood of her belly, both ensheathed in rumpled paper bags. She pulled them and held them to her ear, one at a time.

They were both still ticking.

Good.

The insides of the cans were lined with C-4, your standard military-issue plastic explosive. On the black market circuit, scoring C-4 was as easy as scoring a lid of cheap Colombian smoke. She had turned the inner peripheries of the cans into doughnuts of death, the blasting caps nestled against them like fertilized eggs on a uterus wall.

Most of the rest of the cans were filled with regular black gunpowder, available at any decent sporting goods store. It was tight in Manhattan, but she'd found a place on Long Island that was more than adequate for her needs.

From there, she'd scored the rest of the materials down on Canal Street: a cheap wristwatch, a nine-volt battery, and some wire.

From there, it was a piece of cake.

Diane took a swig from the one real Pepsi in her hand, gave herself a minute to check out *Daddy's Little Girl*. The man looked old, the girl looked young, everything looked almost right. But the girl had ribbons in her hair, which Diane never did; and the man was fucking her from behind, which Daddy never did. He always wanted to look her right in the eyes, reinforcing the power he had over her. Daddy was not a back-door man.

And most importantly, they were missing the terror. There had always been plenty of that.

The years of sexual abuse flashed back over her, filling her with the heat and rage that his memory never failed to inspire. She could see him through the eyes of a twelve-year-old. She could see him through the eyes of a seventeen-year-old. She could see him through the eyes of everything between.

And she could see him on the night that she had followed him from the Brandywine Inn. She could see him drunkenly stagger toward his metallic-blue '67 Plymouth Fury. She could see the back of his head as he drove, weaving slightly, down Interstate 81 at 3:45 in the morning.

She could see the brief flurry of sparks as her front bumper connected with the left-hand side of the Fury's ass-end, sending it hurtling through the guardrail and over the two-hundred-foot embankment to the rocks below.

And, best of all, she could see the explosion. . . .

Diane Beekman snapped back to the present, and the objects ticking before her. A glance at her own watch told her that she had less than six minutes left. If she wanted to get any shopping done, she'd best get out of there soon.

She swigged the last of the Pepsi and slipped the empty can under her coat, where the bombs had been. One went into an outside pocket. The other one stayed in her hand.

The video clicked off, and Diane left the booth. There was a garbage can at the tip of the L, almost overflowing. She gently deposited her first present there.

Then she rounded the corner and headed back toward the bookstore. The guy at the token booth was admitting a middle-aged executive . . .

. . . and it was Daddy, Daddy was back, his dead black eyes boring holes in her lungs to release the burgeoning scream . . .

. . . except that it wasn't Daddy, it didn't even *look* like Daddy, it was just some fat-headed jerk from off of the streets. A laugh welled up to replace the scream; she repressed them both, wiped the fresh cold sweat from her forehead, and started moving again.

She didn't know why she got those flashes sometimes. It was just that her mind was

(SHARP!)

like a monkey, she guessed. It liked to play tricks. Sometimes, the joke was on her.

Chubby Face was still there when she reached the token booth. *No more sales meetings for you, old buddy*, she silently informed him, pulling the second bomb from her pocket. *Won't your secretary be pleased.*

Chubby Face wasn't paying attention. One of the great things about places like Show World was that nobody looked at anybody else. You were expected to be furtive. If anyone looked at her, they did it out of the corner of their eye.

There was another full trash can by the side of the booth. She placed the second bomb daintily within it, then moved back into the bookstore without a word.

The paperback racks were on her left now. The bondage section, in particular, caught her eye. There were a number of titles that she knew good ol' Paula would love: *Mike's Dominating Ways, Sonjia Gets Hers, I Want All-Night Abuse!*

Paula was so funny. Diane had been in the business for years, but she had rarely met such a tight-assed ideologue. Taking your politics seriously was one thing; most Movement people did that, at least at the hard-core level.

But to find such a combination of high intelligence and nonexistent common sense was a rarity, indeed. Her little Hitleresque antics had been transparent from the start, but they'd never been more evident than in the last conversation.

Paula and her cohort had decided that fifteen minutes was the proper evacuation time. Diane had begged to differ. Two minutes, she said, was just enough to get everybody's asses out of there. Anything more and they had time to find the bombs, call the bomb squad, possibly defuse the suckers. It increased the chance of her getting recognized; it increased the chance of the bombs never even going off at all.

But Paula had been adamant. It's the humanitarian thing to do, *she had said.* As if you give a shit what happens to those people, *Diane had countered.* We will do it the way I want it, *Paula had affirmed, scowling authoritatively.* And there will be no more discussion about it.

Which was true.

At least the second half.

"Paula, kid, you are a scream," Diane said to herself as she pulled the three titles from the racks and made her way to the cash register. A glance at her watch revealed that she had three minutes and ten seconds left. Plenty of time. She smiled as she paid for the books.

Then she took a last look at the layout of Show World, wishing she could film the moment as it happened.

The bombs she was using were two-step explosives. When the minute hand struck one-thirty, the blasting caps would set off the C-4. The resultant explosions would be enormous, most likely blowing the doors off every single booth on the floor. Better yet, though, it would ionize every dust particle in the air at the same time that it dispersed and ionized the highly-charged black powder.

Like charges repel. The black powder and dust would react very violently against each other, greatly magnifying the second wave of explosion.

And also greatly magnifying the incendiary effect.

Anyone who didn't die instantly would burn to death in a maximum of fifteen seconds, their hair and clothing brilliant against their cindered flesh.

Nice.

Again, she wished that she could film it.

"Oh, well," she sighed, walking out the door and into the street.

The telephone began to ring.

Diane visualized the conversation as she crossed Forty-second with the light. Paula would inform the man that they had fifteen minutes. He would inform her that she was full of shit, they got threats like that all the time. She would insist that she was serious. She would launch into a polemic speech, and he would hang up midway through. If he lasted that long.

Diane's bus ticket to Chicago was in her breast pocket; her luggage was in a locker at the Port Authority. No sweat off her ass whatsoever. She tried to imagine Paula's face when the bombs went off, right under her ear. It was too funny.

There was a hot-dog vendor on the sidewalk in front of

Port Authority. Diane ordered two, with mustard and relish, then wandered down the street to where she could look in the window of Show World.

The guy was still on the phone.

Wonderful.

She was just biting into the first hot dog when the bombs went off.

THIRTY-TWO

THE HOUSE WHERE JOHNNY LIVED

The ambulance was cruising south on Central Park West, siren undulating in frenetic, constant cadence. Billy couldn't see the red lights from where he stood, well into Seventy-second Street, but he could hear the screeching quite distinctly, cutting a deadly groove against the living night air.

He stood across the street from the Dakota, leaning against the wall of a lesser high-rise. He'd scored a wine-sized bottle of imported Fisher's beer from a neighborhood upper-class deli, and he swigged from it heartily. The night's events had whetted his appetite for something special, and he had something like cause for celebration.

And then again, no, he heard himself think. His spirit didn't ache, but it felt too cold to be proud of itself, either. *You killed eighteen people tonight.*

Nothing faintly like a tinge of remorse went off within him.

The ambulance was very close now. Its siren scraped the perimeter of auditory pain. Then he turned to his right and watched it squeal around the corner, rumbling into the park. Heading toward the source of what it knew.

"Thank God that thing isn't coming for you," said the familiar voice, from behind him.

Billy turned slowly, nodding his head with resignation. *Of course,* he told himself. *Of course.*

"I already did," he said. "Piss off."

"Oh, Billy," Christopher pshawed in patronizing tones. "Come on. Don't you want to know what I think about this latest escapade?"

"Nope."

"Aren't you even the slightest bit curious?"

"Nope."

"Aren't you getting tired," the tone serious now, "of lying to both yourself and me?"

Swigging heavily on the bottle. "Nope."

"Well, then," the angel sighed. "I'll just have to tell you, anyway."

Billy turned and walked away. Christopher followed, pacing him. Billy sped up. Christopher sped up. Billy got an insane flash of him and Christopher, running full-tilt down the length of Central Park. It was too ridiculous.

"Tell you what," he said, stopping and turning to face the angel. "Howz about I tell you how *I* feel about this latest escapade?"

"Fine," Christopher said, leaning against the building and folding his arms across his chest. "Fire away."

Billy had to laugh; the phrase was just too, too appropriate. "Let me put it this way," he began. "For someone who's been stabbed four times and taken three bullets in the face, I feel real perky!"

"And you look *fabulous!*" Christopher camped. "Not a hair out of place!"

Billy ignored him. He was remembering his last victim of the night: the way the bullets had felt when they slammed against his forehead, his nose, his chin. He was remembering the guy's expression, switching from brutal self-confidence to absolute terror in the instant it took for his muzzle flash to fade.

"You know what was strange?" Billy said, his eyes still focused inward at the memory. "I barely even flinched. I know that it couldn't hurt me, so it barely even mattered."

"Nothing left but to lay back and enjoy, am I right?" It wasn't really a question.

Billy nodded, sardonically grinning. "Absolutely," he said. He was being a wiseass, but in fact he wasn't entirely joking. It had been, at the very least, a rewarding experience all around.

And he knew that Christopher already knew that.

"So the idea of urban avenger appeals to you, does it? Killing people doesn't bother you anymore?"

"Not those people, no," Billy answered at once. "Every single one of those fuckers deserved it."

"According to who?"

"According to *me*, man! Remember me: Absolute Judge of Right and Wrong, Master of Mine Own Destiny?" He could feel the anger boiling up inside him, and that was good. Anything to keep the terrible cold at bay. "What, have *you* got a problem with it?"

Christopher shook his head, but his eyes were stern. "I don't have any problem with the deaths, per se. I *do* have a problem with the fact that you enjoyed them."

"There's just no pleasing some people, is there?"

"I also have a problem with the fact that you're turning your back on me, to be honest."

"What do you expect, Christopher?" Hoping that he sounded as disgusted as he felt. "You're a pain in the ass. I can't remember the last thing I did that you approved of. Why don't you just bugger off?"

It was Christopher's turn to look disgusted. "This is beneath you, ace. This is rebellion for the sake of rebellion. It's stupid. It's Jimmy Dean. Why don't you—"

"Why don't you take a hike!" Billy shouted back. "Why don't you take the hint? Don't call us! We'll call you! Is that clear enough for you? Am I getting through to your lighter-than-air brain?"

"Suit yourself," the angel said, hands up in a *whoa, Nellie* gesture. "But I'd like you to keep one little thing in mind.

"The next time you call, I may not answer.

"And it might be when you need me the most."

"I'll take my chances," Billy spat back, but a chill wind

blew through his hollow spine as he spoke. It was not something that the angel could have missed.

Christopher nodded and smiled sadly. "That you will," he said.

And then he was gone.

Leaving Billy, feeling suddenly and terribly alone, to contemplate the entrance to the Dakota. There was a set of ghostly pictures that had been haunting him in the moments before the ambulance and the angel had disturbed him. He returned his attention to them now.

John Lennon was a man who had tried to change the world with his music; and while you couldn't exactly say that the man was a failure, he hadn't quite achieved world peace, either.

The dream had ended for Johnny on the little patch of pavement just across the way. It had ended in a brief but fatal thunderstorm of bullets.

Billy found himself wondering what would have happened if John Lennon had been granted the Power: to both Mark David Chapman and the world at large.

No answers availed themselves.

"We gave peace a chance, Johnny boy," Billy heard himself saying. "Now it's time to try something different."

The beer, as he drained it, felt almost cold as he did.

THIRTY-THREE

CONTACT

It was 2:35 on Friday morning when Rizzo and Hamilton arrived at the Twenty-second Precinct house in Central Park. The Eighty-fifth Street Transverse was down to one narrow lane where the overflow from the parking lot had forced use of the police barricades. Like flies on shit, the news media was there: a buzzing swarm of insects, shoving their lights, cameras, and actions everywhere but up their asses. Which, in Rizzo's opinion, was where they belonged.

There were a lot of patrol cars, as well. Apparently, somebody had gotten the troops ready for a mobilization. Rizzo suspected that it was a case of too much, too late.

But if the carnage was as massive as Detective Bartucci said it was, he could understand the overreaction.

Somehow, they made their way into the station house without being interviewed. The place was a bughouse nightmare. It was hard to believe that anything but pandemonium was actually being accomplished.

Hamilton was the one who spotted Bartucci, hiding in the back of the chaos. "Come on," he said, tugging on Rizzo's sleeve. Bartucci saw them, waved them grimly forward. They followed him into an office and shut the door behind them.

"Okay," Bartucci said in a way that suggested things were not. He looked like twenty years had passed in the last three hours or less. He was a round, balding Italian man who was noted for his big smile and his quadruple chins. The smile was gone. The chins were bristling with unshaven stubble that was coming in gray. There was little difference in color between his dark eyes and the bags beneath them.

"Okay," he repeated. "This is my problem, not yours, though I can't say I'm happy about it. I wouldn't wish this shit on anybody. But I called you in because I want you to hear the tape, see if it triggers off any connections. Alright?"

Rizzo nodded. Hamilton stared at his hands, unreacting. It was starting to be a habit. The Smiley-Face business had gotten under his skin, and that nonsense about the hippie kid was seriously coloring his judgment. Rizzo spent five seconds alternately pissed at and worried about his partner.

Then the tape started rolling.

And the rest of the universe was put on hold.

"*Twenty-second Precinct,*" a voice began. "*Sergeant Reilly speak—*"

"*Don't talk,*" a deep, gravelly voice interrupted. "*Just listen to this.*"

A third voice came in. It was different from the others in virtually every respect: the high warbling of its pitch, the spitfire rapidity of its speech. The reason for the difference was immediately evident.

The owner of the third voice was terrified.

"You gotta understand," it began. *"It was all Toby's idea. He was the one who—"*

"Whap!" There was bone and meat in the repercussive sound. The third voice screamed. Something low and murderous murmured behind it. Then the staccato syllables resumed, faster and more terrified than before.

"MY NAME IS TODD JOHNSON!" Every word was a continuation of the scream. *"AND I'M HERE BECAUSE I SHOT MY FRIEND IN THE HEAD, AND THIS GUY CAUGHT ME, AND HE WOULDN'T DIE . . ."*

The second voice came in, fainter this time. It said something that sounded like, *"Time to eat."*

There was the unmistakable sound of a gun going off, the unmistakable thud of meat against pavement. Both Rizzo and Hamilton put a foot between themselves and the floor.

"There's one asshole who'll never play the piano again," the second voice said distinctly. He'd obviously taken over the phone. *"You'll find him near the playground by Tavern-on-the-Green. I'm using your call box there, as if you didn't know."*

"Holy shit." The voice of Sergeant Reilly. It had picked up a bit of the late third voice's terror.

"You'll recognize him," the second voice continued, *"easily. He's the guy with one end of the gun spot welded to his hand and the other end in his mouth. If you find anyone else who meets that description, check his wallet."* The voice laughed throatily.

Rizzo stared incredulously at his companions. It wasn't just the coldness of the voice and the deed; it wasn't just the fact that he'd caught the audio equivalent of a snuff movie.

What really got to him was the voice. It was, once again, unmistakable.

"Clint Eastwood," he said.

"Exactly," Bartucci agreed, grinning tersely. "Ain't that a pisser?"

"While you're at it," Clint continued, *"you might want to round up the rest of the boys. They're scattered all over the park, but I'll tell you where."*

The next three minutes of tape were spent on descriptions and locations of the dead. If the descriptions were to be believed, the variety of deaths was staggering. The voice kept saying things like, *"I scared him to death. You don't wanna know how."* Odd tickles of laughter punctuated the speech, but the man appeared to remain basically under control.

"All this stuff accurate?" Hamilton wanted to know.

"The locations are," Bartucci said. "Its hard to say what killed a couple of them—Pathology's looking into it now—but from the looks of it, he's pretty much dead-on. He killed them. Or at least he had a part in it."

"There's one other person you might want to look for," the voice continued. *"This beautiful blond woman: the one my little rapist friend was on when I, um, dealt with him."* That laugh again. *"She ran off into the Ramble somewhere. I lost her. You might want to look for her, just in case."*

"You find her?" Rizzo was lighting a cigarette.

"She made it almost all the way up to the Seventy-ninth Street Transverse." Bartucci passed the ashtray off his desk. He didn't smoke. "Multiple rape, from the looks of it. Multiple stab wounds for sure."

Hamilton perked up. "Any similarity to—"

"He's not your pattern killer, no. This was random. Just a bunch of fun-lovin' guys, I suppose." Then Bartucci put a finger to his lips and said, *"Ssssh.* This is the part you wanna hear."

"You're probably wondering why I did it," the voice began. *"No problem.*

"Your hands are tied, but mine are not. That's what I like. The dumb fuckers I cleaned up for you tonight couldn't stop me, no matter how hard they tried. Neither can you. Don't even bother to try.

"The best thing you can do is let the city know—and you can quote me on this—the following:

"I am out here, people. I am stalking the streets. I am looking for the muggers and the rapists and the killers. I am looking for the kidnappers and the pimps and the en-

forcers. When I find them, I will kill them, and I won't lose a second of sleep over it.

"CRIMINALS WILL NO LONGER GET EXAMPLES. THEY ARE EXAMPLES.

"Do I make myself clear?"

Three seconds of silence enveloped the room: dramatic pause on the tape, stunned silence from the men.

"And I've got a special message for Detectives Rizzo and Hamilton, the men assigned to the so-called Smiley-Face Slasher. You'd better move fast if you want him to face due process of law.

"I don't. I want him all to myself."

The click of the deadened phone line followed, and Bartucci stopped the tape.

"So what do you think?" he inquired.

Hamilton was staring at Rizzo. Rizzo knew what his partner was thinking. He refused to acknowledge the stare.

"I think," Rizzo said, "that the guy's a fucking fruitcake."

"Absolutely. Only problem is, he's good at it." Bartucci got up, paced for a second, stopped. "You know, I've seen a lot of strange shit in my life, but this one takes the cake. *We can't explain some of the things he did*. It's driving us nuts."

"Like what?" This from Hamilton.

"Well, like the burned kids, just for starters. Six of 'em, up by the bandshell, burnt black as last week's leftover pot roast. Word from the lab is that they've found no trace of any fire-inducing agent. No gasoline, kerosene, phosphorus, napalm, or anything else. And to make matters worse, they tell me that the bodies had *uniform burns*. It's like the fire started everywhere at once. You follow?"

Rizzo and Hamilton didn't. They wore matching expressions of ugly gaping incomprehension. The shakings of their heads looked choreographed. "It doesn't make sense—" Rizzo began.

"Exactly. And neither does anything else about this case. Take the guy who was scared to death: he sure as hell *looked* like it. There wasn't a mark on his body. Or look at the guy we found up in the Ramble, with the word *RAPIST* carved straight through into the middle of his fucking forehead. A branding iron couldn't do that. It wasn't a knife or a scalpel, either. I've never seen what a laser beam could do, but I'm guessing that it would look something like that."

"So what are you saying?" Rizzo demanded. "The guy's got a ray gun?"

"I don't know what I'm saying! I'm stating the facts, but I don't know what they mean!" Bartucci's face darkened, and a ripple moved through his many chins. Then he realized he was shouting at the wrong man, and a little self-conscious laugh of dismay twitched out of him. "I'm sorry. I don't know. I didn't think about a ray gun. If he's got one, it's like nothing I've ever heard of before.

"And that still doesn't explain— aw, forget it. It's too much." He paused to rub his forehead. Presumably, it ached. His eyes were full of pain as he looked up and added, "You know what this means, don't you?"

Rizzo took a second before answering. "You heard about the bombing, right?"

"On Forty-second. Yeah." Bartucci's chins fluttered as he nodded.

"It means to me that the city's going nuts."

"Yeah," Hamilton interjected. "But the bombing is a separate case. "This vigilante was provoked by the slasher. You can tell."

"Well, that's just spectacular," Rizzo snorted. "Who knows? Maybe they'll get together, wipe each other out, and then all of our troubles will be over. Seems to me like they were made for each other."

Made for each other. Rizzo could feel the words gather mass inside the room, as if they had a life of their own. He could feel them impact upon Hamilton, feel his partner zero in on the thought with the abstract singlemindedness of a tongue worrying a loosened tooth.

And, quite thoroughly despite himself, he felt his spine go cold. . . .

THIRTY-FOUR

HEROES

Friday morning was sunny and cool. It was the beginning of a genuine feel-good day: the kind that mandates smiles as surely as freezing rain brings out the bitches.

So New York was already in a whopping good mood when it flipped on *Good Morning America* or picked up its morning paper. For some, it simply blunted the impact of the slaughter; for others, it was simply all the more cause for celebration.

There was a new hero in town.

Whether you liked it or not.

And they called him the Central Park Vigilante.

The media wasn't able to do anything with the *Dirty Harry* tie-in. Clint Eastwood himself was on the West Coast making a film, so he had a clear alibi; but he made a special point of informing the Powers That Be that they would call this wacko the Clint Eastwood Vigilante at their own considerable financial risk. "Dirty Harry Vigilante" didn't have quite the right ring. So a handful of geniuses from all over the city arrived on the name that stuck at roughly the same time.

Clearly, the Central Park Vigilante was an idea whose time had come.

It was the buzzword on the streets, that glorious morning. Even the thirty-two fatalities from the Show World explosion were left behind by a cool clear margin. Mindless, anonymous terrorism was one thing; fight-back heroism was another thing entirely. It dominated the headline news, the broadcast news, the conversation around the water cooler and the lunch counter at Chock Full O' Nuts. Man-on-the-street interviews and polls were being taken almost frantically. This was clearly an audience-participation event, and everybody was eating it up.

By the time the *Post* finals hit the streets, word was out that popularity polls ran almost seventy-five percent in favor of the vigilante.

It was through this happy carnival atmosphere that Billy Rowe wandered. He felt better than he had for days; perhaps better than he ever had before. He was basking in both the glory and the anonymity: without the latter, he wouldn't have been able to wade chin deep in the former.

Because this was *real* notoriety, played out on the big canvas of the world. This was *real* controversy, inciting shouting matches amongst people who were total strangers to each other, much less himself. This wasn't a bunch of friends sitting around talking about how cool his new song was or how much talent he had.

This was impact. No question about it.

This was the Real McCoy.

And they love me! his mind kept repeating, awestruck and gleeful. *They really do!*

It was flabbergasting. No two ways about it. It was all the recognition he'd ever hoped for. He took a sweeping bow at the corner of Fourteenth and Third, saluting the green veneer of Carmelita's Social Club.

And that was where Lisa spotted him.

"Howdy, stranger!" she hollered, pulling up to the curb. "Bowing to Megalopolis again, I see!"

Billy looked up, saw her, and beamed. "Hey!" he hollered back. "If it isn't the ugliest bike in New York City!"

Which was true. She had a stripped-down racing bike that she'd painted the most dismal shade of puke-green imaginable. That, three top-of-the-line locks, and a quarter-ton of chain were the only things between her livelihood and the bicycle-thieving hordes. It worked. She was one of the only bike messengers she knew who'd never been ripped off.

Its one shortcoming was that it accentuated her beauty by way of glaring contrast. It gave the apes something to shout about, a potential they rarely let go undeveloped.

As if to prove it, a bulldog-headed construction worker

strolled leeringly by, stopped to shamelessly appraise her, and said, "Hey, baby. How ya doin'?"

"Just fine, toots," Billy hissed, staring squarely into the man's eyes. *"How are you?"*

The construction worker's eyes went wide, and he turned a deep maroon. Lisa laughed. Billy kept staring into Bulldog's eyes until the man shuffled away in embarrassment.

"My hero," Lisa said.

"My pleasure, ma'am," he drawled, tipping an imaginary hat. It had only taken the tiniest tickle of Power to make the guy nearly douse his drawers; and *God*, was it fun! "All in a day's work for the Central Park Vigilante—" he continued.

And stopped.

Because Lisa was no longer smiling, and her eyes had adopted that electron-microscope look. It was a look he knew well. He often suspected that it could see through lead: it had never had any problem with his defense machanisms, no matter how heartily he manned them.

It had scared him before: she'd caught him chin deep in his own bullshit before, dredged up feelings he'd been too ashamed to admit to. There are few things scarier than being known like a book in the hands of an apt pupil.

But he'd never been more frightened than he was at this moment.

He'd never had quite so much to hide.

"Aw, come on! Jesus!" he heard himself blurting. "I'm just teasin' ya, kiddo! C'mon!"

"No, you're not," she told him bluntly.

He felt himself reddening under the heat of her gaze, felt laser beams tracing every curlicue and canyon on his brain. The words *you wouldn't believe it if I told you* raised across his consciousness and out of his lips before he had a chance to stop them.

"Try me," she said.

By the end of the first pitcher, she had Christopher's name. Midway through the second, he was really spilling his guts, and the mysteries behind both Billy and Mona had pretty much been revealed. She had nodded her head through most of it, encouraging him without having to say a word. Which was good.

By the time they started the third pitcher, she was nearly drunk enough to speak.

She watched her companion from across the table. His tears had dried, his composure was back, he could almost have been the man that she'd known for slightly more than a year. But not quite.

Because he was not the same man, and now she knew too much to deny it. There was a part of her that wanted a crass display of magic

(*hey, rocky! watch me pull a rabbit outta muh hat!*)

as proof, but that part of her was completely overwhelmed by the knowledge that it *was* true, he *was* the vigilante, he *had* healed Mona, and she *was not* going insane.

But if she saw so much as a card trick, she might just go over the edge.

"Hey, Paleface," he said softly, drawing her out with his eyes. "Talk to me. C'mon. I spilled my guts, now it's your turn.

"Billy—"

"Billy shmilly," he taunted, cutting the edge off of it with compassion. "Turnabout is fair play. The least you can do is tell me what you're feeling."

"I don't know what I feel," she told him honestly. "I mean, you just laid the weirdest story on me that I have ever heard. I had suspicions, but they weren't nearly as crazy as this. I don't know *what* to think! I—"

"Don't think. Just talk. That's what I did. If I'd been thinking, you'd still be guessing. If you keep thinking, I'll be guessing for the rest of my life."

"Oh, Billy. I . . ." He was right, of course, but his rightness did nothing to alter the way she felt. "I . . . I need to know more."

"Yeah, right." His face had *gimme a break* written all over it. "What else do you need, Lisa? There's hardly a spot left in my soul that I didn't just lay out in bite-size chunks."

"I need to know where it's going." She knew the words were right, even as she said them. It made her stronger, surer of where she stood and why she stood there. "I need some sense of where you're planning to take this destiny of yours. Is cleaning up the streets enough, or do you plan to take it further than that?"

It was, once again, his turn to clam up. That was fine: it gave her a chance to try and get her own addled reasoning powers together.

"Is that your definition of a hero?" she added, before he had a chance to respond to the first line of questioning.

"A hero," he said tersely, "is someone who's willing to risk it all for what he believes in, and the ones he loves." His tone was shifting, turning sharper.

"But according to what you tell me," she countered, "you aren't risking shit. Nothing can hurt you. Nothing can kill you. You've got nothing to lose—"

"BUT MY FUCKING IMMORTAL SOUL!" he shouted back. "AND THE LIVES OF THE ONES I LOVE! DON'T TELL ME THAT'S NOTHING, GOD DAMN IT, BECAUSE THAT'S WHAT I'VE BEEN LIVING WITH *SINCE THE WHOLE FUCKING THING BEGAN!*"

He caught himself shouting, went abruptly silent. "It's alright," she said before he could get his apology out. "I'm sorry, too. I didn't mean to bait you like that."

Billy said nothing. He just stared at his hands: one big fist, clenched together on the table before him. He looked so bitter, so stretched to the limit, that her heart flowed out through her fingertips. Very gently, she reached across the table and held his hands in hers.

His eyes slid shut, and he smiled just a little. It was painful with effort. She knew what he meant. *One tear, from either one of us,* a voice choked in her head, *and I think we'll both lose it completely.*

"You know what I wish?" he said, softly breaking the silence. "I wish that there were no such thing as evil in the world. Man, I was havin' such a good time a few days ago. . . ." He laughed, shook his head. A frog came into his throat. "I could've just spent the rest of my life making music, healing little broken people, and rolling Mona all night long. That would have been fine. That would have been nice.

"But no. God had to go and make evil: which, when you look at it, was a pretty shitty thing to do. I mean, it cracks me up when Christians talk about Adam and Eve, and how terrible it was that the Snake got in there and ruined everything. Who do they think made the *snake*, fercrissakes! It was a setup!"

"Even the Devil serves God's purpose," Lisa added.

"Kinda makes you wish you knew what God's purpose *is*, don't it?"

"That it do."

"I think God is the ultimate schizophrenic, to be truthful. All of creation is in conflict because God is in constant conflict with Itself. There's war in the brain of the Creator, and we're all just acting it out."

"So where does that put us, in terms of God's plan?"

"Right in the middle of the battlefield."

Their eyes locked, and they smiled deeply into each other. It was the smile of kindred spirits, in communion with the flame.

"I feel much better now. Thank you," Billy said at last.

"Same to you, mac. I feel much better, too."

"I really needed to talk to somebody human."

"That's me."

"But it scares me, kiddo. How much you know—"

"No psychic lobotomies, thank you," she interrupted. "It was my choice. I *needed* to know."

"I'm just scared of making you a target—"

"Listen, Billy. If I am one now, I'm sure that I already was one. It doesn't matter."

"But—"

"If it's flesh and blood, I can handle it."

"Will you stop interrupting me?"

"*Will you stop trying to be my mother?* Jesus!" She laughed. He didn't. "I'm already a target, if that's what you want to call it, because I'm taking care of Mona. And I'll kill anyone or anything that tries to ever hurt her again."

"I believe that."

"You'd better." She smiled. He tried. "No, really. Billy. Don't look at me as a handicap. I'm a fighter. And in the big fight between Good and Evil, I'm on your side. Okay?"

Pause.

"Okay?" she repeated.

Billy's hands were no longer knotted together; they were now clasped with her own. Wordlessly, he brought all four to his lips and kissed the ones that weren't his.

"I love you, Lisa," he said.

"I love you, too," she said, voice cracking over the words. She could feel the Power coursing between them.

And it was beautiful.

"Okay," he said.

THIRTY-FIVE

STOMPING GROUNDS

It was eight-fifteen by the time Billy got back to his building. Three pitchers of Beck's had left him groggy, highly emotional, and curiously at peace. He noted with pleasure, for instance, that Roxie the hooker was not manning her position at the corner.

And the car's empty, too. Good girl, he mused, putting his key to the downstairs lock and twisting. The door gave, allowing him access to the urine-scented foyer and the second door. It was dark and ripe and horrible in there, as usual; standing in the foyer was like being one of those cakes of soap in a public urinal. He wasted no time in unlocking the second door, moving into the brighter and less fragrant hallway.

Where another scent met him, acrid and harsh and imperceptible to the ordinary human nose.

What the fuck?, his mind inquired. He knew instinctively that he was picking up on something outside his normal range. It made him tingle with Power. He took one giant step toward sobriety and then stood there, head cocked and nostrils flaring, trying to place the smell.

It didn't work.

But it reminded him of a moment just before he'd run into Lisa, standing out front of the Variety Photoplays. He'd gotten a strong whiff of something, *just then; and though it wasn't the same as this one, it had several alarming similarities.*

It didn't seem quite real.

And it was foul . . .

The smell remained a mystery. All he knew was that it was there, it was weird, and it was important. He moved farther down the hallway, his conversation with Lisa forgotten, his heightened senses leading him on.

On the wall to his right, the words ALBERT SHOULD BE ROASTED ALIVE IN HIS OWN STINKING JUICES were painted in big letters, with the appropriate jagged-edged mania. Billy smiled; truer words had never been written. It was one of the coolest things that Larry had ever done, God bless him . . .

Bells began to go off inside his mind.

Albert. DING! The thought and the sound were one. It was as if his skull had become a pinball machine: the silver ball was his consciousness, the flippers were his will, and the truth went DING every time he scored a point on it. *Larry. DING!*

The stink.

DING! DING! DING!

"Bonus points," he informed the hallway, which didn't care. An ugly gestalt was taking shape in his imagination. He didn't know what it meant yet, but he knew that it wasn't nice.

The rent, he thought.

And the bell went *DING!*

But there was more, and Billy knew it. There was a jackpot waiting for him that had yet to be rung up. He batted it around as he moved to the base of the stairwell, to no avail.

That was where the odor split into two distinct directions.

Down the hall, toward Albert's door.

And up the steps, toward his own.

DING! DING! DING!

"Alright," Billy murmured, addressing the challenge. His mind ran over the possibilities while the Power did the work. Albert was the only one who had an apartment on the first floor; that much he knew for certain. There were twelve apartments above him, only one of which was his, any one of which might hold the key to the puzzle.

But the smell is stronger from up there, his mind informed him, and the requisite bell went off. He started up the stairway, trying to visualize the handful of neighbors he actually knew. It didn't work; it didn't matter. The absence of bells assured him of that.

He followed the scent up the stairs.

He was, somehow, not a bit surprised when it led straight to his door.

Larry was not a happy man when Billy came in. He was holding a Baggie full of ice cubes to his left eye, which still prickled and ached. With his right, he was surveying the carnage.

"You're just in time, asshole," he said, very cold. "Maybe you want to break a bottle of champagne across the doorway. This shit should be dedicated to you."

He didn't pick up on quite how crazy his roommate looked. What he did pick up on, he attributed to the state of the apartment. Lord knows that he'd felt a bit on the bongo side ever since he'd come home.

"What happened?" Billy said. It was almost a whisper.

"Well, I'll tell ya what," Larry answered, somewhat snidely. "Howz about if we take a little tour through the battlefield. Then you can see *exactly* what happened." He grabbed his roommate by the shoulders and dragged him toward the bedroom door. "Call it a field trip. Pretend you're back in school."

The kitchen through which they moved was bad enough: every plate and glass shattered across the floor, the refrigerator's door open and contents splayed amongst the shrapnel. But it was nothing compared to Larry's bedroom, which he furiously shoved Billy into now.

"Oh, God," Billy muttered.

"Hey, *that's* an idea!" Larry hissed, contemptuous. "Maybe if we pray real hard, the place will just clean itself up! Whaddaya think?"

It was cruel, the way he was handling it. He didn't give a shit. All he had to do was take one look at what had happened, and all the compassion leaked out of him like helium from a ruptured dirigible. It was not an unjustified frame of reference.

All he had to do was look.

Larry'd built a loft bed; the ceiling was higher than the room was wide, it had made a lot of spacial sense to put as much as possible in the air. At the time.

But not anymore.

Larry'd also had nearly a thousand dollars' worth of uninsured stereo equipment. Again: not any more. The wooden supports that had propped up the loft bed were totaled. When the bed fell, everything beneath was totaled, too.

Including the stereo, all of his records, and a few other choice bits of Larry Roth memorabilia.

"I'm not happy," he said, understating the obvious. "Bet that's tough to figure out. But you still don't know the half of it." He spun Billy around, stared him straight in the eyes, and removed the ice pack.

The flesh around his left eye was a violet rainbow motif, with both red and blue standing out as primary colors. It wasn't as pretty as it sounded, and it failed to esthetically please him.

"This is what happens when you fall three months behind on your rent," he said, hoping to bring the point across by means of subtlety. "Too bad it didn't fucking happen to you."

"What happened, specifically," Billy said. It wasn't a question. He seemed a bit too self-possessed for Larry's tastes, at the moment. It did not sit well.

"Well, let me tell you," Larry said. He grimaced a lot as he spoke. "I got home at about six-thirty. Albert was in the downstairs hallway, talking with some greasy little spick. Both of 'em were looking at me, so I had to ask them what was going on.

"All of a sudden, this big fucker grabs me from behind." He pantomimed the big fucker's grip. It looked awesome. "I tried to get away, but I couldn't. And then Albert asked me where the rent money was.

"So I gave him my share, but it wasn't enough." He paused to emphasize the fact. "Then the big guy whipped me around and slugged me, and they all went back to Albert's apartment."

"And you came up here . . ." Billy continued for him.

"And this is what I found," Larry completed. "Those fuckers were up here, and this is what they left us." He paused to swallow hard. "I just wish they woulda made it half as bad for you."

Billy got a strange look on his face, then: half struggle for comprehension, half hate. Larry felt the ice pick of fear rip a divot out of him, invisible as the source was. He felt himself back off as Billy brushed past him and headed toward his own room.

Whafuck? his mind asked in a tiny, shrill voice, but he couldn't get his mouth to articulate it for him. The terror was sudden and bright and total: a sniper's bullet, from out of nowhere, stunning and mowing him down.

Then Billy disappeared into his bedroom, and Larry's terror diminished into echoing, lingering memory. It enabled his mind to work again, to think about what had happened.

Which produced another kind of terror, gnawing away within him.

Billy's not right, he heard himself saying. *Billy's going out of his mind*. He looked at the locks on the front door, and a fresh wave of strangling impotence overwhelmed him. The locks were for keeping the crazies out.

But if the crazies had *keys* . . .

A low moaning rose up from the deathly quiet that had enveloped the apartment. An animal sound. A thing in pain. Larry could feel his hackles rising as the drone grew stronger and heightened in pitch.

It was coming from Billy's room.

It was coming from Billy himself.

Oh, God, Larry thought, instinctively scanning the wreckage for anything to use as a weapon, not even thinking about what the action meant.

And then Billy started to laugh. Somehow, it sounded very much like screaming.

Only worse.

His albums were destroyed. That was the first thing he saw. All those vintage old Hendrix and Beatles and Airplane and Dead albums lolled out of their crushed covers in

jagged slice-of-pie shards. The floor was littered with them.
The crates that had housed them were kicked over, too, and
one of them had been battered to splinters. Not that it
mattered. There was nothing left worth putting in it,
anyway.

That was when he started to moan.

But it wasn't why.

Because the stink was in the room, invisibly clouding
the air, heady as nitrous oxide and rank as a dead man's
asshole. It burned in his nostrils, made his eyes helplessly
stream. The walls did a hallucinatory bulging outward, a
*Videodrome*ish nightmare sag. It was in the grips of that
vision that the moaning began, and amplified.

He moved deeper into the room. Much of the rest was
left untouched. He followed his nose much more than his
eyes. It led to his desk, where the stench was overwhelming.

There were some photographs there, strewn all over
the surface. The first one his gaze locked upon was Mona

(*DING! DING! DING!*)

and suddenly he knew what the smell was all about, he
knew why it had dragged him by the nostrils to this place.
The ugly gestalt was complete, and it was worse than he'd
imagined.

But it was wonderful, too. Unspeakably, perfectly
wonderful.

And that was when he began to laugh.

"Oh, you bastards," he said, interspersed between
hiccups of cold cold glee. "Oh, God, thou art so kind to
me," he added, and then headed back into the kitchen.

Larry was still standing there. He had an unpleasant
expression of cowardice on his face. He jumped when Billy
stepped through the doorway, and his one unswollen eye
was huge.

"Did you happen to catch the names," Billy began, "of
the two charming gentlemen with Albert?"

Barring the height difference and lack of fur, Larry
looked a lot like Bubba when he'd just been caught
crapping on the floor. Billy laughed. Larry said nothing.

"Come on, big fella," Billy continued, sly and jovial.
"Think on it for a second. Did you happen to catch the
names of either one of 'em?"

Larry's expression remained unchanged, but he took one baby step back. *Boy, you've got a spine of steel*, Billy thought; he didn't say it, but he giggled a little as it rang against the inside of his ears.

"Well, let me ask you this," he persisted. "You say that there was a greasy little spick. Did he have a wormy little mustache?"

Larry slowly nodded his head.

"Now think real hard. Could his name have possibly been Rickie?"

Larry's good eye widened further, just before he nodded again.

"Ah!" Billy smiled. He was pleased. The next question barely needed to be asked. "And the big guy. The big one. Do you think he might have called himself—"

"Rex." The word, from Larry's throat, was nearly inaudible. But the jogging of his memory brought a strange light to his eyes; even the damaged one gleamed with a sudden dawning of comprehension, a slew of unphrased questions that took form within that glow. "Rex," he said again.

And Billy smiled.

"I'm going to pay off Albert now," he said. His hand slid into his pocket, pulled out the enormous wad of bills. "Give him everything we owe him. And then I think I'll settle up with his goons. Sound good?"

"Billy—" Larry began. The unspoken questions were beginning to take shape.

But Billy didn't care to answer them. He had just one more thing to say.

"Don't talk. Just listen. This is something you're gonna want to keep in mind."

He stepped closer to Larry. Larry backed away farther. Billy stepped closer still. He could almost taste the sharpness of his teeth.

"Don't ever fucking push me again, okay?" he said. "Don't push me, don't shove me, don't raise your tiny voice. You may be awfully sorry if you do, and I mean that most sincerely."

Then he turned, leaving his quivering roommate to the rubble, and made his way to the front door and beyond.

THIRTY-SIX

ALBERT

The whole thing went down in less than ten minutes. Like this:

Albert was in bed, his bloated body naked and stretched out on top of the sheets. In the blue light from the TV his sweaty tons of flesh took on an unpleasant sheen. He had a lot of body hair, and most of it was slicked down by the exertion and the heat. He had just gotten laid, and he stunk. Albert wallowed in the fumes like a pig in a poke.

It was a happy coincidence for Cinemax that they'd scheduled *Magnum Force* as their Friday Night Movie leadoff. The vigilante killings had kicked up their share of the viewing public monumentally. Ordinarily, Albert would have been watching *Knight Rider*.

Clint was just blowing off his first young renegade cop when the door of Albert's apartment swung open.

Albert jumped, sat bolt upright. He grabbed the pillow from behind him and used it to cover his crotch. His eyes, when he turned, were wide and huge.

"Hi," Billy said, letting the door swing shut behind him. "I believe I owe you something."

Albert went from fear to fury in the time it takes a fly's wing to flicker. "What the hell are you doin' here?" he demanded.

"Don't you want what's coming to you?" Billy grinned as he said it, and took another step into the room.

Albert was confused, and a twinge of the fear came back. He didn't like that smile, and being naked put him at a very definite strategic disadvantage. "How'd you get in here?" he demanded again, a little less tough this time.

"Through the door. I thought you saw me."

"I—"

"I wanna ask *you* a couple of questions now, okay? You'll want to answer them quickly."

"Listen, asshole!" Albert bellowed. "I don' hafta take dis shit! You can't jus' walk in here without even knockin'— without even fucking *knockin'*—an' try to intimidate me! Get outta here!" It sounded like "gitattahair": one word, with a cheesy Spanish accent. *Intimidate* was pretty funny, too.

Billy laughed. "I think you'd better put your pants on before you try to order me around. It's hard to take you seriously." Albert flushed. "Of course, it's hard to take you seriously, anyhow."

"*Gitattahair!*" Pointing at the door with his pudgy right hand, holding the pillow with his left. His whole body flushed and jiggled. Embarrassment. Rage.

Billy took another half-dozen steps into the room. He wasn't smiling. "You took a couple of guys up to my apartment earlier. I wanna know who they are. I wanna know where they live."

Albert used his patented sneer. "You can't prove nothin'."

"I don't have to prove anything. I already know. I want some names and addresses. Now."

"I don' know what you're talking about!"

"Don't play with me, Albert. I'll waste you right now."

Albert looked stunned. "Are you threatening me?"

"Kinda sounds that way, doesn't it?"

The fat landlord was sweating more profusely now. He slid slowly down the length of the bed, backing away. There was a tiny noise from the bathroom. Roxie. Albert thought about making a dash for it, pounding the door. He thought again. Billy was coming closer. He thought again, and then it was too late.

"You touch me, fucker, you're dead meat!" The notes were shrill and warbling. They packed a lot of volume, but not much power.

But it was the words that got to Billy. He stopped in his tracks, gaze turning inward for a moment. A smile slowly lit across his face.

"No, no, muh man," Billy said very quietly. "You are."

And then he touched Albert, very lightly, on the forehead.

The landlord shrieked. The touch itself was butterfly light, but he felt a spark go off, as if Billy had just struck a safety match off the wrinkles on his brow. His hands came up to touch the spot; and with horror he noted that the flesh of his forehead and fingertips seemed to smush into each other, soft and giving as the feel of bruised plums.

He shrieked again.

"You're dead," Billy said. "You just don't know it yet. You're a walking, talking corpse. Check it out."

Dirty Harry was involved in some serious shooting on the screen. There was the faint sound of whimpering from the bathroom. Billy yanked a mirror that was five feet long and two feet tall from the cheap wooden bureau with a visceral snap.

All of it was drowned out by the screams that persisted as a crackling charge ran through Albert's body, enveloping his head and shooting down to the shoulders as it rocketed up his arms and down his sides. It wasn't pain so much as the feeling that his body was falling asleep: the tingling odd numbness that raced down his torso, overwhelmed his genitals, and made its way rapidly down either leg.

The stench in the room changed slightly for the worse.

"Check it out," Billy repeated, holding up the mirror.

Albert saw himself.

And the real screaming began.

Because he was rotting, the flesh going pale and greenish and slick with something other than sweat. Huge bruises were forming on his ass and thighs; the blood was settling there, purplish and nasty. A vile taste had befallen his tongue. Decay. As he watched, the greenishness became more distinct.

"*NOOOOO!*" he howled, but the effort was suddenly grueling. His muscles didn't work the way they were supposed to, and he seemed suddenly devoid of salivary help. His flesh was starting to bulge, bloating, like a roadside carcass beneath the summer sun.

Which knew no mercy.

"Okay, man," Billy said, holding the mirror steady.

"Give me their names. Tell me where I can find 'em. Maybe I'll reverse the process.

"Maybe."

Albert was having a hard time concentrating. In the reflection, it seemed that his flesh was beginning to crawl. His stomach was bulging in a horrible pregnancy-mode, inch by visible inch.

He looked away from his nightmare image, bug-eyed vision locked on the bathroom door. It was the only locked door that he could retreat behind.

It was his only chance in the Hell that was so rapidly immersing him.

"*Roxie!*" he tried to scream, but the word came out burbled. He staggered to his feet and wobbled there, the pillow falling away. The deterioration of his internal machinery did a number on his motor control. He could barely haul his bulk to the door and slam his fists against it.

"ROXIE!" he bawled, tearlessly crying now. His hands stuck to the door as they struck it, pulled away with a squishing sound. Blotches of goo lingered on the wood veneer.

"Roxie," said the voice from behind him, drawing nearer. It sounded almost wistful, like fond remembering of a favorite dish that Momma used to make. Yes, very much like that.

It sounded almost hungry.

Roxie Wray, a rose by any other name, was cowering naked in the bathtub when the door blew off its hinges. It didn't bulge or boom, as if someone had rammed it; it didn't even crash to the floor.

It blew across the room as if fired out of a cannon, smashed against the opposite wall, and *then* crashed to the floor. A powerful blast of rancid wind swept in behind it, gagging her, blowing her back.

And then Albert staggered into the room.

In the blaring fluorescence of the bathroom light, the crawling of his flesh could be clearly seen for what it was. All the little white maggots squirming in and out were stark counterpoint to his darkening ripeness.

Roxie screamed and screamed and screamed, devoured by the horror. Her eyes bugged out in an unwitting parody of Albert's own, which caught his reflection in the bathroom mirror. His worm-ridden tongue poked out in a grisly lolling raspberry as he let out a scream that had no wind behind it. The result was a gurgling death-rattle.

Then he plummeted to the tiles with a wet smacking sound.

And somebody else stepped into the room.

Oh, no, her mind whispered. *Oh, no. Oh, no.* The presence of the kid made her nightmare complete. The words *Go and sin no more* rippled across her consciousness in a voice that was not her own. And here she was, sinning again: an ugly sin that she hated, that was imposed upon her with force and threat by fucking Albert and fucking Cool . . .

"*THEY MADE ME DO IT!*" she shrieked, and then the wind blasted into her again, the crackling heat spackling against her skin . . .

Billy stopped himself. It wasn't easy. There were several things involved.

Number One: she was a witness.

Number Two: he had touched her, and she had failed him, and the failure made him furious.

Number Three: the Power was roiling and kicking within him. It didn't care who it hit, he realized with sick certainty. It just wanted *out*.

Billy stopped himself, swallowing the ball in mid roll and punting it back. *She's a victim,* his mind reminded him. *You're not supposed to kill her. You're supposed to save her.* He imagined being forced to fuck Albert, and the concept was more revolting than the steaming mound of rot on the floor.

She was babbling her story now. He listened with frigid detachment. All about how she'd *tried* to fight back, but Cool was already punishing her by making her work in the back of the Rambler, and she hated Albert but she couldn't turn him down because Cool would beat the shit out of her—pausing to show him the bruises, going *here* and *here* and *here*, as she pointed them out on her back and thighs—and how she didn't want to be here, and how he *please* should not kill her—

"Then there's no love lost between you and Albert, right?" he asked.

She shook her head emphatically, sniveling back tears.

"And you won't tell anyone."

"No," she whimpered, head still shaking.

Billy thought, for a second, about the six hundred-odd dollars that were still in his pocket. "Was he supposed to pay you something?"

A deep scab of hatred got picked off inside her, bled across her features. She seemed to have deduced that he wasn't going to kill her, and her voice became stronger. "He own the building that Cool work out of. I hadda do him for free." Her eyes still streamed, but her lips curled into a sneer. She brought her gaze up ferociously to meet his and said, "I'm glad he's dead."

Billy smiled tightly and dug into his pocket. He split the pile of bills into equal halves and handed one of them to her. "Get your clothes on and get the hell out of town," he said. "Go home, if you have one. Visit sunny California. You've got a little over three hundred bucks there. Leave this shit. I'll take care of Cool."

Roxie stared from him to the money and back again. Her eyes were still bugging and wet, but it wasn't from terror. She shivered; it was just her central nervous system overloading.

"Oh, thank you," she babbled. "Thank God. Thank God."

"Hurry up," Billy said. He couldn't believe how cold he felt, how removed from her gratitude and his own benevolence. He pointed at Albert's ballooning belly and added, "Looks like our man has got a bad attack of gas in the works. You don't wanna be here when he blows."

Roxie nodded and stood, clutching the money to her bosom. Something went cold inside of her, too; she wrinkled her nose in revulsion, staring at Albert's maggot-festooned back, and then hocked a surprisingly healthy wad of spit at him. Albert didn't seem to notice.

Billy looked at her. Self-possessed again, she really was beautiful. He thought about how far the money would take her, how long she would last on it. He thought *there's more where this came from*.

He handed her the other pile.

"Get straight. Get a job. At the very least peddle your ass somewhere where they pay you what you deserve. But if I see you working that corner again, you're going to look like our friend here. Dig?" She nodded, the terror returning. "This is a new lease on life. You know the terms. Now go."

Roxie nodded, taking the money, and hightailed it out of the room. He never saw her again, but the image of her lithe form's exit burned forever into his brain.

"And now for you," he said, addressing the decay at his feet. He stooped beside it. "And now for you."

Albert was still aware. That was the worst thing of all. The death of his body had not released his mind or soul, such as they were. It wasn't easy for Billy to reach down and touch the back of the festering head. The stench was incredible, and the texture was worse. He pinched his nose shut with one hand and reached out with the other.

And learned everything he needed to know.

When the final grotesquerie went down, both Billy and Roxie were long long gone. Less than ten minutes had elapsed.

But Albert's perception, such as it was, went on and on and on.

THIRTY-SEVEN

A HAPPENING PLACE

It was dark inside the Variety Photoplays. It was just the way he liked it. The lonely men were widely dispersed singly throughout the theatre, their faces indistinct. The only congregations were in the back, near the projectionist's booth, where men paid money to either whack or be whacked off by their companions.

Of course, Stanley Peckard didn't think of it in those terms. All human sexuality fell under the blanket of Nasty Things: unforgivable to do, naughtily gleeful to watch. He was proud to say that he had never done any Nasty Things with anybody else; his mother would have been proud, too. He had done little things with himself, though, and they made him feel

(*bad bad bad*)

excited and tingly and curious as to what it would be like with a woman, or even another man.

Of course, these were Bad Thoughts, which were the second-worst things after the Nasty Things themselves. He had resigned himself to the Bad Thoughts, much as he had to the little things he did with his hand and the things that the Voices made him do with those girls and the Master Carver. He couldn't help but do those things. They

(*had to be done*)

weren't his fault. He hoped that God and his mother understood that.

They weren't his fault.

Stanley sat in the front row, balcony, and watched the beautiful naked people do the wonderful Nasty Things to each other on the screen. They were

(*evil*)

huge, much bigger than life, and their moans and sighs and rhythmic gyrations filled the theatre and flooded his senses. What fun they seemed to be having! How wonderfully wicked were their lives!

Stanley had a Nasty Thing all his own, and he was playing with it as he sat and watched the movie. When he closed his eyes, he could see the girlfriends that the Voices and his Little Friends had given him. They were so pretty. They were just like the girls on the screen. He wished that he were one of the movie stars, doing Nasty Things left and right with his girlfriends, making them

(*smile*)

happy and excited and tingly all over like he was. Then he thought about Lisa, his friend, while he played and played, and his Nasty Thing told him that he was going to

get Sticky soon, but it was good, it was so good, it wasn't
nasty at all, and he saw her moaning and bucking beneath
him like the girls in the movies, and it was

(*SHARP!*)

and it was

(*SHARP!*)

and then he was Sticky, and he wiped himself off, and
he was back in the theatre with the lonely men and the
moaning screen and the darkness.

Tonight would be a Special Night. The Voices had told
him so. He was ready for what was going to happen, ready
as he could be, ready-or-not-here-I-come.

Stanley Peckard stood, turned away from the screen,
faced back toward the huddle to the left of the projectionist's booth. There was a wall behind the last of the seats, and
the men stood behind it, their faces indistinct. A little gray-
haired white man in a business suit and Poindexter glasses
was leaning into a large Korean man who looked like he
drove a truck. Just one big happy family, unilluminated by
the shadow dancers blown up across the screen.

There was a man in a seat two rows behind him, having
a Nasty Thing done to him by one of the working girls who
made the Variety Photoplays part of her rounds. Stanley
moved toward them, fingering the Master Carver in his
pocket unconsciously. He thought about what it might be
like to make them smile, and

(*!!!!!!!*)

the pain was white-hot at the base of his spine. He
staggered, watery kneed, and waited for the pain to pass. It
did. He watched the working girl's head bob up and down,
oblivious. He thought about the Stickiness he had left
behind him. It was no better, and no worse. It was

(*time to go*)

totally beyond him. It was

(*time to go*)

quite simply the way things were.

THIRTY-EIGHT

LAS PUTAS

Rickie Perez sat on the front stoop of 527 East 109 Street. He had a can of King Cobra malt liquor in one hand and a boom box on his knee. The moon was a big round circle of light in the sky over Spanish Harlem.

And all was right with the world.

On a warmer Friday night, the street would have been crawling with people: kids playing on the sidewalk and in rubble-strewn lots, out extra late 'cause of no school tomorrow; older folks, to many of whom English was strictly a secondary language, crowding the little storefront social clubs and bodegas. On a Friday night less chill and imposing, Rickie wouldn't have been nearly so close to alone.

No sweat offa Rickie's ass. The last thing he wanted was a bunch of fuckin' monkeys parading around in his face. As it stood, he had the only ghetto blaster on the block living up to its name. Which meant that he got to Name That Tune.

His favorite tune, cranked up so loud that nothing but tortuous, rhythmic farts could emerge from the blown-out speakers:

> "Oh, Rickie
> You're so fine
> You're so fine
> You blow my mind
> Hey, Rickie!
> Hey, Rickie!"

Rickie upended the can, toasting himself, letting the last drops drizzle down his throat. There was a cluster of garbage cans near the mouth of the alley. He aimed for it and tossed the can. He missed.

"*Shit!*" he yelled, intimidating the garbage. To his left a tight knot of muscle-bound teenage *pendejos* disappeared around the corner, out looking for trouble. To his right, across the street, one lone shadowy figure came around the corner, heading toward him. A car cruised by, and then another. Nobody seemed too concerned about his wrath.

Fuggit, he thought. Didn't matter. He tapped his foot and swayed clumsily to the beat, a hula dancer with hemorrhoids. That didn't matter, either.

The fact was that Rickie felt good. He felt sharp. A hit of crystal meth had taken him halfway home already, and Rex was off scorin' some primo blow that would soon be gracing the inside of his nose.

All of which was very, very good.

Because Rickie was ready to *party*.

He set the blaster down beside him and pulled out his wallet: a big black leather tri-fold with the letters R.I.P. neatly monogrammed to one side. *Ricardo Ignaseo Perez*. There were pictures in there, all neatly segregated in little plastic accordian sleeves. Lots of variations on the same theme. Fond remembrances of parties past.

Las putas. He smiled into their frozen, broken faces. *The whores*.

"I had you, bitch," he informed the snapshot before him. Flat paper eyes stared, horrified, back at him. "You weren't so fuckin' hot." He flipped to the next set of shots, then the next, while the meth cruised through his veins like an accident looking for a place to happen.

Then he turned to his most recent additions—the *before* shot acquired more recently than the *after*—and his mind drifted happily back.

To the source . . .

They'd made short work of the kitchen. What dishes there were had fully turned to shrapnel within the first two minutes. The few nonalcoholic items in the fridge had taken even less time than that.

Then Rex had gone straight to work on the loft bed in the nearest bedroom, leaving Rickie to peruse the other. It wasn't as easily rigged for total destruction. He'd had to scout around.

The record collection had been the first to go: lots of old-looking shit that hadn't interested Rickie in the least. Next had come the desk by the window; he'd rifled through it, looking for money or dope or anything else that might tickle his fancy.

Her picture had jumped out at him from the top of the stack. Even with her nose unbroken, there was no mistaking that face.

Rickie stood there for a good five minutes, laughing and laughing as he compared Before and After. The contrast was striking. Teeth, no teeth. Smiling, not smiling. Fantastic.

When the bed came down in the other room, Rickie decided to help his buddy over there. They didn't need to do anything else to this guy.

They'd already done more than enough.

Rickie giggled; the speed was making his brain jiggle in its case. His vision glitched—once, twice—head snapping involuntarily with each twitch, like a dog with fleas in its ears. He wished that Rex would hurry up and get—

(*RICKIE*)

Thought stopped. Rickie froze in his seat. His vision went gray and murky for a minute while the low booming thunder of the voice between his ears echoed painfully off to oblivion. It was *loud*, like a cherry bomb going off inside his mouth.

(*RICKIE, PAY ATTENTION*)

The wallet dropped to the pavement; Rickie's hands came up to clutch his ears. His body jerked, and the boom box fell over. He could barely hear its ongoing roar.

But the voice was louder than ever.

(*I WANT TO SHOW YOU SOMETHING*)

Rickie screamed, but his eyes snapped open. Dimly, he could see the huge dark shape behind the approaching headlights. Dimly, he could see the man step into the headlight beams.

Time ground down to a stately slow motion in the second before the van plowed into the man at roughly thirty-five miles per hour. Rickie's vision cleared dramatically. He could see the horrified expression on the driver's face, the way that the victim lifted out of his sneakers at the moment of impact.

The smile on the victim's face.

Rickie jumped to his feet and stumbled, unbelieving. There was a crazed half smile on his face, as well. The van slammed on its brakes, tires screaming as it fishtailed forward. The dead guy lay crumpled on the pavement, two feet ahead of where the van finally screeched to a halt.

"Holy *fuck*!" Rickie laughed out loud.

And then the dead man stood up. His lips moved as he spoke.

(*YOUR TURN*)

The van started to back away. Rickie started to back away. The dead man in the street, not dead at all, started to move toward the front stoop of 527 East 109 Street. The wallet and the boom box remained where they were. So did the undead man's shoes.

"Holy *fuck*!" Rickie repeated. He was no longer laughing. His back slammed into the front door of the building, and his fingers dug frantically into his pockets for the keys. The alcohol and Methedrine slam danced through his system, but both of them paled before the rush of adrenalinized terror.

The keys came out. He fitted the right one into the lock. The door opened. He moved past it. He slammed it. He peeked through its window.

The dead man's foot went through the boom box, silencing it forever. The dead man's hand scooped up the wallet and pocketed it promptly. The dead man's eyes bored twin holes through the window with red-hot light, pinning Rickie's own.

(*HEY, RICKIE, YOU'RE SO FINE, YOU'RE SO FINE YOU BLOW MY MIND*)

Rickie jammed a second key into the second lock. It didn't work. It was the wrong one. He cursed in a whimpering high-pitched whine and thumbed clumsily through the rest of the keys on the chain. The right key came into his hand, slipped out of it, fumbled its way back in. He jammed it into the lock. It worked. The second door flew open.

The front door blew open behind him.

(*HEY, RICKIE*)

Rickie shrieked and followed the voice's advice, slamming the second door behind him as he went. He hit the first flight of stairs without looking back, raced halfway up, slipped, banged his right knee against the nearest step. The flesh on top of the bony kneecap stripped away, stinging. He yowled, recovered, and continued to run.

(*HEY, RICKIE*)

The second door exploded just as Rickie rounded the second-floor landing. The rapid staccato of stockinged feet started up the stairs behind him. It picked up Rickie's own pace, pushed him harder and harder, up to the third floor, up to the fourth . . .

. . . and on his way to the fifth floor, he realized that he'd passed his apartment. As if that mattered. As if that locked door or any of the others that slit open and slammed shut before him would have offered any consolation at all. The flesh-covered killing machine behind him was closing in fast. Rickie sincerely doubted that he'd have gotten the door unlocked before winding up, head first, through it.

And there was nowhere left to go.

But up.

Rickie's legs were tiring rapidly, and his brain was severely addled; but midway up the seventh and final flight of stairs, a plan began to take shape. It had fermented in his mind over the many long years spent in stir, just waiting for this kind of Moment of Truth. . .

Pick a cop show. Any cop show. Chances are good that you'll run into a scene where the Good Guy chases the Bad Guy up onto the roof of a tenement building.

And what does the Bad Guy do? He runs straight out into the middle of the roof and stands there, looking stupid. Or maybe he runs straight to the edge, searching desperately for an escape route that doesn't exist. If he's armed, he ducks for cover at the far side of the roof and starts firing off shots that inevitably miss. Not much in the way of options for a television Bad Guy.

But this wasn't television.

And Rickie had a better idea. At least, he *hoped* it was a better idea.

It was, guaranteed, the only chance in Hell he had.

Rickie slammed into the storm door at the top of the stairs with all his might. It was unlocked, as usual. With an alley on one side and a vacant lot on the other, why bother?

The crisp October night twinkled mutely overhead; on a clear night in Manhattan you can almost see the stars. Rickie saw his TV options very clearly, pissed on all of them. He burst through the door, out onto the roof, and stood off to the side. Gauging the distance.

When the Good Guy/dead man raced through the doorway, Rickie grabbed his right arm and spun him violently toward the edge. There was a two-foot ledge there, perfectly suited for tripping. It fulfilled its function admirably. The fucker let out a shout that sounded like *SHIIIIIT!* before disappearing into the darkness below.

There was a moist thud at the foot of the alley.

"ALRIGHT!" Rickie shrieked. He let out a coyote howl. He pounded on his chest in triumph. The image of the man getting hit by a van and living had already receded, dreamlike, into the back of his head.

But like a bad dream, it haunted him, and so he moved to the edge of the roof. Visions of Arnold Schwarzenegger as *The Terminator* minced uncomfortably through his mind.

He peered over the edge.

The body was there.

The body was not moving.

That was good enough for him.

The walk back down the stairs was hallucinogenically fine. It didn't bother him a bit. The aching muscles in his legs were like all-star trophies. The people in the building, well accustomed to chaos, didn't so much as stick their heads out the doors as he descended toward the street.

Which was good. Rickie felt like He-Man and all the Masters of the Universe combined, at that moment. He felt proud of the fact that he hadn't needed Rex to bail him out. He felt like he could take on any stupid motherfucker that got in his way.

He started thinking about the coke, and the fact of how late Rex was. He imagined the gram that Rex would finally bring home, with more than half of it already gonegonegone. It drove a sharp wedge of resentment into the heart of his glee, made him pissed as he swaggered out the front door and down the steps onto the uncaring Spanish Harlem sidewalk.

I'm gonna show you, man, he told the image of Rex that lived in his brain. *I'm gonna show you that I'm bad enough to earn my fair share of this partnership, man. I'll show you a corpse that you'll never forget.*

Rickie giggled and fished into the pocket of his Army surplus field jacket. Out popped the camera. The now-extremely-dead man had his wallet, but that could be rectified easily.

And he was sure he could find an empty sleeve for the poor old Terminator.

"Say cheese," he singsonged, rounding the corner and

(*CHEESE*)

the hand closed around his throat.

Rickie tried to scream. No wind. No way. He was up in the air and slamming against the wall before the word *no* had a chance to form coherently in his brain. The world went white with pain for a terrible second, and then he crumpled to the alley floor.

"Where's your friend?" the killer asked: no longer booming telepathically, but simply speaking in a low, level voice that was all the more terrifying for its normalcy.

But Rickie couldn't answer. All he could do was lie there: pale, bug-eyed, and gasping like a fish out of water. This wasn't a dead man; this was Death Himself, freezing Rickie in place with His terrible gaze. For a moment, he couldn't even remember his name.

But when Death kicked him for the first time, he remembered how to scream.

Rex was staring at the late great boom box and the former front door when the screaming began. He jumped, much to his own surprise. Ordinarily, it was a sound that he much enjoyed; but his nerves were jangling from the toot up his nose, and the voice was unpleasantly familiar.

Then the second scream came, and the pieces fell together. Rex spat out a curse and ran into the alley.

There were two dark shapes near the alley's dead end.

One of them was punting the other one down the lane. He didn't recognize the kicker, but Rickie was the kickee. Under the howls of anguish Rex could hear the sound of breaking bones.

"*Holy shit,*" Rex whispered, hissing through his teeth. He had slowed for a second, stunned, but now he pulled out all the stops. His legs were long and strong. He cleared the distance in twenty seconds.

And in those last twenty seconds his mind was racing, too. He was thinking about his friend and feeling little more than anger. He was wondering where he would find another partner, remembering what it was like to work alone. He was wondering about the man he was about to kill: who he was, why he was here, how much danger he represented.

He was thrilled to note that the man was small.

He decided that this would be easy.

Rickie's screams covered up the sound of his approach beautifully. The man never even knew what hit him. The same hydraulic flesh press that he'd used a million times wrapped around the guy's chest in the form of Rex's massive arms. He'd felt spines snap in that grip before, at least a dozen times.

He was about to feel it again.

But until the thin arms slipped around his back and squeezed, he had no idea that it was going to be his own.

Every nerve in his body went wild, then: a sustained hysteria of pain that hovered well above his threshold. He couldn't feel himself fall like a truncated redwood. When he hit the pavement, the pain notched up another octave, but he had no idea why.

He couldn't even hear himself scream.

But he could hear the voice.

This is how I'm sending you to Hell, *the voice said. So soft. So unspeakably cruel.* This is how you'll feel forever.

And that was the last thing, aside from the pain, that Rex would ever know.

Rickie was huddled against the dead-end wall. Very faintly, through the tears and pain, he could see the dark shape of Death standing over him.

And Death was about to claim him. Oh, yes. His broken ribs were spears that scraped his lungs and poked out through his flesh into the cold night sky. Every breath that he took was a bloody burble. If nothing else came to steal his life, he would drown within minutes, and he knew it.

The knowledge was strangely comforting. The knowledge liberated him from fear. Death was more real than ever, but it had never seemed less real. It brought the closest thing to a smile he could muster to his lips as he watched the dark shape advance upon him, finally.

Something dangled in front of his face. It took him what seemed like forever to figure out what it was.

"*I've got a million good reasons to send you to Hell,*" Death said. "*But I only need one.*"

The dangling thing was his wallet. Open.

To the picture that he'd stolen, only a few hours earlier.

"*LAS PUTAS!*" Rickie roared, through a sudden warm mouthful of blood. "THE WHORES! THEY *WANTED* IT, MAN!"

"*Oh, yeah,*" Death said, stepping back and closing the wallet. "*Just like* you *want* this."

There was a wet explosion at the end of the alley.

In Hell, it never ended.

THIRTY-NINE

COIN OF THE REALM

"**A**nd, yea, though I ride my bike through the valley of the shadow of death," Lisa muttered, "I shall fear no evil." It was a silly thing to say, but she'd been doing a lot of that in the last three hours or so.

Ever since Billy left her at the bar.

And the ramifications of his words began to truly sink in.

If it's flesh and blood, I can handle it, she had said, and she still stood pretty much by that claim. There was only one problem, which neither she nor Billy had posed: *but what if it isn't?*

Variations on that basic theme had taken her through two more pitchers and all but fifteen minutes of the subsequent time, left her in the slowly-intensifying grip of irrational terror. It was one thing to sit there and calmly discuss the supernatural, quite another to cruise the night streets alone with the eyes of Hell upon you.

And in the fifteen minutes since she'd left the bar, she hadn't been able to shake the fear. Every cab, car, or bus that came an inch too near had a demon, in potentia, behind the wheel; every shadow was a possible breeding ground for the evil. The feeble jokes and fractured fairy-tale quotes had helped, but only a little.

"God, I wish I had a gun," she told herself out loud. Not a joke. "God, I wish I were already home." She had less than twenty blocks to go, but the distance had never seemed longer.

She pedaled west on Fifteenth Street, quickly but cautiously. It was nice to escape the traffic for a while; no cars pursued or passed her. Up ahead, the light at the Fifth Avenue intersection was getting ready to change in her favor.

It did, and she wheeled across the avenue. The one car caught at the light politely refrained from mowing her down. At the southeast corner a small group of trendies stepped into the Peppermint Lounge. Other than that, there was no one to be seen. Lisa allowed herself one brief, deep sigh of relief as she reentered the Fifteenth Street shadows.

And that was, of course, when it happened.

The thing was squat and gray and roughly the size of a cocker spaniel. It raced out from under the parked car to her left and straight into her path before her hands could squeeze the brakes. There was the squeal of rubber and something else, a solid thud, a sudden weightlessness . . .

. . . and then she was bouncing off the macadam, the

bike flipping and crashing behind her. She rolled, bracing herself against every impact, half expecting a car to zoom up on her now and finish the job.

None did. She thanked God for that, and that she knew how to land: she could easily have broken her neck.

Her bike wasn't quite so lucky.

Lisa came up cursing the shadows and whatever the hell she'd hit, then limped over to her poor old ugly machine. The rear wheel was still spinning; the front rim was dented, a good two inches off center. A thin smear of blood, shiny black under the streetlights, marked the point of impact. It matched the one on the pavement, which trailed off like an oily ribbon into the shadows on the far side.

"Good!" she yelled at the end of the bloody trail. "I hope I did more than bend your rim. God damn you!" Later on, she'd feel bad about wounding a poor dumb animal. Right now she just wished it had never been born. *If the Humane Society doesn't like it*, she thought, *they can just pay to fix my fucking bike.*

She gave the front tire a tentative spin. It made a half-hearted three-quarters revolution and locked dead-tight as the bend hit the forks. "*Shit*," she hissed, kicking it. Which made no difference. "You ain't goin' nowhere. If you think I'm gonna carry you home, you're crazy."

There was a No Parking sign at the curb, right next to the car that the thing had run out from under. "Thanks a lot, mac," she said, kicking the hubcap. It left a little dent that would have to do. Then she lugged the bike over to the sign, got her locks and chain in motion.

Maybe this is better, it occurred to her. *I don't know why, but a cab ride sounds mighty appealing right now.*

And if I lock you up real good, she told the bike, stringing chain through every available strut and angle, *there's a thirty percent chance that you'll still be here in the morning.*

These were all cheerful thoughts, and they were starting to work their magic.

Until she saw the legs—too close—behind her.

Lisa's reaction time had been pumped up mightily by her trip over the top; the added adrenaline turned her movements into a whirling blur of killing motion. She spun, blocked, and with a short, clipped *keai!* delivered a palm-up, straight-armed blow.

Squarely into the nose of one terrified Stanley Peckard.

She recognized him a fraction of a second too late: too late to do anything but take the lethal edge off the momentum. But she still heard his shrill scream, saw his wide marble eyes, felt the snapping of bone and cartilage.

She felt absolutely terrible.

"I'm sorry—" she began. He didn't seem to hear her. He just stared at her, eyes crawling with panic and pain. The cup of his hands overflowed with blood; she noticed that they were wearing black gloves.

Then he turned and ran away, stumbling over his own feet, smacking into the wall and rebounding. He stumbled off and around the corner, into the service alley behind the Peppermint Lounge. She could still hear him crying.

"Oh, Jesus," she moaned. She could just see his little brain hemorrhaging now. She thought she'd pulled the punch enough, but she couldn't be sure.

And if he dies, her mind droned sickly. *And if he dies* . . .

There was no choice. Not really.

She followed him into the alley.

There were demons in his head, and they'd always taken the bestest care of him.

But now something was drastically wrong.

For starters Stanley refused to believe that they really wanted him to kill her. Even though they kept going

(*NOW*)

and

(*NOW*)

he knew that there had to be some kind of mistake.

Because she was his friend, she was different, she was special, she was the only one who was nice to him at all, and so they had to understand that he wouldn't, he *couldn't*.

The second thing he couldn't believe was that they'd let her hurt him.

Until he realized that, in his moment of pain, the Voices had gone silent.

So he ran, heading for the triangle of shadow at the back of the alley, hoping to hide from both his friend and the Voices forever. Even through the pain, there was something sweet and wonderful about owning his own brain again. It was a feeling that he did not want to lose.

So when the

(*WHAT ARE YOU DOING*)

voices began to

(*GET BACK THERE*)

return, Stanley Peckard fought back. For the first time ever.

Stanley Peckard fought back hard.

But they had strength in numbers, and they were legion inside him: gnawing on his every nerve, poking more of the bleeding holes inside his brain. They had the numbers, and they were much more accustomed to controlling him than he was to controlling himself. They put the knife in his hand

(*NOW!!!*)

and he fought them. They tried to make him stand

(*NOW!!!!!*)

and he fought them. They made him cry out

(*!!!!!!!!!*)

with the pain.

But he fought them.

Through it all, he fought them.

The service alley running between the Peppermint Lounge and the Chelsea Lane apartments was a well-lit, well-tended one: bright floodlamps serviced the rear court/loading area, and a streetlight obliquely covered the entrance. Together they cut a neat swath of overlapping refracted light, with only a narrow wedge-shaped slice from the Peppermint's blind side left over. It was a perfect and pitch-black isoceles triangle, its B-side lightly touching the side wall of the Chelsea.

He was in there. She couldn't see him, but she could hear him. And what she heard was so miserable, so absolutely fucking pathetic that it made her flesh crawl.

"Oh, Jesus," she moaned again, picturing the scene in the emergency room when she brought him in to die. It forced a painful shudder through her body as she stepped into the darkness.

She spotted him, finally, hunkered up against the wall. He had one hand on his face, the other tucked around his middle, while he rocked back and forth on his haunches and wailed.

"Stanley," she said softly, reaching out to touch his shoulder. He jerked away with surprising deliberation, screaming something that sounded like *LEE ME 'LONE!*

"Stanley. No," she persisted. Her eyes were burning, beginning to water. She couldn't help it, any more than she could stop her own body from shaking. "I'm gonna help you, okay? We're gonna go to the hospital now."

She got both hands firmly on his shoulders. He screeched, but didn't pull away. Very slowly she turned him around and started hoisting him to his feet.

"It's gonna be alri—" she began.

Stanley came up.

And the knife went in.

There was no pain at first. Just a horribly clear sensation of *penetration* as the knife came up from out of nowhere and slid between her legs. It took a full second for her to realize what had happened, another to stare unbelievingly into Stanley's face.

And then, at last, his features registered: the stubble, the teeth, the aspirin-sized dimple.

But by then, it was far too late.

The knife pierced her on the inside of the left thigh, sliding in on a line with the uppermost part of her femur, serrating its way across the depression immediately below the fold of her groin. Lisa tried to pull away at the last second, her hands still clutching at Stanley's shoulders. She pushed off.

Her leg gave out.

And the two of them went down, Stanley falling fully on top of her. The force of the impact drove the knife in deeper, severing the femoral artery. Lisa's world went white with pain, came back red an instant later as time itself went rubbery and she dimly heard herself screaming, *screaming* as the first gush of blood spilled across her belly, filling the air with its hot, coppery tang.

All of her senses seemed to amplify, moment by moment. She felt his hot stinking bulk lift up: he was straddling her, one knee on each side of the ruined leg, left arm extended fully, its fat little hand supporting him, his face mere inches from her own. She felt the blade pull wetly from her wound, saw it arcing up and wavering like a cobra preparing to strike.

And in that last precarious instant, without thinking, she moved. . . .

He was off-balance and hesitating, and that was all it took. She pushed off, hitting a bridge with her thighs flexed and her shoulders planted, simultaneously pushing his left arm out and away. The pain in her leg was excruciating, the sensation of blood tracking up her torso even more so. Her ruined leg threatened to buckle, but she managed to bring her right knee in hard, ramming into the nerve ganglia in his left armpit with all the strength she could muster.

Stanley shrieked as the joint dislocated, the force of the blow knocking him sideways and down. Lisa rolled out from under him, reversing positions, straddling his prone form. She yanked his left arm out to its full reach and brought her left elbow down like a hammer once! twice!

Stanley shrieked again.

His arm was shattered. Her strength was spent. She used the last ounce of it to push off and away. Stanley stumbled to his feet and ran, shrieking and flailing, into the night.

She didn't know which way he went. She didn't care. She'd kill him later, if she . . .

If she . . .

All told, a grand total of forty-seven seconds had passed. It was the dispassionate voice of the Master Timekeeper in Lisa's head that ultimately got her up, quoting a litany of statistics on just how little time it took to succumb to shock and blood loss. She knew she didn't have much time to play with, and none to waste. And so, drawing on reservoirs of will she would never have believed possible, Lisa stood.

And, dragging her bloody left leg behind her, made it to the street.

Freddie Brown was, by his own admission, not the greatest guy in the world. He smoked, he drank, he cussed like a sailor, he bet on the horses and got into fights. "If I was any damn good at all," he told his wife at least once a week, "I wouldn't still be drivin' a goddam cab. I wouldn't be always lettin' you down."

But when he saw the young woman collapse at the corner in a pool of her own blood, he didn't hesitate for a second.

"What are you *doing*?" the man in the backseat howled as the cab squealed to a halt at the corner.

"I'm lettin' you out," Freddie said, slamming it into park. He was out the door and around the other side before his passenger had time to so much as fart.

The woman was gaunt and pasty white. Dark hollows surrounded her glazing eyes. When he hoisted her up, she screamed "SAINT VINCENT'S! HURRY!" and nailed him with a hollow gaze. The whole front of her body was covered with blood, from her toes to her chin. In the cold night air, it steamed.

Freddie heard the car door open behind him, felt the passenger come to his side. "*Jesus Christ*," the guy whispered; but he took her by one arm without needing to be asked.

They got her into the backseat in a matter of five seconds. Freddie ran back to his seat. The cab was in motion before the door even closed.

"Hang on, baby. Hang on," he droned, gunning it. He laid on the horn the whole way down Fourteenth Street, running the red light at sixty m.p.h., almost getting broadsided as he flew across Sixth Avenue.

It was less than a mile to St. Vincent's Hospital. He got there in just under four minutes. It was the longest four minutes of his life.

And hers . . .

* * *

The whole way there, the Master Timekeeper kept ticking.

And the blood just kept on flowing.

Lisa hadn't been able to stanch it: no place for a tourniquet, no decent pressure point she could find. She hadn't been able to bring herself to look at the wound quite yet, but she could tell by the blood that it was worse than she dared admit. To admit the worst would be death. And she would not die. *She would not die*. She—

The cab screeched around Seventh Avenue South. The driver's voice was a soothing drone, but she couldn't be sure what he was saying. She was tired, and the world was getting fuzzy, and—

NO! NO! NO! NO! NO!, her mind screamed. *DON'T FADE! DON'T FADE!*

She fought for consciousness, forced her mind to concentrate. Stanley, Stan the Man, Stan Peckerhead— *what was his fucking last NAME???* She had to tell Billy. He had to know. *He's the one, Billy. He's the one you want. He's the one who*—

She reached into her pocket and grabbed her little notebook, her pen. Her arms felt so heavy, so—

NO! NO! NO! NO! NO! NO! NO! NO!

It was hard to write, hard to see in the darkened jostling interior of the cab. But she did it. And she made the driver take it, made him promise to take it to Billy.

Billy . . .

The cabbie was saying the same shit over and over, like a mantra: "We almost there. Don' worry. You be all right. . . ." It was kinda funny.

It reminded her of Gloria, somehow. Maybe the accent. Gloria used to talk about her street smarts and how to defend herself against attackers.

Gloria was good. Maybe not equipped to handle knife-wielding imbeciles and severed arteries, but—

Lisa laughed, a thin trickle of blood showing at the corner of her mouth. She coughed it back. The cabbie looked warily into the rearview mirror. St. Vincent's loomed up in front of them.

The driver practically drove the cab through the Emergency room. He was out of the car and into the double doors before the engine had even died. Lisa tried to smile in appreciation, but he was already gone, and her mouth didn't work at all.

Then he was back, dragging two attendants and a stretcher. Maybe she'd make it, after all. The Master Timekeeper was still ticking.

She tried to think of Mona, but her image refused to come clear. Gloria was hogging her mind's eye: Gloria, in the robes she wore when being, not only her friend, but her *sensai*.

"*Four rules,*" Gloria had said, "*that you've got to remember always. One: you've got to be* ready *for anything.*"

The door of the cab opened. Three sets of hands pulled her out and laid her on the stretcher.

"*Two: you've got to be* willing *to do whatever is required.*"

The double doors slammed open. She felt herself rolling along the corridor, felt many eyes upon her.

"*Three: you've got to be* able *to pull it off.*"

Rolling, rolling. The lights, whipping past her. Too bright. Too bright. The little wheels, spinning.

Gloria's voice faded out. It didn't matter. Lisa remembered.

Good ol' Rule Number Four:
Sometimes, just sometimes . . .
You've got to be lucky.

PART FOUR

THE DOWNHILL SIDE

"An' some folks get bent all outta shape.
Warped out on hatred, lies and rape.
Look out! Here come da killer ape!
The ugliness twists them.
They're never the same . . ."

Billy Rowe
Twisted Toward Life

FORTY

WHAT IT TAKES

He met her on the sidewalk, out front of Emergency. Both of them were too numb to speak or express much of anything. Both of them had been crying. Neither of them were nearly done.

When it was time to go in, they did so silently and without touching.

It was all they could do to keep from dying themselves.

Farley Broome was a wiseass, and had been for many years. Working the morgue had honed his gift to a marrow-scraping sharpness. But he was not without tact, and he knew the difference between an official observer and a genuine mourner. When it came to pain, he knew enough to shut up.

When the young man and woman walked into the room, he did so with casual grace.

Broome had had intimate contact with a lot of dead people in his thirty-odd years of service, not the least of whom was his old partner. Rick Halpern had choked to death on an egg-salad-and-Bacos sandwich not three weeks earlier; the new kid, Louis, was a prettyboy with very little perspective at all. He still fought the gag reflex at the sight of shotgun wounds or major traffic fatalities. He still had a lot to learn.

Louis wasn't too hot with the next of kin, either. So

Broome was left to deal with the mourners and positive identifiers of the late Lisa Traynor.

Tactfully.

Which he did.

"May I help you?" he said.

"We're here to . . ." the male member of the couple began, then faltered. He and his girlfriend/wife/sister/ whatever were as pale as the corpse that they'd come to identify. This was killing them. Understandable.

"Over here," he said, careful to avoid anything like *okay* or *it's alright*. It wasn't okay, it wasn't alright, there wasn't anything remotely okay or alright about it. He turned and walked down the aisle of bodies to the table on which she lay. They followed.

He turned down the sheet.

They both started to cry.

Shit, he thought, biting down on his own emotions. By almost anyone's standards he was a callous sonofabitch, but there were still some things that got through to him. Thank God. Having to fight it down meant that it was still there.

One of the detectives appeared in the doorway. Broome thanked God again. It would give him someone to shuck and jive with when the worst part of the horror was through.

Billy, like Broome, had seen a lot of corpses lately. He had thought himself steeled to the sight of any other.

He was wrong. He knew that now. This wasn't a Rickie or a Rex or an Albert; this wasn't just another anonymous scum. The shape under the sheet was someone he loved.

Too much for words.

Too far gone for deeds.

Mona had turned away, was unable to look any longer. Her sobs were soft and rhythmic and steady; it was the measure of her restraint. She'd gotten the official call minutes before Lisa had died. Dragging herself down to the hospital, so close on the heels of her own collision with nightmare, was nearly impossible. This dragged her squarely to the brink.

Which Billy had just gone over.

The question *why* was in his head, but he already had

it answered. He knew why. He knew fucking well why. She was dead because she knew too much.

She was dead because he loved her.

Just like Mona's rape, the Smiley-Face slashings. They were sacrifices on the black altar. They were designed to drive him mad, to overwhelm him with the hopelessness of his struggle.

Oh, God, his mind whispered in prayer. *Let this not be true. Let this all be a dream.*

God didn't seem inclined to oblige him. The morgue didn't shimmy like a cinematic segue, turn into his bedroom. It remained as it was.

Lisa's body remained as it was.

Oh, God, Billy repeated, not knowing what he was praying for as he leaned over the corpse, spilling tears onto her lips, cupping her white face in his hands. Listening, as he had all those many times before.

Hearing nothing.

It was like holding a seashell to your ear, running a blank tape through your stereo and then listening to it with headphones. It was a dull, constant wash of white noise, too subtle to even be called a hiss.

Whatever there was of Lisa, beyond the body, was gone forever.

That was when all of the walls collapsed, just as he collapsed on top of her. There was nothing left for him to do but cry and

(*avenge her*)

hold her for the very last time and then

(*avenge her*)

avenge her.

Avenge them all.

Dennis Hamilton was standing in the doorway, wondering why he wasn't surprised. At least a little. Actually, he was wondering if anything would ever surprise him again.

At first, the revitalized Marcy Keller had thrown him for a bit of a loop. Then he'd realized that it *wasn't* Marcy Keller, and it had been like hitting the jackpot on a Las Vegas slot machine: *DING DING DING DING,* with all the cherries lining up perfectly. He hadn't cashed in on it yet—it wasn't as easy as calling the casino owner over to confirm his winnings—but he had everything he needed for his own satisfaction. The last hole in the hunch had been plugged.

Did that mean that this girl had been killed by the Slasher? Hamilton believed that it did. His twenty minutes with Freddie Brown had convinced him. Apparently, Ms. Traynor had done a number on her killer before she died. That was both good news and bad news. He wasn't sure which outweighed the other. It was only one of the questions that remained.

For examples: Who *was* the Slasher? What did he have against Billy? He knew they were tied together, but he didn't know how. How?

And if Billy really *was* the vigilante, how had he done the things that he'd done? How had *anyone* done them, Billy or not?

It would not be good form to assail Billy now. However many levels of bullshit there might be on the surface, there was no doubt that the kid was grieving. Hamilton didn't have his senior partner's official sanction, and he couldn't quite whip up the requisite cold-bloodedness himself.

He turned away from the doorway, where Billy Rowe and his nameless dead ringer went through their unassailable anguish together. A little later in the day—at the Rowe residence, perhaps—he would get closer to the bottom of things.

And with any luck at all, survive that dangerous knowledge.

Mona didn't know about Hamilton's suspicions. She knew very little of the subtext at all, but it was enough to assure her that the world had gone mad.

She let Billy make the final identification. She let Billy lead her out of the morgue and back up to the street. She let him hail her a cab, let him accompany her home in it, let him come up with her to make sure that the apartment was safe.

When he hugged her tight and broke down in her arms, she let him do that, too.

They cried each other to sleep, that night. It was good

just to hold him, to not be alone. In the back of her mind, there was a strange subconscious intermingling of terror and love for him.

Later, when her mind came back, she would sort out the pieces.

If her mind ever came back at all.

FORTY-ONE

MASTER OF THE UNIVERSE

By noon on Saturday, Brenda Porcaro had just about had it. Larry was still in the living room, still watching the damned TV, still in his unattractive underwear. She peeked discreetly around the corner, thinking, *my God, he hasn't even combed his hair!*

Larry's matted, frizzy head poked unceremoniously over the back of her gracefully, roll-arm model camelback sofa with the taupe cotton olefin fabric and coordinating throw pillows (which she'd picked up at Gimbel's Total Home sale).

A vague wave of distaste rolled through her. Their relationship was as yet in that delicate phase wherein the sight of the dreaded Morning Roth did more by way of damage than endearment. If things were a little more *serious*, perhaps . . . but as it stood, she'd had him around all week. She wasn't sure that she wanted to make a weekend out of it.

Unfortunately, that seemed to be exactly what he had in mind. He'd shown up on her doorstep last night with that horrible black eye and that even more horrible story about how he'd chased those two hoodlums out of his apartment and gotten in that terrible *fight* with one of them.

Well, she certainly couldn't turn him away. And it

wasn't like she expected him to be gone before she woke up: after all, it wasn't *that* kind of relationship. She really liked Larry. He was funny and bright and he knew how to order in a French restaurant. And after a lifetime of creeps and losers, it looked like maybe she'd found a nice guy. Someone who wanted more than to just bury his face between her breasts and make motorboat noises all night long.

Though he does do a pretty fair imitation of a Chriscraft, she remembered. Brenda giggled and flipped the setting on her True Hue mirror to Daylight, made up and checked her eyebrows. They needed tweezing.

No, she thought further, *I really do like Larry*. And she didn't want to get ugly or anything. But she hadn't bargained on *this*. . . .

Larry had been planted there all morning—unkempt, unshaven, robe hanging open to expose his belly, which was starting to pot—silent and sullen and sucking up every stupid cartoon show that came on. Right then it was some idiotic thing called *HE-MAN, MASTER OF THE UNI-VERRRRRRSSSSSSE* . . .

Or some such silliness. Brenda didn't like cartoons. They were juvenile. She went about making the bed, thinking *not that it needs much making. Not much happened last night to muss it up*.

She was trying to be undestanding: she'd read in *Cosmo* that it happens to a *lot* of men after enduring a heroic, life-threatening situation. But it left her feeling rather unsatisfied.

Not to mention useless. He hadn't said more than three words to her this whole morning, and Brenda was starting to get just a little bent out of shape. He was just *sitting* there like a lump and staring at his stupid cartoons. It was so unromantic.

She saw the pile of clothing he'd left on the wall side of the bed. That actually made her angry. She'd worked hard for her own place, committed major portions of her income to making it nice and *keeping* it nice. Larry's wrinkled ball of outerwear stood out like a pile of day-old doggy doo on her Anso II nylon saxony broadloom. It was a slap in the face to her sense of decor and good hygiene.

Same with the damp, balled-up towels from his shower and the fist-sized squeeze in the middle of the toothpaste tube. Not to mention all the frizzy hairs in the tub. Gross.

She thought about it for a few more minutes, then arrived at an ultimatum: either we breathe some fire into this, or we call it a day.

So Brenda slipped into her new Christian Dior de-micup underwire bra with the matching lace-front bikini that she'd ordered special from Victoria's Secret and checked herself in the mirror. Her breasts jutted fearlessly, without a hint of sag. Pleased with the results, she strolled over to the closet and heaved back the louvered doors. Today she'd be casual, opting for her turquoise Cathy Hardwick bigshirt over narrow stirrup pants with a matching soft-wool jersey halter top (which she'd gotten on sale from Miss Bergdorf Sportswear, just last weekend). A pair of short, zigzag braid boots with three-inch stacked-look heels (from 9 West), and a waxy ranch-leather belt (with silver-tone metal buckle, by Liz) tied it all together.

Some quarter-carat diamond studs and a touch of makeup (*just* a touch, though. Casual.). A dab of Obsession.

She ran some Paul Mitchell sculpting lotion through her hair and gently blew it dry. Then she stepped back and assessed the total effect.

Stunning.

This'll pull him out of his funk, she assured herself. *This'll knock his socks off.*

Or, so help me God, I'll kill him.

The voice wafted out of the bedroom, full of promise. "*Larry . . .*"

No answer.

"*Lar-reeeeeee . . .*"

Subtle innuendo was all but lost on Larry Roth. He sat lumpen on the sofa, eyes glued to the flickering images playing across the screen. The Masters of the Universe had departed for the week; He-Man and Skeletor were quickly replaced by Hulk Hogan and Sergeant Slaughter. A whole cavalcade of 3-D he-men grunted and sweated and bashed it out, live from Madison Square Garden. Larry's eyes watched it all.

But his brain . . .

His brain was AWOL, off in some private netherworld that the dawn's early light had failed to vanquish. And it was busy busy busy, with thoughts of scary things.

Like big greasy bruisers, bashing it out with him. Or roommates and old friends, gone suddenly psycho.

Or peculiar odors, wafting from the landlord's apartment as he fled his own. That smell, like a refrigerator full of spoiled meat, waiting just behind the door

(i'm going to pay off albert now)

which was ajar, and Albert never left the door ajar

(give him everything we owe him)

and he could swear that he heard flies buzzing, and WHAT THE HELL IS GOING ON HERE?

Brenda snuck up behind Larry. She was trying to be understanding. She'd read, in that same article, that many men were often withdrawn and uncommunicative after enduring a heroic, life-threatening situation.

She threw her arms around him.

The article never said anything about shrieking.

Or fainting.

FORTY-TWO

BUBBA KNEW

It was almost five-thirty on Saturday afternoon before Bubba dared to venture into the bedroom. He'd been there for their hysterical return from the hospital, early this morning. He'd watched them cling to each other and cry. They cried until it seemed like they might never stop.

But, of course, they did. The hitching, wracking sobs eventually wound down, and they passed out together on the bed: fully clothed, clinging to each other's warmth like a pair of wet puppies in a storm.

Bubba had sat and watched from the relative discretion of the doorway. His reasoning powers might be marginal, but his intuition was first-class. He knew something was wrong. Very wrong indeed. Their clothes had the smell of death on them: death, and agony, and despair.

Bubba was a Good Boy. He'd gotten out of the way and stayed there, letting them deal with their Bad Thing as he knew they surely must. And he'd sat, on guard and ever vigilant, just outside the bedroom door. Protecting them. It made him feel a little bit better. It was the only thing he knew to do that helped, and he did it wholeheartedly.

But he'd been there a long, long time. Over fifteen hours had passed since Billy and Mona had returned from the Dying Place. Bubba didn't know what minutes or hours were, but he measured time very accurately nonetheless: with his eyes and his belly and his bladder. He'd seen the light come and brighten and start to go again. He'd felt the rumble deep in his stomach that said *yummy* for so long that he hardly felt it anymore.

And he felt the time pass elsewhere: someplace that would not be ignored much longer. Bubba was a Good Boy, but if someone didn't take him out soon, something very very *bad* was going to happen.

So, when he could simply wait no longer, Bubba gently nosed the door open.

And softly . . . *softly* . . . ventured into the darkness.

In his dream, Billy was back in the cathedral.
And he was afraid.
Because it was changing: *growing murkier, more indistinct, with each passing step. The doors vanished: no more memories, no alternatives. No present, save the step-by-step.*

No future, but the one that stretched relentlessly before him.

A path. Straight and narrow.
And sharp as the edge of a razor.
Billy walked, the way stretching taut and thin as an

executioner's garrote, a nightmare tightwire from which there was no escape.

There was only onward.

Or down.

Billy walked. Not feeling the pain as each step sliced into him. Not feeling the tears, tracking down his face.

Feeling only the fear.

And crying all the more, because he could barely even feel that . . .

. . . and then Bubba was there, licking his face like only Bubba could, all hot sloppy tongue tasting of tears and beef by-products. Billy coughed and sputtered and opened his eyes.

"Oh, Bubba," he whispered. "Poor guy." He hugged Bubba's big hairy neck. Bubba wagged his tail.

"You need it bad, huh?"

Bubba wiggled in affirmation. *Now now NOW Billy!*

Billy smiled, feeling such a welcome surge of love from this silly creature that he could barely contain himself.

He looked at Mona; she was definitely out. He'd be back before she was.

Billy rose from the bed.

Bubba did his *oboy!* dance, partly in anticipation of relief but mostly for joy. Billy was back. *Oboy oboy oboy . . .*

"Put a lid on it, Peewee," he chided, grinning. "Lemme get my coat."

Bubba wobbled into the living room. Billy grabbed his jacket and the leash, walked into the kitchen, and opened the door.

For his friend.

It was a Bubba walk. Everything revolved around Bubba. He set the course: a leisurely stroll through the grounds of the Episcopal seminary down the street, followed by a whirlwind tour of all the happening fire hydrants and lampposts in the neighborhood. He also set the pace, the duration of stay at each checkpoint. There was no dragging on the collar, no hustling him off before he'd had a chance to catch up on the neighborhood news. This was a Bubba walk, and Billy was happy to give it his all.

One last time.

Billy's feelings ping-ponged between sheer amazement at how much *piss* that dog could hold—fourteen stops so far—and the simple, unbounded joy he felt as he watched Bubba go through his idiot paces.

And then there was the fear: a quiet, gnawing fear that Bubba was in danger by virtue of his mere proximity.

By virtue of his love.

And Billy couldn't allow that.

They rounded the corner onto Tenth Avenue, and Billy was surprised to find Bubba padding up to the door of the Chelsea Commons. Whether this was a reward for being so patient, or just because Bubba loved his favorite window perch, was a mystery. Billy just shrugged and went in, grabbing a stool at the bar.

Jessie and Julie were on today: the former at the tables, the latter behind the bar. Both were sharp and sweet and lovely beyond belief, and Billy had often mused that he'd risk Hell for a sweet romp with either of them. Or both at once.

Except that now

(*hell is real*)

he couldn't help but view them as he did Mona and Bubba and

(*lisa*)

every single person, place, or thing that he cared for on this earth. They were endangered. They were at risk by virtue of the fact that

(*hell is CLOSE*)

he loved them.

"Howdy, stranger," Julie said. "How ya be?" She set an ice-cold Rolling Rock in front of him and leaned over the bar. "And how are you, Muffin?" she called to Bubba, who shot a panting-dog grin back at her from the windowsill.

"We're both fine," Billy said. It sounded a little bit too low-key to be true. "How are you?"

She turned back to him, melting him with a level gaze that said *never mind about me, you little fibber. Let's hear some facts.* "You look beat," she said.

"Not *yet*, I'm not!" he joked halfheartedly, flexing his muscles. It was good for half a laugh: a quarter apiece.

"How's Mona doing?"

"She's . . . sleeping." He couldn't elaborate. He couldn't bring up Lisa. It was

(*TOO CLOSE*)

too close for comfort.

Julie looked like she wanted to pursue it, but somebody hollered for her at the other end of the bar. She shot him a look that was half reproach, half compassion, then followed the call of the wild.

Billy watched her move off, feeling the like and lust and love careen through his heart and mind. It didn't help when Jessie caught sight of him, smiled and waved delightfully.

They were good people. He loved them.

They were unspeakably, terrifyingly fragile.

He endangered them.

He was under fire.

And they were in the way.

Billy drained his beer quickly, and without another word. He peeled a five-spot from under the dwindling wad in his pocket and slipped it under his glass. He and Bubba were gone before Julie made it back.

There was something very important that he had to do. They were all on the firing line, and he had to get them off.

One way or the other.

Right now.

Mona was still sleeping, albeit fitfully, when they returned. Billy was pleased: he didn't want her to be alone when she woke up. He also didn't want her to be awake right now, so this was probably the best of all possible worlds.

Yahoo.

It didn't take long to write the letters: he'd had all the way home to think about how to say what had to be said. They were short, they were eloquent (if he did say so himself), and they acted upon his soul like Novocain on a rotted tooth. By the time he was done, he half believed them himself.

Bubba sat beside him the whole time. Bubba didn't

know much, but some things he knew very clearly. He knew Love. He knew Friend.

He knew Good-bye.

Billy stood and tucked one letter in his jacket pocket; the other he placed where Mona would be certain to find it.

Bubba whimpered, and the sound of it tugged strings in Billy's heart that he'd hoped would be too numb. He knelt down and skritched Bubba's head.

"You're a good boy," Billy said, choking back the tears. "And I love you very very much."

Bubba whined. He knew that.

"And you're not nearly as stupid as you look."

Bubba knew that.

Billy faltered slightly, skritching Bubba's head all the harder for it. "And now you're gonna have to be extra strong, and extra smart, 'cause you've got to *watch!* for her."

Bubba snapped-to at the Word. Billy smiled through the relentless push of tears. "'Cause it's time, Bubba," he whispered.

"It's time for me to go."

Bubba knew that, too.

FORTY-THREE

BODY SHOP

Stanley sat slumped in his favorite chair, fevered and delirious. The TV blasted before him, refusing to stay on any one channel for more than ten seconds, grafting commercial to program to news broadcast in a lunatic montage of light and sound. He would've liked to watch something in particular, but the tuner wouldn't stay put.

They wouldn't let it.

It was their way of punishing him, of getting back at

him for everything that had gone wrong. For the girl. For his arm. For disobeying them.

For more than he knew.

Stanley threw a halfhearted, bloodshot glance at his decimated right arm. He didn't really want to see. It hurt to even turn his head.

But seeing it, in all its bloated glory, gave Stanley Peckard a newfound sense of perspective.

It was really starting to swell now, encased in the moist material of his trench coat like an enormous slate-gray kielbasa. The elbow was utterly destroyed: ligaments shredded, bones jutting from bruised flesh.

The shoulder wasn't much better. Lisa had quite thoroughly dislocated it, and the pain had spread across his torso like hot bands of molten slag, reducing every breath and movement to just one more cause for agony.

If it were up to him, he would have died on the spot.

But, no . . .

They hadn't let him. They'd made him rise, shrieking and flailing, to stumble off into the night.

They'd made him come home. Unlock the door. Fall inside.

And, once inside . . .

. . . they'd made him do Other Things: things he couldn't have done alone.

Except that he wasn't alone.

They had been with him. They had lined him up and aimed him. They had made him *slam!* and *slam!* and *slam!* into the wall until his mangled shoulder had fallen back into place.

But that wasn't enough. There had still been all the blood.

So they had dragged him bodily into the shower.

And forced him to hose himself down.

And then, when the blood had mostly rinsed away, they'd allowed him to stumble and fall and crawl back to his favorite chair.

And even now—in his shivering cold and torment, some twelve hours later—they punished him. Spinning the channels too fast, with the volume too loud, they punished him. With jeering, yattering cries that clawed through his brain, they punished him.

Through it all, they punished him.

Leaving Stanley in his chair, drifting in and out of consciousness, staring at the horror that his left arm had become. The hand was a vicious, angry red: swollen to nearly twice its normal size, the blood in it trapped by the constriction of his sleeve. With great difficulty, he brought his right hand around to touch it.

Leaving marks that wouldn't, couldn't ever fade.

Stanley just giggled.

The Voices were absolutely furious. The wanted him *up!* and *out!* and *away!*

Stanley wouldn't obey.

The Voices and the Little Ones went truly mad then, shrieking through his skull and rattling the silverware and flipping the channel changer so hard that it snapped off and flew across the room.

Stanley didn't care.

He didn't care if they broke the TV. He didn't care when the pain went

(*!!!!!*)

and

(*!!!!!*)

until he could no longer see straight. *They* had made him do it, made him kill his only friend. And he would never forgive them for that. So long as he lived.

It didn't promise to be much longer.

Stanley Peckard sat in his comfy chair and giggled. The pain in his arm was so excruciatingly unrelenting that anything *they* threw at him seemed to pale in comparison.

It gave him perspective. It robbed them of their only method of enforcement. They had no leverage. They held no sway.

The pain set Stanley free; and in so doing, it left him free to do what he pleased.

He blacked out.

While the demons raged on, and on, and on.

FORTY-FOUR

THE BEST-LAID PLANS

Larry was in absolutely no hurry to get home. It was the most unpleasant option in his entire universe of possibility, with the possible exception of getting torn apart by rabid weasels. But there were some things that he absolutely had to do there. None of them pleasant. All of them essential.

So it was nearly six-thirty when he finally dragged his ass back down to good old Stanton Street. It was already getting dark, fattening the shadows, giving them the strength to conquer the night. Larry's anxieties reacted much the same, gaining weight if not substance as he nervously moved down the street.

The brooding blackness of the construction site unnerved him. He kept waiting for something to jump out of it. The couple of Hispanics hanging out on the sidewalk didn't do much for him, either; it was getting hard to trust in the indifference, much less the good will, of strangers.

But no attacks came from either direction. Which left him only with the one terror that he *knew* lay before him.

The one indicated by the lights shining out from Billy's bedroom window.

There was a long, jittering moment in which he considered turning back. All of his instincts screamed for him to do so; his body language spoke clearly and fluently. His intuition, so often silent, informed him in no uncertain terms that Billy was dangerous, Billy was insane, Billy wasn't really Billy anymore.

And if you go up there, it continued, *you'll be alone with him*.

Alone.

But there was one mitigating factor, and it was a big

one: he had nowhere else to go. Everything he owned—what remained of it, anyway—was up there, as well as the only roof he had to put it under. Foxy Brenda, God bless her empty head, was not yet ready to take him under her wing; nor was he entirely ready to let her, even as a mercenary interim gesture.

No. The place was his, just as much as Billy's, and maybe even more so. *He* wasn't the one who'd fallen three months behind! *He* wasn't the one whose negligence had gotten the place trashed! If anything, he was the only reason that they still had an apartment in the first place!

Among Larry's assets, his ability to produce logical-sounding bullshit at a moment's notice was certainly his finest. He used that sterling talent now on his toughest audience.

Himself.

As he neared the doorway. And the key came out of his pocket.

And he sealed, once and forever, his fate.

There was a tiny bonfire burning in the middle of Billy's bedroom floor. It cast a warm glow on the four walls, smelled sweetly of cedar and pine.

Billy sat, cross-legged, in front of the fire. The last of his tears had already been shed.

Like the last of his recorded history.

The first thing to go had been *The Real War*, his paean to painful naiveté and hopeless, worthless idealism. He'd given it five minutes of spin time when he got home, coddling his maudlin sorrow at having had to say good-bye.

Three minutes into it, he'd begun to get pissed.

Five minutes in, he couldn't listen anymore.

He was laughing too hard.

The turning point had come.

The rest of his works had been dispatched to the flames in short order: all his tapes, all his volumes of lyrics and chord charts. Next had gone the regalia: the posters, the concert photos, the handful of news clips from local Pennsylvania papers.

Last had been the incidentals: report cards, yearbooks, ticket stubs from favorite concerts, love letters, memos, and doodles.

Photographs from days gone by.

Plastic and paper didn't smell so hot; he'd changed the scent to suit his tastes. There was no smoke. The floor was unscathed. The fire was completely under control.

He used it, now, to warm his cold cold hands.

And it was *wonderful* to be so free: unconstrained by mortal bounds, held back by neither love nor death. If they could only get to him through the people he cared for, they could no longer get to him at all. He could not be hurt, and he could not be killed, and his idiot past could not be held against him.

And what an idiot past it was, he mused, grinning harshly at the cinders of his previous life. He'd have thought it would be painful, coming to grips with the fact that he'd been an asshole since the day he was born. It wasn't.

It was, in fact, a major relief.

"Because I'm not you anymore," he said out loud, addressing the ashes. "I'm not the little loser with the big dreams that could never come true. If I want a dream to come true, I just snap my fucking fingers."

Which said nothing about the little dreamy dreams that he'd held for so long to be true: cosmic visions that sounded reasonable as hell, so long as you completely bypassed reality.

End sexism? That's easy! a little voice within him said. *Just change every man on the planet. End world hunger? No problem! Just go make the world a sandwich. End war? Piece of cake! Just get everybody to drop all of their differences.*

Bullshit. Bullshit. Bullshit. People didn't change that easy.

Unless you made them.

Unless you were destined to rule the world.

And that was the great thing; the difference between the old namby-pamby Billy Rowe and the man who he was rapidly becoming. The old Billy Rowe wished that things were different. The new Billy Rowe made *sure* that they were. The world was going to go through more changes than it had since the discovery of fire, before he was through.

All he needed was a little time. Five years, for example. He'd often heard that every budding enterprise required a five-year plan. Now he could see the sense of it. If nothing else, his little *I Love New York* fiasco had demonstrated that he couldn't just go out and do everything at once.

Step by step: that was the ticket. Slowly. Surely. Step by step.

The first thing to do was disappear: spirit a couple million from the coffers of Bechtel or Billy Graham, find a nice little place somewhere, and hole up incognito. Study up on world history and world events. Develop a strategy. Pinpoint his targets.

And, all the while, develop the Power.

In the week since he'd become aware of it, the Power had easily tripled. In five years, God only knew how strong he would be. Christ, by the time he hit thirty-three, he would . . .

He paused. Backed up. Took a look at that number.

In five years, he would be thirty-three years old.

Just like the last long-haired son of God who'd come to change the world.

Billy laughed. He was stunned. It was too perfect to be anything but true. *You have been chosen*, Christopher had said. *A particular man, with a particular purpose: the purpose for which you were born.*

"Christopher!" he called out impulsively, still fighting with the laughter. No response. "Christopher!" he yelled again, dragging his gaze across the naked walls. Firelight and shadow danced across their surfaces, but the angel was nowhere to be seen.

"C'mon! I need to talk with you!" Still nothing. He remembered the last thing that the angel had said to him; it made him simultaneously embarrassed and exasperated. "C'mon! Don't be a jerk! I apologize! I've seen the light! Now wouldja just—"

And that was when the front door opened.

The kitchen was just as it had been when he left it. Larry wondered why he wasn't surprised. His skillful bullshit machinery was in overdrive now, manufacturing

verbal courage at a truly staggering rate. He felt ready for
Billy to step through the door. He felt ready to hand down
the bottom line.

When Billy stepped through the door, it became just
so much windy effluvium. The voice of his instincts came
back, saying GET OUT GET OUT GET OUT GET OUT so
loud that he almost just turned and left.

And then Billy said, "Larry."

And Larry stopped.

And the two of them just stared at each other for what
seemed very much like forever.

"Billy," Larry said, at long last and very softly. He was
amazed that he had any voice at all. "I'm your friend, am I
right?"

Billy smiled. "I don't know. Are you?"

"I always thought I was."

"I always thought you were, too."

"So what's the problem?"

"I don't know. You tell me. Tell me if I'm your friend.
Tell me what is the problem."

"Well, that's very neat, man," Larry said, continuing to
amaze himself, finding it easier as he went along. "Lay it all
on me. As if I created the problem myself." His voice was
coming back. He used it. "It seems to me like we're caught
in the middle of some really weird shit . . ."

Billy laughed.

". . . and we're letting it turn us against each other,"
Larry continued. "It doesn't seem right. That's all I'm trying
to say. We ought to be helping each other, and instead
we're—"

"Larry."

Pause. The air seemed suddenly colder. "What?"

"Cut the bullshit, Larry."

Yes, definitely colder. The fear, coming back. "What do
you mean?"

"I mean that it all sounds great, except that you haven't
given a shit about me in months. Don't try and deny it. I've
been nothing but an inconvenience: a pain in the ass, until
someone like Mona throws a party that you could make
some contacts from if you were any fucking good as a
comedian. Which you aren't. Know what I mean? Then I'm

okay, I get you places. But it doesn't do you any fucking good."

"Whoa." Larry knew that getting furious was called for at this point. He couldn't do it. He didn't have it in him. The room was getting colder, and he was too goddam scared.

"You want me out of here," Billy pressed on. "I don't have to read your mind. It's all over your face."

"Well, that's okay. It's really time for me to go. Besides, you've earned this place. It fits you like a glove." He gestured around at the battered and ratty decor. "You deserve each other.

"But I want you to think about your life, baby, 'cause it's not all that goddam great. You bullshit your way through it. You'll say anything that works. I used to be your friend, but I'm sick of you, because you don't give a shit about anybody but yourself. You lie for a living. You lie to me. You lie to yourself. You lie to your lame-brained receptionist, and that's the only reason on Earth why you ever get laid. If disemboweling your grandmother would get you a promotion, you'd strap her down yourself."

"Billy." It was getting to be too much. The fear was mounting, but it was turning into something that made him want to fight—no, *need* to fight—with every ounce of strength at his disposal.

"*Billy.*" Mocking the sound of his own name, as it had come from Larry's mouth. Mimicking it perfectly. "Billy, *what?*"

It took a second to work up the courage. Larry continued to be amazed that he had it at all.

"Billy, shut the fuck up."

There was a long moment of crackling silence, in which even the air seemed to have frozen in place. Then he felt the first surge of heat against his skin: not painful yet, but mounting by the second. *I'm going to die*, his mind informed him, distant and obscenely casual. His body, less detached, began to form a scream.

The doorbell rang.

Larry's eyes were clamped shut, the thin flesh of his lids feeling the first tingling pain of an imminent massive sunburn. His mind, with that same hideous calm, was now beginning to show travelogues from his past. His nostrils smelled heat, and his ears heard nothing. He was no longer aware of Billy at all.

But he *felt* the heat move away from him suddenly, felt the tangible wave of concentrated light shift suddenly to his left and away. The sudden cool air around his superheated skin was as shocking as the leap from a sauna to a snowbank. His eyes flew open.

The doorbell began to sing again, then stopped in mid-song. There was something not-quite-right about the way it happened. It didn't so much stop as *die*.

Larry looked at the bell, which was mounted on the wall just above the doorframe: a silver circle and its adjoining mechanisms, hanging as it always had.

Except that it was melting, the metal turning soft as a Dali clock, then smoking and slagging and burning into the wall . . .

There was a strange, weightless moment in which his eyes refused to accept it. He was blinking and blinking, as if the flutter of his eyelids would somehow make it go away. It didn't. Molten drops of doorbell plopped on the wooden floor, forming tiny tongues of blue-white flame. The biting-on-tinfoil stink of it filled the kitchen.

"Kinda makes ya think, don't it?" said the voice from behind him. Larry felt a cold hand clap down on his shoulder in mock camaraderie. "There but for the grace of God . . ."

. . . *go I*, Larry completed, accepting it now. Accepting it all. He stared at the smelting metal, and his mind said *that was supposed to be you, Larry ol' chum. He was aiming at you. There but for the grace of—*

And then it was too much, too much, and the scream that had meant to come out earlier sprung full-blown to his lips as he sidled toward the door, not looking at Billy, not looking at the monster that Billy had become . .

. . . until the Billy-monster stepped in front of him, eyes black as night and teeth whitely aglimmer. Larry tried to scream again. Billy touched him on the forehead, and he stopped.

"Shut up," Billy said, "and go to sleep . . ."

* * *

. . . and Larry went crashing to the floor without so much as a whimper. "Just like Bubba," Billy giggled. "Only not as cute."

There was somebody at the downstairs door. It was the only reason why the world wasn't down one Larry Roth. In a big way, that was good: the fewer bodies, or disappearances thereof, the better. Besides, Larry wasn't exactly a hardened criminal. He was just an asshole who was getting in the way.

"I'll get back to you in a minute," he informed his sleeping roommate. "Just let me deal with our uninvited guest."

He moved toward the door, noted that he'd set up the distinct possibility of a fire that would gut the entire building, and extinguished it with a freezing glance.

Then he went down the stairs to the first floor, past the vaguely sentient dust on the bathroom floor of Albert's apartment, and stepped into the fragrant foyer.

Two things, at that moment, caught his eye.

One of them was a slip of paper, dangling from his mailbox.

The other was Detective Hamilton, smiling at him from the other side of the door.

The paper wouldn't notice if he deferred to the detective. The converse, however, was not as true. Billy slipped the piece of paper demurely into his back pocket. Then he opened the front door and stepped outside.

"Well, howdy do!" he exclaimed cheerfully. Hamilton nodded and stepped forward. Billy shook his head and stepped forward as well, letting the door slide shut behind him.

"You're not gonna invite me upstairs?" Hamilton asked, feigning hurt.

"Nope."

"Well, can you come down to the station with me, then?"

"Nope."

"Well, then I guess we'll just talk here for a couple of—"

"Nope."

"Well, then, how about doing Clint Eastwood for me?

The boys up at the Twenty-second Precinct house say that it's a real pisser."

Billy stopped in mid *nope* and thought about it. The detective was all smiles, but there was fear and deadly earnest behind it. He had a hunch—God only knew where it came from—and he was risking his ass to follow up on it. Billy admired his guts, and hoped that they wouldn't have to wind up splattered all over the concrete.

"I don't do Clint Eastwood," Billy said.

"Oh, that's too bad." Hamilton's gaze was level.

"I do a mean Wally Cox, though. Wanna hear?"

"No, thanks. It's Clint or nothing."

"What do you want?" Now it was Hamilton's turn to stop. Billy cocked his head and took a step closer. Hamilton took a step back. Delightful. "I mean, I know what you're going for, but it doesn't make sense. Why me?"

"That's exactly what I was wondering."

"Listen. Dennis." He stepped forward again. This time, Hamilton didn't back off. In its own way, it was equally delightful. "You're a good guy. I can tell. And I don't envy your position."

"You've said that before."

"So I'll say it again." It took a second to realize that he'd trapped himself on that one. He grinned admiringly. "Slick," he said.

"So how 'bout that Clint?"

"So how 'bout those Knicks?" Billy was annoyed and amused all at once. "Man, you don't seem to be getting the message. Don't worry about the Vigilante. He's not your problem, whoever he is. You've got a slasher to catch. You've got millions of innocent people to protect."

"That's just the point."

"Dennis, I think it's time for you to go."

"Billy, I think you'd better watch yourself. Up to now, I've got no quarrel with the people you've killed. I would have liked to kill them, too, I think. But if you step over the line and hurt some innocent people, I'm gonna have to come down on your ass like a ton of bricks."

And just as lifeless, too, Billy mused. He managed to keep from saying it.

"Good-bye, Dennis," he said instead.

"Good-bye, Billy. Take care."

"You, too."

Hamilton turned and walked away. Billy watched him for a minute. As pointless as the bravado was, it certainly was impressive.

Tomorrow, he mused, *when I disappear from your life forever, you'll be a far luckier man. It would be a bitch to have to kill you. The commonweal needs more honorable men like your little bad self.*

Maybe five years from now, we can even get together. The Army's always looking for a few good men.

Then he willed the door open, not even bothering with the key, and headed back upstairs. There were still a few things that he needed to tend to before the night was free to begin.

It was a half an hour later before he remembered the note in his pocket.

FORTY-FIVE

URBAN BUDDY

The transit cop got off the last car of the uptown AA train at Forty-second Street. Ramsey and Clive waited patiently, Ramsey's brand-new Master Blaster tucked firmly between them. It was like trying to hide a steamer trunk with a hankie. The sucker was huge: four-way speakers, dual Dolby cassette, five-band stereo EQ, and a ball-busting seventy watts RMS per channel. It took both of them to carry it, but the motherfucker was *bad*. It could probably blow this car right off the tracks.

And Ramsey and Clive were just the men to test that theory.

Just as soon as the pig trotted back to his poke.

The cop threw them a long admonitory glance before

he left. Ramsey and Clive smiled back, innocent as a maiden aunt's kiss. Then the train hissed, the doors started to close, and the cop stepped out. He continued to stare at them through the windows in the doors until the train lurched into motion, taking them out of each other's view.

Ramsey and Clive just laughed and laughed, throwing in the odd unsavory expletive to punctuate their mirth. The pig was gone, the train was rollin', and it was time to party.

Ramsey kicked in the Blaster while Clive fired the joint. Musky, sweet smoke and ear-shattering music instantly filled the limited air space of the subway car.

People began to move toward the far end of the car. That was fine, too. That was funnier than hell. With their slinking stances and averted eyes, they looked more like whipped puppies than human beings.

Which made them a carload of easy pickin's.

Except for one guy: a young white dude who looked like he needed a shower and shave. He had a scrap of paper in his hand that he wouldn't stop looking at. His face was intense, but it wasn't aimed at them. He seemed like he was barely there at all.

Ramsey laughed, looking at him. *Ain't gonna worry 'bout ol' Barely There*, he mused. *We could pro'bly pick his pocket an' he wouldn't even know it.*

He cranked the Blaster up to full. Clive jumped out of his seat, joint in hand, and started "the *walk*" down the center of the aisle. Ramsey grinned from ear to ear: he knew the moves by heart.

Clive was gettin' ready to fuck somebody up.

The party was about to begin.

The train hissed to a stop on Fiftieth Street. Several passengers got off in a very big hurry. Ramsey doubted very seriously that it was the stop they wanted. He watched several of them scurry up to the car beyond, in fact. No problem. There were plenty left.

As the doors slid shut.

And the train rolled on.

And the real party began.

Billy had already read the note a hundred times in the last five minutes. That wasn't the problem. That wasn't the point.

The point was that he could smell the trouble brewing like fresh-perked Colombian coffee, and he had never been in less of a tolerant mood. The guy at the other end was about to do something ugly; the guy at this end was only about a thousand percent too loud.

The guy at this end was closer.

Billy went for him first.

"Turn it off," he said.

The guy with the Blaster just stared at him, stunned. Maybe it was drugs. Maybe it was stupidity. Maybe it was both. It didn't matter.

"Now," Billy stressed. "And I won't say it again."

The guy just kept staring, and that wouldn't do.

So Billy walked over, took the Blaster away, and rammed it through the nearest window.

Everyone in the car was attracted by that: one brief explosion of glass, and then everything got awfully quiet. Billy could feel the heat of the eyes upon him, none hotter than the man who leapt to his feet before him now.

The man had pulled a weapon. Billy laughed when he saw it. It was a nasty bit of business that he'd seen advertised in the back pages of *Eagle* and *Soldier of Fortune* magazines.

In context, it was one of the silliest things that had ever met his gaze.

They called it the Urban Buddy: three inches of razor-sharp stainless steel on a no-slip neoprene-covered t-bar handle. The ads liked to talk about how a ninety-eight-pound weakling could bring down a Zulu chieftain, sever major muscle groups, dispatch packs of hugger-mugger-pervo-devo-freaks—yes, the Urban Buddy was one hell of a weapon. The survivalist mags loved 'em.

Standing there with the arrow-shaped death-dealer floating inches from his face, Billy wondered just how much the survivalist mags would enjoy the idea of a Zulu chieftain/hugger-mugger-pervo-devo-freak wielding one of their $39.95 specials.

It cracked him up. He couldn't help it. The look of confusion on his assailant's face only made it worse. The guy was practically hopping with rage, but Billy's laughter had him paralyzed.

"Man!" the man cried shrilly. "I'll *cut'choo*—"

"Oh, *Margaret!*" Billy laughed swishily, in his best Bugs Bunny voice. Then he waved his hand limp-wristedly at the blade and said, "Why don't you take that little thing and shove it right up your . . ."

Clive could not believe his eyes. When the Blaster had gone through the window, he'd moved back up, wanting in on the action; this homeboy was clearly some whitemeat that needed to die.

But now Ramsey was screaming, and the back of his pants were running red, and Clive could not fucking believe it. When the homeboy turned to look at him, with those eyes like flaming coals, he started backing up rapidly, thinking *oh, man, you ain't gettin' your hooks into me* . . .

A leg went out behind him, ankle high. He never even saw it. The next thing he knew, he was toppling backward, his head going *clang* against the center pole. The last second of free-fall was blissfully thought-free.

Then consciousness returned, and they were upon him: all those little sheeplike people, turned to werewolves in the space of a second. His eyes opened just in time to watch a black patent-leather shoe slam into his teeth, folding them back and snapping them. Another shoe, narrow and pointed and feminine, dug its spiked heel into his crotch. He tried to scream with his mouth full. It didn't work.

And then they were kicking him everywhere: his kidneys, his ribs, his temples. All four of his limbs were pinned by stomping feet. The pain took him to the edge of unconsciousness, but it also kept him awake a little longer than he might have hoped. The last one he was alive for was the one that took out his right eye.

Then he rose above his body, lingering for a moment of violent voyeurism before toppling back down into Hell. . . .

And as the Vigilante left the car, each of the newborn avengers had their own unique interpretation of just who that person was. He was a Jew. He was a goy. He was a brother. She was a sister.

The Vigilante was a mirror.
The Vigilante was themselves.
And the Power held dominion over them all.

FORTY-SIX

CONCOMITANCE

Dave was entertaining when the knock came upon his door. No big deal: just some close friends and band members over to cut loose and kick some ideas around. But it was nevertheless a closed affair, and everyone who was invited was either already there or accounted for.

So when he opened the door, his first thought was *what the hell are you doing here?*

Followed by *what the hell happened to you?*

Followed by a simple *what the hell. . . ?*

"Dave. Don't talk," his visitor said. "Just take this, okay? And leave it at that."

Dave kept his mouth shut, though his mind reeled in the face of what stood before him. It was difficult to accept that someone could deteriorate so rapidly, in so little time. Just two days ago they had sat in a bar together, Dave marveling at the transformation from shadow to substance.

And *now* . . .

Billy was saying something that Dave wasn't catching. He glitched back to the present tense and heard, ". . . so it's probably all for the best, this way."

"Come again?" Dave said. "I'm sorry. I—"

Billy stiffened, looked like he was ready to take it all back.

"No, really. I'm sorry. I just spaced out for a—"

"Read the note," Billy said, and turned away.

Dave stared at the folded piece of paper in his hand,

stared at the retreating back. He took a couple of rapid steps forward and took his visitor by the slumped shoulders. "Billy, wait—" he began.

Billy stopped and turned. Dave's breath caught in his throat. The expression on Billy's face was annoyance, no doubt, but it came off a thousand times worse than that. Dave imagined that even sublime elation would look like murder on the face that Billy wore just now. It was a terrifying face.

It was the face of a man who had nothing left to lose.

Dave had been thinking about inviting him in: a beer, a toot, a jam with the boys. There was a peace pipe in his heart that he wanted Billy to smoke with him.

But there was no way. Dave could see that now.

"Just take care of her, man," Billy said. And was gone.

Hours later, when the last of his guests had gone, Dave finally worked up the nerve to let the mystery unfold.

By the time he understood, it was too late.

FORTY-SEVEN

NOTES FROM BEYOND

Mona awoke at nine-forty. She awoke suddenly and completely, with no trace of sleeper's cobwebs and no sense of having dreamed.

The bedroom was dark, and she was alone in it. The spot beside her, where Billy had been, had long since gone cold. The neon letters from the digital clock were her only frame of reference, and they only served to disorient her more.

"Billy?" she called out, trying to adjust to the lateness, the fact that she'd slept a solid sixteen hours. "Billy, are you out there?"

Movement, from the living room.

"Billy?" she said again; and as the words left her lips, she knew that it wasn't Billy. Without a doubt. Billy would have answered. Billy didn't move like that.

Whatever it was, it wasn't Billy.

It wasn't even human at all.

Terror stole through her, overwhelming her tongue with its copper blood taste. She sat up in bed, searching beside it for the sock full of pennies that she'd rigged for just such an occasion. Who or whatever it was, she would beat its brains out if it came within three feet of her, so help her God. Her teeth were gritted as her fingers connected with the loaded argyle, tugged at the weight, began to lift . . .

. . . and then the black shape leapt up onto the bed, sticking its cold snoot in her face, bringing its warm wet tongue out to lap her cheek . . .

. . . and she let go of the sock, let it thud to the floor. "Oh, Bubba!" she cried, laughing despite herself. "Oh, Bubba, you scared the *shit* out of me!"

Bubba wriggled and lapped at her face some more, incorrigible. She told him so. It had no marked effect. She stroked his big blunt head and floppy ears, warmed by his brainlessly loving presence. Her fingers ran down the stubby neck, danced over the studded collar . . .

. . . and cut themselves on a piece of paper, folded and tucked beneath it.

"Ow!" she cried, quickly followed by another "Ow!" She sucked at the slice in her skin, then pulled the note out from under Bubba's collar with her left hand while her right flicked on the bedside lamp.

Light flooded the room and assaulted her eyes. Bubba blinked, too, then trained his warm brown eyes intensely upon her. Slowly, unhappily, she unfolded the note. She had a grim, sinking feeling that it was nothing she wanted to read.

She was right.

Mona,

This is the hardest thing I've ever done, short of identifying Lisa this morning. I don't expect it to be any less tough on you.

But my life has gotten too dangerously crazy for us to go on any longer as lovers. Or friends. Or even casual acquaintances. I can't tell you why. You don't want to know. Believe me, baby, when I tell you that finding out would be the worst move you ever made.

So I'm saying good-bye, and that is absolutely final. But I can't let you go without saying that I love you, I will always love you, the heat death of the universe may wipe out all the cockroaches at last but it won't touch a hair on the head of my love for you. Please believe that.

But you're better off with Dave, so I leave you to each other. I wish you all the luck and success that your heart desires. I wish you all the happiness that I will never have.

Don't try to look for me. Let it go. While it lasted, it was the best. Now it's time to move on.

I love you, baby.

Good-bye.

He didn't sign his name to the note. It didn't really matter. By the time she got to the bottom, she could barely focus anyway.

"*God damn you*," she whispered, then said it again. On the second time, she crumpled the note and tossed it at the wall. It hit. So what.

It wasn't enough.

Not nearly enough.

"You bastard," she continued, a bit more of her voice behind it. On the bed beside her, Bubba began to whine. Good ol' Bubba: every last drop of Billy's goodness and innocence, distilled into a ball of wiggling fur and dropped on her doorstep. She hugged the dog tightly, crying as she did it, abandoning herself to the slight consolation he gave.

She wished that Lisa were here to confide in, to hold, to try and make sense of the nightmare with. But Lisa had already been swallowed by it, gone to wherever radical lesbian feminists who didn't believe in God went when their bodies died and their beautiful souls were unleashed into the ether.

Gone to Heaven, Mona thought. *Whether she believed in it or not.*

Then she thought about Billy; and for some reason it made her think about Hell.

It took another five minutes for Mona to drag herself out of bed. It took an additional three minutes for her to make it to the phone. *Believe me, baby,* her mind informed her in a voice that was not her own. *Finding out would be the worst move you ever made.*

It took another thirty seconds to pick up the phone and dial the number.

From then on, it was out of her hands.

Entirely.

Larry awoke at 9:56 to the sound of the telephone's ringing. He felt shards of jagged crockery and glass dig into his back, and moaned. The phone rang again. He put his right hand out to steady himself, felt the piece of paper in it at the same time as the piece of broken glass poked through it and into his palm.

He screamed.

The phone rang again.

"SHIT!" he yelled, pulling out the glass, smearing blood across the note that Billy had left for him. The note, the blood, the glass all mingled into a senseless gestalt that he had no handle for. He stared at them all with equal incomprehension.

The phone rang again.

And the machine clicked on.

"Don't care what the neighbors say:
Roth and Rowe are here to stay.
We can't make it to the phone.
Leave your message at the tone.
BEEEEEEEEEEEEEEEEEEEEEEEEEEEEEP"

"PICK UP!" came the shrill voice over the answering machine's speaker. *"PICK UP, GOD DAMN IT!"*

Larry struggled to his feet, feeling dizzy and drugged. His hand was still bleeding. The white paper of the note was turning red. His flesh tingled painfully, looked darker than usual.

"Answer the fucking phone, you coward! You don't get away from ME this easy!"

The telephone, and its requisite machine, were two of the only things in Larry's room that remained undamaged. Larry staggered toward it, lifted the receiver to his ear, heard the painful whine of feedback, turned down the volume automatically, and spoke.

"Hello?" His voice sounded like a lapidary machine, grinding stone. "Who is it?"

"Larry?" The voice was quieter, but no less shrill.

"Yeah." He looked at the blood, rolling down the sheet of paper. "This is Larry. Who is this?"

"Oh, Jesus. Larry. Is Billy there? This is Mona. I gotta talk with him." The words all came out in a jumble, but the tone dropped to a manageable pitch.

"Mona, Billy's not here." He looked at the note, gauged the silence of the room. The terror came back: a cancerous, bleeding lump in his throat.

He looked at the note.

He read the first words.

"Larry." Not a question. "What's wrong? What's the matter?"

"I've got a note in my hand," Larry said. His voice was calm and even, in complete betrayal of everything he felt. Thank God for the bullshit arts. "I've got a note from Billy, and it's covered with blood. Maybe I should read it to you."

Mona's voice. Very tiny. "Okay."

His own voice, not much larger, as he read her the text.

Larry,
    I don't want to kill you. That doesn't mean that I won't. It all depends on whether you follow these simple rules
    DON'T TALK ABOUT ME TO ANYONE.
    DON'T GO INTO MY FUCKING ROOM.
    Do what I say, and everything will be okay. Fuck up, and I cannot be responsible for what happens.

Take care, man. Be smart.
Obey.

Silence: complete, and all the more hideous for it.
From the other end: the faintest sound of tears.

Larry used the minute or two in which Mona could not speak to assess his own situation. He was more than half inclined to cry himself, but it wasn't in his repertoire. Like his first pair of shoes, his emotions had been bronzed and set up on a mantel somewhere. There seemed no point in breaking them out now.

"I'm on my way," Mona's voice said suddenly. "Before you do anything, wait for me."

"But—"

The phone went dead in Larry's still-bleeding hand. He stared at it for a minute, wanting to sing out the cautionary note that he was not heeding himself.

It was ten o'clock.

FORTY-EIGHT

TIME TO GO

Stanley Peckard awoke, reluctantly, at the twenty-second hour. He could tell, because *Lifestyles of the Rich and Famous* was just starting on Channel 11. Even before the pain, before the stink of his own rotting flesh, Stanley connected with his video programming.

A voice was jabbering on about the joys of owning seventeen limos, but it was all lost on Stanley. There was a crackling band of static along the inside of his brain, thrumming like a high-voltage cable severed and dipped into the ocean. It spoke to him, overriding his own moaning and the voice-over from the tube.

It almost drowned out the demons.

Almost.

When Stanley woke, it was

(*time to go*)

dark in the room, with only the flickering blue light and burble of the TV to moor him down. He already felt light, just as light as light could be. And he felt another light, another kind of light entirely: a distant light, urging him to just leave his body entirely and

(*go*)

fly away, free of both Earth and demon voice, to where the one living force that had ever loved him was waiting with

(*SHARP!*)

open arms.

"No," he whispered. "No, I won't." The armchair in front of the TV was moist and warm. It might have had something to do with the fever that ate at him now, leaving his clothing soggy and his body wracked with chills, reminding him that it was

(*time to go*)

too late for a doctor, too late for a priest. He was

(*SHARP!*)

weak, he was

(*SHARP!*)

dying; the sticky, gangrenous flesh of his arm attested quite convincingly to that fact. There was nothing to do but

(*go*)

sit there and let nature take its horrible course. He didn't have the strength to

(*go*)

do anything but let the comfy chair and the distant light enfold him. He certainly didn't have the incentive. There was nothing that anyone could offer him. He was

(*SHARP!*)

dying. He was

(*SHARP!*)

too far gone to

(*go*)

help them anymore, and too weak to resist. He was

(*SHARP!*)

completely helpless in the face of what the demons told him now.

She would be the Bestest Of All Possible Girls. They made that very very clear. She was the one all along, the one that all the others had led up to: better even than Lisa, his special friend who hadn't been much of a friend at all, had she, what with breaking his arm and nearly killing him and all.

They showed him his Bestest Girl in exquisite detail. Her flesh shimmered like gold against the drowning darkness of her hair. She would come for him tonight, they said. Come to take him in her arms and make it all go away. All the hurt. All the pain.

She would descend from the heavens above, they said. And it would all be over.

The first commercial break was just beginning. Stanley's vision was swimming, but he knew an ad for Burger King when he saw one. He wondered, vaguely, how much Burger King had in common with the life-styles of the rich and famous.

Then he was staggering to his feet, yanked helplessly by forces utterly beyond his control. The pain was horrible. His battered Stetson sat on the rat-bitten couch. The shadow it cast over the top half of his face effectively concealed the tears that bled from his eyes.

It was time to go.

They didn't need to tell him again.

FORTY-NINE

THE DREADED TOLD-YOU-SO'S

Rizzo was weary. Nothing unusual in that. If he was wearier than usual, that was his miserable partner's fault. Between the failure to shut up and the failure to make sense, Hamilton was breaking all the mental health laws that Rizzo demanded from a sane human being.

"Listen to me," Dennis the Menace persisted. "I'm asking a simple favor. Add up all the times that you've patronized me, regarding my hunches. Then line it up with a column that shows all the times I've been right. *Then* tell me that I'm full of it."

"I already told you that."

"But you haven't done the groundwork."

"You haven't told me *anything*!" Rizzo snapped, slamming his fist on the desk. "You haven't given me a goddam thing that I can use! What did you do, throw the fucking *I Ching*? I mean, Jesus!"

"What do you want me to do? Bring him in for a confession? You wouldn't believe it, anyway."

"That's true." Rizzo lit a cigarette, mashed the sweat of his brow with the back of his hand. "The hundred-billion crazies that call in here every second tend to dampen the fires of my faith."

"Nice to know that you put me in such good company."

"Well, hey! I'm sorry! You sound just like 'em! If you came in here and informed me that you'd found the Lost Continent, I'd sit here and wait for the punch line. If you persisted, I'd assume that you don't know how to tell a joke. As it is, you've gone way the hell past the point where it's funny. You got me worried now, Junior. And I don't like that."

The telephone rang, mercifully cutting the conversation short. Rizzo glared at it balefully anyhow, just as a matter of principle. He had come to hate telephones over the course of the pseudoinvestigation. All they brought was heat and flak, heat and flak, twenty-four ball-busting hours a day.

He ran down the possibilities in his mind: the mayor's office, the commissioner's office, the press. The crank calls never made it past the front desk, thank God; though these days they'd have been a welcome change of pace.

"I'll tell ya. That pesky Pia Zadora, she just can't get enough of me," he quipped, reaching for the receiver. Hamilton didn't laugh. He didn't even look. Rizzo shook his head, wearier than ever, and prepared himself for another little slice of happiness.

But when he brought the receiver to his ear, Desk Sergeant Padillo sounded uncharacteristically excited. "We got Dirty Harry on the line here, Frank. He wants to talk to you."

"What?" Rizzo's breath caught, and he felt a bass drum thud in his belly. "Are you sure?"

"I'd practically stake my badge on it. He's crazier than a bedbug, but he sounds just like Clint Eastwood."

"Okay. Okay." Rizzo dragged one rolled-up sleeve across his forehead again, where some fresh beads of sweat had collected. "I'm ready. You got the tape rollin'? Of course you do. Okay. Lemme at him."

Padillo clicked off. There was a moment of silence. Rizzo snuck a glance at his partner, who had suddenly turned attentive.

Then the line clicked on again.

"Hello?" Rizzo said. It was as far as he got.

Because the voice that boomed out of the receiver took him completely by surprise. The voice was too loud.

The voice was all wrong.

"THEEEEEERE'S NO NEED TO FEAR!" it exclaimed, thunderous and wimpy all at once. *"UNNNN-NNNNDERDOG IS HERE!"*

"What the—" Rizzo began again, was met by a gale of

high-pitched and derisive laughter. Rage boiled up inside him, shattering through the tension like a wrecking ball. "Who the hell are *you*?" he demanded.

"Don't fret, sweet Polly. That evil fiend will get his just deserts, or my name isn't mild-mannered Shoeshine Boy—"

"Alright, asshole! Cut the shit!" There was no getting around the fact that the guy did a perfect Wally Cox, but that was beside the point. "You wanna talk to me, talk fast, cause I'm not in the mood to play Name That Goon. Alright?"

"Alright," came the voice from the other end, snapping so abruptly and completely back into the Eastwood mold that it shocked Rizzo to the bone. "Yeah, I got something to tell ya, punk. But first I wanna ask you a couple of questions.

"This is the eighth day of your so-called investigation, am I right?"

"That's right."

"And you still haven't caught him."

"That's right."

"And he just keeps right on killing. Four down, how many more to go?"

"Three—"

"*Four*, asshole. Let me emphasize that. You're forgetting Lisa Traynor." Pause. The sound of a difficult swallow. "The girl who died last night makes four.

"I guess he doesn't see you as much of a threat."

A strange spark of *déjà vu* went off in the back of Rizzo's head. The second he took to dig for a connection gave his caller a chance to go on.

"But that's okay, because I've got his number. You hear me? I know who the Slasher is. You'll be able to read about it in tomorrow morning's papers."

"Wait a minute, wait a minute." The insult was forgotten in the light of this new information. "What are you saying?"

"I'm on my way to his place right now. What you'll wind up finding is a hundred pounds or so of plump link sausage. Yummy nums." A low chuckle.

"You know something, buddy? You're a sick sonofabitch. What makes you think that I believe you?"

"You will."

"I don't even know who you are!"

"Ask your erstwhile partner. Or better yet, don't. I love to watch you fumble around."

"It makes my day."

Rizzo was just about to yell something else when the line went dead. He did it anyway. "*Sonofabitch!* Padillo! Did you get a trace on that?"

"Not enough time, Frank. Sorry."

"Shit. Yeah, okay. Thanks, Ralph. Nice try." Then he hung up the phone and started kneading at his forehead with his hands.

"So what do we do now?" Hamilton asked. His voice was quiet. There was the soft click of his own receiver, settling down in its cradle.

"Same thing we've been doing the whole time," Rizzo said. "Sit around with our thumbs up our asses and wait for someone to make a mistake." He sighed heavily, then turned his wearier-than-ever gaze to his partner. "At least we know who it is now."

"Yeah?" Hamilton said, beginning to grin. "And who might that be?"

Rizzo grinned back sourly, lit another cigarette.

"Rich Little," he said.

FIFTY

REVERSE SEXISM

The cab was a Checker, big and ungainly and solid as a tank. The last several years had seen them slowly phasing away, like the last days of the mastodon; but to Billy they would always be the quintessential New York cab.

So when it pulled over for him at the corner of Park Avenue South and Twenty-first Street, he clapped his hands with glee. The night was young, the timing was perfect; and to top it all off, he had a goddam Checker chariot to take him downtown in style.

"Alright, muh man!" Billy exclaimed, climbing in the back. "How are you on this fine evening?"

"Can't complain," the driver said, uninterested. "Where ya headed?"

"How's First Avenue and Thirteenth Street sound?"

"Yer payin', buddy. Whatever you say."

Not much of a talker, Billy mused, settling back into the darkness of the huge backseat. The car began to roll, and Billy smiled. *That's okay. It gives me time to think think think.*

And there was plenty to think think think about. His nocturnal visit to the office of First Choice Messengers had been just what the doctor ordered. Riffling through the application files had given him the name and address of his prey: something that the phone book had been unable to provide.

And it had given him an insight into the beast that he found quite fascinating indeed.

The guy was a moron. He could barely even write his own name.

Stanley Peckard. Billy let the name roll off his mind's tongue lovingly. *Stanley Peckard. You son of a gun. Boy, are you gonna be surprised to see me!*

The note was still in Billy's pocket; he could feel it dig into his ass cheeks through the tightness of his jeans. He could smell the dried blood. He didn't want to dig it back out again. He didn't want to cry anymore.

But it had made him think about Lisa, and that was really all it took. His emotions were very close to the surface, no matter how hard he tried to repress them: manic, depressive, you name it, he had it. So when he felt the sorrow coming on, he

(*NO!*)

shifted gears abruptly. He made himself think about happy times. The way she smiled. The

(*smiley-face*)

way she stood her ground. God, she was tough! Like when

(i hurt him, billy, you polish him off)

she'd faced down those twits, those man-hating shrikes she worked with. God, that was fantastic. He could still see her face, the way she'd looked when she'd told them to leave. . . .

Billy seized on the image of Paula and Susan. It kept him at a safe distance from his loss and pain, gave him a place to put his rage. He thought about how they'd tried to use Mona's rape as a symbol of oppression, Mona's career as a striking piece of poetic justice, Mona herself as emotional cannon fodder in the grand crusade to rid the world of erect penises. Or even limp ones.

And then a truly hideous thought occurred to him, fanning the spark into a white-hot flame of hatred that grew and grew and grew.

And the thought was: *What if they try to do the same thing to Lisa? What if they make her a martyr to their cause? It would be so easy to do. She wouldn't even be there to defend herself, much less make her own position clear.*

He could picture it with total clarity. He could hear the bullshit now. All the words they would put in her mouth. All the lies they would make of her life.

"Sorry, girls," he hissed, scarcely more than a whisper. "I can't let you do that."

Billy closed his eyes, and Paula Levin's face played crystal clear in the private screening room of his mind. It took a little longer to bring the face of the other woman into focus. But it came.

Somewhere in the city, they were together. From the darkness of that private screening room, he reached out for them.

With the Power.

In the last several seconds before their lives spiraled down into nightmare, Paula and Susan were pleased with themselves. They'd faced a tough decision, but they'd risen to the occasion. They had to. There was a war on, and grief was a debilitating factor.

Diane's betrayal still rankled them, of course: they'd been robbed of their moment of glory. If they took credit for the bombing, they would also have to take credit for the deaths. Aside from the crimp that a prolonged incarceration would put in their agenda, the Movement was liable to frown on such a successful fuckup. Their involvement with the death of Show World had to be kept absolutely secret.

Fortunately Diane had her own reputation to look after. Beyond that, she swore a solemn oath that not a word about the entire affair would leak. Her letter had arrived today, postmarked Chicago, accompanied by a trio of sadistic paperbacks that she evidently found amusing.

The note was short and sweet. It read:

Dear girls,
    Have fun with the books. If you won't tell, I won't tell. Good luck with your next movie. You should stick with them. You're much better at rhetoric than you are at real life.

It was an infuriating footnote, but there was a nugget of truth therein. Making movies was their business; spreading the word was their mission. Once it was clear that they would not be going to prison, they were free to get back down to it.

Hence, their difficult decision. With which they were well pleased.

The bad news was that another beloved sister had died. The good news was that she would have a chance to live on. And *Pieces of Meat* had a new central image: a gut-wrenching true story to dramatize and bludgeon the male-supremist society to its knees with.

The true story of Mona and Lisa.

In the last several seconds before their world went mad, Susan was breaking out the wine. Their nerves were frazzled from two pots of coffee and the meticulous restructuring of their harrowing tale. Making Lisa a hero was a piece of cake: even though they'd often disagreed with her, they'd always respected her inner strength and dedication to the Movement. Correcting her obvious flaws in judgment was child's play; what she'd failed to grasp in life, she'd come to symbolize in death. It was an honor that either of them would have been proud to bear.

Fleshing out Mona was a little more difficult, because

they really didn't understand her. Not that it mattered all that much. Wrongheadedness had held the public center stage long enough; it didn't need to be lovingly spelled out again.

But if the power of her conversion was to come across on the screen, it was important that they make her at least *marginally* deserving of respect. Giving the opposition credit for anything beyond a certain animal cunning was always a problem. It was much easier to simplify, zero in on their faults.

"Well, Lisa seemed to like her," Susan said, acknowledging her glass of Chablis with a terse and joyless sip.

"I think the reasons are obvious," Paula stated. "It was a matter of infatuation. Lisa never quite outgrew the male concept of feminine beauty. You know how slavish she was about her looks. . . ."

Paula had a point that she was circling in on, vulturelike. She never quite got to make it.

Because the pain hit.

And the world went mad.

And the whirlpooling nightmare sucked them in.

The two women screamed, very nearly in unison. The wine bottle slipped from Susan's fingers and exploded against the floorboards. Paula doubled up in her seat. Susan did much the same, but she was crashing to her knees in the process.

In the first quarter of human development that follows conception, the sexes are exactly alike. They share the same organs, the same primordial sex glands. If a person's sexual politics were determined at that point, there would be no war. There would be no other side.

But somewhere in the neighborhood of the eighteenth week, the crafty male supremist Y chromosome imposes itself on slightly less than half of the fetus population.

That early in the person's development, the transition to maleness is both natural and painless.

Undergone some thirty years later, it's another story entirely.

Bones creaked and shrieked and ground against each other: broadening shoulders, narrowing hips. Breasts receded and sprouted hair. Hormones mutated. Cells went berserk.

Both of them were on the floor now, writhing and howling with voices that steadily deepened in pitch. For Paula Levin, the anguish of her rebelling physiology was nothing compared to the anguish of her mind. A different kind of conception had taken place there: an embryonic lunacy that would grow and grow and grow.

Just as something else was growing, in the battlefield between her thighs.

Her enemy was growing there.

And, dear God, it was enormous.

"Hey, buddy!" yelled the voice from far away. "You want out here or what?"

It took Billy a minute to claw his way back to the surface. For one thing, he was in something very much like a trance; for another, he was having a blast there. The visuals, from his private screening room's vantage, were not to be believed.

But he realized that the cab had stopped, and that the cabbie was getting impatient. *It's alright*, he told himself. *Now that the girls are big strong men, I'm sure they can take care of themselves.*

He paid the cabbie and got out. The cab wheeled away, and Billy turned to face the darkness of East Thirteenth Street. He could feel the adrenaline pumping now, and it was the most wonderful feeling in the world.

"Look out, Stanley, cuz here I come," he announced. "Gonna send you to a far better place."

The night, ever tactful, let him go on believing it.

FIFTY-ONE

THE ROAD TO HELL

Another cab was on its way downtown and to the east. It bore no satisfied passenger, no vengeful lunatic glee.

Just a dark shape, huddled alone in the backseat, with one smoking red eye that blinked and glowed.

Over and over and over.

It had been a quarter to eleven when Mona left the apartment, venturing out on the street alone for the first time since the rape. Though the night was cool and clear, she could feel it weighing down on her shoulders like a black woolen shroud. A ponderous night. Foreboding. Foretelling.

God, or whatever powers there be, had seen fit to send a cab her way almost instantly. She'd given her thanks as she climbed in.

And now she was on her way, the cab rolling smoothly through the moderate traffic on the West Side Highway. She stared through her window at the dark waters of the Hudson, while the one red eye stared back at her in silent, somber reflection.

Mona knew that the nightmare was waiting for her. She knew that the worst was yet to come. It was hard to believe, but she'd reached the point where she could believe *anything* now.

And I need some answers, she told herself, while the world whipped past her window. *I need to know what's going on.*

In the minutes following her conversation with Larry, she'd used up the last of her tears. There was so much to hurt about—there didn't seem to be any end to it—but she was getting tired of hurting, she was getting tired of being dragged around and victimized by fate, she was getting tired of standing around in the dark while forces beyond her wildest dreams tore apart everything she loved.

Because she was *strong*, dammit! She was *better* than that! Let some other weeping pussy willow bend to the wind; she had fought her way to the brink of success—a life she loved, a community, a career—and she would be good and God damned if she was gonna just let it all cave in on her.

And as for you, Billy Rowe, her mind harangued, *just who the hell do you think you are? If I want to be with Dave, I'll be with Dave. If I want to be with you—*

She stopped herself there.

The road to Hell was the West Side Highway, blasting down to the Canal Street exit. Mona knew that for a fact. Any road that led to Billy's apartment was the road to Hell, because Billy stood squarely at the heart of all the madness. She knew that, too.

And she was strangely unafraid.

Because whatever dark force had descended on all their lives—making hers a nightmare, stripping Lisa's away entirely—Billy was the first victim of it. Ever since the night of the party, when the first blood was spilled on the street before him, something had taken hold of Billy and transformed him into a creature both beautiful and terrible: an awesome more-than-human, with powers she could only guess at.

And Mona was tired of guessing.

She wanted answers. And she would have them.

Tonight.

The smoking red eye had burned down to its filter. She brought a fresh cigarette to her lips and lit it off the dying spark, then ground out the old in the ashtray. Making way for the new.

"Billy, I love you," she whispered into the darkness. "And I'll save you if I can. But it has to end, baby. The nightmare has to end."

The cab whipped up onto the exit ramp, wheeled left onto Canal Street. The road to Hell stretched out before her.

She knew what it was paved with.

She hoped to God that it was enough.

FIFTY-TWO

TRAILS

The door squealed open before Billy could touch it. He'd had that experience before. He half expected to see Christopher there, smiling and saying *it's alright, man, it's alright.*

But the vibe was all wrong. From the bottom of the stairs, three floors below, that much had been clear.

Christopher would not be here.

Only the horror.

Only the horror.

All the way up the stairs Billy had felt the ugliness thicken in the air, become a semisolid viscosity that he had to force his way through with effort. His previous cheer had given way to an inner coolness that sharpened to intensity and then gave way to out-and-out dread.

And now the door was sliding open before him, as if it were afraid of his touch. Billy smiled tersely at it, stepping forward. He figured it made them just about even.

Because he recognized the smell, and the smell was pure evil. It was the sweat that matted demon-fur, the slime that made them glisten. It was dying breaths and opened bellies, sulfur and sewage. It burned in his nostrils and throat like Drano, made the back of his eyeballs ache.

It made him wish, for just one honest second, that he could turn around and walk back a week in time.

It scared him very badly.

But not enough to stop me, fuckers, he silently hissed, moving into the doorway. *Not enough to keep me from Stan the Man.*

He stepped into the apartment.

The door slammed shut behind him.

A moment of silence.
And then the dance began . . .

*They were lesser demons, one and all: most of them
formless, and brainless as drones. Their functions were as
tiny as their blackened souls; they performed them endlessly, all the while screaming in tones that only the Mad Ones
could hear.*

*They'd all stopped, uniformly, when the Enemy came,
terror coarsing through their tiny maggot hearts. The
Enemy was strong, so much stronger than they were. The
Enemy could make them suffer in ways that they could not
begin to imagine.*

*But they were strong in number, and they could smell
the Enemy's fear. It made them fierce, in their brainless
way.*

The hive-mind buzzed, imperative.
The demons went back to work.

The three drawers of the kitchen cabinet went flying
across the room. Billy whipped around to his right,
watched them hit the wall just as the framed photographs
on the wall behind him exploded. He whirled again, and
the TV changed channels, and the empty TV dinner trays
and crumpled paper bags began to levitate off of the coffee
table that bucked and shuddered and thumped its wooden
feet against the floor in epileptic frenzy. Closets and
cabinets flew open, slammed shut, flew open again. Billy
turned, turned, turned. The TV changed channels.

There was a glass case mounted on the wall behind the
front door. It was crammed full of knickknacks, wide-eyed
and ceramic: kitties and birdies and horsies and clowns.
One by one, their heads flew off and bled: redness thick as
motor oil, oozing from the saw-toothed stumps. Billy
turned and watched them bleed. The TV changed channels. Changed channels. Changed channels. A butterknife
windmilled across the living room, embedded in a newspaper clipping that was Scotch-taped to the wall above the
sofa whose stuffing ripped out through its Colonial flesh and
raced to the ceiling where it hovered like a layer of cumulus
clouds. A rat-thing the size of a cocker spaniel scuttled out

from under the cushy chair in front of the TV and raced toward the bedroom door. The TV changed channels.

Billy stared at the scuttling rat-thing, and it burst into greasy flames.

The apartment went silent.

And nothing moved.

The demons knew terror.

It froze the television dial in place and the stuffing to the ceiling. It stranded the paper bags in midair and paralyzed the coffee table. Closets and cabinets, doors formerly in motion, stayed right where they were.

The Enemy was too strong.

But they couldn't stop screaming, and that was the worst part. Even though they knew that he could hear them, Mad One that he was, they continued to screech and wail. They couldn't help it.

Terror was their frame of reference.

They were learning it anew.

"*Shit!*" Billy yelled, eyes burning, heart pounding, ears ringing with the mewling chorus of tiny demon screams. He had them right where he wanted them; the only problem was, they weren't who he wanted at all.

The one he wanted wasn't here.

"*Shit!*" he reiterated, bellowing. "*Shit Shit SHIIIIITTT!*" He punted the cushy chair, lifting it five feet and slamming it into the TV set, which fell over on its back and died in a shower of sparks. Another of the rat-things had been cowering under the chair; it stared up at him with its black-hole eyes, bared the sharp yellow teeth in its hideous bulging pink gums, and went *skreeeeeee* for one second before its skull flattened out under Billy's boot.

It wasn't enough.

"*Peckard, God damn you! Come out here and TAKE YOUR MEDICINE!*" he screamed. The demons yammered away, but no one stepped forward. No one could. Stanley Peckard was gone.

Billy refused to accept it. He stomped around the apartment, tearing doors off their hinges, overturning furniture. He found seven more monsters and did them in with barely a second glance.

It wasn't enough. It wasn't nearly enough. He felt swindled, stripped, pissed on and left for dead. The Power, thrumming with its own deadly life, threatened to dissolve him into a pool of bubbling fat if he didn't find somewhere to put it, fast.

And he had nothing to go on, no leads to follow . . .

. . . except his sense of smell.

"Ooo, baby," he said softly, allowing himself to smile again. His nostrils flared, savoring the stench of Stanley's apartment, grinding it into his memory banks. He had followed it up the stairs.

He would follow it back out.

This time, when Billy came to the front door, he had to open it by hand. There was a demon in the doorknob, but it was trying to hide. It made a sound like a whistling teakettle when it died.

The door slid shut behind him quietly, and he started down the stairs. The stench was here, yes, noxious and fulsome, leading him by the nose as he descended.

And as he descended, a connection came to him: the place where he had smelled that smell before. It hobnail-booted his memory into recollection, spun him back to a place some twenty-eight hours before.

Just before he ran into Lisa.

Out in front of the Variety Photoplays.

Ah, yes, he mused, remembering the moment. Remembering it very well. The same flaring of nostrils. The same eviscerating dread. With nothing to peg it on, he'd had no choice but to shrug it off.

Now he knew what it was.

And his mind went there . . .

There were thirty-seven men, three working women, a pimp named Cool, and a working blond transvestite by the name of Johnny in the Variety Photoplays when the fire broke out. It started simultaneously in three distinct locations: the bottom of the screen, the rear of the projectionist's booth, and the floor of the ticket taker's cubicle. It did not take its good-natured time. The projectionist and the ticket taker were dead before they had a chance to scream more than a dozen times, much less leave the death traps in which they found themselves flambéing. *Between the actual flames, so rapidly spreading, and the shitty ventilation system that failed to disperse the smoke, every single one of them was dead before Billy reached the bottom of the stairs.*

Not a one of them was named Stanley Peckard.
Billy knew that before he started the fires.
He did it, anyway.

It should not have been a surprise. But it was. When he opened the front door of the building and the stink of evil just upped and vanished, Billy was stunned. He didn't know what to do.

He hadn't counted on the fifteen billion distinctive scents that pervaded any given New York City street at any given moment. He hadn't anticipated the breeze. For some reason he'd been expecting a yellow brick road, and when it wasn't there . . .

"God damn it!" He kicked a garbage can. His foot went through its side. *"GOD DAMN IT TO HELL!"* He yanked his foot away. Some indistinguishable rot had, in that short second, taken up residence on his boot. The stink of it bit quite plainly into his nostrils.

But the stink of Stanley Peckard was gone.

And there was nothing left to do but scream and rant and rave and kick some more garbage cans, all of which he did. His mind started thinking some very crazy things: *What if I just burn every apartment in Manhattan, block by block and street by street, until I hear him scream?* for example . . . and it was everything he could do just to keep from acting them out.

Until a voice in his head said, softly and distinctly, *Go home*.

Which didn't make any sense at all. No, it didn't. If he wanted to catch ol' Stan the Man, it made more sense to just hang around here with the rats and the acrobatic furniture. Didn't it? He felt quite sure. He

(shut up just do it go home shut up)

blinked. There was a voice in his head, and he didn't recognize it. He stared down Thirteenth Street toward First Avenue, and it was very strange, because a thick fog

seemed to have settled where no fog had been before. He
shook his head, and

(*go home*)

the voice was louder, it annoyed him, it seemed to
prickle at the base of his skull. Billy shook his head, as if to
clear it. The surrounding fog seemed to lift for a second.
"Fuck this," he hissed, and

(*!!!!!!*)

the pain was a white-hot seering at the base of his
skull, branding irons in the shape of needles, jabbing
inward and twisting as they dug smoldering holes that

(*go home*)

went away suddenly as he opened his eyes and stared
into the billowing fog. He didn't understand what was
happening. That didn't seem to matter. His legs were
moving, a shambling stride that dragged him bodily toward
First Avenue and the Saturday-night bustle of happening
New York.

A swarm of yellow cabs was buzzing up First. Billy felt
his arm reach out and start to wave. A pair of hookers in hot
pants were flouncing up the sidewalk; he faintly felt one of
them brush against him, heard the sixth-grade sultry voices
ask if he wanted a date wanted a date wanted a—

A cab screeched to a halt at the curb in front of him.
He felt his hand open the back door, felt himself climb
inside. He heard a voice outside his head say *Hey buddy
howya doin' whereya goin'.*

He heard himself say that he was going to Thirteen
Stanton Street, saw the man in the front seat write it down.

*Jeezuz did you see those cunts I don't believe the shit
they pull I kid you not* said the voice from outside of his
head. Undecipherable scenery whipped past the window.
The cab seemed full of smoke. *Lemme tell ya sumpin'
buddy I hate them cunts I see 'em every day they drive me
fuckin' bananas.*

Billy tried to get a grip on himself. It didn't work very
well. The tingling at the base of his skull was still there. It
made him feel like a puppet with a papier-mâché head,
twitching at the end of strings that were impossible to see.

*Every day I'm givin' rides to those fuckin' cunts an' I
don't get a fuckin' thing you know why that is lemme tell ya,*

the voice continued. *Boss has a deal with the fuckin' pimp he gets his blow jobs for free we get to drive 'em around for free do we see anything a tip a blow job not on your life mister sometimes they drag their johns right into the backseat right where you're sittin' an' do 'em up with all this fuckin' and suckin' and they charge fifty a hunnert dollars but do I ever see any of it do I ever even get a fuckin' piece of tail for my trouble pal you better believe I don't it drives me crazy fuckin' cunts.*

Billy felt himself start to get angry. The cab, like the voice, went on and on and on.

Slowly . . . very slowly . . . the fog began to lift.

Know what I'd like to do one day, buddy?, the voice went on. *I'd like to grab one of them bitches.*

Yes, clearer. The world was getting clearer. Billy began to make out the details of his strange new world. The full ashtray in the armrest to his right. The plastic barrier between the front and back seats, halfway open. The meter, reading $1.80 plus the fifty cents it added for driving at night. The hack license beside it, mounted on the dashboard: a black-and-white photograph of an ugly pug-faced man next to the words WEINSTEIN, EDWARD in big block letters.

Eddie, muh man, you're an ugly bastard, he heard himself think in his very own voice. It cheered him up. The tingling was still there, but it had receded into a kind of tactile background noise.

"Beat the shit out of her, an' make her do what *I* want for a couple hours of so. Teach 'er who the hell is boss. Know what I mean?" the cabbie persisted.

The world outside the window was visible now, too. He was on Second Avenue, with Fifth Street whizzing past. He saw the Hunan restaurant, which always smelled like insecticide, about to whiz by on his right; and he realized that if he heard one more word out of the mouth of Weinstein, Edward, there was a very good chance that something nasty might happen.

"This is fine," Billy said. "Pull it over here."

"What?" The cabbie plied his brakes with sudden, jerking finesse. "I thought you said—"

"Never mind what I said. This is fine. This is great."

"Whatever you say, buddy. Your money, not mine." Eddie sounded less than thrilled, but he pulled over to the curb anyway and flipped off the meter.

"Here's your fare," Billy said.

The cabbie let out a sudden, gurgling yelp. It may have had something to do with the fact that his tongue was disintegrating.

"And here's your tip."

The cabbie clutched his groin and tried to scream. No go. A thin plume of smoke wafted out of his mouth. It was matched by another cloud, wafting out of his open zipper.

"And now you won't have to look at 'em, either."

The cabbie's fingers were like meathooks in a long-abandoned slaughterhouse, hanging in the air for no good reason at all. Perhaps it was to indicate his anguish.

Perhaps it was because his eyeballs were frying right out of his head.

Billy left Weinstein, Edward and his idling cab to the caprices of fate and the dregs of Second Avenue. Not even the prickling at the base of his skull could bother him now. He was happy again. He knew just what to do.

He was going home.

And he didn't have very far to walk at all.

FIFTY-THREE

THE TRUTH

The kitchen was dark when Larry opened the door. He stood well back in the shadows, a scarecrow silhouette. "You're not ready for this," he said. He didn't sound like he was kidding.

"I don't care," Mona countered, stepping into the apartment. Her first step in landed on a bloody shard of broken glass. It crunched under her foot. So what.

"No, Mona. You really don't want to see this." Larry, in fact, was in deadly earnest.

She was ready for him to try and hold up an arm to stop her. She was ready to swat it away. He didn't. Apparently Larry didn't even have the wherewithal to do that. Which was fine.

She had a more important battle to fight.

It had been five months since she'd last set foot in this apartment. It had happened only once, and that once had been enough. The destruction barely surprised her—would barely have surprised her even in happier times—if the horror were not raging all around her like tracer rounds in a firefight. Not even the stink, like rotten-egg farts in a closet, could get between her and what she had to do.

"Shut the door, Larry," she said. "Come on."

Reluctantly, Larry obliged. For the first time she noticed how badly he was shaking: the door shimmied in her hands like a Times Square stripper in the instant before he let it go. Whatever he had seen—whatever it was that he was about to share with her—it had made a rubbery strawberry jam of his spine.

I don't care, she reiterated, this time silently. *I need to know. I've come this far.*

"Come on," she repeated, turning impatiently toward him.

And that was when he turned on the light.

"Oh, my God." The words came out slowly, with a lot of space between. "My God, Larry. What happened to you?"

"Oh, nothing," Larry said, following up with a nervous giggle. "Your boyfriend looked at me funny, that's all." He took a step toward her, and the first lump of fear started climbing up her throat.

Larry's skin was lobster red. There was no other way to describe it. He looked like he'd pulled a Rip Van Winkle in the middle of the Mohave Desert. There were cracks in his skin, oozing ever-so-slightly. It was painful to look at; she could imagine what it felt like to wear.

"Come on," Larry said, imitating her tone. "We've got all fucking night, right? You wanna see it? Let's see it."

Larry came closer, and she instinctively recoiled. He

came closer still, and she realized that at least part of the stink was coming from him. It was acrid and pungent and everything she'd never wanted to smell before. It made the lump in her throat identify itself as bile. It made her ill.

"Let's go," Larry said, taking hold of her arm. He sneered, and his teeth shone yellow against the baked skin. Hostility had taken over where the fear left off in his eyes. She could see it. She could feel it.

That was when she yanked away.

"*HEY!*" she yelled, baring her own perfect white teeth. Larry looked startled and alarmed. Pshaw. "Keep your goddam hands to yourself, Larry! I swear to God, I'll break 'em!"

Larry just stared at her, eyes wide and unblinking. "Understand?"

"I'm s-sorry," he said. Blinking now. Blinking back tears. "It's just that—"

"I know," she cut in, her voice softening now. "I'm sorry, too. Come on."

Then they moved, together, toward the darkness on the other side of Billy's bedroom door.

Larry had already seen it, so he knew how bad it was. He had tried to warn her. She'd fought him down.

Now it was time to pay the piper.

The stuff on the file cards was bad enough. It said everything that needed to be said and more about what Billy was up to and what he had become. Coupled with the newspaper clippings, the data laid out in his family tree of lunacy painted an awfully damn clear picture.

Billy was the vigilante.

The vigilante was a loon.

But the photos he'd framed his ravings with were the ugliest things of all. They made his worst tirades seem almost sensible by comparison, showed even his most cogent ramblings to be the blasphemy that they were. He recognized the two men in the underexposed photographs, though he'd never seen the big one so cheesy white or the little one in so many pieces. He knew them for what they'd done to the apartment.

He didn't know what they had done to Mona.

But all the wind seemed to go out of her when she

looked at them. It was like watching a balloon deflate. The supertough woman who had plowed her way past him had decayed into a solid wad of gibbering wet-faced pain.

No. Not quite so easy. She huffed herself back up to her regular height; and though her words wheezed out like an agonizing gas attack, they did so with heavyweight intensity.

"So this is it, huh?" she said. "So this is what's become of my man." She let out a little laugh, then: hideous, bitter as a mouthful of sulfur. "Oh, baby. I suppose I ought to offer you a medal—"

"Yeah. Maybe you should," said the voice from behind them.

Mona turned.

Larry turned.

Billy stood in the doorway.

"I think that I deserve some kind of medal," he continued. His eyes were like taillights: crimson flicker and glow. "I wasted them, Mona. I did it for you."

Billy moved toward Mona. Mona backed away. Without even thinking, Larry stepped between them. Thought came a moment later, saying *what am I DOING?*

But by then it was too late. He had Billy's undivided attention.

"And *you!*" Billy enthused. He had a shark's winning smile. "I thought you were *smarter* than this, man! I thought that you knew how to read!"

"Billy, stop," Larry said. It was all he could think of.

"Stop what?" Billy asked. His smile beamed out and touched nothing, because it wasn't real. "Stop you from coming in here? I already tried that. Stop *her* from coming in here? I already tried that, too. It seems like nobody wants to listen to what I have to say anymore. Breaks my heart. Honest ta God, it does."

"Bullshit," Mona said.

"Oh!" Billy flapped his hands limp-wristedly, made a grand display of his alarum. "Oh! Oh! Oh! And I suppose you know exactly how I feel!"

"I don't think you feel a fucking thing," Mona growled. "Otherwise you wouldn't be treating us this way."

Billy paused for a moment of what looked like reassessment. Larry had no idea what he was going to do, but he leapt at the opportunity to do it.

"Billy," he said. "Come on. We're your friends. We don't want to hassle with you. We want to work things out—"

"*SHUT UP!*" The sheer force of it knocked him back three feet. The flat, soulless red gleam of those eyes put him back beside Mona, very close to the back of the room. "I already *told* you what I think of you, man! If I accidentally stepped on you, I'd scrape my boot off at the nearest curb! You're a turd, man! You're a turd! The line between you and your bullshit has ceased to exist!"

There was Power in the room now. Incredible, killing Power. Larry knew that there was nothing in his repertoire that could even begin to combat it. He felt absolutely powerless. He felt his own death, screaming toward him like a train.

"And how 'bout you?" Mona inquired suddenly. Larry whipped around to look at her. Her features were set. She was a rock. "How about you and *your* bullshit, Billy? Writing your pretty notes, doing your dirty deeds. How clean are *you*, my love, to be throwing these stones?

"Why don't *you* shut up?"

The tingling in the back of his head had been a warm and pleasant thing, like a wicked cocaine buzz that just went on and on and on. Now it was starting to ache. Billy didn't like that.

But Mona's words had punched a hole in him, and that was a fact. He could feel the righteousness leaking out of him like sand from a shattered hourglass. It was a horrible feeling, because it stripped him of his armor; and without it, he felt naked and puny and oh so ashamed

(*NO!*)

and he hated to feel that way, but it was true, it was true. His head was really aching now. He had never felt quite so miserable in his life. Mona was still staring at him with those cold dark eyes, still waiting for an answer. He felt himself wanting to drop to his knees and cry *Oh baby, oh baby, I'm so sorry*

(*!!!!!*)

and the million hot needles ground into his brain, dropping him to his knees after all, quite sure that he was screaming

(*now*)

and then the pain was gone, and a little voice in his head said, *I could kill her*, and it sounded like a perfectly reasonable suggestion.

His head felt nice again.

He stood.

He smiled.

"Mona," he said. Very soft. All strychnine and honey. "Mona, sweets, let me ask you something. What are you doing here? Why didn't you believe me when I told you that you didn't want to know?"

Mona's voice, when she answered, was soft but firm. *Like her tits*, he mused. *Oh, yes. Like her pretty pretty titties.*

"Because I love you . . ." she began.

Billy laughed uproariously. "Oh, you *do*!" he shrieked, clapping his hands.

". . . and because I needed to know what was going on," she continued, slightly louder. She was blushing, her lovely dark skin darkening further as her hot blood welled up beneath the surface. All that passionate lovetalk, no doubt. Billy half wondered if he was blushing, too. He doubted it.

On the other hand, it occurred to him, *if Larry was blushing, nobody'd be able to tell*. It struck him as pretty funny.

"By the way, Lar'," he interrupted. "Nice tan."

"*God damn it, Billy!*" Mona roared. "*Will you STOP AND LISTEN TO ME?*"

"Ummm . . . no," he said, turning back to her. "I don't think so, darlin'. I'm just not in the mood. I don't want to hear about how much you love me, or how scared you were for me, or how your delightfully heaving bosom doth beat with ardor true.

"No. But I'll tell you what I *would* like to do." He smiled and slid his tongue along his top row of teeth. "I'd like to just . . . *look* at you for a moment."

Mona looked properly horrified. Billy's smile increased

to match it. *God*, she was gorgeous! Even now, with her eyes widening and her lips peeling back in revulsion and terror, she was one of the hottest little numbers ever to stroll down the pike. That dancer's body. The dancer's grace with which she commanded it. And that *face* . . .

All the aching had moved from his head to his hard-on. That was good. The mellow tingling at the base of his skull told him so. He remembered all the times that they had made love together

(*no, fucked, that's all it was, only fucking*)

and he realized that he had to be crazy to give up a hot little twat like that. *Uh-uh. No way. Ridiculous*, he told himself.

Thank God it wasn't too late.

"Oh, Mona," he said, moving closer as she backed away. "Oh, Mona Mona Mona. You love it when I say your name, don't you? Of course you do. It's because you love me so very much.

"And you know how I can tell that you love me?" he continued. "I can tell by the way that you run off and fuck Dave every time that I piss you off. I can tell by the way that you respect my every wish. Oh, yeah. You love me, baby. You've said so yourself."

Mona had backed up to the point where she couldn't back up anymore: flush against the open window that led to the fire escape, that same ol' fire escape that had given him the ringside seat for the slaughter of Jennifer Mason. Larry was beside her, also flush against the wall. But Larry didn't matter. If Larry was very lucky, he would get to watch.

"I guess I should apologize for writing that note," he said. "That was silly. Impetuous youth." He grinned boyishly and threw up his hands, dismissing the whole thing entirely. "When two people love each other as much as you and I do, little things like infidelity shouldn't get in the way. Oh, no. And seriously, Mona: I love you just as much as I did the first time I saw you and thought, *damn*, would I ever love to prong that bitch!"

"Billy," she cried. For real. Tears were running down her lovely face. He had hurt her; and, *boy*, did he ever feel bad about that.

"Oh, *yes*, Mona! *Yes!*" He moved closer still, within

arm's reach. "*Tell* me about it! Tell me what a deeply moving experience this is! Or better yet, don't. We don't want to spoil this magic moment, do we?"

"Billy. Please—"

"Oh, yes!" Billy laughed long and hard. "No, please! Don't! Stop!" He laughed some more. "Yes, let's discuss your rape fantasies, my dearingest darling! Let's talk about how *bad* it felt when the mighty Rex dropped his load inside you—"

"*YOU BASTARD!*" Mona screamed, leaping foward and swinging. He could have stopped her, but why bother? It just made the whole thing more exciting.

She slugged him: not a slap, not a namby-pamby little whap. She slugged him across the jaw with every ounce of strength in her body. If he'd been an ordinary human, with an ordinary responsiveness to pain, it very possibly would have floored him.

But he wasn't, and it didn't, and he grabbed her wrists before she could try it again, holding them so tightly that the circulation cut off and she started to whine like the doorknob demon in good ol' Stanley Peckard's apartment.

"No, no," he said. "Don't say anything. Please." He stepped backward, dragging her with him. "Talk is cheap, and we're moving up in the world.

"Just show me how much you love me."

He leaned forward to kiss her.

And that was when Larry jerked away from the wall— good ol' Larry the Lobster, with the cherry-red skin—and grabbed ahold of Billy's left arm, yanking away, screaming, "*BILLY! NO! STOP!*"

Billy pulled away easily. It meant that he had to let go of Mona's right wrist, but that was not an insurmountable loss. He simply hurtled Mona against the wall with his right hand, straight-armed Larry in the chest with his left.

There was only one problem.

His hand didn't stop at Larry's shirt.

His hand didn't stop at Larry's flesh.

His hand didn't stop at the wall of muscle and fat, nor was it intimidated by the breastbone that shattered into a thousand killing pieces of organic shrapnel.

His hand didn't stop until it was wrapped around

Larry's heart, which went *PA-POOM PA-POOM PA-POOM* in the adrenaline-rushing seconds that immediately preceded his death.

And then stopped. In meaty mid *PA-POOM*.

Forever.

Behind him, Mona was beginning to scream. Billy couldn't hear her; he was too busy screaming himself. Larry tried to join in, but all that would come out was blood. After a couple of seconds, he just gave up. His eyes rolled back. The spark went out.

Leaving Billy with 187 pounds of dead meat dangling from the end of his arm. He screamed again, trying to shake the body loose. Larry's limbs performed a lifeless Funky Chicken, flopping and flapping. More blood came up. Billy very nearly slipped in the pool that it formed on the floor. Together, they stumbled toward the wall and Billy's desk like a pair of tangoing nitwits in a Jerry Lewis film.

The desk made a suitable altar. Larry's corpse slumped sacrificially across it, faceup. Billy yanked himself free at last, held his shimmering red hand up in front of his face, and let out one final scream.

And his head, his head, it was going berserk, the tingling turned to prickling turned to

(!!!!!)

the white-hot needles, and it wasn't because he had killed his friend—the murder was fine, the tingling said so—but because he was letting it bother him

(!!!!!)

and then he felt himself moving toward Mona and the window and the fire escape, with the words, "I'm going to kill you now," tumbling off his lips in a dull monotone . . .

. . . and then he heard a voice, his own voice, saying *Don't do it, Billy, you love her, you don't want to hurt her, they're MAKING you do this,* and

(!!!!!)

when he could see again, his hands were already around her throat, smearing her with Larry's gore, squeezing out her life. He was staring into her beautiful bulging eyes, watching her beautiful delicate features contort and swell and move through red to purple . . .

. . . and he fought back with every last ounce of will while his mouth opened wide and screamed, *"NOOOOOOOO!"*

(*!!!!!!!!!*)

and the pain was unbelievable, but he felt his grip relax, and

(*!!!!!!!!!!!*)

he staggered backward, letting go, stumbling to his knees, and bringing his hands up to his temples

(*!!!!!!!!!!!!!!*)

as he felt the Power well up inside him, and the one voice that was still his own said *no, you motherfuckers*, and

(*!!!!!!!!!!!!!!!!!!!!!*)

he flooded his skull with killing white heat, heard it sizzle and sear in the space between his ears, heard the pitiful dying screams of a million demon voices that were *not* his own, *not* his own. . . .

Then silence.

Darkness.

One long, sweet moment of peace . . .

Seven blocks away, on Second Avenue, the night was alive with flashing red lights and police barricades and the squawking of the inevitable vulture contingent. Several cop cars surrounded the object of their attentions, which was a shiny yellow cab that had been idling at the curb for the last ten minutes.

With one extremely dead man inside.

Dennis Hamilton was the one who wound up leaning over the eyeless, tongueless, ball-less corpse of Edward Weinstein. The cabbie's manifest was on the seat beside the body. Hamilton grabbed it, holding his breath against the stench all the while.

He barely even needed to look.

"Thirteen Stanton Street," Rizzo said, reading off the clipboard that Hamilton shoved in his face.

"You know what—"

"Don't say it." There was a look of such intense resignation in the older detective's eyes that Hamilton almost looked away out of compassion. But not quite. "Don't even say it."

"So can we go now?"

"Okay." Rizzo sighed, closed his eyes, and nodded. "Okay."

Hamilton was already running for the car.

Billy woke up to an angelic voice that he knew very well. It was calling his name. For a moment, he was quite sure that he'd died and gone to Heaven.

Then he looked up and discovered that quite the opposite was true.

"Oh, Billy," Christopher said. The voice was weary and condescending, redolent with disappointment. "Oh, Billy Billy Billy. Tell me, why'dja hafta go and do a thing like that?"

Billy blinked. The image wouldn't go away. It filled him with a terror so icy and utter that his mind refused to accept it. "*No*," he whispered, and blinked again.

When he opened his eyes, it was even worse.

Because Christopher was there, as radiant as ever. But Christopher was not alone. He had his friends with him.

His little friends.

His little rat-like demon friends, with their empty black eyes and their pink cleft palates and their rows upon rows of sharp yellow teeth . . .

. . . *and even as Billy watched, the wall behind Christopher faded back and back into an endless dark cavern that stretched and widened and widened and stretched and went on and on forever . . .*

. . . *and it was the cathedral of his dreams, only the doors of memory were nowhere to be seen: just miles upon miles of deepening darkness that chittered and crawled with the emerging legions of the damned.*

They were coming to meet him.

They were coming to take him home.

"Come on," Christopher said. "On your feet, little man. Show a little self-respect, why don't you. Didn't your mother teach you anything?

"You've got company."

Christopher smiled. A tiny lick of flame flickered out of his mouth.

Billy struggled to his hands and knees in a large

cooling pool of blood. *Larry's*, he heard himself think, and the thought brought him back to where he was and what had happened.

The walls on either side of him were still his bedroom walls; the same went for the ceiling and floor. There was a dry heat emanating from the gateway to Hell, but he could feel the cool breeze from the window behind him.

The window behind him . . .

"Omigod," Billy moaned. "Omigod, please, no—"

Then he leapt to his feet.

And he turned . . .

. . . and Mona was staring staring staring into the yawning black abyss. Past the handsome blond devil with the lapping tongues of flame. Past the monster that had stolen Billy's face. Past Larry's body, and beyond all comprehension.

Staring and staring.

Into the mouth of Hell.

Her body was locked in a series of uncontrollable jittering spasms. She wasn't aware of it. Nothing existed but the darkness that had no end.

Staring and staring.

And utterly blank.

"I know what you're thinking," Christopher said, and his voice was full of fatherly compassion. "You're thinking that I sold you down the river. That I came here to destroy you. But that isn't true."

Billy heard the words as if from a great distance. He was too stunned, too broken, to hear them any more distinctly. The madness in his lover's eyes had done what no knife or bullet had succeeded in doing.

It had destroyed him.

"The truth is," Christopher continued, "that I respect you, Billy. And that I'm deeply in awe of your powers: not the least of which is your ability to bring people together.

"Like on the train tonight, for instance. That was spectacular. You didn't even have to lift a finger." Languid whistle of admiration. "What a gift you have."

Billy was still stuck on the phrase "bring people

together." His gaze, scarcely focused, wandered over to Larry, who was still on the desk.

Larry's body was being devoured.

"That's why we need you on our side, Billy. A talent like yours is too good to waste. We believe in you. We can develop you into something like the world has never seen before.

"The man you were meant to be.

"The purpose for which you were born."

And then the terrible truth slammed home to him at last, at long long last. *Not the second coming*, his mind gasped as his lungs tied knots around his heart. *Not the coming of Christ at all.*

I'm the other thing.

I'm—

"What's in a name?" Christopher asked him, all cheerful charm and disarming flair. "A rose by any other name—you know the rest. Don't sweat it, ace!

"You're the one we've all been waiting for.

"So come give your loving Poppa your hand."

Christopher moved toward him, and the hatred seethed like lava in his soul. All the self-delusion, all the betrayal, reached a head that would not be denied.

The Power was his. That much was true. He had been set up for precisely that reason. The realization was a bright light that cut through the terror.

And told him what he had to do.

"You want the Power," Billy said. He was smiling.

Christopher nodded.

"Okay. You got it."

And then Billy let him have it.

At maximum intensity.

It was a solid wall of focused light and heat and death, slamming into Christopher and the front rank of demons with the force of a nuclear blast. The air was alive with the screams of the dead.

But Christopher held his ground.

Billy pushed harder, his whole body taut as a garotte, straining as he narrowed his field of fire, training the full force of the Power on the one target that really mattered.

Giving it all to the fallen angel.

And Christopher began to change. Billy could see it, very faintly, through the brilliance. Christopher's clothing and hair were aflame; his flesh was melting and flowing in runnels toward the back of his head, like wax under a blowtorch.

There was another face beneath that beautiful mask. The true face.

It appeared to be in pain.

But Billy was weakening, he was running out of juice, there was only so much Power in him and most of it was already gone. Fall, God damn you, *he heard himself hissing as he pushed and pushed . . .*

. . . and Christopher began to stagger, ever-so-slightly, backward . . .

. . . and the last of Billy's Power went out in a final blistering wave . . .

. . . and Christopher's hideous jaws went wide, in preparation for a scream . . .

. . . and then Billy toppled to his knees and stayed there, spent.

While the monster before him teetered dizzily on its heels, clutching its hairless skull with long, chitinous fingers. The only sound in the room was its quick, shallow breathing, huge against the silence.

Please, dear God, Billy soundlessly prayed. *Make him fall. Make him fall. . . .*

And then Christopher smiled.

"*Damn*, you're good," he said with open admiration. Then he cocked one hairless eyebrow sternly and added, "But don't ever do that again."

Mona's mind wasn't working very well. She was in a state of pathological shock so profound as to border on trance. The things that were happening before her no longer registered as real. She was watching a movie, only someone had put her on the wrong side of the screen.

Right now, she was watching a horrible monster. It was standing in front of the big black tunnel. Billy was on his knees in front of it, and it was starting to tell him a story.

She just stood there in her space beside the window, leaning against the wall. Watching. Listening.

"What you have to understand," the monster was saying, "is that you're never going to beat me. Ever. And you'll never really get away. Even if I were to let you die, you'd still be mine; I mean, do you really think that Paradise would let you in after some of the things you've done?"

The monster laughed. Mona thought it looked funny. It looked like

(*larry the lobster*)

a giant crustacean, only it had human features: arms and legs and

(*larry's dead he got on the wrong side of the screen and they ate him*)

a big shiny head and a torso

(*but not until billy killed him*)

except that it didn't have skin, it was made out of shells

(*that was when the movie started*)

and the only skin on it hung from the back of its head in stinking, blackened curls that looked like Rastafarian dreadlocks. The shells were bronze; they pulsed and glowed. The eyes were flat and black and had no light in them at all.

"So my suggestion to you," the monster continued, "is to go with the flow. Just give in. Just give in. It'll be fine. You'll see. We'll forget this little outburst ever happened, and get cracking on some of those strategies of yours."

Mona was in shock, but a certain alertness was starting to poke through. There were voices in her head, all of them her own, that were starting to make sense of what they were seeing and hearing.

The monster stepped closer to Billy, held out its horrible hands.

"Come on," it said, voice husky-seductive and low. "Come to Poppa."

Very slowly, Billy took his hands away from his face. He had been crying; she could tell because the palms of his hands were wet. She couldn't see his face, but she knew what was on it. She knew Billy.

He was the man she loved . . .

. . . and several things came down on Mona's head with terrible, crashing clarity. One: *if the monster still had to seduce him, then Billy still had a chance.* Two: *it was the monster, not Billy, that was responsible for the horror.* Three: *if Billy took the monster's hands, it was all over.*

Four: *this was not a movie, and she was not in the audience.*

"NOOOOOOO!!!" Mona screamed, launching forward, away from the wall. It took less than a second to reach the back of Billy's collar, the rest of the second to yank him away. Billy fell on his back with a loud *ka-boom*, and Mona slapped him across the face before he had a chance to blink.

When she looked into his eyes, they were crawling with pain.

So she slapped him again.

And she slapped him again . . .

. . . and then he grabbed her wrists. Not to crush them. Just to stop them.

"That's enough, baby." Very softly spoken. "Thank you."

Then he turned, and stood.

And faced his demon.

For the last time.

"I like you better this way," Billy said, looking Christopher up and down. "Now that I know what you really are, life's become so much simpler."

"Oh?" Christopher said, with his hideous smile. "And what am I, really?"

Billy smiled back. "A subhuman piece of shit."

Christopher started to say something, but Billy shushed him, continuing.

"No, no. Don't get me wrong. You had me *this close*"—pinching thumb and forefinger together—"even after I'd made up my mind. You're at your best when you're feeding on weakness, Christopher. That's probably why I hate you."

Billy took a couple of steps closer to the demon. He had a pretty good idea of what was going to happen. He hoped he was right.

He was looking forward to it.

"You can't have me," he said, stepping closer. Closer. "Not ever. Understand? Not even if I die. Not even in a million years."

"Don't be so sure—"

"Shut up, Christopher! I've had enough bullshit out of you for one lifetime! I renounce you, I renounce whatever Power you've given me, you can take the gift and the guidance and protection and crawl right back down to Hell with it.

"It's over.

"We're through."

Nobody spoke. They just stared at each other. Christopher looked almost sad. *And in his own strange way,* Billy supposed, *he probably is.*

Then the demon sighed heavily and nodded its head. The notebook and the silver pen appeared magically in its hands. Christopher turned to the very last page and scribbled something down.

"Yes, we are," Christopher said, meeting Billy's gaze for the last time. "Good-bye, Billy. It's been fun."

"Fuck you," Billy said.

Christopher smiled. The notebook closed with a startling *snap* . . .

. . . *and Billy felt the center of his breastbone shatter, felt the cold steel sliding inward, sawing back a second, punching through again. He stared down at his chest in horror and agony, watching the black heart-blood spurting out from the hole that had opened there. He felt himself staggering backward, mind reeling, getting flashes of a flat black nonreflective blade some four days past, catching up with him now* . . .

. . . *and his right hand tore open, distracting him for a second, making him stare at the mangled palm as if to confirm its existence. A scream that wasn't his own raked his eardrums. His own mouth, when he opened it, was a heavily-flowing fountain of gore* . . .

. . . *but his mind was suddenly lucid, and it spoke to him even as the roar of gunfire echoed in his ears and the top of his head blew off, striking the window behind him, both glass and bone reduced to twinkling shards* . . .

. . . *and his mind said* good-bye, Mona, don't worry, it's not so bad *as the rest of the bullets, some three days late, made a flying red pudding of his skull. He hoped that she could hear him. He was reasonably sure* . . .

. . . *and then, with eyes and ears that no longer existed, he saw and heard the screeching van's approach, and he thought* ah yes, there's still that, and the other thing, too . . .

. . . *and then Billy's body lifted right out of his shoes and went flying across the room, a skin-bag filled with broken bones and mashed, no-longer-vital organs. It plowed through what was left of the window and impacted against the metal guardrail of the fire escape, snapping the spine in two, sending the lifeless sack of meat pinwheeling three stories down to the pavement below* . . .

FIFTY-FOUR

FROM THE HEAVENS

Flecks of cindered paper flew through the air like shooting stars: the glowing remains of Billy's hellish strategies, cindered off the walls. The mouth of Hell was gone, returning the room to its former dimensions.

Billy, too, was gone, leaving only his shoes and the stench of his death behind.

But the monster was still there: scratching its chin, staring off into the middle distance. "Damn," it said. "We were so close. Every time, we get so *close*. . . ."

Then it turned to her; and for the first time, she felt its cold gaze boring into her own. It smiled, almost kindly, and reopened the notebook to the very first page.

Which was blank.

And waiting.

"How 'bout *you*?" It said. "Care to give it a whirl? Clean up the streets?"

Mona screamed.

"Guess not," it said, shrugging.

Mona screamed again, only faintly aware that her body was moving. Her legs hit the windowsill just above the kneecaps, sent her toppling backward into the night. Her arms flailed back automatically, hands instantly sliced and stained by the meat and broken glass that covered the fire escape landing.

But the fall and the cool night air were a slap across her sanity. The next scream throttled on its way to her lips as she dragged herself the rest of the way out of the room, pulled herself to her feet, hit the first step leading downward and then just kept going.

Below, Stanton Street was silent and empty. The pool of streetlight, the construction site darkness, ran together with the uncaring moon and sky above. The only sounds were her own feet clanging against the metal stairs, the hysterical rasp of her breathing, the distant keening *weep weep weep* of a police car's siren, too far away to matter.

And the laughter, pouring out of the window above her.

She didn't turn to look. She didn't need to see. The second-floor landing was just five steps below her now. Four steps. Three. She jumped the last two and landed with her hands already against the railing, gripping it, hoisting her over the side . . .

. . . *and she was there, just as they'd said she would be: his Very Bestest Girl Ever, dropping down from the heavens* . . .

. . . and the fall itself was painless until the end, her few airborne seconds alive with triumph and exhilaration. Then the ground came up to meet her—too fast, too fast— and before she could get her proper balance, her feet were impacting and the angle was all wrong and her knees were buckling as the pain screamed up her legs and her head traveled the last five feet to the pavement in agony.

She tried to stand. Her left knee refused to cooperate. *"Please!"* she screamed. It screamed back at her, unbending. She put all of her weight behind her right leg, struggling upward . . .

. . . and he was moving out of the construction site shadows, only dimly aware of having done this before or of the hideous completion it implied. His one good hand buried itself in his pocket, pulling out the Master Carver; the other stretched out before him like a fetid, five-fingered Goodyear blimp.

He was dying, yes he was, every shambling step forward weaker than the last . . .

. . . but she was close now, less than six feet away, less than five, and she was beautiful, more beautiful than he'd dared to ever ever hope, even though she was screaming . . .

. . . and she was four feet away . . .

. . . as the car screamed left onto Stanton Street, headlights instantly nailing the two agonized figures in the middle of the block. "Holy shit," Hamilton hissed, focusing on the reflection off the knife, momentarily dragging his attention away from the steering wheel in his hands . . .

. . . as the tires skidded diagonally across the asphalt, Rizzo shouting something incomprehensible in the second before the passenger side of the cruiser slammed into the parked cars lining the south side of Stanton Street . . .

. . . but it didn't stop the nightmare that was dragging itself painfully toward her. She could see the glistening blade that its right hand held aloft, the purpled and elephantine fingers groping at the air less than six inches from her throat.

The motion was automatic. She barely even knew she was doing it. Left hand coming under-and-in to cup the forearm, right hand

(*i'll die before i let this happen to you again*)

locking in on the outside, at the elbow, and *pushing, pushing,* the hideous exploding sounds muffled by the jacket's sleeve . . .

* * *

*. . . and he could feel the demons leaving his mind,
bailing out as his elbow gave and the white-hot pain went
BING down the length of his spine. Rats off an utterly
sinking ship, abandoning him to yowling and spinning
retreat from his Bestest Girl, the one it had all been
for . . .*

. . . as Hamilton crawled out of the driver's seat and
assumed a shooting stance. Legs splayed. Arms loose. Body
balanced.

Finger firmly on the trigger.

"Now," he said, squeezing off the first shot. He couldn't
see the hole, but the jerking of the man's body let him know
that his aim was true. He fired again, and the knife went
flying, and the first hole secreted a bloody red rose that
stood out brilliantly against the tan trench coat.

The second hole bloomed just as the third and fourth
shots took his target to the mat. *I got you, fucker!* he
thought in the second before he realized that he didn't even
know who he'd just killed . . .

. . . but Stanley Peckard was happy. The pain, un-
bearable only seconds before, was slipping away beneath
the cool dark dying waves that enveloped him now. And his
mind, for the first time in as long as he could remember,
was completely his own.

Stanley's eyesight had never been good, and imminent
death did nothing to improve upon it. Even with the night's
sky clear, he could not see the stars.

But the moon was there: a big bright circle of light at
the end of a long dark tunnel. He smiled, and all of reality
funneled down to that one gleaming hole in the sky.
Everything else—the pavement, the pain, the Bestest Girl
that had never been his, no, not even for a second—all of it
simply ceased to be.

When he closed his eyes, he could still see the light:
too beautiful for words as it shone down upon him,
warming him, gently urging him to rise. . . .

Which he did.

Without, even once, looking back.

* * *

The door on the passenger's side was hopelessly jammed. It didn't matter. Whatever had happened had happened so quickly that Rizzo felt strangely like an innocent bystander.

Whatever had happened, it was over.

Hamilton was moving, very slowly, toward the girl. Rizzo took the opportunity to radio in for reinforcements, though there didn't seem to be any particular hurry. One dead man; one wounded girl; another body, just beyond, that he suspected was profoundly dead, too.

Then he slid out the driver's side and stood where Hamilton had been when he'd fired the shots: the first killing shots, Rizzo was quite sure, that his partner had ever fired.

This is gonna be a bitch, his mind informed him in no uncertain terms. Already, Hamilton had dropped to his knees beside the girl, and she had thrown herself into his arms, and it was painfully obvious to Rizzo that at least one of them was crying hysterically.

There was nothing else to do, so Rizzo lit a cigarette and walked over to the bodies, scrupulously steering clear of the living. There was nothing he could do for them, either. The dead, at least, wouldn't mind his hanging around.

Any second now, the vultures would arrive. Already, nearly every window on the goddam block had a light on behind it. It flashed him back to the last time he'd visited Stanton Street at night. The flashing lights. The barricades. The video cameras and microphones. The endless questions.

The white chalk line.

Yeah, there was always a fucking carnival when someone died. It made him sick; but, just like with almost everything else, there was nothing he could do about it. The sense of powerlessness made him feel crazy sometimes: made him wish that he could do something, *anything*, to put an end to the endless veil of tears.

When those feelings came up, he clamped down on them hard.

The first police car wheeled around the corner, immediately followed by another. And another. And another. The first wave of geeks began to pour from the doorways. Rizzo didn't look at any of them.

Rizzo stared at the moon, so distant and cold. The moon stared back.

Neither one of them seemed to feel much of anything at all.

EPILOGUE

PAX

"Some folks is crazy.
Some say I am.
Some say I'm crazy
Cuz I give a damn.
But I ain't here to cry.
An' I ain't here to fight.
I just wanna show you
The twist toward the Light . . ."

> Billy Rowe
> *Twisted Toward Life*
> Griffin Records

All told, it had been an extraordinarily pleasant afternoon for Frank Rizzo. The weather was great. Lunch—Cajun food, a first for Frank—had been fine. The conversation was relaxed and amiable. Even his bursitis had seemingly taken the day off.

Something was bound to screw up.

Then the song came over the radio, and he knew just what it would be.

"Omigod!" Hamilton exclaimed, reaching over and honking the volume up suddenly. "Frank, check it out."

The tinny speakers howled for mercy. Dennis grinned sardonically. Rizzo just groaned and gunned the sedan up Tenth Avenue, slicing in and out of prerush hour traffic like a shark through a barrier reef. He personally hadn't given a warm fart for music, period, ever since that little bomb-shocked Norseman took Glenn Miller and the heart of Big Band on an icy dive into the English Channel back in '44. And his apathy bridged into full-blown contempt when it came to the ultramodern, digitally processed crap that clogged up the airwaves these days. Even *this* tune, which struck him as marginally more soulful than the rest.

Especially this tune.

Sure, it was a ballad. And it was surprisingly lush and haunting; one might even call it bittersweet. But the singer still yowled like a banshee on a washboard when he should have been crooning. And the whole thing still made him uncomfortable.

It reminded him of too many things that were best left forgotten.

He threw a baleful glance at Hamilton, who rocked back and forth and drummed his fingertips on the dash in polyrhythmic accompaniment. "Tell you what," he said. "If you don't turn that down, I'm gonna pull behind that bus, follow it all the way up to Columbus Circle, and let the exhaust fumes kill whatever's left of your brain."

Dennis drummed on, undaunted. "You'll go with me, you know."

"Jesus, I'm trembling like a leaf. I'd rather *die* than listen to this caterwauling crap."

The drumming stopped.

"You know what your problem is, my man?" Dennis said reasonably. "I mean, aside from the fact that you're a sour-faced, insensitive, cranky old coot who doesn't keep up on the current cultural events."

Rizzo shook his head. "Do tell," he said.

"You can't admit that maybe, just *maybe*, you were wrong about him."

Rizzo shook his head some more and ran the yellow light at Fifty-seventh Street, hooking deftly around the bus. He was on the verge of nailing Junior with any of a possible half-dozen stunning retorts when the deejay came up over the fade-out, voice crackling.

"*And that was David Hart and the Brakes here on Ninety-two Rock, doing their new tune, 'Twisted.'* . . ."

And Hamilton watched as Rizzo just dried up in mid comeback. Maybe it was the news that Dennis had plucked straight off MTV; maybe he was just tired of arguing about it.

"Partner," he said at last, "you sure know how to fuck up a perfectly good reunion."

Dennis smiled. He knew that that was as close to a concession as he was ever likely to get. Rizzo returned the gesture. Peace resumed its reign.

The sedan wheeled around Columbus Circle, slowing to a stop as it approached the Central Park West kiosk. They shook hands, wished each other well, and promised to stay in touch.

A minute later, Dennis Hamilton was alone.

The warm scent of early summer beckoned from the park. He opted to walk along the perimeter for a ways, watching the late afternoon sun filter through the trees in fat, golden dollops. He felt good. The humidity was mercifully low today; a sweet breeze rustled up from the bridle path, smelling of cool earth and new grass. That helped.

He'd had a really good time with ol' Frank today, and

that helped, too. Lots of catching up, with a minimum of bull. Nice. Dennis noted, with no surprise and some satisfaction, that Rizzo detested his new partner: a fresh-faced kid named Todd Sweitek. Rizzo nicknamed him the Slug and swore that his reasoning abilities were so slow they exuded a slime trail.

Oh, well, Dennis mused. *Some things never change.* Whereas others changed quite a bit.

Like the park, for example.

Dennis found himself going there a lot in the wake of his early retirement. It was a good place to walk and think: large and lovely despite the decay. And even that appeared less and less prevalent in the past nine months. There was less graffiti, fewer broken bottles and discarded works than there'd been in years. Even the sight of a snatched and abandoned purse, its spilled contents fluttering in the breeze, had become the exception rather than the rule.

It was still light-years from Paradise, and only fools ventured into its bowels after dark.

There would always be fools.

But the others were staying away. In droves.

Because he's still out there, Dennis knew. *Insofar as any of them know, he's still out there.*

And it was true. The fresh statistics that Rizzo had fed him served only to confirm what he and just about everyone else already suspected: violent crime was down.

Oh, people still did one another in with gay abandon. They still abused and misused and mangled one another in the comfort and privacy of their own homes. White collar corporate sleazedom still thrived.

But the streets . . .

They were different now. Subtlely, palpably different. And apt to stay that way, so long as one simple, salient fact remained unchanged.

The Vigilante was never captured.

Billy Rowe died, insofar as the world-at-large knew or cared, protecting his lady-love: the innocent and final victim of the Smiley-Face Slasher. Rizzo and Hamilton ultimately deemed it best to concur with and support that scenario, attributing his condition to the fight and the fall. His charred apartment offered little by way of conflicting evidence: it had burned—walls, floor, and ceiling—to a depth of precisely one-sixteenth of an inch, before putting itself out. Everything else was cindered: his newspaper clippings, his plans.

His music.

It was an anomaly of staggering proportion, and as such, was handled as all such anomalies are: it was ignored. Lost in the shuffle, dumped in the "suspicious origins" file, and forgotten about. Inspectors cited "faulty wiring" in the door bell, and everyone seemed satisfied.

Albert, the landlord, could not be reached for comment.

Dennis Hamilton, as the firer-of-the-fatal-shot, endured his inevitable elevation to media hero with perfunctory grace and precious little said. He weathered the endless questions, accepted the commendations, and resigned quietly at the close of the official investigation. Life went on.

And the carrion-eaters descended. . . .

The lurid cavalcade lasted another six weeks, as every television and newsstand and supermarket checkout lane in the land regurgitated ever-fresher, more highly-speculative glimpses into The World of Stanley Peckard. *Time* and *Newsweek* both bumped the latest summit meetings from their covers to accommodate rivaling variations on the carved-torso theme; and *Time*, in a particularly grisly move, placed that cover strategically into their new subscription-driving commercials, thereby lending a whole new meaning to "*Time* puts it all right in your hands."

Phil Donahue, Bill Boggs, and a host of others tweaked the massmind with the requisite shows on sociosexual violence, all featuring the requisite panels of leading authorities, psychologists, and feminists.

Paula Levin was conspicuously not in attendance.

David Letterman did a disastrously unfunny bit on the "Slasher-Guy."

A hard-core band called The Stanleys made its smash debut at CBGB's, bloodied fans in tow.

Mona de Vanguardia declined to be interviewed. Repeatedly.

And the Vigilante . . .

Nowhere to be found, and everywhere at once. Reports of incidents mushroomed. In every borough. On every street. In every garbage-strewn alley and early morning subway platform. Walking in the shadows. Lurking.

Stalking.

For no sooner had Billy disappeared than a dozen others took his place. The public perception was seamless; the one became a multitude.

And it wasn't long before the spark became a flame became a roaring furnace of raging indignation, as people started looking out for themselves.

And for each other . . .

. . . *and a subway mugger named Royce Buchanan found his escape route seriously altered when a demure young bystander whapped him upside the head with her Italian leather attaché case and pitched him headlong onto the number 6 uptown tracks, only to be held at bay by a bristling armada of umbrellas and feet until the transit police could arrive . . .*

. . . *and the robbery of a BP self-serve in Brooklyn was foiled when another customer suddenly doused the getaway car with premium no-lead and threatened to flick his Bic . . .*

And more. And more. Dozens of tales. Some imagined, most of them not. Some fought well, some fought badly. Many were hurt. Many more were arrested.

It didn't stop.

The mayor cautioned against "copycats" and tooted the perils of "frontier justice"; weapons violations were vigorously enforced.

It still didn't stop.

Public sentiment ran high, and was highly charged. People bickered endlessly in bars and taverns, editorials raged both pro and con. Pop psychologists came off more like TV evangelists: direly warning of burgeoning "Deathwish cults" and lamenting the "rising tide of fear . . ."

Dennis had to laugh, when he thought about it. The climate of fear wasn't really rising, he knew.

It was just spreading out a little more evenly.

* * *

Mona lay alone on the bed, very much awake: eyes wide and staring into the darkness, sweat sticking her back and sides to the sheets despite the air conditioner's diligent hum. She lay like that for some time, just as she had last night.

And the night before that.

And the night before that . . .

Downstairs, she could hear Dave working: diddling with the drum machines and the synthesizers as he laid out a pre-production sketch on the four-track. *Another Billysong*, she realized. *He hasn't let up on those tapes since . . .*

The thought trailed off.

The blanks, at last, filled in.

It had started out, she was certain, as an appeal to her grief: Dave, coming around to the hospital in the aftermath; Dave, listening to her tapes of his music, the sole surviving legacy of Billy Rowe; Dave, telling her how surprised he was at its depth and quality.

Sure, she'd thought bitterly. *Humor the cripple. Grease me up.* She didn't buy a word of it.

That is, until he'd borrowed the tapes. And come back saying that he wanted to use the material, on his next album.

And Mona realized two things in short order. One: Dave Hart was not kidding. Two: Dave Hart could probably do with Billy Rowe's music what Billy Rowe could never quite pull off.

And he did. With a bullet.

Two songs on the latest album. Two more slated for the next. The heart and soul of Billy Rowe, finally getting out where it could be heard. And seen.

And remembered.

"Oh, baby," she whispered. There was a quaver in her voice. "They love it. They really do."

A solitary tear tracked down her cheek. Many more were impending. She fought back a sob, lest Dave hear: the last thing she could handle right then was his concerned, compassionate presence hovering overhead. It was becoming increasingly clear that their falling together was a doomed thing. At first, once she'd gotten over the initial shock and distrust, it had helped: a warm shoulder to cry on, a warm body to keep the ghosts at bay. It was understandable.

But it could never last. That was plain. Dave loved her, she knew; and he did so knowing that she'd never be able to return it in kind.

She didn't want to hurt him. She just couldn't help it. Despite his feelings—or perhaps because of them—she wanted, more than anything, to be alone now. It was important. Too much of her had died back on Stanton Street. She'd lost her love, her livelihood, and very nearly her sanity.

The latter were earned back, in time. Forever and irrevocably altered, but back.

Her love never quite made it. It lay, cold and broken, inside her. And she knew that before the old Mona might ever hope to live and love and dance again . . .

. . . the new one must learn to crawl.

Downstairs, the music stopped. She heard him stand and stretch and sigh. Then came the familiar furry stampede as he quietly called, "Bubba! It's walk time! Whaddaya say?"

There followed a shuffle, a scuffle, and the chink of pocketed keys. Six feet padded down the hall. The front door opened and closed.

And Mona was alone.

She curled fitfully around the pillow and cried, very softly, for a little while. Then, as she had last night, and the night before that, and the night before . . .

Mona dreamed.

(it's not so bad)
The words, over and over like a mantra. Billy's voice, saying
(it's not so bad)
that there was no fear, there was no pain, only the sensation of drifting for a long long stretch of time outside of Time: of floating in a boundless healing void, dark as the womb
(it's not so bad)
and then came the Light. And with it, the longing: to

*let go, to surrender and fly forever into the all-consuming,
all-forgiving Source. But the Light spoke, in a Voice that
was timeless and ageless and infinitely loving*

(TIME TO GO)

*and she felt the pull between what lay before and what
lay behind as the Voice spoke again*

(TIME TO GO)

*and she heard another voice: much smaller, much
closer.*

Billy's voice, affirming

(it's not so bad at all)

*that it was good, it was the way it was meant to be,
even as the Light receded until it was little more than a
pinprick on an infinitely black horizon, like the tiny spark
that is the human soul . . .*

. . . and Mona lay alone on the bed, very much
awake, softly crying Billy's name. As she had, so many
nights before.

With one small difference. One small saving grace.

Tonight, Mona knew where he went.

Somewhere outside the city of Léon, in the foothills of
Nicaragua, a young man sat pensively outside of a hut.
Listening. Waiting. He was thankful that tonight the
fighting was far away.

Inside the hut, his child was being born.

A battered radio lay at his feet, quietly tuned to a
Miami-based radio station that broadcast mostly *yanqui*
rock 'n' roll. The quality of the reception was not so good,
and the radio even less so; but he could hear well enough to
hum along to a song sung in a language he but barely
understood.

"Don't give up!
We need you.
Don't give up!
We need you."

The midwife appeared in the doorway. The look on her
face said that everything was fine. It was over. The man

grinned foolishly, hugely, overwhelmed with the joy and the power of the moment.

The first thing he saw, when he walked through the door, was the face of the woman he loved. It was sweat-slick, superhumanly weary, and the most beautiful thing he'd ever seen.

And then he saw the baby.

The universe opened wide for him, at that moment. His heart reached out and touched Creation, ran its loving fingers along every God-given fold and curve.

He was in the presence of a miracle.

He would never be the same.

And all the heavens be praised.

She was a fine baby girl. Even as they wiped the blood from her, she was the most beautiful thing that he'd ever seen. His wife would understand. He knew that she felt the same way, too.

The baby's eyes were open. She hadn't even cried.

And the music played on, outside.

MORE ABOUT THE AUTHORS

One year and countless nervous breakdowns later, John Skipp and Craig Spector are still working together. Their next project, *We Love the Scream*, will be their first attempt to combine fiction, music, and film in one package. The Bantam novel is slated for early '88, no matter what. Other upcoming projects include a short story collection, another novel or three, a collection of music based on *The Light at the End* and *The Cleanup*, starring roles in films that they also write, direct, produce, and do all the music for, an international fan club, and ultimate world domination.

Skipp is a Taurus/Gemini cusp. Spector is a Cancer on the face of the earth. They enjoy the reproductive act, Bugs Bunny, Tampering With The Forces Of Nature, and Discovering Secrets That Mere Mortal Man Was Never Meant To Know. They are also fond of new Ranch Style Doritos, and have a special relationship with Garbage Pail Kids.

John Saul is "a writer with the touch for raising gooseflesh."
—Detroit News

John Saul has produced one bestseller after another: masterful tales of terror and psychological suspense. Each of his works is as shocking, as intense and as stunningly real as those that preceded it.

You unlock this door with the key of imagination. Beyond it is another dimension: a dimension of sound, a dimension of sight, a dimension of mind. You're moving into a land of both shadow and substance, of things and ideas.

You've just crossed over into . . .

The Twilight Zone

Your companions on this journey to the shadowy tip of reality are these two books from Bantam:

THE TWILIGHT ZONE COMPANION
by Marc Scott Zicree

☐ (34362 • $11.95)

The complete show-by-show guide to
one of the greatest television series ever.

STORIES FROM THE
TWILIGHT ZONE

The short stories in this collection were developed by Rod Serling himself from screenplays for the original television series.

Look for THE TWILIGHT ZONE COMPANION in your bookstore now or use this coupon for ordering direct: